JOY MARTIN

IMAGE OF LAURA

This edition published 1995 by
Diamond Books
77–85 Fulham Palace Road
Hammersmith, London W6 8JB

First published by HarperCollins*Publishers* 1993

ISBN 0 261 66714 9

Set in Palatino
Printed in Great Britain

DEDICATION

For G.S. who also went to Berlin but whose story this is not; and to all those from the worlds of photography, antiques, fashion, design, art, television and film who so generously assisted me as I researched this book.

ACKNOWLEDGEMENTS

Owen Russell-Walling provided much useful information about the early history of Barnes; Michelle Burgess permitted Cassie to take over her role as director of the BBC Antiques Roadshow for the purposes of this book and Bärbel Schrader, Jürgen Schebera, Walter Henry Nelson, Howard K. Smith, Martha Dodd, Madeleine Kent, Sidney Osborne, Susanne Everett and Walther Ruttman were of inestimable assistance to me in researching pre-Nazi Berlin. My gratitude, too, to the Wiener Library, the Goethe Institute and the John Frost Historical Service for their help and interest.

GIVING BACK

CASSIE Stacton was not shy nor was she easily intimidated. The guests, although formidably glamorous, were not responsible for her nervous state.

The party had attracted the rich, the gorgeous, the famous and the outrageous, four hundred people sipping champagne and nibbling cheese *sablés* and talking at the tops of their voices in order to be heard. Some, attired in Chanel and Armani and Yves Saint Laurent, looked stylish and elegant. Others, in outfits by John Galliano and Yohji Yamamoto, were wonderfully ostentatious. Frilly knickers showed under a satin slip dress. Cyclists' gloves and Nike trainers combined with scarlet silk. A blonde, squeezed into an aquamarine bodysuit with wildly plunging neckline, stalked by on matching thigh-high boots. A bearded man with a cane in his hand lurked beneath cover of cloak and Ray-bans.

Fashion editors, past and present, mixed with the celebrities whose pictures had appeared in their publications; agents and models mingled with collectors; the figures of André Leon Talley, Style Director of *American Vogue*, and artist-photographer Michael Roberts, loomed above the crowd. Lord Lichfield, in grey tweed jacket and navy trousers, the collar of his blue and white shirt turned up at the back to discreetly defy convention, had just arrived, and the Irish photographer Bob Carlos Clarke was chatting to Andrew Cowan and Tim Jeffries, the directors of Hamilton's Gallery where the party was being held.

Cassie knew most of these people and liked many of them but she had no intention of letting them know that she had something to hide, that she had spent the day on an emotional

9

weighbridge, tilting between anxiety and elation. At breakfast, her normally compliant stomach had rebelled against its customary fare of orange, toast and black coffee. Walking from her flat in Bayswater to Television Centre, on an upswing, she had been seized by an almost overwhelming urge to skip and pirouette. All of which, she told herself now, was absurdly childish – the overreaction of a small child and quite inappropriate in a cool young woman of twenty-nine.

She talked and smiled and appeared to listen attentively to her companions, her innermost thoughts revealed only from the knees down – right knee pressed against left, big toe of right foot agitatedly tapping on the polished floorboards. This clue to her feelings remained undetected, for the gallery was too crowded for anyone to be able to see her toes or, in the cacophony, to hear so faint a tap.

Had a survey been made of Cassie from the feet up it would have been admitted that they were not her best asset, being too big and too wide for the shoes she was wearing which were just beginning to pinch. But the legs which rose up from the feet *were* admirable – long and slender and adjoined to a shapely body devoid of superfluous fat.

Cassie's figure was painstakingly, ascetically maintained by diet and exercise but her face, which had been pudgy in childhood, was still quite rounded. Her eyes were a very dark brown, her nose was small but distinctive with slightly flaring nostrils, and her full mouth, in repose, turned down at the corners. To balance what might otherwise have been a disagreeable, sulky expression she had dimples in her cheeks, and when she laughed the edges of her lips turned up and her nose wrinkled. Her hair was chestnut brown with red glints, wavy, almost waist-length, and set off by her navy matt jersey dress which Jean Muir had designed to skim the body and enable its wearer to move sinuously.

She stood near the staircase which ran down from the upper to the lower level of the gallery, flanked on one side by her current boyfriend, Dominic Lethbridge, and on the other by a new producer from the Radio Two Arts Programme whom she rated rather attractive.

An interesting *frisson* was developing between the producer and herself and the fact that Dominic was aware of and disturbed by this provided intermittent distraction from her other concern.

'Did you hear the programme?' asked the producer whose name was Jason Walker and whose voice had become raspy from the effort of talking too loudly.

Cassie nodded.

'We had a few problems. Laura isn't easy, is she? But I thought it worked in the end.'

He had very blond hair, unusual in an Englishman. Good body. Long-fingered hands.

Cassie looked away, noted that Dominic was scowling, and returned to the problem of Laura.

Her grandmother was a woman of enormous integrity. Scrupulously honest herself, Laura demanded absolute truth in return. She was extremely independent, resisted any form of intrusion into her life and left others to their own choices.

She could be offended by the white lies and petty concealments of the past eight months. She might conclude, with reason, that there had been grand-scale interference into her affairs. Instead of being overjoyed with the results of that interference . . .

'It *is* an extraordinary story,' said Jason Walker. 'And the pictures are *amazing*.'

Dotted around the walls of the gallery, suspended from steel wires and illuminated by tungsten lights, were thirty-six framed photographs, some in colour and others in black and white. The subject matter varied from street scenes to portraiture to fashion shots from the covers of *Vogue* and *Harper's and Queen* and *Tatler* and *Marie-Claire*.

An exhibition displayed in chronological order and spanning in its entirety nearly sixty years. Depictions of unrelated people in multifarious clothes in a divergence of locations linked by the common element of unabashed sensuality.

Within the frames were men and women, the radiant and the homely, the *soignée* and the less couth, who, when captured by the camera, had been revelling in life. Sweaty road-workers proudly displayed bare torsoes and swelling muscles. Overweight matrons at a café table gorged on cream cakes. High-spirited model girls capered and exulted. A handsome young man, seemingly self-satisfied, leant insouciantly against a bureau on which a vase of flowers had been placed.

The photograph of the young man and the bureau was positioned out of her line of vision but Cassie could see it clearly enough in her mind's eye. The sitter with his old-fashioned movie star looks – Paul someone-or-other, one of Laura's circle of friends in pre-war Berlin – and the handmade bureau.

The bureau, fashioned out of oak, had been mounted on a stand with chamfered posts and block feet. It was at once both delicate and sturdy, with one central panel and two smaller ones on either side. Above the brass handles on its drawers ran a diamond-shaped motif.

Laura's bureau. Handmade for her by the master craftsman Edward Barnsley and for many years her most prized possession.

Next – of course – to her camera. Even today Laura still spoke of it wistfully.

'At the beginning I thought it was only hype,' Jason Walker said. 'I mean, it's barely credible – an anonymous donor returning the photographs after all this time! Posting them to her agent! He must be crazy, letting vintage prints slip through his fingers. Each one of those early shots must be worth more than the rest of the collection put together.'

In photography there was a world of difference between a modern print made from an old negative and a vintage print made shortly after the negative was taken. A vintage print invariably fetched at least ten times in excess of the modern equivalent.

'Did you see the Parkinson exhibition, the one Hamilton's did of *his* Thirties prints?' Jason went on. 'Exactly the same thing

12

happened. Prices like these – £7,500 a print and people queued to buy them. Yet a modern print from that time, *signed*, sold for only £400 just before Parkinson died.'

He paused for breath after this homily and Cassie shifted her weight on to her right foot and began to tap with her left. Covering up was a bore. In that I also despise duplicity, Cassie thought, I am just like Laura, the difference being that, to me, lies simply set up complications, while she is intrinsically honest. I see truth for the purpose of simplification. She is one of those rare people who is, by nature, pure. And resilient. A woman with the personality of a rubber ball, who has bounced back from tragedy and heartbreak with no residue of bitterness. But all the same vulnerable. *I* know that.

'I can't believe she's seventy-five,' said Jason Walker.

'She is. The retrospective was planned to coincide with her birthday.'

Which was why it was so vital that nothing, no reservation, however slight, should mar this night.

'And she's still working – '

'Out of the way, please!' yelled someone above the noise, and the crowd parted to enable a television crew to carry equipment past.

'Where is she, love?' said one of the crew to Cassie.

'Down there.'

'Show me.'

Cassie edged the man between a girl in a silver corset dress and another in fuchsia fish-net, pointed a finger and said proudly: 'There – at the foot of the stairs. That's Laura. That's my grandmother.'

'That's *her*?' exclaimed the cameraman in a tone of disbelief. He looked up at the walls, blinked and contemplated Laura.

Those familiar with the work but not the personage of Laura Conway were invariably surprised on coming face to face with her. Expecting the idiosyncratic, the bizarre, possibly the androgyne, they were disconcerted when confronted with what one interviewer had described as a visual nonentity.

Laura Conway, who was five foot six inches tall, whose body was slender and whose face was kindly lined, might have been a ghost so shadowy was her appearance. She wore only black, grey and white, and since her eyes were grey and her once pale ash-blonde hair had long since turned silver she could have been one of her own negatives.

From the early Sixties people had been used to the famous photographer as a personality, someone who presented his or her self in strong visual terms. Some of them found it strange that a woman who could create such vibrant and lusty images, who was often in the public eye and who had friends of all ages from a multiplicity of backgrounds, should apparently wish to blot herself out.

But Laura Conway's spectral presentation also had its strengths. Although her clothes did not scream out for attention they were selected from the collections of the world's top couturiers. Her hair had been skilfully cut. And even if her personality did not make a powerful initial impact it lingered on after her departure leaving those who had encountered her fascinated and eager to meet her again.

All evening friends and acquaintances and others who were normally wary of her had been hugging and kissing Laura and addressing her as 'darling'. She did not object in the least to any of this. Discriminating in a level-headed way between the sincere and the spurious, adding up the totals, she was heartened by the results. Outsiders sometimes dismissed the fashion world as false and frivolous but behind their criticism could often be detected that jealousy and fear which beauty engenders.

Insiders knew that while top models might look like Hollywood glamour queens, might earn £30,000 or more in a single day, they were still very young women, acutely conscious of the brevity of their fame and as vulnerable to the horror of spots and avoirdupois and broken love affairs as other girls. And while the business itself might be, on the one hand, greedy, exploitive and bitterly competitive, it was also highly creative and stimulating – a magic lantern in a world that was otherwise all too sombre – and peopled by men and women who were, in the main, benign.

'Not *too* benign, I hope,' said Michael Roberts to whom Laura had expressed some of these views. 'Personally, I would feel insulted by that description!'

Laura chuckled. Michael, skilled, too, as a writer and fashion's wittiest critic, was one of her favourite people. They had worked together, fought furiously on occasion, but never lost sight of their admiration for each other's talent.

'Don't worry. You remain fashion's undisputed *enfant terrible*!'

She was enjoying herself immensely. One shouldn't tempt Fate by being over-complacent, she thought, but I do feel pleased with myself. Everything's going so well. All those red stickers. Simply wonderful.

If only Klaus were present to see what I have achieved. And Rebecca. Oh, Rebecca should have been here.

Fool, do not think of Rebecca or you will dissolve into tears, a ghastly prospect. Concentrate, rather, on Cassie. Beloved Cassie.

She looked around, up to where Cassie was standing, took note of Jason Walker's presence, of Dominic's unhappy expression, and frowned disapprovingly. *Cassie!*

'Hi!' said a cheerful voice.

The blonde in the aquamarine jumpsuit caught her by the arm, squeezed it affectionately.

'Cecily. I wondered where you were.'

'Never far away,' said Cecily, who had been running Laura's studio with remarkable efficiency for the last four years.

Seeing her, Laura had an idea. 'Cecily,' she said, 'that man up there with Dominic and Cassie. He's rather your type.'

Cecily considered. 'Mm,' she said appreciatively. 'You could be right.'

'So go on up. Infiltrate.'

'You think I should?'

15

'Certainly I do,' said Laura and, with satisfaction, observed Cecily comply.

'Miss Conway?'

With a sinking heart she faced the television crew. Laura hated giving interviews. Television, which intruded incisively into the psyche, highlighting aspects of it that one would rather keep hidden, struck her as being particularly horrendous.

In turn, she responded badly. On air, in front of the camera instead of behind it, Laura froze. Those who had attempted to interview her in the past had come away frustrated and in some cases resentful. Laura Conway, who should know better, did not play the media game, they grumbled. All agreed that it was a nightmare trying to make her talk.

'What a pity you couldn't come to the studio,' said the unfortunate woman assigned to interview her now for a Channel Four production. 'The noise here is appalling. I can't see what we can do.'

Laura visibly brightened.

'Are you absolutely sure you can't?' said the interviewer, already in despair. 'Tomorrow maybe?'

'Quite sure,' Laura said. 'I'm leaving almost immediately for Paris.' She looked rather as if she would take flight at once.

'Oh, well,' sighed the interviewer, knowing when she was beaten, 'I'll just have to bring you in with a strong intro. Can I just verify some background information?'

She itemised brutally. 'Your husband, Miss Conway – although German – was murdered by the Nazis for opposing their views. Your own life was endangered and you had to flee Berlin. Which was how your portfolio of prints came to be left behind.'

'Yes,' said Laura.

'And then, after the war, you discovered that virtually all your possessions had been found intact, except for the prints and your books and a bureau.'

'Yes.'

'That's the bureau in the photograph, isn't it? Odd that the

Nazis would have stolen that. Popular taste in the Forties was for French polished furniture.'

Once again Laura assented. Blood out of a stone, thought the interviewer. Some actuality it will be.

'Anyway, to get back to the prints – '

Through the gap created by Cecily's departure, Laura caught sight of Richard, a tall, imposing figure with a jowly face and a mane of thick grey hair who at this particular moment looked like a benevolent and harassed lion newly returned to the wilds. She beamed and beckoned.

She's coming to life, thought the interviewer. After all, we may progress beyond the monosyllabic.

From her vantage point on the upper level Cassie, too, noticed Richard reaching out for another glass of champagne and accepting a quail's egg, his fourth of the evening. Thus equipped, he began to make his way in Laura's direction. Cassie watched him ease through the crowd, break up a discussion between two hirsute men, plough steadily onwards. Unlike Laura she did not smile at the sight of him. She viewed her father with reservations, all the more so as, with immense relief flooding his face, he reached Laura's side.

Laura immediately slipped her arm through his. Well, thought Cassie, if it keeps her happy it has its advantages. And she is on a complete high. So my part can only add, surely, not detract, from her euphoria.

Laura is bound to understand my motives. We've always been so close, she and I. Nearly half a century divides us in age and yet, in the way we can relate, we might be contemporaries. We are certainly best friends.

But no one has ever given so much as Laura in the name of friendship. What she has done for me – as a child, in adulthood – is inestimable. The big rescue operation she mounted, the unreserved love provided thereafter, the support and incisive advice, the confidences shared. If it wasn't for Laura, Cassie thought, I know I never would have got into the

17

BBC, wouldn't have been able to fight my way up from researcher to director. She – her affection and sympathy and common sense – turned me from an insecure, miserable little brat into a positive person. Laura will appreciate why I am doing this, why I want to make the big gesture and say thank you to her in public. She will know that in more senses than one I am giving back.

'Hi!' said Cecily who, having been waylaid on the stairs, had finally reached the group. 'Hi, Cass. Hi, Dominic.' She kissed Cassie and Dominic and, honing in on Jason, repeated, 'Hi, I'm Cecily.'

Apart from her accent she was more Los Angeles than London and Jason Walker, who was not used to such flagrant displays of boobs and bottom, looked taken aback.

'Ah – hello,' he said.

'When are you going to do it?' said Cecily to Cassie.

Cassie, seeing the expression on Jason's face, burst out laughing. Her laughter was a delight, unexpectedly deep and deliciously wicked and those nearest her, even Dominic, responded with smiles and twinkles.

'In about ten minutes.'

'I'll make sure the camera crew won't try to come up the stairs again and cause a blockage,' Cecily said sensibly. 'All we need is that lot getting in the way.'

Cecily, a trustworthy person of whom Cassie was fond, had been let into the secret several months earlier.

The others who knew what was going to happen included Laura's agent, the public relations team hired to hype the event and the directors and staff of Hamilton's.

Certain members of the Press, having been tipped off, were aware that something unusual was about to occur. But not Laura. That was the whole point – that Laura would not know, that it would come as a complete surprise to her.

Cecily went to speak to the Channel Four crew. Cassie began to wiggle her way through the crowd to where it had thinned

18

out by the entrance. She stood staring out in Carlos Place, oblivious to the doorman. She thought: This has got to be the best birthday present of the lot. And in a few minutes Laura herself is going to bear testimony to that. There is truly no need for anxiety.

She turned round and was promptly beset by that very emotion. To her left was a desk. And behind it again was a screen. And behind that . . .

What if it isn't there, thought Cassie? What if a thief has dodged past the doorman, taken advantage of the activity within the gallery, carried it into the street and loaded it into a van? What then?

'OK. I'm all yours,' said Cecily, reappearing. 'Let's go.'

Cassie took a deep breath, walked to the screen, peered behind it, sighed with relief.

'All right?'

'All fine,' said Cassie in the voice of one who had never feared otherwise.

And it was fine. Behind the screen, in mint condition, mounted on a trolley and all ready to be presented with a flourish to its rightful owner, was Laura's long-lost bureau.

THE previous year Cassie had signed a contract to direct one of the country's top ten television programmes, the BBC's Antiques Roadshow. The programme attracted audiences in excess of fourteen million. Cassie, who had a twelve-month contract with the show, soon found that she was hooked on its surprise element.

Members of the public brought in antiques which were then assessed by specialists recruited by the BBC. Even at her busiest she wondered what people might produce from crumpled newspaper wrappings and battered boxes.

Some of the items had been found in attics or cupboards. Others were heirlooms handed down through generations. Some of the best finds had been picked up for a few shillings in junk shops. Identifying previously unrecognised or under-valued treasures was the Roadshow's stock-in-trade.

Once, a lost watercolour by Richard Dadd had been produced, valued at £100,000 and later sold to the British Museum. And a pair of tiny enamelled scent bottles in their original shagreen case were proved to date from the sixteenth century – to the bemusement of their owner who had used them as childhood toys.

Sometimes junk turned out to be just that and people were disappointed with the experts' assessments. But the valuable and the unusual continued to flow in wherever the Roadshow went – Tiffany lamps, Irish peat buckets, Blackamoors, miniature chamberpots, a muff pistol hidden in a leather book.

Originally the Roadshow had toured only within the British Isles, but more recently Continental editions had also proved popular. Berlin, coming back into its own after half a century as a huge parochial paradox, was an obvious choice.

The Germans were buying antiques in a big way. Christie's Auction House was in the process of opening a Berlin branch. The city was humming with dealers.

Six weeks before the Roadshow was to be recorded there Cassie, along with the programme's executive producer, the engineering manager, the designer and an assistant, went to Berlin for a planning meeting. Their function was to inspect one of the halls of the SSB, the German television and radio station in the Messengelaende where the recording was to be made, and to check out suitable hotels and restaurants for the use of the full production team in due course.

That was in December. It was Cassie's first visit to Berlin – Laura's city, as she always thought of it, even though, having left in 1939, Laura had never been back.

For this omission Laura had a positive plethora of excuses: 'Darling, I didn't have the money or the opportunity.'

That covered the Forties and the Fifties. Thereafter Laura had relied on the excuse that she could not bring herself to look at the Wall, but in the last two years, after its fall, had been forced to blame lack of time for her failure to revisit Berlin. The real reason, Cassie suspected, was that Laura could not bear to set foot again in the city in which her husband had been murdered.

Naturally Laura would not want to return to Berlin. Although the city had been devastated by bombing so that little of its former splendour remained, there would still be more than enough there to remind her all too poignantly of Klaus. Like the house in which the two of them had rented an apartment.

The street in which that house had stood, Joachim Friedrich Strasse, had been the target of Allied bombs. Most of its big ugly grey Victorian houses had been levelled, but Number 53 was still standing. So Laura had been told.

Cassie was determined to see at least the exterior of her grandmother's old home. So on the second day of her stay in Berlin she slipped off on her own, leaving her colleagues contemplating a black breakfast of Russian Sobranie, coffee and sliced Schwartzbrot in the Schwartzes Café.

Walking along the Kurfürstendamm she thought that – the revivalist cabaret in the Quartier Latin notwithstanding – it was extremely difficult to pick up traces of Laura's Berlin in this reconstructed city. Now, thought Cassie, it's all happening in Potsdamer Strasse but in the old days the action was in the east, around Alexander-platz, not here in the west. In those days the Kurfürstendamm – the Ku'damm as it was called – was simply a shopping centre.

The beerhalls and the cafés of which her grandmother had spoken were all gone forever, the gallery where the work of the Secessionist Painters, Max Leibermann and Walter Leistikow, had been exhibited, the *tanzbars* and the powdered and rouged boys, the naked girls. And in place of the *Jugendstil* architecture of the Ku'damm's Wilhelminian heyday were austere beige and pale grey modern buildings.

Even the trees that lined the wide pavements had been planted after the war. The Hotel Panorama offered fitness and massage treatments in huge lettering. The Be Sexy Nightclub outlined the importance of being happy. There was a prominent sign for the Irish Harp Pub.

Pedestrians were blond and brisk and in a hurry to get to work. Noisy Trabants looking like four-wheeled motor-bicycles pulled up at traffic lights beside brand new BMWs and Mercedes' *coupés*. But there was already a flower-seller out on the corner where the Ku'damm joined Joachim Friedrich Strasse and she remembered Laura speaking of the flowers in Berlin.

'Flowers simply everywhere. The flower shops were so much more beautiful than the dreary ones we had in England then. The flowers and the trees. Berlin was famous for its trees.'

Trees did not proliferate in Joachim Friedrich Strasse. Laura had called it a lamentably dull street pre-war. In that respect there had not been change.

She made the mistake of turning off to the right, passing in the process a red brick building. Halensee Grundschule,

Wilemdorf, said a notice over the door. Grass grew unchecked around the bottom edge of the pavement level windows. Next door was a cobbler's shop. She walked to the end of the street before realising that Laura's house must have been in that part of Joachim Friedrich Strasse which ran to the left of the Ku'damm.

On that side, shabby post-war apartment buildings gradually gave way to the more up-market. She crossed over Westfalische Strasse and saw on the corner of Halberstadter Strasse a grey Victorian house with bay windows, balustrades and an arched doorway. Number 52 – and across the road another similar building which had to be Laura's.

'A large pompous house,' Laura had said, 'usually they were five storeys high and the rooms were very tall. At the front were what we called the respectable quarters. You went through the *Berlin-zimmer*, the final sitting-room, into the back where the bedrooms were.'

She looked up at the house.

'On the third floor. We lived on the third floor,' she remembered Laura saying.

All of a sudden Joachim Friedrich Strasse no longer seemed dull but exciting, animated by the memory of two vibrant people: Laura the photographer and Klaus the film-maker. Cassie tried to envisage them walking hand-in-hand along the street, talking and laughing. Through that doorway they would have gone, followed by their friends, talented people of their own ilk, writers and musicians and artists, as opposed to the Nazis as Klaus had been, though maybe not quite so brave.

In the *Berlin-zimmer* they would have expressed their views forcibly – discussed books and music and art. And afterwards, when the others had departed, Klaus and Laura would have gone into their bedroom ('At the back – the bedrooms were at the back') and made love.

Oh Laura. What you lost.

But, at least, Cassie thought, Laura's pride in Klaus has remained intact. At least she always had that. In this house – up

23

there, on the third floor – Klaus Fleischer had been shot, but his heroic legend had lived on to this day.

The details of this legend – how, precisely, Klaus had stood up to the Nazis – were unknown to Cassie. Laura, not surprisingly, disliked discussing the subject in detail. But the details were immaterial. It was enough to know that Klaus had taken a courageous stance.

My grandfather, thought Cassie, and a lump came up in her throat. She surreptitiously wiped away two stray tears and remonstrated with herself. Enough nostalgia. There was a great deal of work to be done in connection with the recording. She felt in her handbag, pulled out a tissue, blew her nose, began to retrace her steps.

But Klaus and Laura were with her as she went back down the street.

The nature of the Roadshow created a spirit of teamwork amongst its associates. From the viewpoint of those watching, the fun lay in its spontaneity. Those who brought in goods for valuation had to wait to hear the experts' thoughts on camera and this sometimes called for great restraint on the part of those making extraordinary finds.

But the rules were clearly defined. The game could not be given away too early. By the end of the day the whole team was exhausted, having used up every fraction of nervous energy.

Cassie's role was the most demanding. She had to be constantly active and acutely aware of all that was going on. It was essential to remain controlled, cool and collected. A Roadshow director could not afford to be temperamental or anything other than highly professional.

She returned to Berlin at the end of January in a different mood, concerned with the present, not the past. With her was the full team – forty-eight altogether – only seven of whom – the executive producer, three assistant producers, two production assistants and a secretary – were involved with the show the year round, stationed at BBC Bristol.

There was no charge for the experts' opinions, which included date, use, origin and value of items, and no buying, selling or commercial activity was permitted on recording day.

All the same, some dealers came along to have a look, adding to the hundreds of people who invariably poured into the hall from ten A.M. onwards. They would be bound to be out in force in Berlin.

But who knew what might be brought in for valuation? Every now and again in Germany farmers still walked into antique shops with paintings or antiquities which hungry people had swapped for eggs and chickens during the Forties and Fifties.

Unframed paintings on cardboard executed by holidaying artists had been discovered in barns and lofts. What if work by Berlin artists like Henzilow and Bomberger and Zillet turned up? Their drawings of children with roses and plump, complaisant matrons fetched fortunes at auction.

A somewhat dissimilar mural adorned one wall of Cassie's bedroom in the Hotel Mondial, a near relation of the one in the dining-room, green and orange, depicting grinning monkeys.

The hotel, on the Ku'damm, was functional and efficient and the staff went out of their way to be helpful.

Bathing on the morning of the recording, Cassie considered the friendliness of Berliners. It was impossible to reconcile these cheerful, chatty men and women with the image of their near-ancestors. But even during the war, she reminded herself, there had been many decent people caught in a unique and terrifying situation, frightened to speak out as Klaus must have done lest their families be made to suffer for what they had said.

Klaus had not been threatened by family reprisals. But hadn't he considered Laura – the likely danger to her?

No thinking about Klaus and Laura, said Cassie sternly to herself. Not this morning.

She climbed out of the bath, wrapping her hair in a towel. As she did so the loo, which operated electronically whenever it was approached, flushed loudly. Ridiculous system – and now

25

it refused to stop. She silenced it by draping another towel over the sensitive area, and began to blow-dry her hair.

By hired car, by taxi, and in one case by a new BMW motorbicycle which had cost its owner £20,000, the crew made their way to the SSB hall, proceeding along Masuranallee in the direction of the Olympic Stadium.

Their landmark was the skeletal transmission mast of the Funkturm, built as a radio and TV transmitter in the late 1920s and now popular for the views from its one hundred and thirty-eight metre-high observation post.

The huge pantechnicon used for transporting the set and the mobile scanner, resembling a big metal caravan, were already parked outside the hall when Cassie got there. Inside the scanner were sound and vision booths, a control panel and seating for four people. Long before the doors of the hall were thrown open to the public Cassie was ensconced in there, confronting a bank of TV monitors.

Each one gave an output to the four cameras attached to the programme's main unit. From the pictures offered by these cameras Cassie could select those she thought appropriate to a particular sequence.

The scanner was about the size of a small bathroom. Although air-conditioned it could be stressful working within its confines. There was literally no room for personality clashes.

Through her monitors Cassie could see what was going on in the hall. Alec Yirrell, the Front-of-House Manager, was having a word with Margaret Hale, the Press Officer. Hugh Scully, the Roadshow presenter, was walking across the floor, taking care not to fall over the thick insulated lighting wires which ran around it. The experts were taking up positions at tables – Eric Knowles, a Director of Bonham's, who had become Head of its English and European Ceramics and Works of Art department in the early 1980s; furniture expert John Bly who had worked with Sotheby's before joining the family business; glamorous blonde Bunny Campione who specialised in dolls, dolls' houses, miniature furniture, automata and teddy bears. Altogether there were twenty experts on the Roadshow's list, several of whom had been associated with the programme since its inception in 1979.

Some antiques were already inside the hall, those which were too heavy for their owners to carry in with them. A life-sized carving of an upright bear was standing by John Bly's table.

On the dot of ten A.M. the doors opened and the crowd which had been waiting outside filtered through. They did so respectfully, somewhat awed by the serious nature of the recording, taking in the BBC Roadshow insignia, gold lettering on a dark blue background, the souvenir stall with its display of dishcloths, books, badges and fine bone china mugs, the inquiry kiosk to which they were being directed. Here, the treasures they had brought in for valuation were initially inspected and each owner supplied with a ticket itemising the category to which their goods belonged.

Secondary queues began to form to the experts' tables. Alec Yirrell was keeping everyone in order, looking after an old lady in a wheelchair. A woman clutching a silver bowl was rebuking a small child.

By eleven the packed hall was buzzing with excitement. The life-sized bear had been diagnosed as a modern Bavarian reproduction of a Victorian design. Some awful bronzes had been politely dismissed and what had been incorrectly judged a Chinese porcelain vase of great antiquity had been assessed as fairly recent French.

A man had produced an early set of German building bricks made in Leipzig in 1880 and been told that they were worth upwards of £300, and a slightly damaged Staffordshire chocolate pot – the history of which was unknown – had been valued at £2,000 to its possessor's delight.

Cassie called: 'Camera One. Coming to Two. Can you tighten in on the object please. Stand by Three. Cut to Three. Three,' and reached for a glass of water.

The recording was going well. The Germans, as she might

have expected, were behaving in an orderly fashion, which was not necessarily standard practice on a foreign visit. In an average day the experts dealt with 3,500 people, sometimes as many as 5,000, not all of whom enjoyed queuing up. A visit to Malta had involved bringing in the local police to exert crowd control.

'Cassie?' Alec Yirrell on the line.

'What is it?' she said.

'The minute you can take a break pop in and talk to Clive Farahar. There's something he wants to show you.' Clive Farahar was the Roadshow's expert on prints. What could he have to bring to her attention, wondered Cassie.

The conversation at the arms and militaria table was running on a bit too long. She relayed this message to the floor manager who made a mini windmill motion to expert Bill Harriman to wind it up.

She was due for a brief respite. Holding a mug of coffee in her hand she climbed out of the scanner and went into the hall.

Standing by Clive Farahar's table was a tall, slim, grey-haired woman of about fifty. She was wearing a black coat made out of inferior material and large spectacles in cheap plastic frames.

Clive continued the conversation he was having with the owners of a collection of prints of pre-war Dresden. Only when they had triumphantly departed did he become aware of Cassie's presence.

'Cassie, this is Fräulein Eisermann.'

'Guten Tag,' said the woman in the black coat, and smiled engagingly.

'Fräulein Eisermann has brought in some interesting photographs,' said Clive. There was a note in his voice that Cassie couldn't quite pin-point. Clive spread the photographs out carefully on the table so that they faced in Cassie's direction. She glanced at them. Eight photographs depicting Berlin in the 1930s, three street scenes, four portraits and one of a house. Then, as it dawned on her what she was seeing, Cassie stared in astonishment and disbelief. They were without any doubt Laura's pictures. Laura's photographs, confiscated so long ago by the Nazis; not, after all, burnt as her books must have been, but materialising here.

It was quite incredible. There, in one photograph, was the house in which Laura had lived. There was the name of the street – Joachim Friedrich Strasse – and the number 53 quite clearly visible on the gate post, as it still was to this day. And the other photographs – the one of the singer in the sequinned gown who might or might not be a man; those overweight café matrons – they could not have been taken by anyone other than Laura.

Equally astonishing was the high quality of this early work. Hadn't someone once said that certain photographers, unlike artists, were at their best at the onset of their careers?

Except that Laura always maintained her supreme standard . . .

'They are valuable?' inquired the woman in the black coat.

She was polite to the point of being deferential. But Cassie's surprise was turning into puzzled indignation. Who *was* this woman? What was she doing with Laura's pictures?

Showing none of the confusion she felt Cassie ignored the question and said coolly:

'How fascinating. Tell me, how did you come across these prints?'

'They belong to my father,' said Fräulein Eisermann, wide-eyed behind her glasses, innocent as can be and speaking English extremely well.

'Fräulein Eisermann's mother died a few weeks ago,' explained Clive. 'She found the prints when she was tidying out her parents' apartment. People have told her that old photographs are valuable, particularly pre-war prints. However, she is aware that I can't at this stage commit myself to a price. As I said to her, the background to these discoveries can affect their value.'

A further wave of indignation engulfed Cassie. *Value*, she thought – morally the woman isn't entitled to sell Laura's prints. But legally she may be. Possession is nine-tenths of the law, a maxim which presumably also applies here in Germany.

However, it doesn't necessarily follow that I'll be involved in wrangling. There may be a perfectly reasonable explanation as to how Laura's photographs fell into Herr Eisermann's hands.

If there was, Fräulein Eisermann did not know it.

'You wish to ask him – yes?'

Do I not, thought Cassie. But she must not sound too eager. 'If that's possible.'

'Of course. But my father is an old man now and we live on the eastern side of the city. So the morning, I think, is better. You can come tomorrow?'

'Yes, I can manage that,' said Cassie, even though this would mean making arrangements to stay on in Berlin for another day.

'So, in the meantime, you keep these pictures,' Fräulein Eisermann said. 'My father has many more. These, you understand, are a selection.'

Well, she was certainly coming over as a surprisingly trusting and decent person.

And there were other pictures – many more. Trying to contain her excitement Cassie remembered that before the arrangement to meet Herr Eisermann was set in concrete she must first obtain permission from Christopher Lewis, her executive producer.

In the event it was given. Cassie tried to put Laura's photographs out of her mind and returned to work.

In bed she mulled over the possibilities of how Herr Eisermann had laid hands on the prints – found them abandoned in a house after the Nazis had gone, or bought them out of pity from a starving thief just after the war had ended?

Or simply been interested in collecting memorabilia of pre-war Berlin?

The rendezvous was to take place at 16 Metzer Strasse. Looking it up on the map Cassie saw that Metzer Strasse was in the heart of what had once been the Jewish quarter of Berlin. In the same vicinity was the Moorish-Byzantine synagogue burnt by the Nazis on Kristallnacht in 1938 during their all-out attack on the Jewish community, and the old folks' home used as a temporary rounding-up post for concentration-camp victims.

Was Herr Eisermann, Jewish by name and back again in what may have been his old stamping ground, a survivor of Dachau or Auschwitz, wondered Cassie as she prepared for their meeting. Did he have a number and a special double triangle tattooed on his arm and who knew what horrors engraved on his mind? He and his wife and daughter had survived the war as a family unit, the lucky few, but had other of his children perished?

Cassie shivered – then hardened her heart. The old man might not be as charming or as compliant as his daughter and his business instincts would probably be aroused by her report. He would be bound to demand some form of payment for the prints. On the other hand he might not have any idea of their true worth.

Cassie reminded herself that, until comparatively recently, the Eisermanns had lived behind the Wall, as cut off from western culture as most Russians were. What Muscovites had heard of Parkinson or Penn – or Laura Conway?

Still, it was outrageous to think of having to pay out even a relatively small sum for Laura's own prints.

Contemplating these things, she set off for Metzer Strasse by the U & S Bahn, getting out of the underground at Senefelder Platz. From that stop she only had to walk around a block to reach her destination.

The removal of the Wall had not transformed the shabbiness of eastern Berlin. Sixteen Metzer Strasse might once have been a reasonable address but Communist rule had turned it into a number of small flats.

The entrance hall was clean but drab, the carpet on the stairs mud-brown. She made her way to the first floor as she had been directed, tapped. Fixed to the outside of the door was a little round metal container which was, she knew, a *mezuzah*. Inside it would be a blessing on a piece of paper.

The door was opened by Fräulein Eisermann, smiling broadly. 'Welcome,' she said, holding out her hand. 'Please come in. My father is waiting for you.'

She led the way through into a tidy but sparsely furnished living room. The beige curtains were as dull and synthetic as the well-worn carpet. Two wooden-legged sofas had been draped with cloths. There were three functional chairs.

On a bookshelf were several candlesticks, another indication that this was a Jewish home. A pair for *Shabbat*, Cassie recalled from a programme on which she had worked. You light both and two other candlesticks. And the *menoah*, seven-branched after the seven tribes, and the *hannukiah* which has room for nine candles. Hannukah is an eight-day festival but the ninth candle is needed for lighting the other eight.

'*Willkommen.*' An old man with thin white hair and faded brown eyes had entered the room. He was stretching out a blue-veined hand.

In New York people incessantly tell one to 'Have a good day' thought Cassie; here they continually bid one welcome.

She shook hands. His was bony, his grip non-existent.

'I have here all the photographs,' he said, gesturing towards a table in the far corner of the room. 'You wish to examine them?'

'Please.'

It was a repeat performance, with more material, of the previous day. Supplementary street scenes: a cleaner working energetically with two brushes, women brushing down their doorsteps with fierce intensity, girls in pale cloche hats and short-skirted suits. Portraits – altogether of three young men, one with dark hair.

'Berlin of the past,' said Herr Eisermann unnecessarily.

Cassie was bemused. This was a treasure trove of Laura's work.

'Where did you get these?' she asked politely.

'Why do you wish to know that?' inquired Herr Eisermann. 'Either they are valuable or they are not valuable.'

'Look,' said Cassie, gritting her teeth, 'my grandmother took these photographs. She lived in Berlin before the war and this is her work. So naturally I'm curious as to how you got hold of it.'

The old man gaped at her, then felt for the nearest chair, sat down on it, said finally, 'Your grandmother?'

'Yes,' Cassie said. 'My grandmother. Laura Conway. Well, that is her maiden name. She reverted to it when she went back to England. Her married name was Fleischer.'

She was conscious of over-explaining, thrown off-balance by the odd look on the old man's face.

'Fleischer,' repeated Herr Eisermann, 'Laura Fleischer. She is alive?'

Now Cassie, too, had an urge to sit down. He *knew* Laura, she thought. He knew her as Laura Fleischer.

'Yes, she's very much alive. She's living in England.'

'Alive,' he said, wondering, 'I thought – so many are dead.'

He was there, sitting on the chair, but somehow not present. He was back in the past.

'I will bring coffee.'

Fräulein Eisermann slipped away discreetly.

Her father was staring into space, looking backwards. Eventually he reached into his pocket, drew out a handkerchief that had obviously been in there for some time, and buried his nose in it.

He knew Laura, Cassie said to herself again, and presumably Klaus as well. Apart from Laura she had never met anyone who had known her grandfather. But all these years, on the other side of the Wall, she thought, there was this man. And Laura was unaware of his existence.

'Tell me about your friendship with my grandparents,' she said. 'It's so exciting for me to meet someone who knew them when they were young. Laura won't believe it!'

The old man started. He's still in the past, Cassie thought. I must not force him to return too quickly.

All the same, the questions she wanted to ask kept bubbling up inside her – how did you meet Laura and Klaus? Were you close friends? Were you looking after her photographs all these years, hoping to see her again, and if so why didn't you try to locate her?

She kept glancing at him, willing him to return to the present.

But he was still silent when Fräulein Eisermann bustled back into the room carrying a tray laden with coffee and buttered slices of stoffen cake.

Cassie said, 'We have just discovered that your father knew my grandmother long ago.'

Fräulein Eisermann looked startled, as well she might.

'This is so?' she said, and lapsed into German, apparently asking her father to embellish what Cassie had said.

He spoke briefly to his daughter who glanced at Cassie and smiled, glad perhaps that her father had received news of an old friend.

So many died, he had said. And amongst them now was his wife. He was no doubt lonely, missing company of his own age. Well, now he could hear more about Laura and maybe in due course the two of them could get together and catch up on the past.

Meanwhile, Laura was going to be fascinated by the dual discoveries, thought Cassie, already mentally making her report from Berlin.

The conversation between father and daughter terminated and Herr Eisermann reverted to English.

'Please,' he said to Cassie, 'drink your coffee. When you have done so there is something else I wish to show you.'

There was no Berlin-room between the one in which they had met and the old man's bedroom – only a short, dimly-lit corridor.

He opened the bedroom door and stood back to allow her access and to see what stood against the wall facing the doorway.

Cassie heard herself gasp. She was looking at a handmade oak bureau, mounted on a stand with chamfered posts and block feet.

Surely it *was* Laura's bureau?

'*Bitte*,' said Herr Eisermann, 'take out the top drawer.'

There were seven drawers inside, she remembered Laura saying, *and a little cupboard in the centre. Edward Barnsley wrote the history*

*of the bureau, who had helped him make it, whom it was for and the
date, on the back of the top centre drawer.*

Cassie's legs were suddenly pliant and unsteady. She stepped
forward, pulled out the drawer and there was the inscription:
For Laura Mary Conway. 25 September 1930. Edward Barnsley.

'It can't be true! My God! You mean – you've had it all this
time? As well as the photographs?'

She turned, expecting an explanation.

Instead Herr Eisermann said:

'Laura is happy? Her husband is also alive?'

'Oh no,' Cassie said, 'Klaus died. He was murdered by the
Nazis before she left Berlin. Didn't you know?'

'Not Klaus. Her husband in England.'

'But she didn't remarry.'

He thought about that. 'Then you are?'

'Klaus and Laura's granddaughter.'

Once again, he stared intently at her. He said *'Ich verstehe dich.'*

'It's quite simple. Laura was pregnant when Klaus was killed.
Her daughter – my mother – was born after she got to England.'

She was answering his questions in a dazed kind of way
instead of putting her own to him.

'Anyway,' she said, 'you must tell me the whole story. How you
all met. How well you knew my grandparents and, of course,
how it was that you ended up looking after Laura's possessions.'

But Herr Eisermann was shaking his head.

'It is in the past. No, let me speak. I wish to make a bargain
with you, Fräulein Stacton. You may take the photographs and
the bureau and return them to your grandmother. Today before
you leave the apartment we will make arrangements for this. But
there is a condition – '

So it's like that, is it, thought Cassie. After all that –

'You want to be reimbursed?'

'No. I require only that you do not tell your grandmother of our
meeting. I would prefer that she does not know of my existence.'

'But that's impossible. Ridiculous. And *why*? It doesn't make
sense!'

35

'Not to you, but to me – yes.'

'But *why* can't you tell me? *Laura* will want to have all the details – '

'That will be a problem for you,' he said. 'But it is still my condition.'

In vain, Cassie argued and probed. He was quite adamant. In the end, she was forced to comply.

'All right. If that's what you want,' she said. 'But I'll give you my address and phone number in London all the same in case you change your mind and want to contact Laura. I'm sure she'd be delighted.'

Instead of replying he shuffled out of the room. Cassie followed him to where Fräulein Eisermann was sitting, waiting.

'*Was ist los?*' she said, surveying her father. '*Was fehlt Ihnen?*' He shook his hand at her.

'*Es ist nichts Ernstes.*'

Fresh coffee was brewed. A slightly mystified Fräulein Eisermann was informed that the true owner of the prints and bureau had been located and that they were to be handed back. With her assistance, Cassie made arrangements for packing and transport.

Fräulein Eisermann saw her out. '*Gute Heimfahrt*,' she said. *Safe journey home.* She really was a very nice woman.

'*Danke*,' said Cassie. '*Vielen Dank*,' which was more or less the sum total of her German.

The full implications of her *coup* came to her on the underground. The prints would make a magnificent and valuable addition to Laura's planned retrospective. And maybe that was the way out of her own dilemma – to hand them over to Laura's agent and suggest that he fabricate a feasible explanation for having laid hands on them. He would be so ecstatic at the prospect of his commission that he would take on the dirty work. Cassie – like Herr Eisermann – could stay out of it, at least for the present.

As for the bureau . . .

It used to stand in one corner of the Berlin-zimmer, Laura had said. *Our belongings were strewn all over the place – books, cushions, ashtrays – and the armchairs were covered in white chintz with red and mauve and yellow flowers, all clashing horribly!*

But before that the bureau had been in Laura's bedroom in Barnes. When she was thirteen years old.

It was entirely appropriate that, having been given to Laura on her birthday, it should be returned to her on that day.

Which had the added advantage of giving Herr Eisermann seven months in which to change his mind about revealing his involvement and thus, thought Cassie, getting *me* off the hook with Laura.

But she had an unpleasant suspicion that Herr Eisermann was not going to be so obliging.

And indeed, as the months drifted by and the plans progressed for the opening, the bureau remained where Cassie had put it in storage, and there was not one word from Berlin.

'L ET'S go!' said Cassie to Cecily, and the two girls pulled and pushed the trolley out from behind the screen. 'Excuse us,' they said. 'Sorry – we have to get past.'

The guests, naturally nonplussed by the sight of a mobile desk, gave way. Conjectures as to its significance were voiced by several.

'It's a prop for the TV presenter.'

'*Wicked* piece of wood!'

Isn't it just, thought Cassie. She was no longer nervous. She was glowing with the expectation of giving back.

Laura and Richard had been joined by Laura's photographic assistant, John Dodgson, commonly known as Dodgy John.

Dodgy, who was West Indian, was 'A Talent', one of the few in her field not decried by Laura, who bristled at competition. Dodgy was different. He brought the exuberance of the Caribbean into his work. Laura opened doors for him to designers and fashion editors, and everyone knew that one day he would take over her studio. He was also a survivor of the *Marchioness* riverboat disaster. His wife had been one of those drowned, but this evening he was once again on top form.

'Gotta have a blinder,' he said to Richard, and patted his pockets in search of cigarettes. He lit up and sighed with satisfaction.

'Why do you call them blinders, Dodgy?'

'Man, do they have eyes?'

Richard chortled. He was still laughing when he became aware that the noise level in the gallery had dropped. Cassie had not let him into the secret so he wondered why she was becoming the focus of attention up there on the top level and what Andrew Cowan – in the process of commanding complete silence – was about to say. Then he noticed the bureau.

Meanwhile Cassie had been introduced to the crowd and was beginning to speak herself. 'Those of you who know my grandmother well will have heard that she was once given a very special birthday present . . .'

Richard listened attentively, joined in the applause which followed the end of Cassie's speech. Like everyone else, he was exultant at the bureau's return.

'This is wonderful news!' he exclaimed, turning to Laura.

As a matter of course, he had expected Laura to be over the moon. She was moved all right – but not in the way he had hoped.

Laura was trembling with the wrong kind of shock. Pale at the best of times, she was now completely devoid of colour. She might have had news of the death of a friend instead of being the recipient of a presentation, so distressed did she seem.

'Laura?' whispered Richard and because she looked as if she might actually faint he put his arm around her waist, 'Laura darling?'

'It's all right,' she managed to say.

Her eyes were opaque and without expression. It certainly wasn't all right. He held her firmly.

Cassie, waiting for Laura to respond with glee, was horrified by her reaction. Anger would have been preferable to the pain she saw etched on Laura's face.

What have I done, she thought wildly. My God, why is she so upset?

Her own impulse was to take flight. 'Get me out of here,' she said to Dominic.

The party had resumed with renewed zeal. Dominic, serious rather than sulky, took her hand and drew her towards the door and out into Carlos Place.

'Where's your car?' she said.

'We came by taxi – remember?'

'No,' said Cassie. She burst into tears.

'Come on. It isn't such a disaster.'

'It's a complete fuck-up! And I haven't got a tissue.'

Dominic produced a handkerchief and she dabbed her nose and eyes. The tears kept coming.

'*Shit!* I won't be able to go out to dinner.'

As a contrast to the glitz of the opening Laura had opted for a quiet family meal in a cosy restaurant and booked a table at Maggie Jones's in Old Court Place off Kensington Church Street.

'Yes, you will. But we'll go back to my flat first and get you cleaned up.'

A taxi with its light on was approaching. Dominic hailed it.

'Get in, woman.'

Still sniffing, Cassie obeyed.

Maggie Jones's, with its refectory tables, hunting prints, baskets and earthenware pots, was an agreeable place. The waiters were handsome young men in dark green aprons. The wallpaper downstairs was green and red, depicting peacocks strolling between flower arrangements. On their table were geraniums, a magnum of house-wine and reassuringly large glasses.

Richard and Laura were already seated when Dominic and Cassie arrived. Cassie had done a professional job on her face and was hoping that her red eyes would not be noticed in the discreetly lit room. Although her tears were under control her stomach was playing up massively. But mercifully no one else was aware of its gyrations.

'My dear, we missed you. Where did you disappear to?' Laura's voice was not altogether natural but she sounded friendly.

'We just popped by Dominic's flat.'

'So I didn't get the chance to thank you, darling.'

All highly artificial, thought Cassie. This is just terrible, Laura and I pretending to one another.

'You're pleased?' she said, continuing the artifice.

'Of course, I'm pleased. Why wouldn't I be?'

Why indeed?

In the normal course of events Laura should now begin her interrogation. *OK, darling – tell me how the hell you got hold of the bureau?*

Cassie, who had been dreading this question and been intending to keep mum, no matter how heavy the pressure, found herself wishing that Laura would probe and insist.

Instead, Laura retreated behind the huge menu. 'What a selection!' said her too-cheerful voice. 'Let me think – haddock mousse? Is the mussel soup available or maybe the artichoke hearts?'

The waiter, who had been hovering, closed his eyes, shook his head in mock confusion and informed them that, for the record, Maggie's Tart tonight was a hot little number.

'Actually cheese quiche. And the mussel soup *is* on.'

'Mussel soup then.'

'And for you, madam?'

'Iced cucumber soup,' said Cassie dully, and her stomach heaved again.

'My tastes are plebeian, I'm afraid. I'll have a prawn cocktail.'

Under the table, Dominic's hand reached out for hers.

'Don't *tell* me you're going to order a pepper steak! We haven't got Black Forest gateau and don't, whatever you do, ask for a gin and tonic!'

The background music was what Cassie called Fogey Forty-Four Years Back.

'*Paper Doll!*' Richard said, '*With those flirty-flirty eyes* . . . dum-de-dum . . . *real live girl!*'

It couldn't be worse, Cassie thought. Soon, however, Richard, diverted by the sheer brilliance of the artichoke hearts soaked in hot melted butter and served in a soup bowl, gave up trying to inject some sparkle into the evening.

Laura, noticed Cassie, was tucking in heartily to her mussel soup. Although she often forgot to eat, could apparently survive all day merely on air, when food was put in front of her she was surprisingly rapacious. Her appetite had not been affected by her distress.

I should have taken her age into consideration, Cassie berated herself. At seventy-five perhaps people find it difficult suddenly to face the past. The bureau must have brought back too-vivid memories to Laura, made her recall it being in the apartment, made her remember Klaus.

'Mange-tout, cauliflower in cheese sauce and *sauté* or new potatoes,' the waiter said. 'Just those three. They'll be enough to share between all of you. Otherwise you waste money and I *hate* people to do that.'

'I'll just have a green salad,' said Cassie.

Laura guzzled all her steak-and-mango casserole and ordered a *crème brulée*. She had a touch of colour in her cheeks induced by the wine.

Maybe it's going to be all right, thought Cassie. Maybe the past, having rushed back to destroy Laura's equilibrium, is now in retreat.

Richard, thinking along similar lines, finished his pudding. 'One thing about you, Laura,' he said, lovingly teasing, 'is that you've always been so deliciously greedy! I like that! Actually, most men secretly fancy greedy women!'

If he had expected Laura to smile, he was disappointed. Instead her eyes grew big with hurt and her mouth turned down. She didn't speak. Nobody did.

Laura got up. 'Excuse me,' she said, 'I must go upstairs.'

Still no one rushed in to fill the conversational gap. The silence was broken only when Richard, with uncharacteristic clumsiness, knocked his side-plate on to the floor.

'*Naughty!*' said the waiter.

The ladies' cloakroom was two floors up. Laura walked up the sanded steps holding carefully on to the rope banister.

Having been to Maggie Jones's before she was aware that there was only one ladies' loo and she was praying to a God in Whom she sometimes believed, sometimes did not, that it would be vacant.

The upstairs restaurant was full. Panting slightly, Laura began to wend her way between the tables, heard a woman hiss, 'That's Laura Conway the photographer. She looks very *dull*, doesn't she?' and made her escape into the cloakroom. The lavatory was vacant.

'Thank You,' she said.

She locked the door, sat on the pine seat, lid down, and contemplated the walls, which were painted cinnamon.

She thought, Where did she find it? What does she know? How can I ever explain?

But, no: if she had found out, she would have told me.

All the same, she found the bureau so she must have made some connection.

She closed her eyes. Like snowflakes in the wind her thoughts fluttered round. Does it matter so much if she has stumbled on the story? It doesn't appear to have altered her attitude towards me. All the same . . .

There was the sound of a door opening, the clatter of high-heeled shoes. After a few minutes a woman coughed.

I can't ask her, Laura thought. I just cannot. Silly old fool that I am, getting upset all over again because of one word.

Greedy, he said. And, of course, he's right. If I'd not had such a large appetite for life none of it would have happened.

LAURA

1930 – 1939

WAKING in her iron bedstead, Laura already had misgivings about the day ahead which, from her point of view and despite what her mother said to the contrary, was bound to prove tedious.

This was an opinion she had to keep to herself, although she knew that if the circumstances were favourable and she could express it to her father, he would agree. But the circumstances were *not* favourable . . . Remembering that, she sighed, pushed the bedclothes aside and swung her feet out on to the bare floor.

At twelve, Laura was a thin child with a face that was neither pretty nor plain, ash-blonde hair and – her best feature – deeply set grey eyes outlined by long, decently dark lashes.

When Laura looked serious, as she did at present, she gave the impression of being studious, which she was not. The only school subject which really interested her was art and that, as her headmistress said, was entirely natural, her father being an artist.

There were some people who still spoke with respect of Tim Conway's work, basing their judgement on his pre-war reputation.

Before the Great War there had been a vogue for Tim's delicate watercolours. But in the war he had been wounded in more ways than one and when he came home he was drunk more often than he was sober, more frequently in the Red Lion public house than in his studio. Commissions were postponed or forgotten – half-finished canvases abandoned forever. The Conways were nearly always in financial difficulties.

When Tim was sober he was marvellous company and the

world was painted in colours far more brilliant than those he employed in his work. So his youngest daughter thought. Laura adored her father. Tim's best days were also hers.

This would not be one of them. Tim had been drinking all week. In the mornings he was frowsy and bad-tempered. When he returned from the pub he ignored the family and went upstairs to bed. No, today her father would not be receptive to her confidences, thought Laura, opening her bedroom window and sticking her head out.

She could just see the Common. The Conways lived in Barnes and the Common had been her playground. It was still a source of fascination for anyone with an imaginative streak. Once – until a hurricane had overturned it – a mill had loomed up to compete with the walnut trees and elms and to look down on the miller's house alongside it. In the cemetery was a grave where an Arab boy was buried. His name had been Yussef Sirree and his grave was diagonal to all the others so that, even in death, he could face Mecca.

If the Common was an attractive place, so was the village of Barnes. The shops in the High Street and Church Road sold flowers and hosiery and books and sweets. In the window of the grain shop, seeds and grains were arranged in constantly changing patterns.

In a previous era French Huguenots, fleeing from persecution, had settled in the vicinity, and some roads and buildings still paid tribute to them by name.

But it was the Anglican Church, not the Huguenot, which dominated village life now, in 1930, and which was also dictating how Laura was to spend most of this fine July day.

Under the aegis of the church a fête was going to be held in the rectory grounds in Church Road. Margaret Conway, Laura's mother, was a member of the committee organising the fête, and all the Conway children had been recruited to help. It was not a prospect that appealed to Laura.

Having checked the weather, she dressed and went downstairs. Her older sisters, Caroline and Harriet, and her

48

younger brother Willy were already eating their porridge and her mother was sitting with them at the table.

'You're late, Laura!'

'I'm sorry, Mother.'

'You must discipline yourself to wake up early like everyone else!'

Laura, being like Tim, worried her mother. In turn, Laura was frustrated by her mother's extreme conservatism.

The more Tim drank the more tightly Margaret held on to the security of upper-middle-class values. Where once she had been intrigued by romance and creativity, now she feared them. In the years since Laura's birth she had turned from an easy-going, loving wife into a woman made pedestrian by too much responsibility.

Pitying her mother, Laura secretly wished that Margaret was more like Tim when sober, less concerned with her place in society and with doing the right thing.

Or – better still – like Kitty, Laura's aunt, who travelled to exotic places and appeared every now and again in Barnes to report on what she had seen. But Margaret, thought Laura, could never emulate her light-hearted sister-in-law.

'Are you sure you know what to do, Laura? I don't want you annoying Mrs Barton.'

Mrs Barton was the vicar's wife.

'Yes, Mother, I'm sure.'

'Laura doesn't want to go to the fête,' Willy announced.

This statement, although accurate, did nothing for Laura's case.

'Why doesn't she?' Margaret demanded.

'Too much noise!' said an aggrieved voice. Tim, still in his dressing-gown, was standing in the doorway with his hand to his head.

The topic of the Anglican church fête was temporarily shelved. As if by common assent the Conway children rose from the table and solemnly carried their porridge bowls through to the kitchen. Doing the washing-up was infinitely preferable to proximity to Tim.

*

Whenever she walked along Glebe Road Laura had a vision of herself disembarking from an ocean liner in a foreign port.

This was because the Lion Houses there, with the stone heads perched on the roofs and gate-posts, put Africa into her mind.

Aunt Kitty had been to East Africa and visited Zanzibar which had smelt pungently of cloves and reeked of the weird and wonderful.

Oh, to travel to unfamiliar locales. Instead of which she, Laura, was going to assist the vicar's wife in running a Hoop-la stall! She had nothing against the vicar's wife, or the vicar either. But the afternoon of enforced jollity was somehow woven in with her mother's desire for respectability; Margaret's need to prove to the people of Barnes and Mill Hill that, despite Tim's lapse from grace, the Conways were worthwhile. Inherent in this was disloyalty to Tim.

The five Conways turned into Church Road, Margaret and Willy leading, Caroline and Harriet following and Laura lagging behind. Younger children in fancy-dress costume, Bo-Peeps and clowns, Cupids and Red Riding Hoods, were being scurried along the pavements by their mothers. A red streamer with white lettering drawing attention to the fête had been mounted above the rectory wall.

The Conways filed through the gate. Inside, a keeper of the portals was receiving monies and offering admission to the freedom of the revels. Tea tables had been positioned around the lawn, ladies stood behind stalls laden with goods and, in that corner of the grounds where giant trees offered good shade, Miss Beatrice Brown's pupils, attired in gauzy draperies, were already dancing on the green turf.

'Ah, Mrs Conway, you're here! Could you whip some cream for the strawberries? Laura, dear, come along with me.'

Don't give any trouble to Mrs Barton, warned Margaret's face.

Don't worry, Mother, signalled Laura's. She had no desire to add to her mother's woes by staging a rebellion. With complete resignation she accepted her fate.

*

At the end of the afternoon the children formed a procession to march around Barnes prior to participating in the 'Battle of Flowers'.

The results of competitions were announced and prizes awarded, after which the children would leave, fairy lights would be lit, and the grown-ups would dance under the trees on the lawn.

'Well, that was a great triumph!' exclaimed Margaret, rounding her brood up. 'Lady Lowther's speech went down very well. And her daughters are absolutely charming. You talked to them, Caroline. How did they get on playing Clock Golf?'

'Quite well,' Caroline said smothering a yawn.

Having worked hard all afternoon, they were keen to get home. Only Margaret chattered away animatedly as they went, pleased with the fête's success.

In the same order as they had set out they reached Rock's Lane.

'The Railway School play was excellent,' Margaret was saying, 'I do think . . .'

She stopped in mid-sentence. The vivacity drained from her face. Her expression became impassive. Sitting on the side of the road in a drunken stupor was Tim, his shirt partially unbuttoned and his mouth half open, emitting gentle snores.

Willy giggled nervously. Caroline and Harriet exchanged rueful glances. Laura reached out to take her mother's hand.

Quick as a flash, Margaret snatched her hand away. 'Don't!' she said coldly, and while Laura was still grappling with this rejection, she added, 'Quickly, let's get away before anybody sees us.'

She began to half walk, half run along the lane, hotly pursued by Willy.

'Come on,' Harriet said. 'It's no use standing here.'

She and Caroline set off at a brisk trot, leaving Laura and Tim.

Father, thought Laura. She wanted to scream at him, berate him for throwing his talent away, for shutting the doors between them, allowing the world to become drab and grey. At that moment she was convinced that life would never again be infused with colour. And here was her father fast asleep, not minding a jot!

She left him to his slumbers, stomping gloomily in the direction of home. The others would all be equally depressed by what had happened. Groaning inwardly, she opened the back door, walked through the kitchen into the corridor and there paused.

From the sitting-room came the sound of a merry voice. Seconds before, Laura had been weighed down by pessimism. But now her spirits were lifting. She rushed forward, opened the sitting-room door, held out her arms – and Aunt Kitty came forward to embrace her.

She smelt delectably of French perfume, and Laura thought that her knickers were bound to be silk with slits up the thighs. Aunt Kitty's stockings were held up by garters which had bows on the side and she did not wear a bust flattener as other women did but let her bosoms go free. Laura could feel them, small and firm, as she held on to her aunt.

'Good heavens!' said Kitty, finally releasing her. 'You *are* tall!'

'Do you think so?'

As usual, Kitty was fashionably clad. She loved clothes, both as garments to be worn and as *objets d'art*. Sometimes she ran them up out of fabrics purchased on her travels; more often she had them made for her in Paris where the smartest women in the world went to be dressed. She was wearing now a vivid green dress with a V-shaped neckline and a box-pleated skirt which was tied round the hips with a deep contrast sash. Her fair curly hair was almost completely covered by a bonnet-shaped cloche hat with a wide pointed turn-back brim, the same shade as her dress. Her shoes had T-straps and a small bunch of artificial flowers was pinned on her right shoulder.

At thirty-one, Kitty Bellamy was a pretty woman. Her husband, who had died three years previously, had left her well-off.

'How long are you going to stay?' Laura asked.

Kitty's visits enriched the household in a number of ways. On Tim, she had a positive effect, keeping him out of the pub. She was generous with her money, more than paying her way with household expenses and buying everyone gifts. All this compensated for what Margaret described as her tendency to flit.

Kitty lived a mercurial existence, drifting not only from country to country and city to city but from man to man. Sometimes one of these suitors would accompany her to Barnes and inquiries would be made as to the nature of the relationship.

Each time, Kitty would say, 'He's a darling man but I'm not in love with him,' and the suitor would fade out of the picture, not to be seen again.

But now she was here on her own. Lovely.

'How long will I be staying?' repeated Kitty, thoughtfully. 'Until the beginning of September, if your mother doesn't mind. Then I'm going to Paris for a few months, spending Christmas there, and in the New Year I'm going to Berlin. And after that – '

The family listened, distracted from the problem of Tim.

It wasn't until Kitty said, 'Where's that brother of mine? Not upstairs in bed, is he?' that they remembered where they had left him.

With all the talking they got to bed late and it was not until the following day that Kitty unpacked properly.

Laura sat on the edge of her bed, watching her lift out silk nightgowns, beige-coloured stockings and slinky sheath dresses.

'Tell me more about Berlin and Paris.'

'Berlin is carefree and emancipated!' Kitty said. 'The cafés are full of young men and women holding passionate discussions about music and art and painting. So civilised!'

She pulled out a crêpe-de-chine slip, threw it on to the bed and considered what had been underneath it. It was a small box and at first Laura thought that it must contain jewellery.

'I must show you my Leica,' Kitty said, and while Laura was still wondering what she meant, her aunt opened the box.

Instead of jewellery a tiny camera was lying on the red plush lining.

'Small it may be,' said Kitty, 'but it's formidable! Can you believe that it takes pictures of moving objects? In Germany, the magazines are illustrated by photographs instead of drawings and all the photo-journalists there use this camera. I was dying to own one but then I mislaid the instructions and . . .' She paused and looked exasperatedly at the little Leica.

'You don't know how to use it?' Aunt Kitty had never been good with gadgets.

'Actually not.'

'Let me see.'

Kitty passed over the box. Until then the only camera Laura had ever seen was a Box Brownie. Kitty's was much heavier, being made out of metal. Numbers and letters and words, in both German and English, were minutely imprinted upon it. On its front was a circular cap.

'I think you take that off,' said Kitty vaguely, 'and look through there.'

Following these instructions, peering through the viewfinder window, Laura saw that it was divided into two sections, providing a duplicate image of Kitty.

'Why should there be two of you?'

'I don't know. I think you have to fiddle around until you get one picture. You can experiment with it if you like. More excitingly, I want to take all of you shopping. Shall we go in to London, have lunch and pay a visit to Peter Jones?'

'Lovely.'

All the while Laura was playing around with the camera, inexpertly turning its lens. Suddenly, the two images of Kitty merged into one. Encouraged by this she experimented further, pressed a knob. There was a soft 'click'.

'I think,' said Kitty, 'that you've taken a photograph!'

'Have I?'

Even then, Laura was fascinated by the camera. Kitty said that it was loaded with sufficient film to run off thirty-six frames.

'You can use them all, as far as I'm concerned. Take lots of photographs! We can always get more film. But never mind about it now, darling. Let's get back to important issues. Where are we going to lunch?'

That summer the Conways were thoroughly spoilt. Expeditions to London on the open-topped bus were followed by shopping at Peter Jones, a sombre red brick and stone building with a green slate roof. Inside were carved walnut and ebony cases, potted palms and polished counters, alongside which were ranged chairs for customers.

Lulled by luxury, Margaret relaxed. Coaxed into sobriety by his sister, Tim reformed. They all pretended that the idyll would continue even when Kitty left.

Every so often she did so temporarily, abandoning the family for her own circle of friends. Once she went down to Petersfield for the weekend and returned bubbling with enthusiasm.

'We drove over to Froxfield to see Edward Barnsley's workshop. He's making the most exquisite furniture, all hand-crafted. I fell madly in love with a walnut and macassar ebony cabinet and I told him I wanted to buy it.'

'And you did?' Margaret asked.

Kitty shook her head. 'It was a special piece. He made it for the exhibition at Wembley four years ago and – can you imagine – no one wanted it then! Now, *he* wants to keep it. Such a pity.'

'I can't believe you gave up so easily,' Tim said, smiling at his sister. 'After all, Edward Barnsley is probably England's greatest craftsman.'

'True. And I didn't exactly give up.'

'So you did buy something?'

'I ordered something. You'll see!'

If Laura had been paying more attention she might have seen Kitty give a meaningful glance in her direction.

But Laura's thoughts were elsewhere. She had become obsessed with Kitty's Leica and was coming to terms with handling it. After much puzzling over the various controls on the top of the camera body she had finally worked out how to wind the exposed film into its container.

Reloading was even more complicated. The cog-like teeth of the camera had to be carefully slotted into the holes of the film. And having the film developed proved to be problematic. Mr Battersby the chemist had regarded the fruits of Laura's labour with deep suspicion, pointing out that foreign film could not be processed in England, let alone in Barnes.

The roll had been posted to Leica's headquarters in Weimar and, after a three-week wait, the photographs had just been returned.

To Laura's amazement and Kitty's delight they had all come out. Kitty had said that the camera was Laura's on the basis of a natural rapport, and pressed it into her hands.

'I'd rather have a piece of jewellery!' Harriet had said.

But, in a way, the camera was a jewel. Not for nothing had it been presented in a box lined with red plush lining. All her life, Laura would think of the camera in this way. All summer, she roamed Barnes Common with the Leica in her hand.

And then the summer ended and Kitty left. Having grown accustomed to being pampered the family was left with a sense of anti-climax.

Nothing special was planned for Laura's thirteenth birthday. When the bureau arrived the family felt elated, as if, after all, the era of extravagance had not passed. They surveyed the bureau, commenting on the ease with which the drawers slid out.

'It smells really nice,' Harriet said.

'That's because the drawers are lined with cedar,' said Tim.

'Oh, Kitty is too generous!' exclaimed Margaret. 'This is too valuable a present for someone of Laura's age.'

'It's beautiful,' Caroline said, 'I wish it was mine.'

It *was* beautiful, Laura thought. And there was, too, the novel experience of owning a piece of furniture on which her name had been inscribed.

She was incredibly lucky. She thought then that she would treasure the bureau all her life.

In May 1932, she parted with her thirteenth birthday present, but only briefly. The bureau was packed and shipped and Laura embarked on what she thought of as the Great Adventure.

She sat bolt upright in the compartment, peering out of the window, while on the seat opposite Kitty continued to doze. Through the billowing smoke which emanated from the funnel of the train she could see telegraph wires, a blur of trees, dolls' houses placed with precision in the middle of tiny gardens which were much too neat to have been tended by children. A sign, rushing towards her, proclaimed that Berlin was twenty-five kilometres away.

Ever since Kitty had begun rhapsodising over her photographs, insisting that *yes*, she had talent, and must be taken to Berlin to enhance her knowledge, Laura had been anticipating their arrival.

Although she was still only fourteen (fifteen in September, she reminded herself) she felt extremely grown up. This was partly due to the fact that she was wearing clothes more appropriate for a young woman than a girl of, theoretically, school-going age. Her sleeveless pinafore dress, with button closure at the back, was exactly the same shade as her rose red hat.

There had been ructions over this attire from her mother, just as there had been trouble over Kitty taking Laura out of school before the term had ended.

Laura's premature metamorphosis into an adult – worse, the proposal to introduce her to a city known for its wicked ways – had been too much for Margaret to accept without demur. She had protested and argued and waved her hands to reinforce her point, and Kitty had listened patiently and talked her down.

For Laura, Kitty had said, was going to become a superb photographer. Since this was her obvious bent, what point was there in keeping her at school? Berlin might have a notorious reputation, but it was years ahead of any other country as far as photography went.

Eventually Margaret had sighed and bitten her bottom lip and tried not to think of pimps and prostitutes and lesbian love and nude gambolling in pursuit of Free Body Culture and all the other horrors she associated with Berlin. And while she had been visibly weakened, Kitty had pointed out that by arriving in May, Laura could take an intensive course in German before beginning work as a darkroom assistant to one of Kitty's friends – an arrangement scheduled to start in September.

'In any case, we'll need to find an apartment,' Kitty had said to Laura. 'And you must get to know the city. I just love Berlin in the spring!'

The first sight of this much-loved city was not that encouraging. Laura wrinkled her nose, staring out at sombre warehouses, at huge, as yet uncompleted structures draped in scaffolding, at a vast billboard advertising a mysterious product called 'Welt-Hölzer'. It was exactly five A.M.

Yes, well, naturally it would be, said Kitty, waking up. German trains always ran on time and when the Germans maintained that something would happen, invariably it did.

As organised, a car was waiting to take them to their hotel in Pariser Platz. All the way there, Laura tried to form an impression of Berlin. The streets were lined with trees and the lofty buildings spoke less of decadence than of sobriety. At this early hour the city was silent, grey and semi-deserted. Wooden shutters were still drawn over shop windows. A black and white cat padded past on the pavement. A man walked a dog.

They drove along a wide boulevard and drew up outside an enormous, imposing edifice. 'Hotel Adlon' said the sign over its portals. A splendidly attired doorman stepped forward, opened the door and assisted them out. It was all quite intimidating.

In the foyer a uniformed bell-boy of about her own age was sorting the morning newspapers, each of which had been neatly wrapped round with a sticker. The manager came forward. Kitty was recognised and welcomed back. They were taken up to a bedroom on the third floor.

'I never do manage to sleep on trains,' said Kitty inaccurately when coffee had been ordered and they were on their own again. 'I'm going to have a hot bath and get straight into bed. I suppose you're longing to explore!'

Laura grinned. 'How did you know?'

'I just did. But do you want to go straightaway?'

'Why not?'

'Why not indeed? Then off you go. If you get lost, ask for the Adlon and someone will point the way back.'

Laura shot off. Her Leica was in her pocket. She needed no other company. In a few minutes she was retracing her steps along the wide boulevard. The trees which lined it were covered with clusters of cream and gold flowers which were emitting a most delicious fragrance. But apart from the trees the boulevard was too austere for her taste. The buildings had an official air about them. She was relieved when, after a brisk walk and several turnings, she reached a more heavily populated area.

The city was just waking up, washing its face of sleep. Women were winding up shutters and shaking out sheets and brushing down steps, and men were throwing buckets of water over the cobble-stoned streets. Berliners, Laura observed, were chunky people: the women sturdy with low waists and short legs, the men large and powerful.

Whatever their shape they all seemed to be obsessed with cleanliness. After she had observed them for a few minutes she decided that not only the streets, the houses and the white lace curtains appeared to have been newly-scrubbed, but also the people. Even the children were pristine clean, off to school with satchels on their backs, the boys in short trousers with crossed straps and the girls in crisply ironed dresses and dainty white socks.

The streets were filling up. Men on their way to work wore caps on their heads and many smoked pipes. Most were walking, some cycled in the wake of trams and double-decker buses. A policeman in a helmet, assuming a stern façade, waved the traffic past.

In the shop windows all sorts of unusual goods were suddenly revealed. Mechanical dolls bobbed their heads. The eyes of the dress dummies, bodies displayed from the waist up, were luminous and seductive.

Laura meandered on, stopping every now and again to take a picture. No one noticed, or cared. They were too involved in their own affairs – the fruit-sellers with their stalls, the flower-vendors with their baskets, the men offering the morning papers and the shoe cleaners working manically with brushes in both hands – to appreciate the significance of a young girl recording the life in the streets.

By July Laura had acquired a basis of German. When she went shopping for clothes she wrote *ein Unterrock* and *Strümpfe* on her list instead of petticoat and stockings.

Her knowledge of Berlin had extended considerably. She knew now that the two towns which had originated on either side of the Spree river had later grown into one which became the Prussian capital. The river and its valley enthralled her. The Spree was inundated with rowing boats and pleasure craft. In what had once been the river's swampy valley was a beautiful park, the Tiergarten.

In the old days this part had been a forest where hunters had stalked deer and wild boar, and in more recent centuries a formal garden laid out with geometrical avenues in the French manner. Then it had taken a few paces backwards to become a much more natural, albeit well-cultivated park, famous the world over for its trees and shrubs and waterways and flowers and for the *'Berliner Luft'*, the invigorating Berlin air.

For the last two months Kitty and Laura had gone riding every morning in the Tiergarten, so that its winding paths were now as familiar as the roads in Barnes had once been.

Barnes had receded well back in Laura's memory. Home was the smart apartment Kitty had rented for them in Grenadier

Strasse, near Alexander-platz. The area was not as obviously fashionable as Pariser Platz but Kitty said that it was not only more lively but more convenient for Laura when she started work.

The apartment itself belonged to one of Kitty's friends, an architect who had studied at the *avant-garde* Bauhaus in Dessau, and Laura was taken aback by the starkness of its décor. The carpets and curtains were unpatterned. There were no pictures on the bedroom walls, and the furniture – which Kitty said was designed by Marcel Breuer – was made out of tubular steel.

Like many of Kitty's Berlin friends the architect was a Jew. That was the other thing Laura had learnt about Berlin – that it was largely run by Jews, as were many of Germany's great provincial cities. The Jews, it seemed, worshipped intelligence: the most brilliant financiers, scientists, doctors, lawyers and artists in Berlin were of the Jewish faith.

'Which makes people jealous of them, naturally,' said Kitty. 'I can't bear anti-Semitism!'

'Herr Hitler is against them.'

At the mention of the Austrian leader of the National Socialist Party – Nazis, for short – Kitty snorted.

'I can't think why they ever made that nasty little man a German citizen. He and his ghastly friends will resort to any tricks to get into power. When they want to break up a political meeting they release white mice! Everyone, particularly the women, rushes out of the auditorium. What minds dream up such strategies?'

'But I've been told that the Nazis will find jobs for everyone when they get into power.'

Over six million people were unemployed. Every day Laura saw men and women slumped dejectedly on benches, epitomising defeat.

'Who tells you?' Kitty demanded, 'is it Frau Ullrich?'

This was the woman they had taken on as a maid-of-all-work.

'Yes. She supports Herr Hitler.'

'Does she indeed! It's just as well we employ Frau Ullrich for brawn, not brain! I don't want to be reminded of Herr Hitler. The night's still young and I want to go on enjoying myself!'

That was easy in Berlin. The city offered virtually unlimited pleasure. Sailing and tennis clubs abounded. In spring the country landowners poured in to attend the horse show and to dance all night at the Aristocracy Ball. There were fifty theatres, superb orchestras, excellent cinema, provocative cabaret, dozens of lively nightclubs and one hundred and twenty newspapers. Every foreign actor, composer, musician and journalist aspired to work in Berlin.

That evening Kitty and Laura had been to the Zaruck Club, where Adolf Glaisbrenner, the satirical cabaret artist, had been performing. Laura had missed much of the subtleties inherent in his act and had to have them explained to her. And now they were wandering along the Motzstrasse. The street musicians were out in force and a barrel organ was just starting to play.

'What does *Zaruck* mean?' Laura asked.

'It's a bowdlerisation. *Zurück* means backward and *Zar* means emperor and – '

That was when the beautiful women sauntered down the street.

There were three of them, all about six feet tall, and they were dressed, more or less identically, in long satin evening gowns with very low necklines. Laura stared. The women's gowns were extremely tight, like wallpaper pasted on, and their faces were heavily made up with much emphasis on the eyes and a startling amount of rouge.

'Are they actresses?'

Kitty shook her head. 'No, darling, they're not.'

She waited until the trio were out of earshot and added, 'They're men – not women.'

'Men – in women's clothes?'

'My darling, this is Berlin, where anything is permissible. Anyway, they're doing no harm to anyone so what does it matter?'

'But if they're not in the theatre *why* are they doing it?'

'I suppose because they'd rather be women if they had the chance.'

Laura thought about that. 'How awful to be a man and wish you weren't. Are there many men like that?'

'Oh, yes,' Kitty said. 'Just as there are many men who would prefer to marry a member of their own sex. Given the chance, that is.'

'Frau Ullrich says Herr Hitler would get rid of all the queer people in Berlin. Is that what she means?'

'More or less,' said Kitty, 'God forbid that he should get such power into his horrible hands!'

The darkroom work Kitty had obtained for Laura was in the headquarters of Dephot, a cooperative set up to train photojournalists and to sell their pictures to the illustrated magazines. Its founder was Simon Guttman, a Hungarian Jew and one of a group of intellectuals who had started the German Dada movement.

Kitty had gone to some pains to explain Dadaism to Laura. The movement opposed the belief that the world was spiritually ruled and that art was sacred. Instead the highest art was to be that which concentrated on contemporary problems. The movement had been supported by the left-wing artist George Grosz, whose caricatures highlighted the degradation of the poor and the cynicism of governments. It had played cat and mouse with the authorities – an international Dada fair held in Berlin had contained blatantly political and anti-militaristic exhibits which had greatly upset the conservative officers and men of the Reichswehr.

While Laura was still assimilating the concept of Dadaism, Kitty had gone on to speak of Simon Guttman himself. He was enormously intellectual. He had introduced poetry into the Dada group. At Dephot he initiated the ideas and told his photographers exactly how to carry them out.

'If he sees a glimmer of talent, something that he can expand and stretch, he will encourage it,' Kitty had said. 'He's seen your photographs and on the strength of that he's willing to take you on. Remember, it's an honour to work at Dephot, even in the darkroom, so for heaven's sake don't mention your real age to Simon or he'll start having qualms!'

With this weight of information and instruction pressing down upon her shoulders, Laura was sitting in the reception room at Dephot trying to look poised.

In an attempt to appear at least seventeen she was wearing a navy blue crêpe dress with a tight bodice and puff-shaped oversleeves, a matching wool beret, cream stockings and pointed shoes. Kitty had lent her a strand of pearls and a navy blue envelope bag but she still felt vulnerable beneath this disguise and convinced that the girl behind the reception desk suspected her true age. Deception was an altogether miserable business.

'Herr Guttman will see you now,' said the girl, so meticulous that she even wore sleeve protectors.

Until then Laura had been confident that her suede shoes were *schick* and *modisch* but now she wasn't sure. But perhaps the man behind the desk didn't notice such irrelevances. He was a little, round man of about forty with a balding head. He surveyed Laura over the top of his glasses.

'You look extremely young,' he said right away. 'I find it difficult to believe that *you* took these photographs.'

They were laid out on his desk. Could she laugh her way out of it? No, she thought. In spite of his appearance, Herr Guttman is not a comical man.

'I can tell you I did.'

'*Vielleicht*,' he said thoughtfully. 'We will see how you progress in the darkroom. You will have to work long hours and I will not pay you. That was the agreement I made with your aunt.'

'I understand that.'

'Fine printing requires delicate hands and total concentration.'

Laura nodded.

'Come back tomorrow morning at eight A.M.,' said Herr Guttman. 'Please be punctual.'

The interview was over. She supposed it had been a success.

And perhaps it had been, for the following morning the receptionist greeted her with a smile. 'I'm Magda,' she said in English. 'My mother is from London so I can help you if you have trouble speaking German. When André comes he will explain your work.'

'André?'

'André Friedmann. He is from Hungary also. But last year he fled to Berlin. He was involved in *Politik* – he is *links*, of the left – and he is a Jew so – '

She stopped as a young man came in.

'*Hallo!*' he said.

He was about eighteen, with an attractive, impudent face.

'*Guten Morgen, André,*' Magda said. '*Darf ich Ihnen Laura Conway vorstellen.*'

'*Freut mich!*' he said.

'André does not speak English,' said Magda. 'When he came here he did not speak German either but he learns very fast.'

'I hope I can do the same where my work is concerned.'

'He will teach you very quickly – so he can forget about the darkroom and only be a photographer!'

And in fact André was already looking impatient. Hoping fervently that her limited knowledge of German would get her through the day, Laura was led to the darkroom. She knew nothing whatsoever about the developing process. The strong smell of chemicals which emanated from the room assaulted her nostrils and eyes. At the end of an hour she still could not differentiate between pyrogallol and alkali, sodium sulphite and potassium bromide, but she was as enthusiastic as André about the pictures he was processing.

Within the week these photographs would appear in various illustrated magazines. Kitty subscribed to two of them, *Berliner Illustrierte Zeitung* and *Neue Jugend die Illustrierte*, which Laura studied as if they were textbooks. It was fascinating to see the illustrations for the next editions before their editors had the chance!

One day, she thought, *my* photographs will be developed here prior to publication.

'How was it?' Magda said at the end of the day. 'Come with me for coffee and you can tell me. *They* all go to the Romansche café after work – Simon, André, Gerda Taro and the rest. Gerda is André's sweetheart from their schooldays. You know that he is already a brilliant photographer! He taught himself and then he pleaded with the Homunculus to give him assignments – '

'The Homunculus?'

'That is our name for Simon – and the Homunculus refused until one day everybody else was occupied and he *had* to use André. It was good for the Homunculus to learn that he is not always right! He is – I warn you – a martinet. So you must be careful!'

I'll be careful, Laura thought, and one day *I'm* going to follow in André Friedmann's footsteps.

Or in Kurt Hubschmann's or Otto Umbehr's, she might have added a few days later when she had met some of the other photographers associated with Dephot.

Magda was a fountain of information about these men. Kurt Hubschmann had served in the German cavalry and won an Iron Cross. His wife, Mutti, was an Austrian seamstress who made dresses for Marlene Dietrich, the actress whose performance as a callous prostitute in the film *The Blue Angel* had caused such a furore.

'Umbo' was a sweet roly-poly man, much nicer than the autocratic Felix Mann who looked down his nose at those he considered lesser mortals.

Magda chattered away. She took it for granted that Laura was at least seventeen, an alarming state of affairs which led to inquiries about boyfriends and suggestions that Laura wear trousers, as smart women did, and buy a cigarette holder.

'I don't know what to tell her,' Laura said to Kitty.

'Least said soonest mended,' said Kitty, insensitive to her plight.

Kitty was getting ready to go for a drive with one of her admirers. She had so many friends of both sexes that Laura had lost track of them. Some were Jewish intellectuals and artists, others diplomats and members of the foreign Press.

Several of her German friends were members of the liberal Social-Democratic Party, opponents of the Nazis. This party was running sadly short of funds. The majority of its members were out of work and unable to pay their subscriptions. Many were resigning and becoming Nazis instead.

'Is Herr Fritsch a Social-Democrat?' asked Laura, referring to Kitty's admirer.

'I'm not sure. Why?'

'I just wondered. Frau Ullrich laughs at the Social-Democrats. She says they eat raw food and constantly wash their hands!'

On this occasion Kitty chuckled at Frau Ullrich's remarks. 'Some of them *are* like that – the ones who say that high heels and corsets are signs of spiritual decadence!'

With that, off she went in Herr Fritsch's open car, holding on to her hat. Laura was left alone and uneasy, as always happened whenever Kitty went out with a man.

What if Kitty should fall in love, marry, and decide that a young niece was an encumbrance round the house? I'd have to go back to Barnes, Laura thought, sinking further into depression. I'll never experience the fun – dancing at the Ambassadeur and the Barberina and the Press Ball – that Kitty promises I'll have when I'm sixteen. And I'll certainly never be taken to see the topless dancers at the Apollo, as Magda has been. My career as a photographer will come to an end before it's even started.

All that Berlin had to offer was suddenly very precious, and the need to record it vital. Laura dragged on the bright red coat with the black fur collar which Kitty had just bought for her, grabbed her Leica and rushed downstairs into the street.

Within minutes she had reached Alexander-platz and was already feeling less gloomy. The square, with its modern shops and colossal figure of Berolina, was busier than ever. She could see the square tower of the Town Hall and, in the west, the domes of old Berlin.

A woman in a white cape and dress offered a cigarette from which her escort could light up his own. They smiled at each other, unaware that they had been models for Laura.

She lingered in the square for the best part of an hour, then made her way along Kaiser Wilhelm to the Unter den Linden, striding past the banks and hotels and the Kaiser-Galerie arcade and the Café Kranzler, pausing every now and again to take a picture of something that caught her eye.

Her destination was the Tiergarten, the best place in the world to be when things went wrong, although by now she had almost forgotten her earlier despondency. In the morning it had rained. Now, the sun was shining on the glistening trees and waterways of this loveliest of gardens, and on the golden figure of the Siegessäule perched high on top of her column.

Laura's spirits soared. She stopped by the star-shaped roundabout, observing a child learning to skip – a girl in trousers. Completely in her element she wandered from the Column of Victory towards Charlottenburg.

She had already reloaded her camera when she spotted the young man swinging up one of the pathways in her direction. She was struck first by the confidence of his gait and then by his beauty. He was tall and wide-shouldered and his hair – which her mother would have judged in need of a good cut – was dark brown, thick and curly. When he was closer she saw that his eyes, too, were brown – almost black – with thick lashes, and his skin sallow. He had a rather narrow nose and a wide, sensual mouth, and he was so handsome that he must certainly be a film-star from one of the Berlin studios, having a day off.

She pointed her camera at him, hoping that he would not notice or, worse, object. He did neither. Instead, most obligingly, he sat down on a conveniently placed bench, reached in his pocket and produced a book which he proceeded to peruse.

A text-book. She crept a little nearer. A medical text-book. He was a student, a would-be doctor, not an actor and, far from needing an audience, he was so engrossed in his studies that he did not hear her clicking away.

He was so good-looking . . . She hovered, camera in hand, willing him now to become aware of her presence, to get into conversation with her, ask her to join him in coffee at the Café Bauer.

But why should he? I'm not beautiful, Laura thought. I'm not even pretty. He would only take heed of a girl who could match him for looks.

Still, it was sad that they would never meet, that he would forever remain a record in her portfolio. She slipped her camera into her pocket, feeling that she had taken her best photograph of the day. The young man remained oblivious to her, and of all else but his book and leaving him to his studies, Laura walked away.

By November the city was covered in snow and the darkroom was making sense. Simon, in his reserved way, had inferred that she was making progress, and everyone was talking about André's first-ever photograph of the exiled Russian politician Lev Davidovich Bronstein – more familiarly known as Leon Trotsky – speech-making in Copenhagen.

Herr Fritsch had disappeared from Kitty's life. Kitty had been to the Carl Hofer *Maskentanz* – the masked ball – with another man in whom she had as quickly lost interest. Laura was coming round to the view that Kitty, having deeply loved her husband, would never develop strong feelings for another man.

She and Kitty had been to the cinema to see the latest box office hit, *Peter Voss der Millionendieb*, and to the State Opera House, and to a concert in the Philharmonie conducted by Wilhelm Furtwängler. A new gramophone had been purchased and Laura could not get out of her head a silly song about a parrot who would not eat hard-boiled eggs.

'These foolish politicians!' exclaimed Kitty, describing the political parties and coalitions of parties who, in turn, had attempted to govern Germany in recent years. 'After five months in office, Herr Papen's resigning.'

'What will happen now?'

'Oh, they'll form a new cabinet – and *that* won't last either! The next thing we know we'll be governed by the Nazis!'

'Will we?'

'It could happen. And then where will we be?'

'You wouldn't want to leave Berlin, would you?'

'Of course I wouldn't. Horrible Herr Hitler isn't that much of a threat. I'd just hate to think he had the satisfaction of succeeding, that's all.'

Given that reassurance, the Nazi party reverted to its customary position of insignificance in Laura's mind.

Of major importance was the need to escape from the darkroom, to follow in André's footsteps, if not all the way to Copenhagen, at least on to the streets of Berlin and its environs. But Laura's ambition to become a professional photo-journalist was daily thwarted by Simon who, while encouraging her talent, seemed perfectly happy to keep her in the darkroom.

She considered going elsewhere for work. Dephot was not the only photo-agency in Berlin. Ignaz Gidalewitch was selling his pictures through Weltrundschau, which was owned by a Rumanian. Could she throw herself on Herr Gidalewitch's mercy, beg him for an introduction?

Before she could put this plan into action, Kurt Korff, the editor of *Berliner Illustrierte Zeitung*, a man so dedicated to his job that he was said to seldom leave his chair, succeeded in startling Simon.

'Hats!' Simon was muttering one morning when Laura got to work. 'Kurt Korff wants a full page spread devoted to hats! He must be mad even to consider it – and what's more I haven't got a photographer available!'

It was the obvious opportunity for Laura to seize. 'What about me?'

Simon considered. 'One doesn't want to turn down commissions. I suppose you could. I'll give you a letter to take to the millinery department of the Ka-De-We. Bring back a selection of hats and Magda can model them here. We don't want to *pay* someone for doing that!' He shook his head at the absurdity of such a notion.

Laura returned from Wittenberg Platz with a collection of felt cloches, soft berets, and hats with pointed crowns, and Magda tried them on, commenting on the prices.

'Eight marks fifty! Do you think it's worth it?'

'Please look as if it is. Just pretend you're Marlene Dietrich.'

'I'm more like Lilian Harvey, I think,' Magda said, and posed in imitation of the English actress.

'That's lovely. Stay like that.'

It was all very different from street photography. The other photographers would regard the assignment as irrelevant; Simon would be quite justified in condemning the procedure as artificial; but Laura was enjoying herself.

'I've got a new boyfriend,' said Magda. 'He's Jewish.'

'Is he?' Laura was only half listening.

'My father should be pleased. He's always said he could do with influential Jewish friends and he hasn't got any. Do you want me to smile?'

'Yes, please.'

Magda, when she was not discussing her love life, was an excellent model.

'I hope Simon's paying you for this,' she said darkly. 'Don't let him take advantage of you.'

'No, I won't.'

But when the sitting was over the excitement of developing her own prints as part of a professional assignment eclipsed Laura's other priorities.

The pictures were not bad – were, really, rather good. Simon said so, pronounced them technically competent, and sent them to Kurt Korff. Laura was relegated again to the darkroom.

It was like being back at school, waiting on examination results. She had never excelled at exams.

'You've been biting your nails,' Kitty said critically. 'And look at your hands – the tips of your fingers are brown.'

'It's developing fluid. I'm in a state, waiting!'

The results were better than any she had received at school.

'Kurt's using them all,' Simon said. 'You did well. Next time we get a request like that you can handle it.'

She had not yet escaped. After Christmas she would plan a new campaign.

More snow was forecast. The skies were lead-grey and the temperature plunged. In the streets stall-holders blew on their fingers to warm them and offered ginger-bread and apples and nuts and hot sausages and decorations for Christmas trees.

Kitty wrapped presents. 'Not all for you, darling. In fact, the majority are for Frau Ullrich and her family. I do love buying gifts for children at this time of year. Mind you, the Germans do it all year round. Children get presents at Easter and for their birthdays.'

'But at Christmas they're allowed to keep their toys for only two weeks!'

'That's their *best* toys. And then they're put away until next Christmas. Turn off the radio, would you, darling? It's becoming a tool of government policy. Schleicher's talking his usual nonsense about negotiating with the trade unions. He'll never prevent the strike movement spreading. The working classes can't stand him. Mark my words, *his* cabinet won't last any longer than von Papen's! What news do you bring from work?'

'Something horrible happened to Magda.'

'Oh yes?'

'You know I told you she had a new boyfriend?'

'A Jewish boyfriend? It's something to do with that?'

'How did you know? Someone came up to her in the street and shoved a card into her hand. She showed it to me today.'

'What did it say?'

'That she is being watched – that it's unworthy of a German woman to mix with a Jew and that her name has been put down in a register of women who possess no pride of race.'

'How outrageous!'

'It's worse than that. The card said that in the new Germany a sign will be branded on the faces of women like that.'

'I've heard about these cards,' Kitty said, straightening up.

'They're being handed around. Magda isn't the only one to have this experience.'

'But who's distributing them?'

Kitty shrugged. 'Nazi fanatics. Anyway, cranks. Don't look so worried, darling. Anyone who'd do such a thing is mad, and there aren't that many crazy people, even in this city! I hope Magda is being a sensible girl?'

Laura grimaced. '*She* thinks so. She's told her boyfriend that she'd better not see him again.'

'*Stupid* girl!'

'You don't think there is such a register?'

'Certainly not! And Magda should be ashamed of letting herself be intimidated! I can't imagine *you* giving in like that! Oh, I don't want to even think about it. I must finish my presents. Do you think Frau Ullrich will like this jersey?'

'I'm sure she will,' Laura said.

It was silly to worry about Magda and her card, just as it was to dream about the handsome young student she had seen in the Tiergarten.

But every so often she did. His photographs were in her portfolio – not newsworthy, and of value only to herself.

In the New Year she would take pictures that *could* be sold. In 1933 she would nag Simon into giving her assignments of real validity.

Kitty was already making forecasts for the year ahead. Laura could go to at least one of the spring balls. No one would guess that she wasn't quite sixteen. And when she *was* sixteen she would be able to mix in society as an adult.

Nineteen thirty-three, Kitty said, was going to be Laura's year – when everything changed. Even then no one envisaged how rapidly everything could do so.

It was mid-January when it began. On the 15th, voters went to the polls in the tiny province of Lippe. The Nazis had organised a huge electoral campaign in which the entire party leadership had joined, and the resultant victory was promoted throughout

Germany so that people felt something momentous had happened.

A week later Herr Hitler's party staged a provocative mass rally in Berlin, while the leader himself and representatives of President Hindenburg negotiated an agreement on the composition of yet another new cabinet.

Counter-demonstrations followed as the Antifaschistische Aktion, comprising Communists, Social-Democrats and unaffiliated sympathisers, took a stance against Fascism. On 28 January the Schleicher cabinet resigned. On the 30th President Hindenburg confirmed Herr Hitler as Chancellor of the Reich.

Kitty groaned. 'What did I tell you? The Nazis are on our doorstep!'

'Only one of them.'

The feeling in Berlin was predominantly anti-Nazi. Three out of four voters in the city had rejected the party in the last elections.

'All the same,' Kitty said, 'I want to see the procession. I must know what's going on.'

That evening the Nazis' Berlin Gauleiter Goebbels were to hold a victory march down Unter den Linden towards the Chancellery.

To prepare them for this horror, said Kitty, they should dine out first at the Coq d'Or restaurant. The Coq d'Or was a Russian establishment, one of several designed to cater for the huge cross-section of White and Red Russians living in Berlin. The sound of the balalaika, the taste of borscht and blinis and shashlik had become for Laura as much a part of the city as the *Flohkinos*, the 'flea cinemas'; and the Romanisches Café at the Kaiser Wilhelm Memorial Church where the doorman, Herr Nietz, welcomed only the famous; and Königin and Ria Rita, the erotic *tanzbars*.

So many Russian restaurants, tearooms and bars existed that the city had been nicknamed Berlinograd, and they always seemed to be packed.

'Don't you love Russians?' Kitty said after dinner when they were walking towards the Brandenburg Gate. 'They *feel* so strongly. Heavens, darling, look at the crowds!'

The Unter den Linden was solidly packed with curious by-standers. They squeezed in amongst them.

'Most unpleasant!' Kitty had time to complain before the night sky was illuminated by a myriad of torchlights and Herr Hitler's supporters goose-stepped past.

As they marched they sang in jubilation: *'Smash the red scum to pulp! When Jewish blood spurts over the knife we'll all be feeling twice as fine!'*

Kitty said, 'That's *enough!* Push your way through the crowds, darling. We must go home.'

Some of the changes were vast, affecting all of Germany, and some small, peculiarly relevant to Laura's own life.

Overnight Berlin became the capital of Fascism. The propaganda and inscriptions which instantly appeared on the city walls confirmed this fact. On 1 February the Reichstag was dissolved; on 27 February it was set on fire, an event proclaimed by Herr Hitler as a sign from God, affording the Nazis an opportunity to arrest 10,000 of their opponents.

In March, President Hindenburg announced that the swastika and the black, white and red stripes of the Nazis were the official emblems of state, and opened the new parliament with Herr Hitler to whom the Reichstag gave the absolute powers of a dictator.

Jews were attacked in the streets. In April a boycott of Jewish shops was organised and a new law removing 'politically unreliable' and 'non-Aryan' civil servants from their posts came into force.

The same week Magda resigned from her job.

'But why?' asked Laura, surprised.

'I don't think it's advisable to carry on working for Jews.'

'There's no law against that!'

'All the same, I want to keep out of trouble. Look what's happened to André.' André had been involved in several street fights and was talking of leaving Berlin.

'That's just thugs.'

Magda sniffed. 'Sometimes I think you're younger than you pretend, Laura. Don't you know that it pays to be on the winning side? A lot of my friends admire Herr Hitler.'

'I hope they agree with his taste in films!' Laura said.

Films dating from the Weimar Republic had been banned, as were the works of directors or actors who had emigrated. The new Reich Ministry of National Education and Propaganda had invented the word *'Gleichschaltung'* which meant 'switching into line' and particularly applied to control of press and radio. *Die Weltbühne* had already ceased publication and other newspapers were rumoured to be following in its wake. Bruno Walter had been prevented from conducting at the Berlin Philharmonie and the composer Richard Strauss put in his place. Libraries and bookshops were being purged of so-called subversive writing.

'Maybe they do!' said Magda in an unfriendly voice.

After lunch she was gone and Simon was in the throes of recruiting her successor. It was not the appropriate moment, Laura thought, to beg her employer for further photographic assignments. Stefan Lorant, the editor of *Münchner Illustrierte*, had also used some of her fashion pictures – dresses rather than hats – and there had been one half-page spread commissioned by Kurt Korff which had fallen into her hands.

But otherwise nothing! And here was Simon being diverted by Magda's defection! It was all the fault of the foul Herr Hitler who was intent on ruining Berlin, a city he apparently disliked and even planned to rename 'Germania'!

Her work in the darkroom was finished for the day. Simon, on being apprised of this, nodded curtly to a request for an afternoon off. She was going to spend it looking for a dress: not an everyday, run-of-the-mill frock, but a truly spectacular gown to wear at next week's spring ball.

The party for this ball had already been arranged and, apart from herself, consisted of people of Aunt Kitty's age. No matter! The fact that she was going at all was testimony to being –

almost – grown-up, virtually Kitty's equal.

Since the Nazis had come to power she and Kitty had grown even closer. It was frequently remarked that they could be sisters instead of aunt and niece, except that she had never felt as relaxed and happy in Caroline and Harriet's company as she did in Kitty's.

Altogether, Kitty had replaced the family in Barnes. Although Laura dutifully wrote to her mother twice a month, she seldom thought of her otherwise, and of her father only with a heavy heart.

At Wertheim's department store she was thinking only of herself and of how she would look in a ball-gown. There was a huge range from which to choose: satin and lace and organza, some with long evening gloves to match.

She vacillated, torn between a square-necked model – black lace lined with pink silk – and a blue satin gown with a bias-cut bodice and narrow shoulder straps, and decided finally on the latter. The blue was quite pale. Deeper blue gloves and shoes would complement it.

'Excuse me, madam, but aren't you the lady who came here to select dresses for *Münchner Illustrierte*? The photographer?' the saleswoman said when her purchases were being wrapped.

'Yes, I am.'

'Are you going to take photographs at the spring ball?'

This had not been mooted but – 'I am,' said Laura, 'I am!'

If Simon would not give her assignments, she thought, she would dole them out to herself, and present him with a *fait accompli*. If her pictures of the ball were up to standard he would automatically offer them to one of the magazines and afterwards she would increase her pressure on him in this regard.

Kitty roared with laughter when she heard about this. 'You'll spend the whole evening sitting on the stairs, taking photographs through the banisters!'

'I might indeed!'

'I hope you're not going to become a *voyeur*!' Kitty said, and laughed at her own remark.

Laura smiled, too, and said, 'Certainly not!' in mock protest, but her own participation in the ball had indeed already taken second place to ambition, so that the evening remained forever in her mind as a series of selected images: chandeliers sparkling on bare, plump shoulders; the hem of a ball-gown burnt by a cigarette; a man's hand daringly caressing his girlfriend's breast; sedate and abandoned dancers.

Almost without her recognition her pictures were taking on a new, sensual connotation. She was barely aware of sex on a personal level, and yet mature enough to be able to record the erotic perceptions of her models.

At three A.M. the dancers were still on the floor. Laura was not tired either, just eager to escape to the darkroom, develop her prints, and make her selection for Simon's approval when he came to work.

Kitty was amongst the dancers. Laura scribbled a note for her, outlining her plans, and crept away. She was still wearing her blue satin evening dress when she laid her photographs on Simon's desk.

'What – ?'

'The spring ball,' Laura said. 'And, please, Simon, will you give me the chance to cover other assignments?'

She did not expect an easy victory. When Simon said, 'I will. I'm going to need another photographer immediately. André is leaving. He and Gerda have decided that Paris is a better town than Berlin,' her joy in winning was mixed with regret that André was opting to depart.

André was in the forefront of the exodus. In that year of change 100,000 people left Germany, amongst them the cream of the country's intellectuals, artists, writers, composers, scientists and politicians.

One after the other, the Jewish photo-journalists joined the queues at stations and airports. Felix Mann, Kurt Hubschmann and Stefan Lorant – who had been imprisoned by the Nazis – had headed for London; Ignaz Gidalewitch to study for a PhD at Basle University. Dephot and the other agencies mourned the loss of these men. Simon, struggling to keep going, was under Nazi surveillance.

The new regime ensured that the content of the illustrated magazines had altered. There was much less emphasis on gaiety – much more on political rallies and those events attended by the Führer.

Laura, covering the Berlin circuit, became accustomed to taking pictures of those sports deemed healthy by the Nazis. The irony of getting her chance to work in a less stimulating environment than heretofore did not escape her.

But it was dangerous now to take photographs indiscriminately in the street. The Gestapo, the notorious secret police, had their hands not only on Berlin's throat but on that of the whole country. The bullying SA – the Brownshirts – under the leadership of Ernst Roehm, had three million members. Everywhere men were marching – and watching.

The year of change had unsettled Laura. Berlin was irrevocably altered and yet she knew that she could not bear to leave it. The more it shook under the Nazi onslaught, the tighter she held on to it – and on to Kitty.

Only too well aware of the daily threat to her security, she was still unprepared for the next developments awaiting her at Dephot. Taking some pictures of masked fencers in to Simon she found him slumped at his desk.

'Are you ill?'

He looked sick. His face was pale and he was rubbing his fingers over his brow as if he was trying to ease a headache.

'No, I'm not ill,' he said, unhappily, 'it's more serious than that.'

'How could it be more serious?'

'It can be. It is. The Nazis have taken Dephot over.'

All sorts of invectives came into her mind. She wanted to shout them out.

'I know,' said Simon, reading her thoughts. 'As you can imagine, I feel the same.'

'But what will you do?'

'Probably go to Paris – eventually. I still have things to sort out here. What about you? They'll use your work.'

'They will not. I'm not going to take pictures for the Nazis. There are other agencies.'

'For the moment. You must be careful, Laura. This is only the start of it. It's going to get worse.'

It can't, Laura thought obstinately. This is the worst of it. It can't go further than this.

But – on a purely personal level – all of a sudden it did.

Looking back, she realised that there had been clues and that she had been too busy, or too obtuse, to pick them up.

Kitty had been abstracted, but happily so: if she had been distressed her condition would have been more noticeable.

That June day Laura had been to Laubenheimer Platz in Wilmersdorf where the Bohemian colony had formerly lived. But the colony had been broken up and its members attacked, just as the list of books by Jewish and other 'undesirable' writers had been used as fuel for a giant bonfire in Kaiser Franz-Joseph Platz.

Laura had watched the furnace being lit. Afterwards dozens of students, urged on by storm-troopers, had danced around the flames.

In Wilmersdorf there had been little to see – no picture material. Ahead of her two men with masks on their faces were wobbling on stilts, causing enormous amusement amongst the by-standers. She glanced at her watch, remembering that Kitty was having coffee with her friend, Sigrid Schultz of the *Chicago Tribune*, and that she had arranged to join them later.

Looking up she saw that a crowd was gathering further along the street. People were shouting and gesticulating. From the midst of it a man ran out clutching a bundle of newspapers.

'*Was ist los?*'

'*Achtung! Vorsicht!*'

In spite of his protests the papers were snatched from his

hands. Now she was nearer and able to read the headlines:
CHIEF-OF-STAFF ROEHM DISMISSED!

This was astonishing news. Ernst Roehm, the creator and commander of the SA, was the Führer's bosom friend – a friendship which provoked caustic comment since Roehm was homosexual.

Laura sidled up to a woman immersed in the report and peered over her shoulder.

Executions, she read. *Three hundred men . . .*

'Spreti's one of them,' somebody said. Count Spreti – known amongst the English-speaking community of Berlin as 'Count Pretty' because of his curly hair and ladylike mannerisms – had also been homosexual.

She bought a paper of her own, moved into a corner and read on. Other names were mentioned on the list of the dead. Heines, Heydebreck, Hayn – military men who all along had been Herr Hitler's staunch supporters.

Around her the crowd had dispersed into groups talking about the news.

'Roehm!'

'He deserved all that's coming to him,' a man spat.

'Filthy pig!'

At that a scuffle broke out. The newspaper vendor shouted again: *'Vorsicht!'*

Laura folded the paper and walked on. Sigrid, she thought, would be bound to have heard the news already. She and Kitty would be mulling over its implications. Mrs Schultz, who shared her daughter's apartment, would have plenty to say on the subject, as she usually did.

The Schultzes lived on Dornberger Strasse. The windows of the apartment were open. As she approached Laura could hear voices raised in exclamation, amongst them Kitty's.

'Laura, come in,' Mrs Schultz said warmly. 'Kitty, Laura is here.'

Kitty was sitting at the far end of the room. Seated around her were several men and women, most of whom Laura knew. But next to her on the sofa was a complete stranger, a middle-aged man with spectacles and greying hair.

Neither he nor Kitty looked up as Laura came in. That in itself was unusual – much more so was the way Kitty was gazing at the stranger, as she had never before, to Laura's knowledge, regarded any man. Admiration was written all over her face and the awful thing was that her approbation – rapture was a more suitable word – was reflected on the countenance of the stranger.

Laura's throat went dry.

'Coffee, dear,' said kind Mrs Schultz. 'And you must have a piece of my delicious cake.'

'Thank you.'

'Kitty!' Mrs Schultz called. 'You're dreaming over there! Laura's arrived.'

Kitty started, as if she had been miles away in a foreign land and been summoned back peremptorily.

'Darling! There you are. Come and sit with us. Leo, this is Laura. Darling, this is Leo Bennett. He is a senior editor on the *Chicago Tribune* and he has taken a year off to come here to research a book.' Her voice was high-pitched, the words tumbling out over-excitedly.

Leo stood up, smiled down at Laura. He had a charming smile. His eyes – nice greeny-brown eyes – twinkled. All the same, Laura froze.

'I've heard a lot about you,' Leo said.

'Have you?'

'And about your photography.'

His friendliness did not help. Kitty moved up and pulled her down on the sofa. 'Sit between us, darling.'

Laura sat on the edge of the cushion, her body rigid.

'You've heard the news, I suppose,' Leo said. 'What's the reaction out there on the streets?'

'I saw the start of a fight.'

At that everyone began to express their opinions on the situation. Norman Ebbutt of the London *Times* arrived and afterwards they all adjourned to the Taverne, the favourite meeting place for foreign journalists.

All evening Leo and Kitty sat side by side, exchanging covert glances. Once, Leo's hand brushed lightly against Kitty's. They smiled at each other in a misty kind of way. Laura – or anyone else, for that matter – might not have been there as far as the pair of them were concerned.

Later on they all returned to the apartment and listened to Paul Josef Goebbels, the national propaganda chief of the Nazi party, rationalize the arrest of Roehm, describing how the Führer had rushed at midnight to Munich and Bad Wiessee to attend a conference of his storm-troop commanders.

In a shocked voice he graphically described the terrible discoveries of Heines in bed with a boy – of the vivid flash of light which this incident had thrown on Roehm's circle, and of how the other commanders had proved to have been mutinous at heart.

'His voice was real shaky,' Mrs Schultz said when the broadcast stopped.

'No wonder,' said Sigrid. 'Goebbels was in agreement with Roehm and the rest. They were all mighty fed up with the way things are going in the party. But that's only the half of it. Wait for the next instalment!'

Roehm was executed two days after that. And in July the SS was set up as an independent organisation under Heinrich Himmler. A skull and crossbones were emblazoned on the caps and uniforms of its members, some of whom had been posted to Dachau, near Munich, where a concentration camp had been built to house five thousand prisoners.

All these things Laura heard of and partly observed. A campaign was under way to purge Germany of homosexuals – so it was said. But Laura was seeped in her own problems. Leo and Kitty were falling in love. With that realisation came a flood of the insecurities that had always threatened Laura.

As Berlin reeled from the blows of the Nazis, her old fears swamped her.

THE inevitable had happened. Leo and Kitty had announced their engagement, and Norman Ebbutt of the London *Times* and his friend Mrs Holmes were arranging a celebratory party.

Leo was planning to stay on in Berlin after he finished his book. He had plans for another one, a novel this time, set in contemporary Germany.

All this Laura learnt from Leo himself. Kitty was less communicative. She was already living in another world, one apparently inhabited only by Leo and herself.

'What shall I wear to this party?' she said, returning from the other world to open her wardrobe door. 'It's so important. I should have bought a new dress, shouldn't I? What time is it, for goodness' sake? Oh well, too late now.'

In a bemused state she took a black satin evening gown out, frowned at its low back and returned it to the rail.

'You're better off with one of your old dresses,' said Laura. 'The ones in the shops are all so dull.'

The Nazis were doing their best to curtail female adornment. Fashion was severe and forbidding. Women's noses were shiny. The use of cosmetics and jewellery was frowned on by the Führer.

'What about this?'

Kitty pulled out a peach-coloured crêpe gown with feathers sewn on to the cuffs.

'Yes, that's one of my favourites.'

Laura's own party dress was cream, which she privately thought made her look a bit washed out. But who was going to notice her? All the attention was going to be on Leo and Kitty.

'Are you any nearer to setting a wedding date?'

'I think now not until this time next year. I mean, I know Leo's been divorced for years and years but we'd still like to get his children used to the idea.'

Leo had two children, a boy and a girl, who lived with their mother in America.

'But they're grown up!'

'She's only eighteen,' said Kitty. 'It's quite a sensitive age. She might resent me. Anyway, Leo wants them to spend a month here at Christmas so we can get acquainted.'

'Does he?'

'I'm looking forward to it,' Kitty said, insensitive to Laura's lack of enthusiasm. 'We'll have such fun.'

She wafted into the bathroom and began to run a bath, singing as she did so. 'It will be nice for you, too, darling, having young people around,' she called when she got to the end of the refrain.

But Laura didn't hear her. Convinced that she was being excluded from Kitty's plans she retreated into her bedroom.

She laid the cream dress out on the bed. It *was* uninteresting and it was a pity that she had allowed Kitty to talk her into it. With her ash-blonde hair she would look like a bottle of milk. It was so uninteresting being fair – so commonplace. German women were desperate to appear authentically Nordic and sales of peroxide had soared.

She put the dress on and added a string of large plastic beads. Another mistake. *Glass* beads maybe? But what did it matter? Kitty might think Mr Ebbutt's parties splendid, but all the guests would be over thirty and therefore old. There would be no one of her own generation – there never was.

'Are you ready?' Kitty cried. 'Leo's here!' She spoke as if one of the gods in Greek mythology had dropped out of the clouds!

The party was two hours old. Everyone else was enjoying themselves immensely. Laura stood by the fireplace trying to think of something other than Leo and Kitty, around whom all the action was taking place.

What was she doing here, she asked herself? No one would notice if she left, least of all Kitty. She was on the verge of doing so, was beginning to edge her way round the perimeter of the party, when the doorbell rang and Mrs Holmes, Mr Ebbutt's friend, ushered in three newcomers: a woman and two men.

The woman was red-haired and exceedingly glamorous. She was wearing an exquisite black satin dress with a beaded motif. The other women at the party ran their eyes over the dress, taking note of the sequins and rhinestones forming an asymmetrical pattern down one side of the low neckline and around the waist.

'My darling!' the red-haired woman exclaimed, embracing Mr Ebbutt.

'Lucia! I'm glad you were able to come.'

'I nearly could not,' Lucia said, pouting. 'These Germans make me work so hard!'

She fluttered her lashes pseudo-reproachfully at her companions, one in his early thirties, Laura deduced, the other younger by a decade. The younger one was tall, slim, fair-haired.

'It's not true!' the older man protested.

'But it is!'

She must be an actress, Laura thought. She sounded Italian.

Lucia slipped her hand through the older man's arm and said engagingly, 'I will forgive you.'

The party swallowed them up, separating them from the fair-haired young man, who accepted a drink from Mr Ebbutt and then retreated into a corner, rather as Laura had done.

He moved elegantly. They were close enough for Laura to observe that he had beautiful, long-fingered hands and nice blue eyes. To her embarrassment, he became aware of her scrutiny. As she blushed he smiled and she thought that he had a sympathetic aura.

To get to the door she would have to walk right past him, a daunting prospect in view of having been caught staring. He might think she was pursuing him. On the other hand she could simply sweep past him, smiling vaguely, and leave as planned. But that would be a pity, throwing away the chance of getting to know him.

While she was still hesitating the fair-haired man took a decision of his own and came towards her.

'*Guten Abend!*' he said. 'My name is Klaus Fleischer.'

'I'm Laura Conway. I'm sorry if I was staring.'

'Why should you apologise for being curious about people? No one is having pangs of conscience for staring at Lucia!'

He *was* nice.

'Is she an actress?'

'A very well known Italian actress, yes. Which she doesn't let us forget!'

'Her dress is beautiful.'

'I like *your* dress,' he said. 'It's so delicate. It suits your fragility.'

Coming from him this statement seemed considered and sincere rather than sycophantic.

'Thank you.'

Not a milk bottle, after all, Laura thought.

'Are you a journalist? Everyone else here is, I think.'

'Not all of them,' Laura said, thinking of Kitty. 'I'm a photographer. A news photographer. I work mainly for the magazines.'

'An interesting job.'

'Not as interesting since – '

' – *the Nazis came into power*,' she had been about to say. But these days one had to be careful about making such statements, even to nice young men.

' – as it was when I started,' she said instead.

'For me, also.'

'You're a newspaper man?'

He shook his head. 'I work for Ufa.'

This was one of the large German film companies.

'You're an actor?'

'No. An assistant director.'

'That's exciting.'

'It used to be,' he said drily.

The Nazis had revolutionised the film business. The art-house productions of the early 1930s, mostly designed for export, were as frowned upon as the writings of Thomas Mann. *Volkisch* – people's films – bland substitutes, were being made for the home market.

He couldn't be one of *Them*. Still she said cautiously, 'Is that because the industry is in financial trouble?'

'No. And Ufa is big enough to be able to survive. It's the small and medium-sized companies who cannot. Although it's true that top artists command high fees. Lucia does! And patent costs and studio rentals are increasing all the time. But it's not that. It's the quality of the films we're making that I object to. What's happening in the industry is a tragedy for art.'

No Nazi would express such opinions.

'Anyway,' he went on, 'you should stop me talking about it. I can be very boring on the subject. You're English, aren't you? What brought you to Berlin?'

Laura explained, trying to keep the story relatively short. But Klaus kept intervening, asking for more and more information, until she found herself telling him about Leo and Kitty and her own complicated reactions.

'I know,' he said. 'I also have problems with my family. My father and I do not get on.'

'But your mother – '

'My mother is dead. I have a sister but she is much older than I.'

He was twenty-three. He was much more than nice. He was intelligent and compassionate and fun to be with, and what an error she would have made had she gone home early!

'You're always with Klaus!' Kitty complained. 'I hardly ever see you any more!'

It was the end of March, 1935. Leo's children had been to Berlin and long since gone. During their visit they had taken Kitty to their hearts and been friendly to Laura. But in contrast to Klaus they had seemed extrovert and boisterous. Laura had been glad to wave them off.

Kitty said continually how much she missed them and Laura was convinced that they had replaced her in her aunt's affections. But instead of Kitty there was Klaus.

'I do love being with him,' Laura admitted. 'You like him, don't you?'

'Ye-es,' said Kitty. 'Yes, I do. It's just – it doesn't do to have such an intense relationship at your age.'

'It isn't intense.'

Serene and comfortable, rather. Klaus, Laura thought, was her best friend. They were at ease in each other's company.

'You know what I mean.'

But Laura didn't. She was still only half awake in terms of her own sexuality. Klaus's kisses comforted rather than excited her.

'We're just happy together.'

'Seventeen is very young,' Kitty went on. 'At your age I had dozens of boyfriends.'

'I'm not much good at that. I'm not a flirt. I like being with one person.'

'Klaus is not being drafted for military service?' All able-bodied men between eighteen and forty had been drafted.

'No, he failed his eye-test. Haven't you noticed that he's been wearing glasses lately?'

'Now you mention it, I suppose I have.'

Glasses suited Klaus. The need to wear them had caused further friction between Klaus and his father. The older man had been convinced that Klaus was dodging the draft.

Laura had not met Herr Fleischer but Klaus had told her that she was missing nothing, that his father was a hard industrialist, a Fascist who despised his son's liberal attitudes and disliked his circle of friends, most of whom were actors, musicians and writers.

Some – like Nikolaus, who had been at the Ebbutt party with Klaus and Lucia – were German by birth. Others were not. Klaus enjoyed exchanging ideas with people from outside his own country.

'It's the only way to keep sane. Germany is closing in on herself. All this talk of *Dein Volk is alles*. The nation is not everything to *me*. I want to reach beyond it.'

Du bist nichts, the Nazis counselled – the individual is nothing.

'You don't believe that,' Klaus said thankfully. 'Most German girls do. They're all so obedient. *You* have a mind of your own, Laura. That's why I love you.'

Being told that she was loved was still a novelty, a lovely gift, a balm that soothed the pain of Laura's fears about Kitty's forthcoming wedding. This was now scheduled for the end of the year. Leo and Kitty were discussing buying a house in Berlin. It would be sad, Laura thought, to leave Grenadier Strasse.

In April, Klaus left Berlin for three months to film in Dresden. He wrote frequently: long, affectionate, amusing letters recounting the latest gossip from the set. The leading lady had been rejected by her current lover and was so hysterical that production was being held up. The producer's wife, suspecting his fidelity, had arrived in Dresden to check.

Without Klaus, Laura moped. She lay in bed at night remembering what he looked like and casting him in the lead role in her own life, a part for which his intelligence and gentility rendered him ideal.

It was spring, then summer, but Berlin was bleak. Tensions were mounting within the city. Nikolaus said several artists from the old Laubenheimer colony had been taken away by lorry to unknown destinations and not seen again.

On a more mundane level certain foods were proving hard to obtain, and the cost of dairy products had risen. Kitty's friends sneered at the latest fad introduced by the Nazis, the *Eintopfgericht*, the one-course meal, designed to save money so that it could be donated to the winter relief scheme for those in need.

'If the country was properly run there wouldn't *be* needy people,' Kitty said. 'Or shortages either. Anyway, catch me eating Irish stew at the Bristol!'

Members of the Nazi party were prohibited from attending parties in the homes of diplomats and journalists.

'They're not allowed to get drunk any more!' Kitty laughed. 'Leo says . . .'

Leo was openly critical of the Nazis, particularly in regard to news censorship. An argument between him and a German journalist had brought them close to a punch-up.

'Frau Ullrich has been giving Leo dirty looks!' Laura said. 'You don't think she's a Nazi informant? You just never know . . .'

Kitty snorted. 'How dare that old bag glare at Leo! She's here to keep our apartment clean, not to pass judgement! A man like Leo isn't going to be intimidated by dirty looks. Darling, when is Klaus coming back?'

'In ten days. I can't wait.'

Laura felt slightly let down at the sight of him. In her imagination he had assumed a more heroic status, become as handsome as the leading man in an Ufa production. In the flesh he was simply Klaus.

They hugged. He smelt familiar, primarily of Crème Mouson soap and Kalodorma razor cream.

'It's *good* to see 'you,' he said appreciatively. 'I have been missing you such a lot.'

'And I you.'

'I'm starving! Let's go to Pschorr Haus.'

This was a big *buergerliche* restaurant on Potsdamer Platz, hardly romantic, or compatible with Laura's dreams of the last three months. But when they were seated at one of the white wooden tables and had selected from the menu, Klaus squeezed her hand.

'*Meine kleine Schwester,*' he said – *my little sister.*

That was not romantic either but it hit the right note. It was secure and reassuring being with Klaus. It was wonderful having him home.

In several directions the pattern of life in Berlin continued to change.

The lime trees along Unter den Linden were cut down so that the triumphal procession which would mark the Olympic Games the following year could proceed more easily. The sight of the barren boulevard reduced Kitty and Laura to tears.

The Nuremberg laws were enacted, forbidding marriage between Jews and non-Jews and describing sexual contact between the two groups as a crime of racial desecration. Several of Kitty's Jewish friends departed to make a new home in America.

In October Leo was served with deportation papers.

'Two days to get out of the country!' Kitty said furiously. 'He's protesting – naturally. But I think we both know it's pointless. We'll just have to go ahead and make our arrangements on that basis.'

'What arrangements?'

'My darling Laura – think! We must give notice on the apartment. Organise packing. Masses and masses of things! I doubt if you and I will be able to follow until the end of the year.'

'You and I follow?'

Kitty said exasperatedly: 'What else? Oh, my poor Leo. He hasn't finished his research.'

Leo, Leo!

'It's bad enough,' Kitty said, 'without *your* looking so stricken! Let's just say to ourselves that it isn't the end of the world. I'm sure you'll love America.'

'You really want me to go with you?'

'Good heavens, of course I do. You don't think I'd leave you behind?'

A year ago these would have been reassuring words. But –

'What about Klaus?'

'What about him?'

'*I* can't leave *him*!'

Kitty closed her eyes and took a deep breath. 'Darling,' she said, 'you're very young. You're going to have lots of boyfriends before you settle down. You can write to Klaus. He can pay us visits.'

'I won't desert him,' vowed Laura.

Why didn't Kitty understand that Klaus had become the pivot of her existence? *She* should appreciate the importance of love.

But Kitty's mind was running along another track. 'Be reasonable. What would your parents say if I abandoned you? Your mother would have a fit!'

This was altogether the wrong argument. Laura might have listened, at least, had Kitty begged and pleaded and declared deep affection and a desire to have her company in America.

But Kitty was distracted by the arrival of Leo and Laura went off to meet Klaus.

Klaus had his own answer to the problem.

'He wants to marry me,' Laura announced. 'We've talked and talked about it and we're going to have a quiet wedding before you leave Berlin.'

Kitty protested volubly, attacking from all sides. 'Why get married at this stage of your life when there's so much to see and do? Photographers do well in America. Lee Miller is back there from Paris and she's being inundated with assignments in New York. Leo had marvellous contacts at Condé Nast. He'll introduce you.'

'But I'm engaged to Klaus.'

Kitty shamelessly resorted to bribery. Laura could have a magnificent studio in America with the latest photographic equipment. Didn't that have appeal?

It did, but Klaus had more.

'Your parents won't approve of your getting married.'

'You said that already, but I don't think they'll care.'

Nevertheless, Kitty wrote to them, expressing her reservations. But Tim was quite beyond having any opinions on the subject and Margaret had given up.

'All I can say is that some sort of provision must be made for you,' Kitty said, 'just in case.'

'It's not necessary for you to make provision for me. Klaus would be offended.'

'Let him be offended! I'm going to make arrangements with my English bank and – no, I don't want you to argue with me, darling. In this climate one doesn't know what might happen.'

All this should have spelt out to Laura that Kitty cared enormously for her. But Laura had drifted too far in the direction of Klaus to read the meaning of what Kitty said, let alone alter course.

When they were married they were going to live in Klaus's apartment in Joachim Friedrich Strasse. The flat had a cosy, old-fashioned appearance. The *Berlin-zimmer* looked out on a sombre but meticulously maintained backyard, and was hard to air, so that it constantly smelt of coffee and smoke. It was furnished in a haphazard style with shabby armchairs and rugs left over by a former tenant and the curtains and cushions clashed; yet this lack of deliberation gave it a charm of its own.

'It's as well you think so, since I can't afford new furniture!' said Klaus.

For the same reason they were not going away on honeymoon. Klaus had turned down Kitty's offer to pay their wedding costs.

Kitty was the only relation coming to the wedding. His sister lived in Munich; his father was not invited.

'You wouldn't like him any more than I do,' Klaus said when Laura questioned the wisdom of this decision. 'He's always been vile to me.'

In Klaus she sensed a core of loneliness to which she could relate. He was not unsociable – he had dozens of friends – but he was a private person at heart, and this solitary aspect of his personality, Laura thought, also explained his emotional reticence. He was loving but not intense. He was not wildly impatient to take Laura to bed but seemingly content to wait until they were married before making love.

Before then Laura was to relinquish her British passport and become a German citizen. On the front of her new brown passport was a black eagle with a swastika clutched in its claws.

Kitty shuddered at the sight of it. 'I wish you weren't doing this,' she said, but then she hugged Laura. 'Darling, I want you to be the happiest girl in the world.'

'I will be,' said Laura earnestly.

'I do hope so,' Kitty said, but there was a dubious note in her voice that secretly infuriated Laura.

Still, they were about to go their separate ways and they should part amicably. Laura managed to restrain herself from snapping at her aunt. Just you wait, Kitty, she thought. I'll soon be writing to you, saying how happy I am.

I know you had reservations about my marriage but I am happy.

Having only just started her letter to Kitty, Laura paused to beam at the photograph of Klaus which stood on her bureau. He was by nature a harmonious person, easy to live with. Instead of complaining about her own deficiencies in the kitchen, he made up for them by helping with the cooking and even ironing shirts.

He brought her flowers and said regularly how much he loved her. And it was enormous fun having his friends around. The apartment was invariably crowded with visitors, particularly at weekends. Quite frequently they stayed overnight, camping out on the sofas in the *Berlin-zimmer*. Sometimes, going in there in the morning, she stumbled over bodies asleep on the floor.

Klaus suited her. Their lifestyle was perfect. She was – content. Happy, content, peaceful.

Such gentle words. Gentle Klaus. So gentle, so – tender in bed.

With him she was safe. She thought fleetingly of her childhood. Klaus was a haven by contrast.

So, of course, I'm happy, she wrote. *Truly ecstatic*, and started a new paragraph.

But, all the same, you wouldn't believe the things that are going on here. The SS – there are 3,500 of them now – have orders to act as studs for childless women. An organisation called the Spring of Life has been set up to care for these women and the children they'll have. And an institute has been

founded to deal with the problem of gypsies! Klaus has heard
that Himmler, who is head of the SS and the police force these
days, is going to have all gypsies rounded up and sent to
Dachau.

In two months' time the Olympic Games will start, so the
anti-Semitic signs are being taken down and the homosexual
bars are being reopened! Such hypocrisy!

She stopped again, considering what next to say. Kitty knew
none of Klaus's friends. She would not be interested in hearing
about them.

The German film industry then? The films Klaus was forced
to make were technically proficient and creatively uninspiring.
But at least they did not contain the propaganda dished out in
the newsreels and documentaries.

– still he maintains that they are a danger because they give
people an idyllic and false view of Germany. The old fantasy
and crime films were more truthful, he says. And we're losing
our best actors and directors. Peter Lorre, Paul Wegener,
Murnau and Pabst are all getting out.

Now I'm sounding negative, Laura thought. Kitty will never
believe I'm happy if I continue like this – but I am, I am, I am!

For another year she was. And then the hurricane of change
which was hitting Germany struck her relationship with Klaus.

The *tanzbars* were all closed down again. Himmler had
announced that homosexuals were a danger to the German race
and should be eliminated. The liberal group who gathered at the
Fleischers' were sickened by such statements, but only Klaus
was visibly depressed, his old serenity gone.

At the end of the day he complained of tiredness but at night
he lay awake on his side of the bed. He didn't want to make love
any more. He was detached and withdrawn, affected – so Laura
believed – by a combination of work frustration and the political
events.

But gradually his depression, instead of easing off, grew noticeably worse. He stopped confiding in Laura. He hardly spoke at all so that the friends who came and went commented on his state.

Nikolaus raised the subject with Laura. 'Klaus is in a bad way. What do you think is bothering him?'

'I don't know.'

'Don't you think you should ask? You can't go on pretending that all is well. He's desperate. He needs to confide in someone.'

So Laura confronted Klaus one evening after work. He was standing by the window of the *Berlin-zimmer*, gazing down into the sombre courtyard. She went to him and put her arm around his waist.

'Please tell me what's wrong.'

He shuddered. The tremor went through him like an electric shock.

'Klaus?'

She insinuated herself between his body and the window so that he was forced to face her. His expression was so miserable that she, too, was shocked.

'You must talk to me,' she said, 'I'm your wife.'

The blue eyes filled with tears. 'I can't,' Klaus whispered. 'I can't talk to you.'

'Why not?'

'Because it would be impossible for you to understand.' He covered his face with his hands.

Another woman, she thought suddenly – he's fallen in love with somebody else. His work at Ufa brought him into contact with many beautiful girls. She remembered Lucia.

'Don't hide from me, Klaus. I can bear anything but lies. You know that.'

'I can't tell you.'

She had to ask. 'Are you in love with someone else?'

Klaus started. He was very pale. '*What?*'

Surely he had heard? It was awful asking the question a second time. 'Are you in love with another woman?'

He blinked – shook his head. 'No. I'm not in love with another woman. What made you think that?'

He still looked agonised but Laura was momentarily relieved, almost irritated. If it was not illness and not another woman it couldn't be so bad.

'Because you're not here, not with me any more,' she said impatiently, 'and we never make love so – '

'But I love you,' Klaus said desperately, 'I love you and I don't want to lose you.'

Now she was exasperated. 'But why *should* you lose me?'

'Laura – '

His tears spilt over, ran down his cheeks.

'*Why?*'

He swallowed. 'I don't want to hurt you.'

'But if you're not in love with another woman, why should I be hurt?'

'I think you're going to be,' he said. 'Because – there's a side of me that's always been there. It's stronger than I am and now – I can't control it any more. I don't know what to do. Laura – I've met this man.'

The floodgates were wide open and Klaus the stranger was pouring his story out.

'I kept running away from it. I was frightened, can you understand that? I said to myself – it's just a phase. It will stop. It has to stop. At the same time I was looking for warmth, for affection, for the sensation of being loved. You must understand that I was happy with you. I still am.'

'Who is he?'

'His name is Gebhard Brandt. He's my age – an actor. He has a small part in the film we're making now.'

'How long have you been seeing him?'

'For the last few months. Laura, I didn't want to lie to you. And yet – I love him. I have to see him.'

She was angry then, hating him – hating Gebhard.

'We made love,' she said.

'I wasn't lying about that. Sexuality is a lot less clear than people suppose. I was attracted to you. I enjoyed sleeping with you. It was – something wasn't there. A part of me wasn't being expressed. I'm only fulfilled when he and I make love.'

'I hate you!'

'I still love you,' said Klaus sadly. 'How could anyone not? Laura, I truly don't want to lose you.'

So much had already been lost. The sparkle had gone out of Berlin. The flowers in the Rosegarten retained their beauty but the Tiergarten Café was closed and there were few boats on the lake which Lenné had created.

The 'Yazz-Band' musicians had put away their trumpets and cow bells and guitars and cap-guns and quietly slipped away; in the pubs the drinkers listened to the sound of marching in the streets outside.

The satirical art of Otto Dix and Georg Grosz had been dropped as topics for conversation. In February 1938 people spoke of the annexation of Austria.

Spring came. But that year Laura remained insensitive to seasonal signals, being too concerned with her own.

When her initial anger with Klaus had died, when she had stopped crying and he was a stranger no more but his old familiar self, he had put a proposal to her. He could not leave Gebhard but Laura and he need not separate. The affair could be conducted out of her sight in Gebhard's apartment.

When Gebhard visited the flat in Joachim Friedrich Strasse – and Klaus had wanted him to meet Laura, had been anxious that his lover and his wife become friends – the two men would behave as if their relationship was platonic.

Could Laura live under such circumstances, Klaus had asked? Because if she could – and he hoped and prayed that this would be the case – nothing need change. Except that it was a lot to ask of her – *he* knew that.

With her hand in his Laura had said she could. There had been enough upheaval. Klaus was *family*; she loved his circle of friends.

She had truly believed that she would be better off staying with Klaus than moving out, but she had expected as a matter of course to hate and fear Gebhard.

Klaus had described him in glowing terms: *'Gutaussehend'* – good-looking, handsome – and that in itself had served to increase her antipathy. She had put off meeting him for as long as possible.

Gebhard, confronted, had proved to be more *hübsch* – pretty – than handsome, and every bit as nervous and insecure as herself. Although he was the same age as Klaus he was less mature, more overtly feminine than Klaus – nothing like as intelligent.

For mental stimulation, Klaus needed *her*. This was flattering. It made it that much easier for Laura to like Gebhard.

Easier – not easy. It was almost impossible not to scream in protest at the image of Klaus and Gebhard in bed, Gebhard (it had to be Gebhard) stretched out on his stomach with buttocks raised, Klaus, cock stiff, poised above him. In her presence Klaus and Gebhard were consideration personified, yet the couple on the bed made a mockery out of their measured politeness.

What about *me*, she thought. What am *I* meant to do about sex?

But she didn't listen to the answer – *take a lover, Laura*. When, as she sometimes did, she considered reneging on her agreement, she recoiled from the idea of living on her own.

She needed Klaus and he – and Gebhard – were in need of her protection. Their affair, discreet as it was, put their lives at risk. If it came to the notice of the authorities Klaus and Gebhard could be transferred to a concentration camp after serving a prison sentence. Or they could be shot.

All of these things were on her mind when a letter arrived from Simon Guttman in Paris in response to one of her own. Simon was running an art magazine in the French capital but he had retained his links with photography and Laura had asked if he could put her in touch with a picture agency there who might be interested in using photographs of Berlin.

Simon came up trumps.

– *Gerda, André's girlfriend, worked for the first one I've listed,* Laura read.

> *André has a new name as a result – Robert Capa! Gerda and he concocted the story that a famous and rich American photographer called Robert Capa – who doesn't exist, of course! – would be insulted if she offered his pictures for less than 150 francs. The going rate is 50 but the editors in Paris have paid up and André – alias Robért – has made his name! Now he and Gerda are in Spain, covering the war . . .*

For the first time in ages Laura giggled. André – *Robert!* – and Gerda had such spunk. Their initiative started her own engines up. She would do a picture story on an aspect of Berlin and send the spread to Paris. It was just a question of finding the right theme, something topical.

That same week a new law had been enacted forcing Jews to register their possessions. Anti-Semitism was spreading like a noxious weed. Many Berliners found the trend disgusting but some had closed their doors on their Jewish friends.

In smart restaurants and night-clubs, visitors who chose to dine with Jews ran the risk of being given the worst tables or refused permission to enter. A government edict had prohibited Jews from bathing at Wannsee, the popular lake just outside Berlin. A black notice had been posted on the edge of the beach: JEWS NOT ADMITTED. She had seen it herself.

And yet sensible people knew the facts: that the Jewish birth rate had dropped, that Jews were being assimilated into the German race instead of being a threat. Nor were all Jews rich. The Jewish hospital was situated in the working-class district of Wedding.

Thinking of Wedding Laura found her theme: the less affluent Jewish families living in Berlin.

The hospital was a big general institution catering for everyone, but she would start there, all the same, and work her way around the district until she found what she wanted.

She decided against telling Klaus about this expedition. Klaus would fuss and try to put her off taking pictures in a Jewish district.

The district of Wedding was beyond Oranienburger Strasse, the site of the largest of the city's twelve major synagogues. The Jewish Hospital was on the corner of Exercier Strasse and Schul Strasse. It was a three-storey building sub-divided into several sections. The administration block faced Exercier Strasse with the nurses' residence, the gynaecological wards and those reserved for infectious diseases on one side. A huge Cypress tree loomed above the entrance, the sign *Das Jüdische Krankenhaus* confirmed that she had reached her destination, but the appearance of the hospital was neither here nor there. Laura's interest was in the patients who were going to be admitted.

Making herself as inconspicuous as possible she watched members of the hospital staff – senior nurses in black dresses with white collars, cuffs and caps, juniors dressed in white – enter the building.

A car pulled up and a man got out, opened the passenger door and assisted another man on to the pavement. Nothing there. The second man was clearly sick but he was too well-clad to qualify as one of Laura's contenders.

A second car disgorged a small boy, kicking and screaming protest, with spots all over his face. It could take ages before she got a picture.

She had been outside the hospital for nearly two hours and was considering going for coffee when three figures walked in from the Schul Strasse side: two women, one heavily pregnant, and a little girl holding on to what must be her mother's hand.

They were as shabbily dressed as Laura – for the purposes of her photograph – could have wished, and to add to the atmosphere the pregnant woman was clearly in distress, probably in the early stages of labour.

She stopped, groaned and, removing her hand from the child's, pressed it to her stomach.

'*Mir reicht's!*' – 'I've had enough!'

'*Already?*'

The other woman raised her eyes to heaven. The little girl was silent and solemn. They made an excellent picture.

One! Laura was thinking. *It's been slow but that was a good reflection of what I want.*

'What do you think you're doing?' a voice demanded, and she started convulsively.

'Taking a photograph. You gave me a terrible fright.'

He was so close to her that for a few seconds all she could see was his white coat.

A doctor. Well, thank God for that. A Jew when it could have been a Himmler Brownshirt.

Not that I'm doing anything illegal.

'Why?' said the man. 'That woman is in labour. She doesn't want her photograph taken,' and Laura looked up from a white coat to a disapproving face.

She started again. She couldn't help it. Glaring at her was the handsome – the incredibly handsome – man whose photograph she had once taken in the Tiergarten.

'It's part of a photographic feature I'm doing for a French agency,' Laura said defensively.

'Even so. It's intrusive. Do you have permission to be here?'

'No, I don't.'

He was horrible. Beautiful he might be but he was cold and harsh.

'Then I must ask you to leave.'

'I don't think you should be so judgemental. You haven't seen my work. You don't know what kind of photo-feature I'm going to present.'

His mouth twitched. He was still frowning but: 'That is right,' he conceded, 'I have not seen your work.'

How serious he was! He was as sunny as a funeral on a wet, wintry day.

She pressed home her point. 'If you did see it I think you'd change your mind. The Nazis have been depicting German Jews

104

as affluent and grasping. I am trying to show that there are less privileged Jews in this city. Like those women . . .'

'We look after our people,' he said. 'What favour can you bestow upon us by depicting Jews as poor?'

'I didn't say poor – I said less privileged.'

It was too bad of him to pre-judge her pictures. Having been as intimidated by his looks at the beginning of this conversation as she had been long ago in the Tiergarten she was now incensed. No one, she thought indignantly, must condemn her work until he or she had seen it. Or be prejudiced about her motives, either, before they were fully explained.

'What other photographs were you considering taking here?' asked the doctor.

People assumed that you could plan a picture in advance. But her photographs were spontaneous happenings. They were depictions of life as it was being lived at a particular moment. This was going to take much explaining to her listener.

'I didn't have anything specific in mind,' said Laura. 'I was going to wait and see what images the day brought me.'

Which made the whole procedure sound fey – not what she had intended. And now this humourless man would see her in that light and send her about her business.

'That does not sound so heartless,' he said.

'What I do is not heartless. For example I would also like to photograph the woman's baby when it arrives. But that would be inside the hospital and if you have such objections to my taking pictures out here I suppose that is out of the question.'

'We could ask Professor Strauss for permission,' said the doctor, taking her by surprise.

'Professor Strauss?'

'He is in charge of the hospital. He has been here since 1911.'

'*You'd* assist me in that?'

'If I approved of your photographs,' he said, still judgemental and slightly pompous but much more friendly.

'You're welcome to come and see them,' Laura said. 'My husband and I would be glad if you did.'

She had no ulterior intentions. Just as he had been in the Tiergarten he was, to her, a man out of her league because of his good looks. She was quite sure no man – handsome or ugly – would ever again be attracted to her on a sexual basis.

She told the doctor where she and Klaus lived, slipped her Leica into her handbag and was about to say goodbye when a junior nurse in a white uniform came out of the hospital and called out, 'Paul! I've been looking for you!'

'Oh – have you?' he said. 'What for?'

'I wanted to talk to you,' the nurse said, coming up to them and glaring at Laura.

There was a proprietorial note in her voice. And yet she was a very dull-looking girl with no outstanding features and mousy-brown hair.

Something took hold of Laura. If this dreary girl could assume a possessive attitude about her companion maybe he was not so far out of her reach. A tiny flicker of confidence came to light inside her.

'Well,' she heard herself say, 'I hope you do come to visit me.'
Me, not *us*. What was happening to her?

Whatever it was it yielded a positive response from Paul. 'I will,' he said. 'I'd be very interested to see your pictures.' Still solemn but managing to raise a smile for her before she finally left.

At home the flicker of confidence burnt itself out. Laura soon convinced herself that Paul would not call. On the basis that he would be worried by what she had done, she did not mention their meeting to Klaus.

Gebhard and Klaus were spending most evenings with Laura and their friends, most of whom were aware of the nuances of the relationship. That Wednesday when she turned into Joachim Friedrich Strasse Laura was expecting them both to be waiting. She had been shopping. Gebhard was going to cook.

The light rain which had been falling as she walked along the Ku'damm had metamorphosed into a heavy shower. Her hair was a mess, the little make-up she used was being washed off.

She heard the sound of voices inside the apartment before she opened the door. Good. *They* were home. She would pass over the foodstuffs and get straight into a bath in order to warm up.

'Hello!' she called out.

'Laura?'

'Who else?'

With the parcels still in her hands she walked into the *Berlin-zimmer*.

There were three men present: Klaus, Gebhard – and Paul.

And I look *awful*, Laura thought.

'Well – ' she said, and ran out of words.

Gebhard rushed in to fill the conversational gap.

'Paul explained that you told him to call.'

Admiration for Paul's beauty was written all over his face.

'I did. Has he explained where we met?'

'He has. He's been with us for *ages*,' Gebhard said in his slightly affected way.

Klaus was looking offended as if Laura by failing to share confidences had let him down.

She put her parcels on the table and felt her wet hair. 'I'll just go and dry this,' she said, and fled into the bathroom.

Towelling her hair she wished that she had thought of grabbing a clean dress before she went in there. The one she was wearing was creased. She was wearing her oldest pair of shoes.

Even when she was relatively presentable she hesitated about rejoining the others. She sat on the edge of the bath, drumming her toes on the floor.

She could hear snatches of conversation: '. . . do in the Reichstag is applaud the Führer . . .'

'. . . our Parliament . . . the country's most costly choral group . . .'

When she came out Gebhard, who was a clever mimic, had broken into his impersonation of Adolf Hitler singing the Nazi anthem.

The parcels were where she had left them. Gebhard was studiously avoiding her eyes so she carried the food through to the kitchen, chopped up some onions, prepared the mince and began to make *Hackepeter* to serve on buns.

Gebhard was talking in an over-animated way when they all sat down at the table. It seemed to be taken for granted that Paul would join in the meal. Klaus was polite but reticent, taking heed of Gebhard's reaction to Paul.

Who knew what *he* was making of it all, Laura thought. She passed over his plate, conscious that he was watching her. His arrival and the tensions at the table had the effect of putting her off food altogether. Paul said little. Gebhard's monologue was almost unbearable.

'I'll bring in cheese,' she said, pleased to have an excuse to get up.

'Not for me,' said Klaus unexpectedly. 'Gebhard and I have to go.'

'Do we?' Gebhard looked like a small boy being deprived of a treat.

'I think we do.'

Laura's escape was momentary. She returned with the cheese to find Gebhard and Klaus blocking the doorway.

'You'll be all right?' Klaus said mechanically. He kissed her cheek.

'I'll be fine. Don't worry about me.'

'All right. Goodnight, Paul.'

'*Bis gleich!*' Gebhard said boldly. *See you soon!*

'Good night,' said Paul stiffly.

Laura put the cheeseboard on the table and sat down wearily. What an awful evening.

'Is Klaus really your husband?' Paul asked suddenly.

'Yes,' she said, 'yes, he is,' angry with him for being inquisitive and with Gebhard for his lack of discretion. Gebhard never behaved like that with Klaus's heterosexual friends. But none of those friends looked like Paul . . .

'Would you like some cheese?'

She pushed the cheeseboard in Paul's direction, wanting to hit him with it, smack Gebhard hard the next time he turned up.

'When can I see your photographs?'

'I'll fetch them,' Laura said coldly.

They were in her bedroom, along with her other pictures. Including the one she had once taken of Paul. I was only fifteen then, she thought. A lot has happened since that day. I've changed. I'm not the innocent little girl I was that afternoon, when my only worry was whether or not Kitty might be falling in love with poor Herr Fritsch.

Leaving Paul to stew in his own juice for a few minutes she leafed through her portfolio until she found his picture. He was even more handsome now than he had been then. If she wasn't so angry – so humiliated – she would have asked him to pose for her again. As it was . . .

Oh, never mind, Laura thought crossly. She left the portfolio where it was and took the photographs she had taken for Paris into the *Berlin-zimmer*.

'Here they are.'

She made space on the table and laid them out. Paul stared at them, examining each one with intense concentration.

'They're wonderful,' he said eventually. 'You're a very talented woman.'

'So you'll speak to Professor Strauss?'

'Of course. I promised I would and I will.'

'And afterwards will you phone me and tell me what he says?'

'I will.'

'I told you I wasn't heartless,' Laura said.

'I understand that now. By the way, that woman who was in labour – she had a son. I thought you'd like to know.'

A few minutes later, after refusing coffee and without any preamble, he, too, departed.

Laura was left alone not only for a few hours but all that night. That was the first occasion on which Klaus stayed until morning at Gebhard's apartment – but not, as it happened, the last.

*

On her second visit to the Jewish Hospital there was no sign of Paul, although Professor Herman Strauss, bearded and bald, knew all about her, and the new mother posed proudly for the camera along with her baby son.

Laura posted her pictures to the Parisian agency suggested by Simon and resumed her other work. Klaus and Gebhard went to Munich on location. Nikolaus called round as did several of their other friends. In the streets signs and banners called on true Germans not to buy in a Jewish shop.

Out of the blue there was a telephone call from Paul. 'I haven't seen your second batch of photographs.'

'I didn't think you wanted to see them. I've already sent the pictures to Paris.'

'All of them?'

'The best of them.'

'But you do have some left?'

'The left-overs,' Laura said relenting. 'You can see those if you wish.'

'I do. When could I call?'

He was so formal! He had none of Klaus's and Gebhard's natural lightness and charm. Laura had forgiven Gebhard for the ghastly evening and so, it appeared, had Klaus.

'Whenever you like.'

'In that case I will come this evening at eight o'clock,' he said and put the receiver down before Laura could reply.

At seven she bathed and changed into a yellow dress with a large berthé collar and a bow at the neck. Not that Paul would notice what she was wearing, she thought. He would look at her photographs, say something complimentary about them and depart.

She plumped up the shabby cushions. The apartment was as orderly as it ever could be – and as empty as it always was when Klaus was away. It was ten to eight. Paul would be here in a matter of minutes. Like all Germans he was bound to be on time.

But he was nothing of the kind. It was eight, then half-past and there was still no sign of him.

110

A quarter to nine. He wasn't going to turn up. It was too early to go to bed. A fine spring evening and she was alone – as usual. Other women of twenty had boyfriends or husbands for company. I could be like this all my life, Laura thought. Unless I do something about it.

The doorbell rang so loudly that her heart missed a beat and her stomach was still churning when she went to answer it.

'I'm sorry I am late,' Paul said. 'I was delayed at the hospital. It happens frequently. I should have mentioned it.'

It was the longest speech he had ever made. She noticed that he was still wearing his white coat underneath his mackintosh.

'It doesn't matter. Come in.'

'Isn't your husband here?'

'He's in Munich on location.'

'For how long?'

'He won't be back until July,' Laura said. 'Six – seven weeks.'

'You seem to spend a lot of time on your own. Doesn't he have any relations in Berlin that you could stay with?'

'No, he doesn't. Do you find that strange?'

'Very strange. In Jewish families it's different.'

'I daresay it is,' said Laura, irked by these questions and comments, 'but Klaus is an individualist. He has always said he wants to operate from that position, not from the standpoint of nations or groups.'

'Only a privileged man could make a remark like that,' Paul said. 'Your husband can afford to stand alone. We Jews can't. No one's going to call him a *Judenjunge* if he stands up for his rights. There are no signs up to warn Ufa against using his services as there are against Jewish doctors and lawyers.'

'That's not *his* fault.'

'No,' said Paul. '*That's* not his fault.'

Such direct confrontation was new to Laura. She was feeling altogether strange, angry once again with Paul, threatened and excited. She put her hand up to the bow at her neck and checked that it was fastened.

'You didn't come here to talk about my husband,' she said. 'I was going to show you the photographs I took at the hospital. Do you still want to see them?'

He nodded, and then yawned. It struck her that he was tired. Perhaps he worked long hours at the Jewish Hospital which might – just – explain and excuse his rudeness.

'Sit down and I'll get them.'

'Can I hang this up?'

He had taken off his mackintosh.

'Give it to me.'

He yawned again and collapsed on to one of the sofas. The phone rang in the bedroom.

'Excuse me. I must answer it.'

'Laura, is everything all right?'

Klaus, in Munich. She kicked the bedroom door closed and sat down on the bed for a chat.

'Yes, it's all right. And you?'

'The usual problems,' Klaus said. 'The film will have to be re-cut before it's passed. Not that you could call it anti-Fascist . . .'

'But it's a *comedy*!'

'Of a kind . . . !'

When the conversation was over she took the photographs she had selected for Paul's perusal into the *Berlin-zimmer*.

He was lying on the sofa, fast asleep, curled up like a foetus, vulnerable and almost indecently handsome. She was immensely touched by the sight of him. He wasn't in the least threatening. She put the photographs on the table, located the spare eiderdown, and draped it over him.

HE was still asleep in the morning when Laura got up, immobile and in the same position, as if he had not stirred during the course of the night.

She stood by the sofa, debating with herself whether or not to wake him. She had an eleven o'clock assignment and he, presumably, had to be on duty at the hospital.

Eventually she whispered, 'Paul?' and he was awake immediately, pushing the duvet aside and sitting up.

'I'm *here*! I didn't go home! What will your landlady say?'

'She won't mind. Our friends often stay the night.'

'I'm sorry. I've been a nuisance.'

'No, you haven't. I'm only concerned in case you're late on duty.'

'Not until midday. What time is it now?'

She told him and he stood up, adjusting his rumpled white coat. 'I must go home and change. You're quite sure I haven't caused problems for you?'

'Visitors staying are never a problem for us. Don't you want breakfast?'

'No. I have to go,' he said. 'My parents will be wondering where I am.'

'You live with them?'

'Yes, and with my younger brother and sister.'

'Don't you want to phone them?'

At that, he appeared relieved. 'Yes. Please.'

She directed him to the bedroom and poured coffee for both of them, wondering what his family was like. She had still not met either Klaus's father or his sister. He and she were an isolated couple in comparison to Paul.

'Were they worried?' she said when he reappeared from the bedroom.

'A little. My mother especially.'

He drank his coffee hurriedly and asked for his coat. He was quite obviously in a hurry to be gone.

But then at the door he stopped. 'Your friends often call round?'

Laura smiled. 'All the time.'

'So you wouldn't mind if I did?'

'Why should I mind?' Laura said. 'I'd be pleased to see you.'

She could not quite make him out but it did cross her mind that, in spite of his astonishingly good looks, he might be a shy man.

Ever since the annexation of Austria, the Czechoslovakians had been nervous lest the Germans attack. That May, President Benes ordered partial mobilisation.

The fragrant pink and white magnolia blossoms fell to the ground and were trampled under foot. Spring turned into summer. Simon wrote from Paris with sad news. Gerda Taro had been killed by a landmine in Spain while covering the civil war. Paul got into the habit of dropping in to the apartment once or twice a week.

When Klaus and Gebhard returned from Munich he had become as much a fixture of Laura's life as their other friends. She had even persuaded him to pose for her, leaning against her bureau.

Taking the photograph Laura thought how misleading appearances could be. Paul *looked* self-assured, almost blasé, but he was neither of those things. His father was a jeweller. His younger brother worked in the business. Much of Paul's free time was spent with his family. Otherwise, he was devoted to medicine, so obsessed as a student, he said, so determined to obtain the highest grades, that the culture and artistry of Berlin had virtually passed him by.

And now he was reaching out, through Laura and her friends, for what he had lost. That was how Laura saw it. It was the only explanation she could find for his visits to the flat.

These visits disturbed Klaus, and not only because they affected Gebhard. Laura thought Klaus was jealous of Paul being *her* friend, monopolising her attention. His advent had disrupted the more-or-less even tenor of their existence, but that was just too bad, was a small price to pay for having someone who stayed on to chat with her when Klaus went to Gebhard's.

No, *not* chat: chatting implied light-heartedness, and Paul was a serious man. *Converse*, thought Laura. *Discuss. Theorise.* Talk about music and books and art while strictly observing the restrictions on their friendship laid down silently by Paul.

Keep talking, Laura, while you silently will him to take you to bed.

Since this didn't seem to be getting her anywhere she tried a different approach.

'I want to tell you the truth about my marriage,' she said, but the truth merely led back to further discussion. Paul said she should leave Klaus – that their marriage was nothing but an offensive charade. Laura said Paul was looking at it from a puritanical point of view.

By September they – like most Germans and many in the West – were talking of Herr Hitler's antipathy to President Benes and the threat to Czechoslovakia.

Mr Neville Chamberlain, the British Prime Minister, arrived in Germany to meet the Führer. At the end of the month an agreement signed by Mr Chamberlain, Herr Hitler and the French and Italian heads of state forced Czechoslovakia to cede to Germany all districts of Bohemia and Moravia which had a fifty per cent or more German-speaking population. On 5 October President Benes resigned.

All this almost distracted Paul from the latest anti-Semitic action taken by the Nazis. Jewish physicians had lost permission to practise.

'It means that I'll have to leave Germany.'

'Now?'

'Not yet. I must stay on at the hospital for another two years. My parents are already talking of selling the business and going to America. My uncle is there, my cousins . . .'

'But not for two years,' Laura said, relieved. 'I don't want to lose any more of my friends.'

They still did not anticipate what would happen. A month later the real horror began for Berlin, for the Jews, and for Paul.

The excuse for it was a killing in Paris, not Berlin. The third secretary of the German embassy, Ernst von Rath, was murdered by Hershel Grynszpan, a displaced Jewish youth. Reprisals followed fast, unbeknownst to Laura who went to bed early that night.

In the morning she realised that there was no bread and went down to the Ku'damm in search of it. New posters had been put up during the night: GERMANY AWAKE. DEATH TO THE JEWS. People were standing around in a bemused way, talking in whispers. Laura could smell burning. Further down the street smoke was puffing up into the sky.

Forgetting her errand she walked in that direction until she reached the Czardas, the Jewish-Hungarian restaurant. The place had been demolished. There was glass on the pavement from broken windows and bottles and a red stain that might have been made by red wine or blood.

'What's happened?' she asked another woman who had also stopped.

'Don't you know?'

'If I did I wouldn't ask.'

'Men in *Räuberzivil* have ransacked Jewish businesses,' the woman said, choosing her words with care.

Räuberzivil – the clothes of thieves.

'Just on the Ku'damm?'

'Everywhere in the city. Also the synagogues. People have been arrested.'

The thieves, Laura presumed. It was not until much later in

the day that she learnt the truth. Twenty-three out of Berlin's twenty-nine synagogues had been destroyed in the night, along with thousands of Jewish homes and shops. More frightening was the report that twelve thousand Jews had been rounded up and sent to concentration camps.

'Mainly Sachsenhausen,' Klaus said, speaking of a camp north of the city.

He was deeply depressed by what had happened, as were most Berliners. Now, on the Leipzigerstrasse and the Fasanenstrasse, every block seemed to have its share of charred beams, collapsed façades and burnt-out walls.

'I'm going to phone Paul,' said Laura.

His parents' number would be in the phone book.

'I don't think you should intrude. It's *Hanukkah*. His mother won't like it if you phone.'

'I'll try the hospital.'

Klaus buried his nose in a book. 'It's up to you. I wouldn't have thought doctors liked being phoned on duty.'

'You're probably right,' Laura said. 'Do you think that report is true, that so many Jews have been arrested?'

'Who knows what's true any more? Don't think about it. There's nothing any of us can do.'

Except wait, Laura thought. Nobody else *was* taking action of any sort. There was no looting. Shop windows were hastily boarded up. The news that the Jews were to pay compensation for what had been done was greeted with embarrassment, as was the announcement that Jewish businesses were to be handed over to 'deserving' Nazis.

Laura, sleeping alone, was haunted by nightmares of Sachsenhausen. Nikolaus called, Gebhard flitted in and out, but there was no word of Paul for over a week.

One interminable evening she threw cushions onto the *zimmer*-room floor and lay on her stomach reading until well after dark.

Eventually she began to doze off. Well, why not sleep where she was? It was infinitely cosier on the cushions than it was on her own in the double bed. She fetched an eiderdown, spread it out on the makeshift mattress and as she did so the bulb in the standard lamp blew, leaving the room in semi-darkness.

She half-undressed and snuggled down. But now, ironically, sleep eluded her. Lying on her back she was more alone than ever. In the half-light the sofa and the shabby chairs and the Barnsley bureau were alien shadowy forms staring down at her.

Why did everything have to change?

Tim would have said that man was a mutant, that nature was in a state of metamorphosis, but he had not survived the onslaught of violent change any better than his youngest daughter. His lugubrious youngest daughter . . . She turned onto her side, supporting herself with an elbow, and savagely plumped up one of the cushions.

The doorbell rang. She jerked into a sitting position, hands clenched with apprehension. Once she and Klaus would have welcomed late arrivals. Now a ring on the doorbell at night might mean that Klaus and Gebhard had been arrested.

She reached out for her jumper, pulled on her skirt. The doorbell rang again.

'I'm coming,' she said, although no-one could hear her, and padded barefoot through the connecting rooms to face whatever horror was waiting on the other side of the door. It was no bogey – no demon.

'I know it's late,' Paul said. 'I hope you don't mind?'

'How I do not! You couldn't begin to understand!'

She led him into the dim room.

'The bulb went. I'll fetch one from the bedroom.'

'No. Don't. It's better like this.'

She stopped in her tracks, swung round to face him. She could barely see his features but she knew that the situation between them had changed.

'You have beautiful hair,' he said. 'Almost the colour of pearls. Laura . . . ?'

'It's all right.'

It was hardly a romantic reply but it seemed to be the right

118

one. In any case, they had talked enough these last few months.

Paul must have thought that, too. He stepped forward, pulled her into his arms and kissed her purposefully. From that point on it was, in both senses, a short distance to bed.

Klaus smelt of Crème Mouson soap and Kalordorma razor cream – Paul of fresh sweat, which added to the excitement. But it wasn't odour that made the difference, nor the degree of energy that went into love-making, or the time expended, or the length of the lovers' erections. It was the contrast between one man fucking with his whole being and another who, during the act, had only been able to give part of himself.

It was the change in her own willingness, from then on, to take risks.

All life – all *real* life – is risk, Tim would have said. Tim the escapist . . .

Laura shivered. Paul was lying across her, his head on her shoulder, his hand shielding his face. In spite of their intimacy she thought that he was deliberately cutting himself off from her. The curtain of loneliness dropped.

Just now, Laura thought, he will get up, dress, and leave me.

She tensed, waiting for this to happen. Paul stirred, as if he had momentarily fallen asleep and had woken abruptly. With his hand over his face he mumbled something unintelligible.

'I didn't hear you,' Laura said apprehensively.

'I said I'm sorry.'

'*Sorry?*'

He rolled off her, lying on the cushions from the sofa, looking up at the ceiling.

'I took advantage of you. I – these last few days have been a strain.'

'At the hospital?'

'No. I haven't told you. I haven't had the chance to tell you. The other night – my father's shop was smashed. It's been taken away from us. My parents have lost everything.'

'That's terrible.'

'And standard – for people like us.'

'So what are they going to do?'

'What can they do? They're getting out. They're going to America – all the family.'

'And you?' Laura said in a small voice. 'What about you?'

'I can't leave the hospital. I don't want to desert what I'm doing. My work there is more important than anything in my life. The worse it becomes here the more I realise that I have to stay on. I know *you* can understand that feeling. That's why I wanted to see you. Why I got carried away as I did. I shouldn't have made love to you.'

'I'm glad you did,' said Laura. 'What else would I be? Please don't say you're sorry because I'm not!'

She felt light-headed and happy again but part of her was cold-bloodedly calculating how the practicalities of an affair with Paul could be carried out.

She had to tell Klaus. Gebhard was making a film for one of the other film companies and the two men were seeing less of each other as a result that particular month.

'What's for dinner?' Klaus said when he came home.

'Steak-and-kidney pudding. English dinner!'

Klaus brightened. He loved stodgy food, the more fattening the better, although he never put on weight.

'Marvellous!'

He could have been any young husband returning from work, looking forward to a meal. But he wasn't a typical husband and the dilemma facing his wife could hardly be called normal.

'You're lost in thought,' he said. 'What else have you got on your mind?'

An ordinary wife would not have to reveal such scandalous thoughts: *I'm in love with Paul. Now that you're home again we're going to have a problem about where to make love.*

Making love was altogether a complicated business, Laura mused. When you were occupied with it what you and your lover did seemed to you spiritual and pure and unique.

When you contemplated discussing it with a third party all that changed. Because you couldn't explain to an outsider the emotions and thoughts that went with the physical act. An attempt to do so would only leave the listener with a clumsy and grotesque image of two people coupling. Which was why it was wiser never to talk about making love at all.

'Is it Paul?' Klaus asked gently.

Laura was sitting on the sofa where she and Paul had lain. Now that Klaus was home the old sofa was the same cosy piece of furniture it had always been. The under-stuffed cushions were their same faded selves, reassuring in their antiquity.

And Klaus was the same . . .

'Yes,' she said. 'It's Paul.'

'Do you love him?'

'I think so.'

In that moment she was unsure. Her affair with Paul represented further change and she resisted that.

'We have enough to contend with as it is,' said Klaus, 'without you taking a Jewish lover.'

This was perfectly true and Klaus stated it without animosity but Laura was annoyed. In the back of her mind a small petulant voice said, *You started it first!*

'It's too late for me to worry about that. We *are* lovers.'

Klaus crossed his arms defensively. 'You should have given it more thought.'

'I have. *We* have. What I'm trying to say to you is . . . we want to – meet here – '

She floundered helplessly. Klaus wrapped his fingers so tightly around his biceps that his knuckles turned white.

'I know what you're trying to say to me. All right, then we must be practical. I'll make sure I don't come home on those evenings. After all, I'm often at Gebhard's as it is. It won't make that much difference.'

But already it had. They had set up a conspiracy but, in an odd way, the old trust that had existed between them was gone.

*

The practical problem of where to make love had been solved. Finding the time to be together proved to be another dilemma.

Paul worked long hours and was often tired. In the winter of 1938-1939 Laura was quite frequently out of Berlin on sports assignments.

More than ever, it was dangerous to be seen in the company of a Jew. The Führer had announced a policy of extermination of European Jews in case of war. All Germans between ten and eighteen were conscripted into the Hitler Youth. There was a feeling of preparation for conflict. And out of that came the desire, spreading amongst their friends like a virus, to live for now.

Laura could feel herself being infected by the virus. She was not satisfied by the snatched hours she spent with Paul. So when Nikolaus offered the use of his family's chalet in the Harz Mountains to his circle of friends she leapt at the chance.

'We could go there together for a weekend,' she said eagerly. 'It's not that far from Berlin.'

Paul frowned. 'I don't know if I can get away from the hospital.'

'Only for two nights.'

'Please try to understand that, for me, work comes before everything else: before you, before love, before my friends.'

'Yes,' Laura said impatiently, 'I *do* understand, but even doctors can get away sometimes. No one should be that committed to their careers.'

'That's what you think, is it?'

But in the end Paul did take a weekend off and they travelled together to the Harz.

Laura had been there before, in springtime, but now the sunny flowered meadows of the herb-scented valleys were covered with snow and the forested foot-hills were white.

More snow was falling as they reached the chalet: fat, puffy flakes. An outside table and two chairs were barely discernible as forms. Inside, the walls had been painted white.

Icicles like jagged blades of glass hung from the eaves of adjacent chalets. It was so silent that Laura could hear the gurgle of the small brown stream that ran through what she could see of the garden.

They made love and slept and made love again, kept warm by an old eiderdown.

In the morning the sky was clear. The sun shone on crisp, sparkling snow and the forest was a huge family of emaciated children walking towards them, wasted arms outstretched.

In a cupboard they located skis and boots.

'I can't ski.'

'I'll teach you,' Paul said.

In this environment Paul was very much more relaxed than she had ever seen him before. He proved a competent instructor, demonstrating how Laura should find her balance, and how she should proceed uphill, taking tiny, sideways steps.

Coming down even a gentle slope, stopping with skis pointed together in front, was hazardous at first. She tumbled again and again.

'I can't do it!'

'You can!'

He hauled her up, transformed from his normal serious self into a young man having fun in the snow.

'I want to stay here forever!' Laura said, extravagantly, her face tingling and her bottom just beginning to ache.

'I, also,' said Paul – and then he seemed to withdraw as if he was cross with himself for having unbent.

Because she was at her most confident on this holiday, Laura reached certain conclusions about this reaction of Paul's.

He came from a background infinitely more conventional than her own, and he had not been influenced by a libertarian aunt. Much as he loved her, he would have reservations about introducing a *goy* girlfriend to his parents. And if that girlfriend was married . . . ! So naturally he would withdraw every so often, wondering how he was going to cope with the prospect of a shared future with Laura.

She would have to relieve him of part of the burden. She would have to divorce Klaus.

Back at the chalet she brought the subject up.

'You said in the past that I shouldn't remain married to Klaus. You were right. I'll have to make the break. Perhaps I should see a lawyer.'

Paul did not react as she expected. He frowned.

'Is that wise? What will it do to Klaus? It might focus attention on him.'

'What about me? What about us?'

'I don't know if any of us are free to act independently any more. We have to protect others.'

He was withdrawing again. What a frustrating man he was. But perhaps he was right about Klaus. Laura sighed.

'I don't want to go back to Berlin,' she said, 'I wish we could stay here.'

'We *have* to go back,' said Paul reasonably.

He was already there, Laura thought. Unlike herself he was not unhappy at the prospect of sleeping alone.

There could be no shared future in Nazi Berlin. But Paul was adamant that he did not want to leave. He was deeply entrenched not only in his work at the Jewish hospital but with the community in Oranienburg Strasse, and that side of his life he kept very much to himself.

Laura was once more intent on broadening her outlets for work. All year round she had been toying with the idea of visiting Paris and doing the rounds of the various photographic agencies. In August she applied for an exit permit for the following month.

'Is this because you want to get away from Paul?' Klaus wanted to know.

'Why ever should I want to do that?'

Klaus became vague. 'I don't know. I just wondered.'

'Why should you wonder?'

'You really want to know?'

This was infuriating. 'Naturally, I do!'

'I thought that perhaps it was over. I – well, the other day I saw Paul in Alexander-platz with another woman.'

This was a body blow.

'Truly with another woman?'

'Perhaps she was only a friend,' Klaus said promptly. 'She was very unattractive – uninteresting. Mousy hair. Dull clothes. Someone from the hospital perhaps.'

'Perhaps,' said Laura, dogged by the memory of a junior nurse with a proprietorial manner.

But Paul wouldn't be attracted to a girl like that. It was odd enough that he would be interested in her! In any case, why shouldn't he talk to someone he chanced to meet in the street? She did not refer to the girl when she next met Paul. The hours they spent together could be better used. That August they made wonderful love.

On the thirty-first of the month Laura was granted her exit permit for September. On 1 September German tanks rolled into Poland. On the second Laura, turning from the Ku'damm into Joachim Friedrich Strasse, was seized by the wrist and Nikolaus said, 'Laura! Thank God I've got hold of you!'

There was a suitcase at his feet.

'What on earth do you think you're doing?' Laura said indignantly. 'You gave me the fright of my life grabbing me like that.'

He picked up the case. 'Come,' he said and, taking her by the elbow, he guided her back on to the Ku'damm.

'Nikolaus! I want to go home!'

'You can't go home,' he said in such a serious voice that she stopped protesting.

When the traffic permitted they crossed the road. Nikolaus propelled her to the left, away from the main activity towards a small café. When they were ensconced in a corner and he had ordered coffee he took her hand.

'You're going to have to be very brave,' he said. 'And you mustn't break down, even in here.'

Her heart began to thump. 'It's Paul, isn't it? He's been arrested?'

125

Nikolaus shook his head. 'Ssh. No, it's not.'

The coffee was set down in front of them.

'*Danke schön.*'

When the waiter had gone Nikolaus said, 'It isn't Paul, it's Klaus. You're going to have to control yourself because this is a terrible story. *Klaus is dead, Laura.* Don't try to say anything. *Just don't cry.* This is what happened. I'm sorry. I have to tell you . . .'

His voice broke. His face was devoid of expression.

'Tell me.'

'They were on their way to Gebhard's apartment. A group of Brownshirts stopped them. I think they sensed something about Gebhard. Klaus and Gebhard went on into the apartment but two of them followed and one taunted Gebhard. Klaus went wild. He picked up a knife. He was trying to protect Gebhard. He stabbed one of the men – killed him. The other Brownshirt shot him.'

'*Klaus killed a man?*' Laura said. That, above all else, didn't make sense.

'Protecting Gebhard . . .'

'But how do you know?' In spite of her thumping heart she was quite calm.

'Gebhard told me,' said Nikolaus. 'He got away. He came to my apartment. He's hiding there now. Laura, listen to me. The Brownshirts take reprisals. One death won't be enough to satisfy them. They'll look for you. I've been to the apartment. I've packed a suitcase for you. Your passport's inside – and your exit permit. I've got some money for you, enough to get you back to England. I'm going to take you to the station. You've got to make a run for it.'

The train, white smoke puffing magnificently skywards, had pulled out of Berlin.

Laura was huddled in a corner of her compartment, trying vainly to warm her hands and staring vacantly out of the window. Fields and trees and houses she had first seen seven years earlier sped by in reverse without her being aware of them.

Klaus is dead, Laura. Klaus is dead, said the wheels passing over the joints in the lines.

And, equally unbelievable: *He stabbed a man.*

'You're cold, *Mädchen,*' the elderly woman in the seat opposite observed with concern.

She opened a basket at her feet, took out a flask and a cup. '*Der Kaffee?*'

'*Nein danke.*'

'*Ja bitte!*' one of the two men sharing the compartment interspersed.

If Klaus really was dead, Laura wondered, why was she not feeling his loss? But she felt nothing, only fatigue, as if she had been enveloped by a cloud of lassitude.

Odd fragments of her conversation with Nikolaus drifted in and out of her mind.

Klaus went wild.

Will you ask Paul to look after my bureau?

I think they sensed something about Gebhard.

Tell Paul I'll write.

'*Ich schwitze!*' one of the men in the compartment said, which quite contradicted her own reactions to the temperature, and the train suddenly stopped.

The two men exchanged anxious glances. The door of the compartment was slid open to reveal three members of the SS.

. . . reprisals. One death won't be enough . . . They'll look for you.

'I'm here,' Laura said – or thought she said. But if she spoke aloud nobody heard.

'Get up!' one of the SS said to the two men.

The elderly woman gasped and put her hand to her mouth. The men were bustled into the corridor. The door slid shut.

'*Mein Gott!*' said the elderly woman and made the sign of the cross.

A few minutes later the train shuddered and recommenced its journey away from Berlin. Within the hour it stopped again on the line. Peering from the window Laura saw men in SS uniforms dragging passengers off. But these actions, too, did not touch her. Like everything else that had occurred within the last twelve hours they were without reality for Laura.

The train pulled into a station and the elderly woman said, '*Auf Wiedersehen!*' and got off the train, leaving the door to the corridor open.

Shivering, Laura got up to close it. Boots thudded. More uniformed figures came into view. She backed away as five generals stomped angrily past, their thunderous faces indicating that they, too, could have been the recipients of terrible news.

Klaus is dead, the wheels ranted. *He stabbed a man.*

She returned to her seat. Apart from herself the compartment remained empty. Hours passed. There were long blanks. At some stage she must have fallen asleep.

In this shocked condition she reached Hamburg from where she was to catch the boat for England.

The port was buzzing with speculation and fear. Even Laura registered what people there were saying, what was at that moment making headlines around the world, and what presumably had caused the five generals to look so distressed.

The Western powers had objected to the invasion of Poland. War had been declared.

It would all be over in a few weeks, so they said in England.

Laura, back in Barnes, had only to make a brief statement. Klaus had been murdered by the Brownshirts. The family took it for granted that he had been shot because of his anti-Nazi views.

As her frozen emotions began to unthaw, Laura heaped blame on herself for forcing Klaus out of the apartment in order to facilitate her own love affair. If she had been able to talk it over with someone she might have been persuaded that it was hardly her fault, but there was no one in whom she could confide.

She could not make contact with Paul. All postal and telecommunication with Germany was cut off. She retreated into herself. The rest of her family – having expressed sympathy – were preoccupied with the war. William was joining up. The girls were making black-out curtains. The likelihood of air-raids was higher on the agenda for discussion than Laura's introspection.

And Laura herself was brooding too deeply about Klaus to take heed of the signs made by her own body.

Light gradually dawned that she might be pregnant. The doctor confirmed it. The family took it for granted that the father was Klaus. For Laura letting them think so was the easiest way out, obviating the necessity for long explanations and revelations about Klaus. Like the family, she thought that the war would soon end. When it did she would write to Paul and tell him about her pregnancy.

She thought that he would want to marry her, although she was not sure that she deserved so happy an ending. They would probably emigrate to America to join Paul's relations.

But those who predicted the duration of the war were proved incorrect. It became more difficult, not less, to attempt to make contact with Jews in Germany.

Before she could stop it, Laura's explanation about Klaus, about the baby, even about the bureau, had turned into a legend. And Laura, who had never set out to deceive anyone, found herself locked into a labyrinth of lies.

REBECCA

1954 – 1965

REBECCA Conway, said her grandmother, must have inherited her outstanding beauty from her father's side. The veracity of this statement could not be proven – no photographs of Klaus Fleischer had ever been produced – but there was nothing of Laura in Rebecca's looks.

At fourteen Rebecca was tall – five feet seven and still growing – slender and fine-boned. Her hair was dark brown, naturally curly, her eyes so deeply brown as to be almost black, and her nose a perfect retroussé. Her skin, just that touch darker than that of her classmates, was gloriously unblemished by acne as theirs was not. Even in her school uniform – the clumsy navy-blue box-pleated gym dress, the white shirt and the maroon and navy-blue tie – Rebecca gave the impression of being older than she was, of knowing much more about life than others of her age, although, in reality, she knew very little.

This carefully cultivated air of sophistication, coupled with her superior attitude and her German blood, made her unpopular at school.

It would have astonished her classmates to know that Rebecca envied them – that she was as jealous of their positions as ordinary girls with conventional parents as they were of her beauty. She also wanted a sober-suited father, a mother in a thick wool double-breasted costume with a hip-length jacket and a domed felt hat. She longed for siblings and pets and a lively, clamorous household. Her home in Barnes, where she lived with her mother, her former nanny, and a black cat known as Her Vileness, was not in the same league as those of her classmates.

133

Wanting a father was top of her list. Some of her classmates were also fatherless, because of the war. But these fathers had been alive at the time of their daughters' births. Photographs of *them* were prominently displayed in silver frames in these wretched girls' homes as Rebecca had seen on the rare occasions when she had been asked there for tea. *Those* pictures had not been lost by mothers fleeing Berlin.

Having no image of her father on which to reflect, Rebecca was left with the feeling that he had never existed. With this went a vague suspicion that her mother was at fault.

It was to Laura's discredit that she, Rebecca, had not taken her father's name. On the premise that Conway was more socially acceptable than a German surname, Laura had reverted to her maiden name before Rebecca was born. Somehow, this action had further served to obliterate Klaus. Not that it did any good, Rebecca thought, since it had got out anyway at school that her father had been German.

In the last year Rebecca had been looking more closely at Laura than heretofore and had observed in her a whole host of irritating defects.

It was not that Laura disgraced her by wearing exotic clothes – on the contrary, Laura's were dull and colourless, grey and black – but her views on life were different from those of other mothers who described her as *avant-garde*.

Unlike them, she worked for a living, and as a photographer, which was an oddity in England although Laura said it would not be in Germany or France. Nevertheless, taking pictures was not in the same respectable category as raising money for charity like other mothers.

Worse was Laura's absorption in her work. Laura lived life entirely through her lens. She was always either taking photographs or developing them.

If she was not in Shoe Lane, where *Picture Post*, the illustrated magazine for which she did most of her work, had its offices, she was in her darkroom, or in the new studio which she had built on to the side of the house.

Her friends all came from this photographic world. Some were acquaintances from her Berlin days: disdainful Mr Mann, and much nicer Mr Hutton and Mr Gidal, who had changed their names from Hubschmann and Gidalewitch after leaving Germany. The founder of *Picture Post*, Mr Stefan Lorant, had also been a refugee from the Nazi regime and Mr Guttmann, whose photographic agency, *Rapport*, sold Laura's pictures, had been her employer long ago in Berlin.

All these people Rebecca met when they came to the house in Barnes. She never went to Shoe Lane or to Fleet Street, which was a depressing part of London with bomb craters round the corner.

Laura's photographs were *not* dreary: anything but. Even in her worst mood Rebecca admitted that.

Laura specialised in fashion and in portraits of personalities, some of whom came to Barnes to be photographed in her studio. On other occasions Laura went to the homes of the famous and, once in a blue moon, took Rebecca with her.

One such blue-moon sitting was scheduled for this forthcoming autumn weekend in 1954. Early on in her school career, Rebecca had discovered that Famous People Assignments impressed the other girls. On Friday afternoon, just before school broke up, she made an announcement.

'Tomorrow I'm going to meet Dirk Bogarde.'

The class was every bit as stunned as she had hoped. Dirk Bogarde was the idol of the Odeons, the number one box office star, devastatingly handsome, whom they had all seen in the hit film *Doctor in the House*.

'I suppose that's because your mother has to take his photograph,' one of the girls said, trying to sound withering.

'We're going to his house for lunch.'

Unable to control herself, somebody moaned. They all dreamt of waking to find Dirk Bogarde at the foot of the bed with a stethoscope in his hand.

'*I* prefer Rock Hudson,' said one of the stalwarts.

'He probably knows Rock Hudson,' Rebecca said airily.

'Masses of famous people go to his house. Rock might be there but if he's not I'll ask for his address.'

She smiled sweetly at them, shook back her hair and picked up her books.

At home in Barnes, life was proceeding on a more mundane level. The house, on the corner of St Mary's Grove, was within easy walking distance of where Laura had lived as a child. It was, Rebecca conceded, a cheerful place, the walls painted in pretty, warm colours, the furniture rustic, a few – a very few but pleasing – paintings well-positioned, but it was still very different from other girls' homes.

In the kitchen Eileen Minogue, the Irish woman who had reared Rebecca and put the fear of God into her in the process, was doing *The Times* crossword like the expert she was.

'You're late home. Your stomach must be falling out of you with the hunger.'

'I'm not a bit hungry.'

'If you turned sideways and stuck out your tongue you'd be like a zip-fastener, you're that thin!'

'I am not.'

This always went on and invariably ended with Rebecca being firmly sat at the table and plied with food that she didn't actually want.

On this occasion she succeeded in fending Eileen off. She went into the sitting-room where her aunt and uncle were sitting, chatting to Laura.

Aunt Harriet was the only one of Laura's relations still living in the British Isles. Uncle William had been killed in the war and after Grandfather's more recent death, Grandma had gone to live in Rhodesia with Aunt Caroline who was married to a doctor.

Uncle Charles, Aunt Harriet's husband, was a farmer with land in Ireland. With the harvest just over he had been persuaded to take the kind of holiday approved by his wife.

'Hello, dear,' Aunt Harriet said. 'We were just debating

136

whether Charles and I will go into London tomorrow.' Aunt Harriet conducted debates – she never just talked.

'One would be frightfully bored all day going around the shops,' said Uncle Charles who, whenever he wanted to get out of something, referred to himself as One.

As a child Rebecca had believed implicitly in the existence of Wun, an Oriental Person with a perverse streak.

'Yes, but what are you going to *do* otherwise?' Harriet went on, anxious on Charles's behalf.

'Not sure,' said Uncle Charles. 'One misses the country. No offence to you, Laura my dear, but One does.'

'You could always come to Amersham with us.'

Charles looked dubious. 'Fella there might not appreciate the intrusion.'

'I'll phone and ask,' Laura said. 'He's very charming and I do know him reasonably well.'

Uncle Charles was duly invited to lunch. The following day was frosty, then sunny. Mr Bogarde's house turned out to be truly magnificent, a Queen Anne manor in a ring-fence of fifty acres.

'I say, what!' said Charles, impressed. 'Fella has taste. Splendid garden.'

'He's keen on gardening,' Laura said, putting the handbrake on. 'He's a superb actor. Roy Nash said in the *Evening Standard* the other day that he is one of the three best young actors in British film.'

Who were the others, Rebecca wondered idly? Laura knew so many famous people – Ava Gardner and Diana Dors and Richard Attenborough and Audrey Hepburn.

A figure appeared on the steps of Mr Bogarde's house and Laura hailed it. The man himself. He was quite slight but he was even more attractive in the flesh than he was on the screen, with black hair, intelligent brown eyes and a wide mouth.

He shook their hands. Rebecca was already playing a role in her own production of *So Long at the Fair*, taking over the part played by Jean Simmons.

Indoors there was no sign of Rock Hudson but Mr Bogarde told her that Judy Garland, Cary Grant, Rex Harrison, Kay Kendall and Olivia de Havilland were frequent visitors at the house.

One Sunday, he said, Gene Kelly and he and other friends had all gone for a walk after luncheon and Gene Kelly had danced up and down the stairs of an unfinished house they came across on a building site.

Rebecca took note of everything to relate at school. The drawing-room was papered in red brocade paper with curtains to match. The study, where pre-lunch drinks were served, was a Regency room with striped dark green flock paper, white woodwork, polished brass and glass that even Rebecca recognised as good. There were flowers everywhere.

Usually Laura was the one who commanded attention on these occasions but Mr Bogarde, as if sensing that, made a point of including Rebecca in the conversation.

'I read in the paper the other day that a girl was found hiding in your woodshed!'

Mr Bogarde nodded. 'The gardeners found her. They called the police. She wanted me to get her a job with a vet because she loves animals, and I did.'

At luncheon a houseman in a white linen jacket, black striped trousers, a black tie and gloves, waited on table. The food was superb: smoked trout, a baron of beef from which Mr Bogarde carved the fillet, four different vegetables, and four sorbets – raspberry, greengage, lemon and orange. The savoury was a mushroom tart, followed by cheese and port.

What a sensation this report would cause at school! Rebecca almost forgot about being Jean Simmons.

'You have an Indian trumpet tree?' Uncle Charles said as Laura produced her camera.

This was the signal, prearranged, for Rebecca and Uncle Charles to make themselves scarce.

'I'll take the Child for a drive,' said Charles at once.

'Yes, but should you?' Laura demurred.

Uncle Charles had imbibed rather a lot of the Sauvignon, the Mouton Cadet and the Dom Perignon.

'Certainly I should. You know me, Laura my dear. I never drive fast.'

'Oh, all right then,' Laura said.

Jean Simmons was thus forced to exit from the set. Uncle Charles and she had no particular destination in mind. For half an hour they meandered amiably about the Buckinghamshire countryside, discussing Mr Bogarde.

'His father was an artist, too,' volunteered Rebecca. This meant that he and Laura had lots in common. Not for the first time she felt eclipsed by her mother's seniority.

'I say, Rebecca, we need petrol. Isn't that a garage over there?'

Without signalling, Charles turned right. The car behind, a smart green Rover, followed in their wake.

'Fill her up,' commanded Charles. 'Good to be in the country. I can't understand the attraction of Oxford Street, can you?'

He released the handbrake, turned the ignition key and reversed with a resounding crack into the green Rover.

'Damnation and blast!'

They both got out. The occupants of the other car – a tall auburn-haired man and a pneumatic young woman with tightly curled blonde hair and a camel-coloured suit with a waist-nipping leather belt – were doing likewise.

'How could you be so stupid?' demanded the woman in a shrill voice.

'Vivienne, please don't interfere,' the man said evenly.

He was tall and not bad-looking with a heavy-jawed, affable face. He had exceptionally nice green eyes and was, Rebecca reckoned, in his late twenties. She liked the way he spoke. His was a well-educated voice but devoid of arrogance.

'I say I'm terribly sorry,' Charles was saying, 'but I don't think it's bad.'

'Actually, it isn't,' said the auburn-haired man, surveying the damage. 'Only a slight dent.'

'Twenty pounds would straighten it out.'

'Hardly even that.'

'Not my car,' Charles said. 'Belongs to my sister-in-law. Have her permission to drive it. Staying with her. Better give you her address.'

'It's only a *minor* dent,' said the auburn-haired man. 'Both our no-claim bonuses will be safe-guarded if we don't make a claim.'

'In that case I'll give you twenty pounds and we'll call it quits.'

'If you insist.'

'My dear chap,' Charles said, feeling for his wallet and failing to find it. 'Rebecca – ?'

'You left it in Laura's handbag. Don't you remember? You said your pockets have holes.'

'So I did. I'm frightfully sorry. Look, I will give you my sister-in-law's address. She lives in Barnes. You're not going that way, I suppose? If so, call in – have a drink.'

'When would you suggest?'

Before they parted the auburn-haired man opened the passenger door for Rebecca and waved her farewell.

By then she had given up being Jean Simmons. Quite interesting things happened when you were simply Uncle Charles's niece by marriage.

Rebecca considered what to wear when the auburn-haired man called. She did not possess that many non-uniform clothes. In the end she settled for a pair of tight knee-length trousers which a model had conveniently left behind in Laura's studio and added a sleeveless blouse of her own with a high round neck.

'Will you look at yourself!' said Eileen on seeing this attire. 'Won't you freeze to death, and is that lipstick you've got on your face?'

'I'm not in the least cold and I've only a tiny bit of lipstick on.'

'*You* didn't turn up to get it when sense was given out!'

Mercifully, the other adults refrained from comment, although Aunt Harriet blinked when Rebecca entered the room.

The auburn-haired man arrived. His name, it transpired, was

Richard Stacton, and he worked for a mining subsidiary based in London.

Remembering the way he had opened the car door for her, how Mr Bogarde had treated her, Rebecca was expecting a certain amount of attention from the visitor, but he talked to Laura instead. The fact that she was a photographer and had trained in Berlin intrigued him no end.

'But you were a photo-journalist,' he said. 'Why did you change over to fashion and personalities?'

'I think I'd had enough of grim reality,' said Laura. 'Fashion isn't frivolous but it can be fun.'

She didn't tell Mr Stacton that there had been an eight-year gap between her photo-journalistic career and her current line of work. When Rebecca was a little girl Laura had done no serious photography. There had been no demand for her skills during the war. It was only in 1947, when Mr Dior had introduced his New Look and friends at *Picture Post* had persuaded Laura to take pictures of women adapting their existing skirts and dresses to the new fashion that she and her camera had become inseparable again.

Rebecca was waiting for her mother to find these photographs and show them off to Mr Stacton. They were funny enough – odd pieces of material sewn on to hemlines or half-way up a skirt; waists bulging over tightened belts; petticoats hanging down – but they would only add to the amount of notice Laura was getting from this third guest.

Then Uncle Charles said, 'Not frivolous? Can't understand why you women *need* all these clothes!' and Aunt Harriet rushed in to defend her shopping expedition.

Later on Mr Stacton mentioned that he was being transferred to Rhodesia for the next few years and Laura asked him whereabouts in Rhodesia.

'Salisbury.'

'What a coincidence! My sister Caroline lives in Salisbury – and my mother.'

'Do they really?'

'You may come across them.'

'I hope so. I hardly know anyone out there apart from the chaps in the office.'

'In that case won't you look them up? Caroline's very sociable. She and her husband are always giving parties. Shall I write you a letter of introduction?'

'Yes. Please.'

A few years, Rebecca thought. Richard Stacton had no potential for her as a leading man. She lost interest in him. It had been a waste of effort getting dressed up.

Lucie Clayton's charm course was Laura's idea. At seventeen Rebecca, having left school, was without career ambition.

'You'll have to find *something* to do,' said Laura in the voice of one whose patience is running thin.

'I expect I'll get married before too long.'

'Early marriages are a bad idea.'

'Yours wasn't.'

'Well, I don't want *you* getting married too young. Anyway, you don't like any of the boys you know, let alone love one of them.'

'They're so gauche. They don't know how to behave with a girl.'

These boys – brothers of classmates – were avid enough for her, but otherwise her social life was not that good. Girls of her own age were nervous of her and she was intolerant of them. She did not get invited to many parties.

What she wanted to do, she thought, was marry a rich, older man and have a big family – at least four children. They would live in a beautiful home with landscaped parkland and antique furniture and back and front stairs. It was just a question of finding the right man.

'If you do the charm course you can model for me.'

'You only want to avail yourself of my services for free.'

'That's not true, darling. You can work with any photographer you like when you've done the course. If John French or anyone else wants to hire you *I* won't mind.'

That was then.

'All right. I'll think about it.'

The course ran for a month. Still, anything would be better than hanging around at home all summer with only Eileen, *The Times* crossword and Her Vileness for company while Laura disappeared into her studio or rushed off to do a Famous Face portrait for a magazine.

Modelling opened doors. Models found wealthy husbands, some of them titled.

Lady Rebecca? It didn't sound right. She would have to change her Christian name. *Lady Margaret*?

She enrolled at Lucie Clayton's.

At charm school she learnt about make-up and how to walk with a book on her head. At the end of the month she was one of the stars put on the books of the model agency which was attached to Lucie Clayton's.

The other girls who had also made this transition were arming themselves with composite sheets to put into their portfolios so they could make the rounds of the photographic studios. They dreamt of posing for Norman Parkinson or Cecil Beaton or Angus McBean, for Laura or for John French. They were looking forward to being discovered by Penn or Avedon, the famous American photographers.

'Your mother is going to take your photographs!' they said. 'You're so lucky!'

'Why do you need a composite sheet?' Laura asked. 'I have enough work to keep you fully employed.'

'What about working for John French?'

'John French? He's a dear, dear man but you don't have to do the rounds of the other studios. I know the kind of work most of the other girls are going to get – mail-order catalogues and knitting patterns for *Woman's Weekly*. I'll get you covers.'

It was a take-over from the start. Models were putty in the hands of photographers. They were not encouraged to have identities of their own. The beauty might be Rebecca's, the hair and the make-up her creations – she had a way with both – but Laura was in control. Never sure who she was, Rebecca became less certain.

Otherwise modelling was not so bad. Laura was a perfectionist who never tired herself and did not expect those who worked for her to complain about fatigue, but she was surprisingly patient and never shouted or threw tantrums when things went wrong. Rebecca never exited from the studio in tears as models sitting for more irascible photographers were seen doing.

And Laura was true to her word about the covers. Rebecca soon got used to the sight of her own face on the front of *Woman* and *Woman's Own*. These magazines had huge circulations – nearly five million each. *Woman's Own* ran an article on Laura and Rebecca as a mother and daughter team. For a while Rebecca enjoyed the idea of fame.

But although she continued to smile down from the news-stands her own life did not change very much. On wet days other girls traipsed into London to do catalogue and advertising sittings at Odhams' Press and Carlton Studios. Rebecca, with hair and pancake make-up perfectly in place, walked along a corridor and opened a studio door. This was comfortable on a windy day but it was not conducive to meeting eligible men. After two years Rebecca's ambition to marry a rich, older man was still being frustrated. She was not content with her lot. And then, in the autumn of 1959, Richard Stacton returned from Rhodesia and called to pay his respects.

Rebecca had forgotten all about him. When she went into the sitting-room and found him with Laura she couldn't remember his name.

'Richard Stacton,' he said, getting to his feet and taking a few steps towards her in order to shake hands. 'And you're Rebecca.'

He had put on a little weight. She liked that. It gave him a slightly regal appearance. Henry the Eighth, she thought, might have looked like Richard Stacton in his earlier days, before he had grown obese. They had done the Tudors at school and it had struck her that the eighth Henry must have had terrific sex appeal as a younger man.

Henry's hair, too, had been red – or auburn. Richard had pretty glints in his, although he wasn't a 'pretty' man but more of an outdoor type.

'Richard has been telling me about Caroline and Duncan,' said Laura. 'They saw quite a lot of each other in Salisbury. I can't believe my sister water-skis!'

'You should see her whizzing around Lake McElwane!'

Laura chuckled. The details of their last encounter with Richard were coming back to Rebecca. Then, as now, she recalled, her mother had monopolised him. Why hadn't Laura remarried? She was forty but not beyond it. After twenty years she shouldn't still be mourning Klaus.

Perhaps she wasn't. She was showing every sign of having emerged from that state – too many for Rebecca's liking. Her conversation with Richard Stacton was too animated, her response too prompt. That remark of his about Caroline hardly rated a smile, let alone a guffaw.

'What else is Caroline up to?' Laura said.

'Golf. Tennis. It's a wonderful country for sport. I had a terrific time there although I must say I think the Federation is a tenuous arrangement.'

'It can't possibly last.'

'But in the meantime Salisbury is quite a civilised place for a single man.'

The telephone rang in the hall and Laura went to answer it.

'Are you back in England for good?' asked Rebecca.

'For the foreseeable future. Although I'll still have to do a fair amount of travelling. And you – your mother tells me you've been modelling for her.'

'I *am* a model, yes.' And a person, she wanted to add – not a package as Laura would have you believe.

'You work for other photographers?'

'You do have to move on,' Rebecca said. 'It has been suggested that I sit for Cecil Beaton.'

This was a downright lie but she didn't care.

'I remember seeing a magnificent photograph he did of Fiona Campbell-Walter,' said Richard. 'In *Vogue*, I think it was. She was wearing a fur coat and holding a Pekinese.'

'I'm glad about that,' Laura said in the hall, and returned looking triumphant.

'Cover for *Woman's Journal*.'

'I'm sure that calls for a celebration,' said Richard. 'Why don't I take you girls out to dinner?'

Where they should eat formed the basis of another dialogue between Richard and Laura.

'What about that restaurant Terence Conran started – The Orrerry? I like that place.'

'I think he may have sold it,' said Laura. 'But I agree with you. It was one of my favourite restaurants.'

'Very white – very simple. Black and white chequerboard floor and black metal furniture with cane seats.'

'The door was yellow.'

'So it was. But the tables had black and white tiled tops. Conran's sister was a photographer, too. She did those still lifes of vegetables and cookery equipment which he used as panels . . .'

'And there was a view into the garden. Plane trees – and a barbecue. And they served globe artichokes with vinaigrette and ratatouille which was regarded as exotic fare! People used to eat the artichoke leaves and send the hearts back!'

'Terence Conran has designed the new Mary Quant Bazaar,' Rebecca intervened. 'There's a lot of black metal there, too, and wooden slats on the ceiling. And the dressing-rooms have louvred panelled doors so you can catch glimpses of people changing! It's very *risqué* – I always get the feeling that I'm being watched when I go in there!'

After that, Laura was less forthcoming with Richard, but she didn't give up. All through dinner – they ended up in Barnes village, not on the King's Road – Rebecca was conscious of competing with her mother.

She wondered if Richard noticed. He was not altogether relaxed himself. In between courses he straightened his tie and rubbed the nail of his index finger with his thumb. But he talked equally to both of them – she couldn't accuse him of concentrating exclusively on Laura. And when he dropped them off he said it was such fun that they must do it again and what about next week – meaning all three of them.

For a while they were a trio, two women silently waiting for the man to make a move. Which of them did he want? Rebecca couldn't tell. Perhaps Richard himself did not know the answer. But she was becoming more and more interested in him. He was physically attractive, nicely mannered, well-spoken. At thirty-four he fulfilled the qualification of the older man and, if he was not madly rich, he was quite well-off.

The situation was still not resolved when Laura accepted a *Vogue* assignment in Majorca.

'It will still be sunny there, darling,' she said. 'Nice break for you.'

Rebecca concurred, schemed, and went down with what she insisted was the 'flu.

'The 'flu, is it?' said Eileen caustically. 'And you the one that is looking as hardy as a mountain goat.'

'I ache all over.'

'Like a man that fell over a straw and a hen pecked him!'

Laura, agitated, phoned one of the agencies for a replacement and Rebecca lay back on her pillows waiting for the moment when she could get hold of Richard and tell him that she was on her own for the next ten days, recuperating from illness.

'Poor old you!' he said. 'You've missed Majorca!'

'I know. And now I'm fine. But it's too late. Laura got someone else and they've already gone.'

'Never mind. We'll go out on our own,' said Richard on cue.

Rebecca rose from her sick-bed in order to buy a new dress.

It was draped and strapless, with an overskirt split at the waist and a bow trim. She put her hair up and added a long necklace with matching earrings.

'Didn't I say you were as tough as a snipe that wouldn't tear in the plucking!' commented Eileen, but Richard said straight away that she looked terrific.

He had a degree in metallurgy. In reply to her prompting he explained how refined copper was sold on world markets through the London Metal Exchange.

Africa was better. Before Richard, Africa had been grey-green greasy rivers and fever trees and Mau-Mau. With him it was splendid rock outcrops, baobab trees, orange sunsets and the Zimbabwe Ruins.

'And the Kikuyu.'

'That's Kenya. Around Salisbury it's the Shona people. Their god is Mwari and they believe that he came to earth thousands of years ago in search of a bride. The world wanted a bride price – in Africa they call it a *lobola* – so he offered it rain – a commodity of which Rhodesia is often pretty short.'

She liked his stories. Klaus, had he lived, would have told his small daughter fairy tales before she went to sleep.

'So Laura won't be back until the third?' said Richard when he dropped her off.

'No,' she visibly drooped. 'I do so hate it when she goes off.'

'Does that happen often?'

'Too often. It was worse when I was young. But I did have Eileen.'

'Poor old you,' said Richard again, more seriously.

The message, she thought, had sunk in. And Laura did put her career before all else. On that score there was no need to lie.

Beauty and wistfulness were too strong a combination for a man of Richard's chivalry to resist. They had nine days before Laura returned. They spent six evenings together.

On their third date he kissed her goodnight in a way that showed his interest without pushing his luck. Rebecca would have resisted French kissing at this early stage but Richard did not attempt it.

Parked outside the house on the fifth night she lingered for longer in his arms. There was a fine line to tread between losing his respect and failing to keep his interest, between maintaining her persona of aloof sophistication and drawing attention by lack of experience to the fifteen-year gap in their ages.

The other problem was that she was becoming more and more attracted to him. She had no intention of going all the way until she was a married woman, but she was already aching for Richard to stroke her breasts.

'Go and get your beauty sleep,' he said instead. 'Not that you need it, God knows. You are – you really are – the prettiest girl I've ever met. And I'm cradle-snatching. What will your mother say when she comes home?'

Rebecca had been wondering the same thing.

'Laura will be delighted. She likes you very much.'

'I feel the same about her.'

'She's completely open-minded. She doesn't make rules for me. She doesn't think – and I don't – that age has anything to do with – ' better not say *love* – 'it.'

'Doesn't she? Don't you?'

'*No*! Nor should you. You know my father was older than she was – and she was eighteen when she – ' better not say *got married* – 'and he became serious about each other.'

'And it worked out?'

'Wonderfully. That's why Laura has never again – been serious about anyone. Because she loved Klaus so much.'

'And that's why she immerses herself in work?'

How had they got so deeply into the subject of Laura?

'*Yes*!' said Rebecca and held up her lips to be kissed.

'I hear you've been seeing a lot of Richard,' said Laura. 'Eileen tells me – ' Eileen would! – 'that you've been out with him virtually every night while I've been away.'

No obvious hurt or indignation, just – regret? resignation?

Whatever it was, the blow could not be cushioned.

'That's right. We've become rather fond of each other.'

'Isn't he a little old for you?'

'*I* don't think so and neither does he. I've always preferred older men. You know that.'

'You've never had an older boyfriend before.'

'Now I have.'

Please, Rebecca thought, leave it like that.

Her wish was granted. Laura subsided. On her next date with Richard her mother appeared only briefly in the house – to say how busy she was in the studio.

The other contestant had withdrawn. The courtship progressed with Rebecca's vision of the future focused on her big house (modified, in view of Richard's income, to an early Victorian detached residence on an acre of land). In her mind's eye she furnished the house traditionally and filled it ebulliently with children and puppies and noise.

On 22 March 1960 Richard took her to dinner in the Savoy River Room. She sensed a special occasion. She was sure he was going to propose.

As the meal proceeded he spoke about Africa – not about sunsets and the Shona people and their tribal beliefs, but about South Africa. The day before the South African police had shot and killed forty-seven Africans in a place called Sharpeville. Nearly two hundred others had been wounded. Richard said the carnage was iniquitous, whatever the provocation. It would have long-standing repercussions on the stability of the republic.

Rebecca expressed horror and shock. It *was* awful about the poor Africans but she was still not certain why the police had fired and too concerned with what might be about to happen to herself to concentrate on the news.

Over coffee Richard dropped the subject of Africa and became more personal. He reached across the table and clasped her right hand. 'There's something I want to ask you.'

This was going to be it. And sure enough Richard duly

produced from his pocket a small box in which there was a three-diamond ring.

'That's just gorgeous,' said Rebecca.

Not for nothing was Richard a metallurgist. She stretched out her left hand, slightly elevating the third finger. He slipped the diamond ring on to it.

'It fits perfectly. It *is* beautiful.'

'You're the beautiful one,' said Richard, mellow from the wine. 'Darling Rebecca, I do love you.'

'And I love you.'

She was sincere in that statement. She thought of their big house and all that would go with it. She was convinced that their home and their babies and their dogs and the happy hullabaloo that must result would satisfy her needs.

I T had not occurred to Rebecca that Richard might question her vision of the future. Until she suggested house-hunting he did not.

'*House-hunting*? What's wrong with my flat?'

Richard's flat – in Cadogan Gardens in the heart of Chelsea – was on the third floor of a red-brick Victorian building. It was conveniently located – just off Sloane Street and five minutes from the tube – and spacious: large sitting-room and dining-room, and two big bedrooms. It was a marvellous flat. It just failed to conform to Rebecca's dream.

'I hadn't expected to live in town.'

Richard frowned. 'And I hadn't anticipated living out of it! I don't want to spend hours commuting, Rebecca.'

He sounded stern. He usually called her *Rebecca darling*.

Nevertheless, she persisted. 'It's just that I had thought of a family home – a house.'

She could see it quite clearly in her mind's eye. It was shaped like a foreshortened E with a heavy stone arch (recumbent lions at its base) to mark the entrance. A large hall (with a marble fireplace in which a fire continually glowed) led off on the one side to a drawing-room (creams and pastels and a full-length gilt mirror covering most of one wall) and to a dining-room (masculine – mahogany and leather; hunting prints) on the other. From this hall the main staircase swept up to the first floor; stairs from the back hall went down to a huge kitchen with a double oven and innumerable pots and pans: Rebecca was a good cook, improving with the aid of Elizabeth David.

'It's unrealistic,' said Richard firmly.

He had a habit of going along with situations for a considerable length of time like an owner taking a dog for a walk on a very long lead. Then quite suddenly and often unexpectedly the dog would be reined in. Richard would have walked as far as he wished along that particular pathway and no amount of coaxing would persuade him to go on. But, on this issue, they had gone no distance at all. His attitude was a severe blow to Rebecca. It had the effect of making her slightly breathless, as if someone was putting a light blanket over her head.

She stared at her hands – at Richard's ring glittering on her finger. He loved her. But he had been a bachelor for longer than most men and he would need gradual prising out of his set ways. In a couple of years from now he would realise that a house was more suitable for family living than a flat. Babies would lead him to that conclusion. And perhaps it was all to the good because in the meantime they could acquire furniture.

Richard's furniture was modern and functional and elongated. The grey sofas had spindly legs. The three-legged kidney-shaped coffee table was prone to falling over. The carpet – paler grey with yellow and black triangles – was meant to contrast with the walls, three of which were a curious shade of pink and the fourth duck-egg blue.

Rebecca could not wait to change the décor.

'Shall we go to some furniture sales?'

'Whatever for?'

'It's better to do it that way round and adapt the colour schemes to what we find.'

'I don't see any need to redecorate.'

'Richard, it's a Victorian apartment. It cries out for brocade sofas and Wilton carpets and a big brass bed with a patchwork quilt.'

'I hate fuss!' Richard said. 'The Victorians were tasteless vulgarians. They built terrific homes but they filled them with bourgeois rubbish.'

Rebecca very nearly lost her temper. Not all Victoriana was

over-fussy. It was possible to pick out good pieces which did not fall into that category. She had a natural sense of colour. She knew that, given the go-ahead, she could do wonders with Richard's flat.

'Anyway,' said Richard, 'buying new furniture is a waste of money and, what's more, even if I was prepared to spend it, which I'm not, I don't have time to spare for going around sales-rooms.'

His work pressure was building up, and so was the requirement for him to travel. He had been out of the country three times recently.

'Don't you care about what I think?'

'I do – very much. But I also feel that your taste may change and that what appeals to you now won't in another couple of years. Then what will we do with a house full of Victorian junk?'

'A flat-full!'

'All right, a flat-full. Whatever you like!'

He was growing impatient. He had no idea how much the refurbishment of Cadogan Gardens meant to her.

Anger and frustration reduced her to silence rather than to tears. If she had had money of her own she would have gone out and refurnished the flat according to specifications while Richard was abroad. Once he saw the results he would know that she had been right. But she did not have that kind of money in her bank account. Modelling for Laura had not made her rich. Laura was not mean but she was parsimonious, in the way of the war generation. She had ensured that Rebecca had been well-educated, and thereafter given a generous enough weekly allowance, but that was where it had ended.

Laura, even if begged, would not provide the cash for such a shopping spree, not behind Richard's back. She would maintain that the flat was adequately furnished. She agreed with everything Richard said. These days, when they met in Barnes, they chatted like long-lost friends. Soon they would not get the chance to meet so often. There would be less opportunity for cosy chats when Rebecca moved into Cadogan Gardens.

When they were married – that was when she should raise the subject of furniture again. Start with the odd piece. Build up slowly.

When they were married she wouldn't suffer from breathlessness any more. It was only due to pre-marital nerves.

They were married in September. Rebecca's white-watered silk gown had a high Mandarin collar and short bell-shaped sleeves. Bystanders sighed as she came out of the church.

Their honeymoon was spent in Deauville. The high season was already over, the horse-breeders and the racing enthusiasts had left the week before but Richard and Rebecca could stroll down the broadwalk with its gaily coloured umbrellas and fluttering flags, stop for aperitifs at the Bar du Soleil and visit the Casino. At the baccarat table in the *Salle Privée* they spotted the film star Gloria Swanson, smoking a cigarette.

Richard promised that he would take her to Jamaica for the winter sun the Christmas after next. The honeymoon was a success. Sometimes in the afternoons Rebecca rested (after all the love-making she was often quite exhausted) while Richard, whose energy was boundless, played a round of golf.

She returned to England in the certainty of being a chic woman of the world, more thirty than twenty.

In the lead-up to the wedding and during the honeymoon she had not got round to mentioning her desire for puppies. Maltese poodles, she thought, as she was unpacking her suitcases. Two, so they can be company for each other when we're not at home.

'Can we go to Harrods' pet shop on Saturday morning?'

'Pet shop? Why would we do that?'

With a feeling of *déjà vu* coming on, Rebecca explained.

'No puppies!' said Richard.

'But why not?'

'For one thing because it wouldn't be fair to have them in a flat – a third-floor flat – and for another they'd be an encumbrance. What if we want to travel?'

'We could put them in kennels.'

'And what about exercising them? Do you really see yourself trailing them along Sloane Square on a wet day? But if you didn't they'd piddle all over the carpets.'

'I hate the carpets anyway!'

'Now, darling, be reasonable. Puppies are *out*!'

She tried to catch her breath. All of a sudden the flat was airless and stuffy. She said so to Richard.

'I'll open some windows.'

It was a breezy day but the onrush of fresh air did not alleviate Rebecca's breathlessness.

'Come on, let's get the unpacking over with,' said Richard cheerfully. 'Then we'll go out for supper. I don't want you becoming a complete slave to the kitchen.'

As he unpacked he hummed. There was no more talk of dogs. But one of Rebecca's ambitions was fulfilled sooner than even she could have hoped.

She had been frying bacon and eggs for Richard's breakfast when, without warning, the floor rose up and the earth engulfed her. She came round to find herself lying on the bed with Richard gazing anxiously at her.

'Darling Rebecca, thank God you've revived. You gave me the fright of my life. Sit up, sweetheart, and drink some water.'

She sipped obediently.

'How are you feeling?'

Her limbs were leaden. 'Worn out.'

'Darling!'

They didn't consider pregnancy, which they associated with morning sickness rather than black-outs, but they were both delighted when this was diagnosed.

'Clever girl!' said Richard. 'I must phone my mother and tell her.'

Richard's mother lived in Godalming and was obsessed with gardening. She expressed pleasure at the news and promised to send Rebecca a book on flower-arranging for special occasions.

They phoned Laura and got hold of Eileen.

'Laura's off somewhere. I'll tell her you rang.'

Rebecca could not contain herself. 'Eileen, I'm pregnant!'

'God between us and all harm, aren't your troubles only starting.'

This prediction proved only too right. The next morning Rebecca blacked out again.

'My poor darling,' Richard said. 'You must spend the day in bed. Maybe Laura can come round.'

'If she isn't working. Otherwise Eileen will.'

Eileen did. When she went back to Barnes at six o'clock Rebecca had recovered.

It was two days before she suffered a recurrence, then two more. For the next four months these fainting spells, from which she emerged dazed and weary, occurred without warning.

Deeply concerned, Richard forbade her to drive the car. During the week, Eileen stayed with her, at Laura's insistence.

In the later stages of pregnancy she fainted less frequently but she was always on edge, waiting for it to happen. The damage to her psyche was greater by far than the strain on her body. Rebecca had always acted out a superior role and succeeded in her performances. As Richard's chic, woman-of-the-world wife she had convinced herself, as well as others. In pregnancy she was floundering under the pressure she had put on herself to be perfect.

She had always kept her innermost feelings to herself, a habit she had got into as a child, living with a mother who had immured herself against love. In any case she would not have dared share her current thoughts with anyone – not Laura, and certainly not Richard – in case he or she was disgusted and repelled.

How could she tell anyone that the baby had become a parasite to her, a hostile entity; that the lunges and punches he made with his tiny hands and feet were not swimming movements but bellicose attacks? She was monstrous to think of an innocent creature in this way but she couldn't rid herself of the thoughts. She grew to fear the baby and she hated herself.

The cause of all this trouble was due to arrive on 17 August. Laura and Eileen were both on stand-by. Laura had taken the unprecedented step of cancelling a sitting.

The first pain was no more than a twinge. Laura was bemoaning the fact that East Germany had closed the Berlin border – that week's big news – when the second one came.

Rebecca felt calm. She was pleased with herself about that. Could it be that, having failed lamentably for nine months, she was going to succeed at the end?

'He's on schedule!' she said to Laura – and her mother got into a dither.

'Goodness! Eileen, where are you? We must phone Richard. We should get you to hospital, darling.'

In the car she had another twinge.

'I'm *OK*,' she said in reply to Laura who was at the wheel.

'Oh my God, I forgot! We should be heading for the Fulham Road, not the Embankment!'

'Don't panic. We're not in that much of a hurry.'

The twinge came back as a spasm of pain. Rebecca winced.

Richard was already at the hospital. Forms were filled in. She was extracted from Richard and Laura, conducted through a swing door and down a long corridor. The pain was intensifying but she clenched her teeth, determined to behave well.

'Come on then,' said the nurse, a grey-faced woman with cold opaque eyes. 'It's not started properly yet, has it?'

'I don't know.'

'You'd know,' said the nurse grimly, pushing open another door and shunting Rebecca inside. 'Here you are. Take off your clothes and put on this gown and get into bed.'

Another nurse came, and a doctor who felt her stomach and said, 'A fair way to go yet,' in a flat, phlegmatic voice.

They abandoned her. The contractions continued to come and go at twenty-minute intervals. They were not unbearable but her isolation was. She was more alone than she had ever been in her life.

The first nurse looked in.

'How long will it be before my baby is born?'

'You're still only in the first stage! Your waters haven't broken yet.'

She was naïve, ignorant, asinine, but she still wanted to acquit herself according to rule.

Another spasm. Where were Richard and Laura? What were they doing? What were they talking about? The image of them together connected with the next wave of pain.

But there was, as the doctor had said, still a fair way to go, although other adjectives would more aptly have described her journey – lacerating, punitive. Rebecca's vision of life became a nightmare.

Her waters did not break until the next morning by which time she had given up trying to behave well.

The grey-faced nurse was back on duty. She gave instructions: *'Bear down. Breathe deeply. Stop crying.'*

Rebecca wept and screamed and swore. The nurse pursed her lips. The nightmare endured.

Eventually, doped with Demerol, she gave birth to an eight pound thirteen ounce baby boy.

They cleaned him up and put him into her arms. He was raw and red and apparently as fed up with her as the doctor and the grey-faced nurse.

'He's a *beautiful* baby,' said the nurse, as if Rebecca was about to oppose that fact.

Beautiful? She couldn't see beauty in that scarlet countenance. She couldn't feel or react. She was – there was no doubt of it – an all-round flop.

The baby howled and his face turned from red to purple.

'Give him to me,' said the nurse.

In a way, she was taking not only Rebecca's baby but Rebecca's vision of life. She didn't want a big family, she thought – not any more. She didn't even want a second baby. The Pill was freely available on prescription. Thank heaven for that!

She refused to breast-feed, a decision that resulted in a fierce fight with the grey-faced nurse. Rebecca stuck to her guns. She had given nine months of her life to Peter Elliot Stacton and she wanted her body back.

This, as the nurse let her know, was another instance of Bad Behaviour. She came home in the knowledge of Being In Disgrace.

Eileen came to stay until Peter slept through the night, which Rebecca privately thought he never would do.

His complexion had paled but his temper did not cool. Eileen said it was wind. Gripe water was purchased. Peter was burped.

How to burp was another skill Rebecca couldn't learn. The baby, Eileen said, was best held with its stomach pressed against one of your breasts. But for that you needed a generous bosom which Rebecca lacked.

She perched on a cushion – she had been torn and restitched and where she had previously been soft and pink she was knotty and hard – watching Eileen give Peter his bottle.

'Isn't he the fine fellow?' Eileen crooned, an observation that applied to anything Peter did, be it a soiled nappy or a quality burp.

Lately, Rebecca felt as if she had been cut adrift from the mainstream of life. It was as if Richard and Laura and Eileen and Peter were living on an island and she was a passenger on a ship that was cruising past. Richard lived on that part of the island she couldn't see from the deck . . .

She was further apart from him than from the other three. He was extremely busy at work. He was about to go overseas again on a business trip. She didn't much care. She didn't care about anything. As long as Eileen was there she could sail aimlessly on with no particular port in mind.

When Peter was eight weeks old Eileen put a stop to her circumnavigation with the announcement that he had slept through the night.

'So that's it then and I'll be off back to your mother.'

'You can't. Richard's away. I'm all on my own.'

'No use complaining. You'll get nothing for it. I have no call

160

to be in London tomorrow, I can tell you!'

A massive Ban-the-Bomb demonstration was planned for the following day.

'But – '

'No buts.'

Rebecca was forced to accept the *fait accompli*. Eileen was not given to changing her mind once it was made up. She was like Richard in that.

Having been forced to come ashore Rebecca found herself on a bleak island. No Richard, no Eileen, and Peter sleeping.

The next day she was nervous of going out because of the march. She heard on the News that eight hundred and fifty people had been arrested.

The day after that it rained. At four A.M. Peter woke in a rage and remained awake. If only babies were more like electric kettles or toasters or irons which you could switch off at will.

The rain had fizzled out by nine-thirty but even if it had been belting down she would have put him into his pram and taken him for a walk.

Up until then this had been Eileen's prerogative. Rebecca discovered that walking in London was a tricky business if you were pushing a pram. The pavements were uneven, the wheels baulked. Shop doors had not been designed to facilitate the movement of mothers and babies. You couldn't take a pram into a coffee bar or a boutique. Everywhere she went she saw people of her own age on Vespas or in bubble cars.

In spite of this she walked along the King's Road and then – because she loved the pretty houses there – along Godfrey Street, heading for Knightsbridge Green.

She was only going to stroll past Bazaar but when she reached the shop she realised that there was a fashion show in progress. She stopped and looked in. There was a balcony at the back and a mezzanine floor from which models were making their way down to the lower level. There a simple chandelier made out of flex with naked light bulbs highlighted their vivacity and their confidence and their youth. The oldest models looked seventeen, at most.

Seventeen . . .

Peter woke, snuffled and bawled. She hadn't brought a bottle with her. She would have to take him home.

She practically ran there with the pram, Peter grumbling all the way. While she was changing and feeding him she was formulating a plan. It was not ideal. It never had been. But it was better than trundling around London with a ululating child every day of the week.

When Peter had finished his bottle she wrapped him in a blanket, took him downstairs into the street and hailed a taxi.

'St Mary's Grove, Barnes, please.'

Laura had been missing her in the studio – or so she said. Well, that could be rectified. She, Rebecca, was about to resume her modelling career. Eileen could be coaxed into babysitting. She'd enjoy having Peter in Barnes.

It need not be every day – just twice a week for a start. And it need not always be Laura who employed her. That would do for a new beginning. Once she was reinstated she would persuade other photographers to put her on their books.

'I DO see,' said Richard, 'that it will give you something to *do*. It must be lonely for you, with my having to go abroad so often. I do see that babies aren't exactly stimulating company. But why not the Chelsea Babies' Club – you'd meet other young mothers there?'

'No thanks!'

Richard, being busy, did not labour the point. Rebecca fell into a new routine. Every morning she set off for Barnes with Peter in his carrycot and her model bag neatly packed with black and white shoes and gloves, stockings, hairpieces and make-up. *Every* morning because, almost immediately, she realised that twice a week was out. It was not possible to model for Laura on a modified basis. Laura was incapable of doing anything by halves and she did not allow those associated with her to act otherwise. She was even more ambitious, more obsessed with photography than she had been before. The success of other talented photographers – Brian Duffy, Terence Donovan and David Bailey – fuelled her competitive instincts.

But the fashion editors had taken with renewed enthusiasm to the mother and daughter team. There were sittings in the *Vogue* studio and – when the spring of 1962 permitted it – outdoors, in one of the parks, as well as in Laura's own studio.

Rebecca's earnings were quite impressive. *Vogue* paid her ten pounds for a day's work, advertising more.

Richard protested that she was over-doing things. 'It isn't as if we need the money. It's going to push us into a higher tax band. The net result won't be worth it.'

Rebecca did not argue nor did she cut back on her work, even though it *was* a strain sustaining two roles. She did feel split in half. The young wife and mother who set off in the morning metamorphosed in the course of the day into a young, carefree Sixties child. Her hair had been recently cut. Her fringe was long and straight, her eyes heavily outlined with black and her mouth very pale. It was a look which she knew Richard did not really like, although he did not say so.

When Richard was not in London Rebecca lingered on at Barnes, waiting until Peter had eaten his last meal of the day. Every now and again she slept over in St Mary's Grove, ready to start work early in the morning.

Even so, that was as far as she had intended to go in terms of self-realisation. She was not that personally ambitious and she had not considered working anywhere other than London. It was Laura who, by purchasing an apartment in Paris, unwittingly unlocked the other door.

The apartment, in rue Jean Mermoz, near the Champs Elysées, hardly merited so grand a nomenclature. On the eighth floor – to which a lift designed for two very small people ascended with crunching reluctance – it consisted of one reasonably sized room. A sliding door led into a tiny so-called bathroom, with shower and loo.

'All I need,' said Laura happily, 'when I go over for the Collections.'

Actually, she covered other assignments in Paris. She had photographed Maurice Béjart, the French ballet dancer and choreographer, and the actress Simone Signoret, and Edith Piaf.

'Piaf is extraordinary! That little body and the enormous voice.'

She sang two lines of *Je Ne Regrette Rien* in an off-key voice.

'One of these days, you must hear her sing in person. Have you and Richard been to see *Last Year at Marienbad*?' This was the new Alain Resnais film in which past and present fused.

'No, we haven't.'

Laura was always a step ahead in terms of what was happening. And it was Laura who said now, 'Would Richard mind, do you think, if you worked a week or so in Paris this summer?'

Rebecca looked down at her boots. They were white plastic. They went well with her Quant pinafore 'Cad' and collarless cotton shirt.

Would Richard mind? And would she care if he did?

Richard, she thought, had a tendency to think of her as an object rather than a person. A precious object, to be sure, a work of art pleasing to the eye – an object which he had purchased for his apartment. A pretty picture which, if she had not taken action to prevent it, might have been left dangling while he was abroad.

Men of his generation were like that. They assumed control. As Laura did . . .

'Don't worry about Richard. What's the job?'

'The Pierre Cardin Collection.'

'You're doing it?'

'Of course!'

But it didn't happen like that. Two days before they were to leave for Paris Laura slipped and sprained her ankle. She was furious with herself.

'What an idiot I am! I can't bear to think who will go in my place! I hope you'll cope without me – '

'I will. Never mind.'

'– but you don't have to worry about using French because you won't need it. And stand up to the French models. They always sneer at our choice of clothes. *I* say to them: "My dears, they're all *French* clothes, after all!" and then it's all right. It's pointless being too polite. The French simply don't understand "I'm frightfully sorry" and all that nonsense we go on with. They appreciate *strength*. So shout if you must but for God's sake don't burst into tears.'

'I hardly ever cry.'

Peter was walking by then. With Eileen stalking him he toddled to the gate to see his mother off.

She had the key to Laura's apartment in her bag. The other

models, she knew, would be booked in to l'Hôtel de la Trémoille. Except for the *Vogue* team who headed for the Crillon.

What was the saying: *'The Nazis stayed at the Crillon during the war. In peacetime, Condé Nast'?*

And here was she, on her own, in an eighth-floor flat.

As soon as she had unpacked she walked to the Champs Elysées and bought new stockings from the Elle Boutique. It was a warm, humid day, but in spite of this she wandered further along the great, wide avenue from the Place de la Concorde to the Rond-Point, taking pleasure in its elegance, in the pavilions and the trees and the grand old chestnut alleys and, this above all, in the novel sensation of being on her own in a strange city.

She was aware that men were watching her. They did not whistle, as happened in London – their admiration was more subtle and because of it more seductive.

Some of them were young. Her own age. A decade and more younger than Richard. She shied away from this realisation, turned back, and stopped in a café for black coffee before going to bed early. In the morning she had an appointment for fittings at the Cardin salon in Faubourg Saint-Honoré.

Cardin was the first of the French designers to show his Collection that year. Since he was a couturier who was often one or two seasons ahead there was an all-too-justifiable fear of pirating at the salon. A kind of black-out had been imposed on the designs. Turning up for her fittings, Rebecca was conducted into a room in which all the shutters had been closed.

The room was decorated in black and gold and further dramatised by Venetian torch-bearers and exquisite pieces of Boulle furniture inlaid in ebony, tortoiseshell, brass and pewter.

The thirteen other models had also assembled, amongst them a friendly, talkative Irish girl called Brigid and the Japanese Hiroko, Cardin's favourite model vedette.

Brigid knew Laura. 'I hear she's hurt herself, the poor pet. Does that mean she's not coming over?'

'I'm afraid not.'

There was no getting away from Laura.

'She's a fine woman but it must be strange having her for a mother. What's she like at home?'

Talk about being direct, thought Rebecca. She couldn't be so herself, couldn't say what her own image of Laura was, couldn't explain to a stranger that she was so overpowering a personality, or that part of her was cordoned off, locked away in sadness; that they were not that close.

'I don't suppose she's any different from your mother.'

'You're having me on! Listen, my mother is in the kitchen all day long. The youngest of us is four.'

'How many are there?'

'Seven and six are girls. I'm the third. I was born on my old fellow's birthday. "Another girl?" he says. "What kind of present is that?"' She laughed without resentment.

'That's a big family.'

'You know how it is with Catholics. There was a girl in my class at school who had twenty brothers and sisters. But they had lashings of money so that was all right.'

Twenty-one children, Rebecca thought, appalled. How could any woman face a life like that?

'Aren't you roasting in here?' Brigid said. 'We'll die with the shutters closed.'

The fitting session was expected to last between ten and twelve hours. In between fittings each model put on a shirt-bag with a tie-string round the neck to hide the clothes from would-be pirates who might break in.

The shirt-bags added to their body heat. Every so often Hiroko rushed to the shutters and opened them, breathing in fresh air. Each time she did so the fitters panicked and shouted, '*Interdit!*'

'Have you got a fellow over here, Rebecca? There's loads of good-looking men.'

'I'm married.'

'*Married*? Aren't you old before your time?'

'And I have a baby.'

'Ah, sure what good are you!' Brigid dabbed her face with

Crème Puff to counter perspiration. 'You won't be able to come out with me, spotting the talent.'

The session dragged on. In the semi-darkness the other models fanned themselves with magazines, yawned, and chattered in French.

Pierre Cardin called and the models revived. He ran a professional eye over the garments, exchanged words with fitters.

Brigid sighed. 'Isn't he the most gorgeous fellow you've ever laid eyes on? Is he still going with Jeanne Moreau?'

'I don't know. I think so.'

'What hope is there for the rest of us with her around? I love her pout. Did you see her in *Jules et Jim*? That film would give you a few ideas, Rebecca, you being married and all!'

But not that day. When the session was over Rebecca wearily turned down Brigid's invitation to go out on the town, and collapsed into bed.

The showing of the Collection was in stark contrast to the apathy of the fittings. Out front the salon had filled with famous clients, show business personalities and fashion journalists. Backstage designer, dressers and models whirled around in a boiling pot of simmering excitement. One model, already overcome, had dissolved into tears. Last minute alterations were being made to some of the many garments swinging on the rails near the long table on which accessories – stockings, shoes, hats, jewellery – had been laid out. It was to be a lengthy showing. Cardin, as Laura had said, was an innovator, not an editor: ideas poured from his sketchbook out on to the ramp.

'*Vite!*' he urged. '*Vite!*' and Rebecca herself was on the ramp. Bulbs flashed. Photographers jostled for better positions. Tomorrow their pictures would appear in publications round the world.

Seemingly serene, unblinking, Rebecca wafted along the catwalk, pirouetted, glided back, returned to semi-hysteria.

'Someone's taken my shoes!'

'Jesus, Mary and Joseph, there's a pin sticking into me!'

'*Vite!*'

A spy returning from an out-front foray brought news of a positive response, eliciting a different kind of excitement. Only Hiroko managed to remain totally calm.

At the end of it Rebecca was both exhausted and exhilarated. Temporary snags and disagreements were forgotten. They were all going to dinner at La Coupole.

The brasserie was already crowded with foreign buyers and photographers and those who simply wanted to look at beautiful people when Rebecca and Brigid threaded their way between the green and gilt pillars and the white-clothed tables.

'*Bon soir, cherie! C'était magnifique!*' people called out. '*Sublime! Prodigious!*'

Brigid recognised one of the South American buyers who hugged her tight and maintained that he was in Paris only because of her.

Rebecca was propelled onwards to one of the tables which had been reserved for their party. She sat down and instantly a young man eased himself into the adjacent chair. He was both ugly and attractive, with straight black hair and what Eileen would have termed a bold look in his eye.

He introduced himself: '*Ça va* – I am Alain Bergé.'

'And I'm Rebecca Stacton.'

'Your name I know. Because of you I am making superb pictures. For me you were the best.'

Frilly flattery, Rebecca thought. All the same she thanked him for it.

'Everyone talks of you,' he said. 'Madame Collange, the woman editor of *l'Express* – you must know – she is very influential. Her husband, you understand, is editor of *France-Soir* – she tells me "That one is *fantastique!*"'

'That's kind.'

Rebecca's mind was beginning to clear in terms of the Collection. Right now, she realised, Richard and Laura would be dining together in Barnes. Afterwards Richard would take Peter home.

Tomorrow at this time she too would be back in London, would have cooked Richard a special meal to mark their reunion.

Roast pheasant? Stuffed breast of lamb? And they would eat the Brie de Melun which she had bought already.

Alain Bergé tapped her arm, pointing to the menu. 'What is it that you wish? Cassoulet? Here it is superb. Or maybe the fruits de mer or the croustillant de ris de veau?'

'Cassoulet.'

It was disgustingly fattening and just what she felt like eating at the end of such a day.

She peered around in search of famous faces. She knew from Laura that the brasserie was frequented not only by fashion personalities but by film stars and artists. Salvador Dali had dined there with his two leashed cheetahs and so, quite often, did Brigitte Bardot.

'There, you see, in the corner is Alain Delon,' said her companion.

'Truly?'

'But of course. Anouk Aimee, Romy Schneider, Vittorio Gassman – they all come here. On Sunday night it is very smart. That is when the real Parisien *noctambuliste* begins the week – one night before the others!'

'Does that mean you, as well?'

'Sometime. When I am young I come here with my parents. They have then a waiter. Ali. He is black. From Senegal. And the children love him. He walk, you know, like a cat! And each day one dozen *ensembles*! He serve here the Café Cona and he is the big attraction of La Coupole.'

'He's not here any more?'

'It is very sad. He become sick. He has a small operation – *simple* – but he die. And after they return to making coffee from the machine.'

The cassoulet was placed in front of her just as she had decided that she liked Alain Bergé, his stories, his confidence, his bold eye and the fact that he was young. Older than she was. Maybe twenty-five or twenty-six, but of her own generation.

All around her people were flirting. She had never been good at that. *You're old before your time,* Brigid had said. But she wasn't old. She was a wife and a mother but she was still only twenty-two.

'Rebecca. I would like very much to work with you. To find the right model is not easy.'

'Come on!'

'I am serious. It is the combination – the good model, the good photographer, who make the picture come.'

Rebecca thought about that. The combination. Not just the photographer. It would not be Laura's point of view.

'So you come back to Paris – yes?'

'Maybe.'

'I take your number,' said Alain. 'We keep in touch.'

There was a dance floor in the basement.

'Dance with me?' he said.

He was smaller when he stood up. His legs were not long. But his arms were strong and his chest broad and he was undoubtedly attractive. As a rule Rebecca discouraged advances. Richard's colleagues sometimes made mild passes when they had had too much to drink but she always fobbed them off.

Alain did not make a pass. He did not hold her too close. Other couples were melting into each other but she and Alain were quite circumspect on the floor. So there was no necessity for guilt unless you counted enjoyment as a sin.

'You stay in Paris – where?'

'In my mother's apartment.'

She did not tell him who Laura was. It was nice to be free of the association, just for this evening.

'I take you there in my car.'

'No thank you,' she said, the dutiful wife again, 'I've made arrangements.'

Leaving Brigid behind with her South American she caught a taxi to rue Jean Mermoz.

She had behaved impeccably – unlike Brigid who insisted on

going to Confession before going home to Dublin – and yet she knew that she would not tell Richard about Alain.

There was nothing sinister in this, she reasoned. It was simply that Alain was part of her respite from being old before her time, and she was not obliged to share him.

Richard and Peter were waiting for her at Heathrow, Peter with his auburn curls clinging to the nape of his neck looked like a diminutive edition of his father.

A wave of affection for them broke over her.

'It's so good to have you back,' Richard said.

Red roses were waiting in the flat to be arranged in vases. She bathed Peter and put him to bed and settled down with Richard to watch 'That Was The Week That Was' with David Frost compèring.

'So what else happened in Paris?' said Richard when they were undressing for bed.

'Everyone's talking about Yves Saint Laurent. He left Dior this year to open his own couture house.'

'Oh yes?'

Richard did not sound that interested. He had no inkling of the designer's importance in terms of new stimulation. Alain had rated Saint Laurent as unbelievably gifted.

Alain kept drifting in and out of her thoughts in a way that was beginning to alarm her. He had made more of an impression on her than she had realised. She had no business thinking of him at all . . .

'You know,' Richard said when they were in bed, 'we should have another baby.'

Rebecca stiffened. Another baby? Another hideous pregnancy and excruciating labour? Hadn't she vowed – never again?

'Peter needs a brother or sister,' said Richard.

'Ye-es.'

Peter had looked so adorable tucked up in his cot. And Richard was a darling. Those roses . . . Somehow she could not imagine Alain buying flowers.

Alain again! This was dreadful. A dam was threatening to

burst within her. By whatever drastic means its wall had to be reinforced.

She said again, 'Yes. You're right. We should.'

'Tell you what,' Richard said, taking her into his arms. 'Next month when we go to France, leave your Pills behind.'

The day they left for Provence Rebecca heard on the News that Marilyn Monroe had died.

'That's awful.'

'Poor woman,' said Richard, putting their passports into his pocket. 'All those marriages and affairs. I suppose she craved stability. She couldn't have children, could she?'

'I think she miscarried.'

'Anyway, very sad. Let's talk about something cheerful. This is my plan for the holiday. One, listen to the cicadas, two, sip *pastis*, three, watch *boules*, four, make love to you!'

It proved too hot to do much else. While it was pleasant to drive into Barjols, find easy parking on the tree-lined Place de la Rouguière, listen to the cool splashing waters of the fountain – one of twenty-five in the town – and explore the maze of tiny streets and alleys, the atmosphere soon made them sleepy. They went to bed early and got up late.

Rebecca reckoned that she became pregnant the very first week. Within three she was back in her old routine of fainting and exhaustion.

The baby was due in May. She heard nothing from Alain until December when, out of the blue, he phoned asking her to fly over for a week's work.

'I can't.' Her bulge was just beginning to show.

'But why not, Rebecca? Are you so booked?'

'It's not that.'

'Then *why*?'

She explained, thinking ruefully that she would not be available in New Year for the spring Collections in Paris or Florence or London. But at least she was able to put down the phone in the surety that her life had a stable base. The dam wall was holding.

She forced her thoughts away from Alain on to the problem of maternity clothes, most of which were quite ghastly. Why did pregnant women have to resemble kangaroos?

Richard said she was lovelier than ever, that he was crazy about her bulge.

'It could be twins,' said the doctor in the New Year.

'Twins?'

'It could be.'

Three children, she thought. How could you ever take three toddlers for a walk?

And what would Eileen have to say on the subject? But it wasn't twins.

'Now that's unusual. The placenta is exactly the same size as the baby,' said Dr Hudson when the birth was over. 'That's why I thought there were two. See for yourself, Mrs Stacton.'

How strange doctors were, expecting a mother to show interest in a placenta after she had produced an eight-pound baby girl.

' "Cassandra. Greek Kassandra. Possibly a feminine form of Alexander", said Richard, consulting the Dictionary of First Names. 'What do you think, darling? "Name of prophetic daughter of Priam and Hecuba. Used in Britain in the Middle Ages." Cassie for short?'

Anything. Oh, the wonder of having one's body back.

She had done her duty, to Richard, to herself, to Peter. A boy and a girl. She need never, never get pregnant again.

The new baby had her mother's colouring.

'So like you at that age,' said Laura, who was already besotted with Cassie, far more so than she had been with Peter and more, Rebecca suspected, than she had ever been with her own child.

'But this is like having you arrive again!' Laura tried to explain. 'Only the circumstances are happier.'

'If you feel like that you should come to Ireland with us and help babysit!'

174

This suggestion was made in jest but Laura took it seriously. They had planned to go to Ireland in September to stay with Charles and Harriet who lived in the rich farmland known as the Golden Vein in County Tipperary.

They hired a car at Shannon airport and dropped Eileen off to stay with her family in Clare, then pressed on.

Even with Eileen gone the car was over-crowded, the carrycot vying for space with Laura's camera equipment.

A signpost at Dundrum told them that it was eight and a quarter miles to Cashel. The countryside was visibly lusher. The fields were brazen with gorse. Black crows flew low over stone walls encrusted with ivy. Horses, chestnut and grey and dun, stood sleeping and grazing.

'Studland,' said Richard, 'and I see the first cow traffic jam looming up ahead!'

Sitting in the back with the children Rebecca was quite content, even though she felt thoroughly sat on and Cassie was leaking.

A grey outline of tower and turrets appeared on the horizon.

'The Rock of Cashel,' Laura said. 'Do let's have a look at it.'

Richard concurred. When they pulled in by the massive fortress complex Rebecca was full enough of *bonhomie* to offer to remain in the car with the children while Richard and Laura explored.

'You don't mind, darling?'

'Not a bit.'

It was much more than a rock. It was friary and abbey, cathedral, sarcophagus and much else combined. Which no doubt explained why Richard and Laura had been so long in there.

Half an hour went by. Peter was fidgety and Cassie smelt. Rebecca wound down the window and stared up at the rock, willing Richard and Laura to reappear.

Eventually they did. By then Cassie was yelling for a bottle which had to be heated and Rebecca was snappy.

'You two took your time!'

Richard and Laura exchanged conspiratorial glances, for all the world like two naughty children who had wandered away from home.

'Darling, it's so fascinating inside. We went right up to the top of the tower. There are a hundred and twenty-seven steps! Our poor legs – '

'I could have done with stretching mine!'

At that Richard closed up. He took his place at the wheel and drove without speaking through Golden and Bansha and Rath Dermot. No one expressed delight at the rise of the pale blue Galtee mountains out of the mist.

In this uneasy state they reached the Glen of Aherlow where Charles and Harriet lived. The trees were rouging and primping with autumn in mind. Rebecca almost forgot that she was annoyed, almost said, 'Isn't it lovely?' as they turned off the road and drove up a long wooded slope at the top of which was a two-storey, three-bay, gable-ended house.

As Richard drew in the front door opened and Uncle Charles and Aunt Harriet came out crying, 'Welcome, welcome!' and getting thoroughly in the way as the boot was unpacked.

Still, Rebecca's spirits lifted once she was inside the house. It was the kind of home of which she had once dreamed, painted in strong Georgian colours – the hall golden yellow, the dining-room Roman red and the drawing-room Chinese blue. The furniture and artefacts were a mish-mash – good pieces of Dutch marquetry and nineteenth-century Chippendale mixed up with Indian papier-mâché gilt chairs and a bust of a Roman emperor standing on a cantilevered Italian table – but the overall effect pleased her.

'Hope you'll be happy here,' Uncle Charles said. 'A word in your ear. The Kitchen is going through an experimental phase. Some of the food produced for One is delicious. Other meals not. Fortunately One can count on the Cashel Palace Hotel.'

With this warning about Harriet's cooking ringing in her ears Rebecca prepared to settle in. Richard remained cool towards her but everyone else was catching up on news and Charles's culinary misgivings proved unfounded.

'What are you going to do tomorrow?' Harriet said when Charles had finished deriding the Fianna Fáil party, and observing that the Irish Censorship of Publications Board was sex-obsessed.

'I must take some photographs while I'm here,' said Laura.

Rebecca knew what that would entail. Laura would fiddle around for hours finding the right location, waiting for the sun to come out, worrying about angles and balancing perilously on wobbly walls and toppling ruins.

'Count *me* out on that expedition! I'm going to stay put tomorrow.'

'I'm afraid I have a church meeting,' said Harriet. 'And Charles is tied up on the farm.'

'I'll come with you,' Richard said to Laura. 'Where were you thinking of going?'

Rebecca was taken aback. Richard, going off and leaving her, just like that? Not that he wouldn't live to regret it once he fell into Laura's clutches. This thought warded off what would otherwise have been resentment.

'I saw this blue hand-pump on the side of the road. And Bansha village green is worth investigating, and that castle, wherever it was.'

Hours, thought Rebecca. Poor old Richard. Rather him than me!

They went off early. Harriet left, and Charles set out to supervise the harvesting of the corn, telling the reapers, who did not need instructions, what to do.

Rebecca, going into the kitchen to make some tea, found the sink stuffed with nettles. As she filled the kettle they stung her arm.

Cassie fell asleep. Only Peter remained active, preventing Rebecca from reading the latest gossip about Richard Burton and Elizabeth Taylor.

Harriet shot in, clattered around in the kitchen and rushed out again. At three o'clock Peter, frazzled and over-tired, was still holding out. In spite of his vociferous protests Rebecca put him to bed, went downstairs and opened the newspaper.

Burton and Taylor were reportedly living in Puerto Vallarta. The paper carried a picture of Elizabeth in a bikini with beaded thongs on her feet and black flowers in her hair. Across her breasts were looped gold chains.

'Here I am!' said Peter defiantly.

'You bad boy. Go back to bed at once.'

'*Won't!*'

Rebecca had used up most of her store of threats.

'God doesn't like children who won't behave.'

'Shoot *Him*! Bang, bang, bang!'

She dragged him back to bed and locked the door from the outside, standing in the corridor listening as he kicked it. Eventually the clamour died down. Peering in she found Peter asleep on the floor.

It was not exactly how she had imagined spending the holiday. Having not minded when Richard and Laura set out on their expedition, now she did. It was even more irritating when they came home and Richard said blithely that he had enjoyed the day. Laura launched into a eulogy about the wonderful Irish light.

'We're having nettles for dinner,' Harriet said. 'The French prefer them to spinach. They purify the system.'

Oh God, Rebecca thought, loathing spinach.

The nettles were tough and under-cooked. Rebecca only just managed not to throw up.

'Must have a wee,' said Charles, and Harriet went back into the kitchen to make coffee.

'Oh dear,' Laura said. 'What does One say about that?'

Richard grinned. 'Let's just hope she hasn't got a recipe for gorse!'

They howled with laughter at this. Rebecca did not join in. Their compatibility was reminiscent of the days when Richard had first come calling, before she had done Laura out. She knew that their friendship was completely innocent but it still rankled. It was as if Laura had a line to Richard on which his wife could not talk.

Let them get on with it, she thought. They were nearer in age to each other than Richard and herself, could share references which came out of belonging to nearly the same generation.

They weren't the only people who could thus participate. Her thoughts – which she had previously prevented from doing so – went back to Alain. It was over a year since they had met. He had probably forgotten all about her. He might be married himself. Or perhaps he, too, had come to the conclusion that it was dull being stable.

F OR a couple of months this leak in the dam wall exuded only a dribble of fantasy and conjecture. Rebecca half convinced herself that she wanted nothing more.

But it was clear that the division between Richard and herself was widening. London was a youthful city. She had read that thirty per cent of its population was between fifteen and thirty-four.

Richard was a year off forty. *She* was young. Richard would look ridiculous with a Beatles haircut. The 'In' words – fab and groovy and with-it – did not feature in his vocabulary.

She had to admit that he took an interest in the new music and the plays and the films and the fads, seeing what they added up to as a renaissance. His approval was not altogether to her liking. She was at a stage where she wanted to enlarge the divide.

Not that she was seeing much of Richard. He was travelling more frequently. Rebecca fell back into the habit of commuting to Barnes and leaving the children with Eileen.

'When are you going to start working again?' Laura said.

'Not just yet.'

'Isn't Audrey Hepburn the most enchanting creature?' Laura said. 'Look here she is looking quite Japanese in a Givenchy lace dress! Why are you putting it off? I need you.'

Given the chance, Rebecca thought, her mother would ingest her. The whole family – Richard and the children as well – was whale-like in outlook. If she was to survive as a personality she must swim beyond its reach.

Hadn't she intended to work for other photographers? Alain

had tried hard enough to recruit her but she had let the chance slip. Was it too late to take up that option? The door flew open. 'Mother of God!' said Eileen dramatically. 'The heart of me is stopped with the shock!'

'What is it?'

Eileen made the sign of the cross.

'President Kennedy's after being shot.'

They turned on the television for further details of the assassination. There was no more talk of work. But Rebecca had arrived at a decision. Once home she phoned Alain.

'Rebecca! *Quelle surprise!*'

He sounded genuinely pleased to hear from her. When she asked if they might work together his voice became warmer.

'When can you come to Paris? I can find work for you *immediatement* with *Elle*. But you are sure that you will do this? You will not change your mind – have more baby?'

'No more babies,' she said. 'That I promise! Tell me about this work.'

'Evening trouser. Short to the knee. You have – I remember – the *superb* legs.'

They fixed the date. Not immediately. In the New Year.

Richard didn't mind. The Federation of Rhodesia and Nyasaland was in the process of breaking up. Northern Rhodesia was to become independent Zambia and his company was opening up an office in the capital, Lusaka. A series of meetings were being held about this in the London office and he was too preoccupied to raise objections to anything that she did.

Laura fumed. 'You're going to work with another photo-grapher? Who is he? Alain Bergé? *He's* doing a job for *Elle*? Wonders will never cease. And what about me?'

'We hadn't made any plans.'

'That's beside the point. Alain Bergé – really!'

'You did say – '

Laura did not want to be reminded of what she had once said.

She gave Rebecca the key to the flat in rue Jean Mermoz but she was still being sniffy when they parted company.

Rebecca, having built Alain up in her mind in quasi-romantic terms, soon discovered that he was a serious photographer who had been sincere in his professional liking for her.

They did not meet until the studio opened at eight A.M. Alain arrived on time followed by two girls with clothes draped over their arms.

Lights were turned on together with a recording of Charles Aznavour singing *'J'attends'*.

Rebecca was already made up. She checked her face in the mirror. Sooty eyes stared back at her. Her lashes were so long that false ones were unnecessary. She had powdered her own and applied a second coating of mascara.

A hairdresser came and fiddled around with her hair, asking her if she had it cut at Vidal Sassoon. At nine they were ready for pictures. Alain had set up the lights. Charles Aznavour had been replaced by Edith Piaf.

'So,' said Alain, 'we begin.'

It was not in the least like working with Laura. For one thing no instructions were called out. Alain hardly spoke at all and when he did it was only to say *'Bon'* or *'Superbe!'*

Rebecca looked expectant (off to a party), nervous (is *he* here?) and ecstatic (he is!), counting the clicks of the camera until Alain had taken all twelve of the first exposures.

They worked all day. It gradually dawned on Rebecca she was of real value to Alain; that in his perception of her she was more than just a clothes-horse.

At one stage, while they were having a break, this subject came up.

'But I told you when we met – it is the combination.'

'That's not how all photographers think.'

He shrugged. 'They will change their minds one day. You must go, I think. We will have more work together?'

'I hope so.'

She had found what she wanted – someone who took her seriously as a person, put a value on her, and yet she was both tantalised and thwarted.

Alain had respected not only her personality but her marriage. She tried to remember how he had been at La Coupole. Hadn't he offered to drive her home? But perhaps she had misread his intentions?

She went, as he had said she must, in a state of some confusion.

Laura thawed and they took up the threads of their working relationship on the understanding that Rebecca was free to accept assignments with Alain.

London throbbed with excitement and creativity. A Labour government came in under Mr Harold Wilson. Pirate radio stations, Radio Caroline and Radio Atlanta, offered pop music and commercials from battered boats moored five miles off land. She saw the new James Bond film *Goldfinger*, watched Cilla Black, the Liverpool singer, top the charts, and listened to Bob Dylan and the Rolling Stones.

Twice more that year she went to Paris to model for Alain. Their relationship did not change.

She thought about him a lot when she was at home. Richard was spending an inordinate amount of time in Lusaka. He had friends there whom Rebecca had not met, George and Chloe Meredith. He worked with George and stayed at their home for weeks on end, and every so often he said that they must all have a holiday together when things were less hectic. It was not a proposition that particularly appealed to Rebecca. The Merediths were Richard's age, *his* friends, not hers. Their lives, she thought, were veering in different directions. They had the children in common – not much more.

She was brooding about this when she went to Paris at the beginning of 1965. She was tense anyway, pre-menstrual and generally viewing life in negative terms.

The session was not arduous but when it was over Rebecca

went into the loo and wept. It made her mascara run. For once she didn't check her appearance in the mirror before emerging, and she was unaware that two thin black rivulets were running down her cheeks. In this condition she bumped into Alain.

'I thought you'd gone.'

'I thought *you* had gone,' he said, looking at her intently. 'Rebecca, you are crying. What is happening with you?'

'Nothing,' said Rebecca, thinking that *nothing* summed up what she felt about the vacuity of her existence.

'You have trouble with family?'

At that moment her marriage to Richard did indeed seem irksome. She tried to explain. The effort prompted more tears and a flood of shame.

'I think,' Alain said, 'that you are hungry. So we will go and eat.'

'Don't you have to go straight to the darkroom?'

'After we eat.'

He did not hold her hand, did not help her into the car but something had already happened between them. Even in her deranged state she knew that. She understood too that he would take her not to a restaurant but to his apartment. They drove to the Croix-Rouge intersection without exchanging another word, pulled up in the rue du Sabot.

Alain was as good as his word. In the apartment he produced the basics – wine, bread, pâté, cheese. The meal helped. Rebecca calmed down, washed her face and repaired her make-up.

'You are still unhappy?'

'Not now.'

'You must go?'

This time it was a question, not an order. She shook her head.

'*You* must go to the darkroom?'

'Not now,' he said.

Which was all rather predictable. But then she had known all along that they would go to bed.

*

Having done so, having established a romantic rapport with Alain, she did not feel as if she had fallen in love.

She was puzzled by this reaction. Was she a tart or was it just that she wanted a small measure of excitement in her life?

She wasn't sure of the answer – only that sex with Alain had the effect of putting her off sex with Richard.

It wasn't, she thought, that Alain was a superior lover or Richard an inferior or insensitive one, or even that Richard's body was in poor condition in contrast to Alain's. Wasn't it because making love with Alain was a liberating experience; that she was enjoying the sensation of freedom more than the actual sex?

Whatever it was she spent the first half of 1965 contriving to be in Paris.

Oblivious of this urge Laura steered her towards Milan for a Gala Lipsticks campaign.

The original plan had been for Laura to fly on to Florence on the Thursday morning and for Rebecca to return alone to London later the same day. Laura was still packing when the phone rang in Rebecca's room.

'Rebecca, it's me – Alain. Are you finish with your mother?'

'Yes. We're leaving today.'

'Come to Paris.'

'I can't,' she said thinking how fortunate it was that she and Laura had booked separate bedrooms. 'The children will be upset.'

'They are young. Come for two day.'

She hummed and hawed. Eileen wouldn't mind. She never did. Richard was away and Laura wouldn't be back either.

And Peter and Cassie really would not know the difference.

'All right. I'll come.'

'We will have special times. I have already made a booking for us at l'Hôtel de la Trémoille.'

'Why not your apartment?'

'You are not the only one with a mother! My parents have come to Paris for two week. So, when can you arrive? I will meet you. I will be so loving . . .'

'Don't meet me,' Rebecca said. 'Wait for me at the hotel.'

All the way from Milan she was seeing in her mind's eye the map of the hours ahead.

Her luggage coming through on the carousel, the taxi ride into town, the cobblestoned street that led to the hotel, herself pushing open the revolving doors, Alain waiting with outstretched arms in the lobby. Perhaps, after all, she *was* in love with him – or with the concept of romance.

In France the airport baggage handlers were on strike. After she had waited for half an hour a dispirited voice announced that luggage was to be deposited on the pavement outside.

It was raining heavily. On the edge of the pavement a crowd of exasperated, shivering passengers were glumly surveying a stack of a dozen or so suitcases, none of which was hers.

Nearby was a van and beside it three of the striking *bagistes* and a depressed officer waving his hands about. A heated discussion ensued. The cases on the pavement were heaved into the back of the van which took off with its rear door open. As the crowd groaned in disbelief the cases wobbled and tumbled one after the other on to the street.

To hell with this for a lark, Rebecca thought. She could do without luggage for tonight. She hailed a taxi.

'L'Hotel de la Trémoille.'

Alain was not in the lobby but a note at the desk informed her that he was in room five hundred and nine. She took the lift to the fifth floor.

'*Mon Dieu,*' he said, 'you are wet!'

'Don't tell me. And don't ask me about my case, not till I've had a bath.'

Or made love. Or had dinner in the room. Or made love again. She fell asleep with the matter of her luggage unresolved.

In the morning she was woken by the sound of church bells. Alain was still asleep. She got out of bed and drew the curtains, opened the door on to a balcony with a wrought-iron railing and traced the bells to a church spire on the corner where rue de la

Trémoille met Avenue George Cinq. The rain had stopped and the sun was out. Even then the weather took precedence over her cases.

When Alain woke they made love again. Propped against the pillows, surveying the odd-shaped, almost triangular room, the chandelier that tinkled each time the door was opened or shut, Rebecca felt like a caged bird who had made a bid for freedom.

She wasn't really in love with Alain, she decided. He was rather too much in love with her, which could be confining unless she was careful. But she would be . . .

It was Alain who phoned the airport.

'No *bagages*.'

'I'd better get up and go and buy something to wear.'

It was evening before she remembered packing her Pills in one of the missing cases.

'Oh God!'

'There is a problem?'

She had taken seventeen of the twenty-two days' supply and this was the unfertile stage of her cycle.

'I suppose . . . Not really.'

'Maybe the *bagistes* have finish the strike. I phone the airport again.'

Richard was away for another two weeks. Rebecca's period had not come on although she indicated that it had. It couldn't – surely – be happening to her again, she thought. And not with Alain . . .

'You're looking peaky,' Richard said. 'Poor darling. Listen – you're going to hate me. I've got to go back. For a month. I feel terrible about it.'

Not as terrible as I feel, thought Rebecca. Richard left and one ghastly day followed another. Nothing changed, or not in the way she wanted.

One morning, getting up to go to the bathroom, she collapsed in the doorway.

*

The options that were open to her were either unsatisfactory or objectionable.

In two weeks Richard would be home. She could not and did not want to pass off Alain's baby as his. If she confessed to Richard he would be repulsed. That would be the end of it as far as their marriage went. She would be forced to go through this new pregnancy on her own.

In this light Richard as a husband assumed a renewed importance. Too late she re-evaluated the worth of the family, which she had discarded for a flighty affair.

That she did not reciprocate Alain's depth of feeling was further proof of her own shoddiness. She did not want to tell Alain about the baby any more than she fancied confessing to Richard.

Abortion then? Backstreet abortions were available. She knew at least one other model who would know where to go.

Eileen would say abortion was murder. Not that she had any intention of confiding in Eileen.

Round in her mind went the cheap-jack options like clothes in a tumble-dryer and all the while she was taking the children to and from Barnes and trying to behave normally.

Her last resort was Laura. She held out not because Laura would be shocked – not worldly Laura – but because she could not bear the idea of showing herself as a failure to someone who was herself such a success, not only professionally but morally.

Laura would sympathise. She would offer advice. Perhaps suggest acting as a go-between with Richard. Maybe even salvage the marriage. And as she did so she would be thinking what a fool Rebecca had been. Her kindness and her love would not mask her contempt. Laura's feelings were always clear to decipher. Her scorn would be as difficult to face as Richard's revulsion.

Even so.

She phoned Laura.

'It's me. I need to chat. Can I come round?'

'Yes, do. *Nova*'s on the other line so I must rush. Berkshire stockings. We can have great fun. Of course you can come round. Why do you have to ask?'

Theoretically, it was perfectly feasible to call and talk to Laura. The reality was quite different. Every few minutes the phone rang and Laura leapt up to answer it. When she sat down again she bubbled away about her work.

Rebecca gazed at her bleakly wondering how, even when she was married, her mother had found time for love. She had an image of Laura with her camera welded on to her hand. Click, click, click . . . And in the background the phone incessantly ringing.

And that was without the added problem of the children. Peter and Cassie had been deposited with Eileen in the kitchen. But no sooner was there a break between phone calls than one or other of them came into the sitting-room.

'Cassie is *so* intelligent,' Laura said. 'She's getting the hang of pronouns. I'm knocked out by the quality of her speech!'

Cassie was two and a half and Peter four. They were both in the room on this occasion and Peter, who objected to his sister stealing the limelight, said, 'Last night she wetted her bed,' and Cassie kicked his shin.

Retreating from his venom she knocked Rebecca's handbag on to the floor and stood on the mirror which had fallen out of it.

'Why don't you children play outside?' Rebecca said, suppressing a scream and picking up pieces of glass.

'It's cold outside.'

'Or in the kitchen.'

The phone rang. Laura left the room. Her voice filtered back. 'Meriel McCooey tells me that Ernestine – *Way* ahead on trends . . .'

The subject of fashion editors assumed major importance for over ten minutes.

Rebecca again rehearsed what she had planned to say: 'Laura, I want to have a serious talk with you. I'm in the most terrible mess,' and, 'For Christ's sake don't answer the phone for the next half-hour!' which should arrest even her mother's attention.

'Good Lord, what a morning!' said Laura, reappearing. 'Let's get Eileen to make us another cup of tea, shall we, and then we can relax. What did you want to talk to me about? I hope you're not going to work exclusively for that Frenchman?'

'No!'

'That's something anyway!' Laura said and, most cruelly, the phone went again.

It was impossible to talk under these circumstances. There was no chance of peace in Barnes. Laura would have to be enticed to Cadogan Gardens.

'Where were we?'

'I think you should come and have supper with me tonight.'

'Tonight? Is that why you came – to ask me to supper?'

'I wanted to ask you something. But it's awkward here.'

'Why is it awkward here? I don't think,' Laura said, looking for her diary, 'that I can manage tonight. What about tomorrow evening, or Monday, better still?'

'Tomorrow.'

'All right then. Are you going? Why are you rushing off? Stay for lunch.'

'I can't,' Rebecca said, suddenly desperate to be on her own for a few minutes. 'Can I leave the children with Eileen?'

'Of course. See you tomorrow, darling. 'Bye.'

The effort of trying to behave normally in the lead-up to confession took its toll. In the car she was trembling. As she reversed out into St Mary's Grove she was already feeling odd. She headed for home, drove along Castlenau in the direction of Hammersmith bridge. Her ears seemed to be blocked. Instead of the noise of traffic she could hear the sounds of buzzing and bells. She thought fleetingly of the church bells that had chimed when she had been in bed with Alain.

She was slightly dizzy. She considered pulling in but other cars were coming up behind her, forcing her to drive on. The buzzing drowned out the bells. And it wasn't cold as Peter had said but too warm inside the car. Hot and muzzy. Her vision was going. She put a hand to her head, pushing back her fringe.

So hot. And the buzzing . . . A car horn hooted. She had a vague notion that she was driving badly, was swinging from one side of the road to the other. On her left was an intersection – a bollard . . . Muzziness enveloped her. The car went out of control.

Richard, staying with the Merediths in Lusaka, had become thoroughly enmeshed with their servants' lives.

There were three of them: James the cook, Joseph the house-boy (*boy*, Richard thought – the fellow is my age) and Frank the gardener.

James's fifteen-year-old daughter who lived in the familial *kyah* at the bottom of the Merediths' two-acre plot, had recently given birth to a baby boy in the back of Chloe Meredith's car en route to hospital.

During this diversion three plastic buckets disappeared from the house. Chloe suspected that they had been purloined for the purpose of making and selling kaffir beer, a foul smelling and highly intoxicating brew consumed in large quantities in the beer halls over weekends.

The servants pleaded ignorance. But later the same day Joseph discovered that his wife was running her own modest beer hall on the corner of the road two blocks away. He lashed out with his hand and Mrs Joseph fell over one of the buckets, spilling the contents and breaking her leg. Richard took her to hospital to have it re-set.

On the day Rebecca went to Barnes he sat on the *stoep* with Chloe.

'You must bring Rebecca out, Richard. The children would love it here. It's sad to think of their being cooped up in dreary old England.'

The English in Africa often ran down the United Kingdom as if to demonstrate how wise they had been to leave their motherland.

'Mm. Young children can be a menace. I don't need to tell *you* that.'

The Merediths had four children, all grown up.

'I don't mind small menaces. Yes, Joseph, what is it?' No one ever heard Joseph arrive. He seemed simply to materialise.

As calmly as if he was announcing the arrival of a visitor he said, 'Police is coming, dòna,' using the Portuguese term for lady as servants did. 'Is accusing me of murdering son-in-law.'

'What nonsense!' Chloe said briskly. 'You wouldn't kill anyone. Bring tea and anchovy toast.'

'Yes, dòna.'

'Somebody's always dying,' Chloe said. 'They have so many relations. It's the extended family thing, cousins counting as brothers and sisters and all that. There's a funeral every week.'

'But not a murder.'

Death and murder seemed that day incongruous subjects for discussion. The garden, still steaming after a heavy shower, blazed with summer flowers, pink and purple bougainvillaea, red cannas and poinsettia, pale yellow frangipani. The jacaranda, purple contrast to the yellow of the sun, toned to the blue of the sky.

Richard yawned. In the night his sleep had been broken by a tree frog croaking in search of a mate. The sound was like that of heavy cardboard being savagely rent apart. The frog, located on a leaf at dawn, was less than an inch long. In Africa, he thought, nothing, however small, was understated.

'I daresay,' said Chloe, 'that it will all blow over.'

In this she was proven wrong. Joseph came back. 'Police is coming to funeral.'

'*Today*? But we've got a dinner party tonight. Oh never mind. Richard, I'll have to take Joseph to the funeral and have a word with the police myself.'

'I'll come with you.'

Mrs Joseph was trundled to the car in a wheelbarrow and put on the back seat. Joseph and several children squeezed in beside her. A baby was passed through the open window, rejected by Mrs Joseph and delivered back to its mother by the same route.

They drove along a road called Leopards' Hill and through the gates of a cemetery. Two large crowds of Africans were gathered inside, the women in Liberty print dresses and Zambian national dress.

A police-car pulled in and a young black officer leapt out. Chloe accosted him.

'. . . absolute nonsense . . . had a party . . . worked late. Didn't you, Joseph?'

'Yes, dòna.'

'You tell those in-laws that it's not Joseph's fault. I won't have him being beaten up.'

A hearse had stopped in the road outside. The four pall-bearers were carrying the coffin through the gateway, preceded by a young African man, magnificently built with the face of a black god. A grieving god, crying out his sorrow, raising one hand heavenwards as if to reprove those up there for the death of the one he loved.

Richard stared, moved by the young man's pain and envious of his ability to express so freely what he felt. How incredible, he thought, to be so free – not to care what onlookers thought.

But they, too, were moved. They sighed in sympathy, the women swaying in what might be the onset of a mourning dance.

'So that's all right then,' said Chloe. 'We'll come back for you at two, Joseph. You'd better get the wheelbarrow out of the boot.'

That was the other thing! The need to keep up appearances was less evident here. No one laughed at Mrs Joseph being trundled along. What if one was to transpose the scenario to Sloane Square?

He and Chloe drove home in high spirits. On the *stoep* George was hovering.

'Something's happened to one of the children!' said Chloe, getting out of the car.

For it was perfectly obvious from George's face that something was wrong.

'Not the children. Richard, I don't know how to say this. There's been a phone call. Dreadful news. An accident.

Richard – Rebecca is dead . . .'

Somehow, he managed to maintain control, not to call out, not to embarrass George and Chloe by breaking down.

RICHARD

1965 – 1970

RICHARD was assailed by guilt as well as by grief. Guilt mounted an attack on two fronts. He could defend himself against neither.

Yes, he thought, he had opted for beauty and become mildly bored with the immaturity that had accompanied it. Yes, he had used work as an antidote, had (on a number of occasions, M'Lud) prolonged his stays in Africa, had neglected Rebecca.

Guilty as charged.

He had cared more for his wife's body than for her mind and, yes, it was true that this attitude had resulted in a third pregnancy which she would not have wanted, and in her death.

Guilty.

The wounds inflicted by guilt were still not adequate to satisfy his need for punishment. Surely he should be made to pay with his head for these crimes? It did not occur to him that he bore the cost on a daily basis, each time the children demanded when Mummy was coming back.

Doing without sex was a minor, automatic atonement. In the year after Rebecca's death Richard shied away from encounters with women. He concentrated on work, continued to travel and, when in London, devoted his weekends to his children. Otherwise, Peter and Cassie lived in Barnes.

Sooner or later, Richard told himself, he would have to move out of the flat with its communal garden through which the children rampaged, shouting and arguing. The neighbours had been splendid about the rumpus but their patience must be running thin. The children needed their own garden in which

197

they could romp and fight at will. He would have to look round for a house.

But whenever he was about to phone an estate agent he would hesitate, hand on receiver, reminding himself that he was once more about to set off on his travels. Maybe when he got back?

And there were other reasons for vacillation. The continuity of the set-up in Barnes with Eileen and Laura – when she was in England – was surely preferable in terms of the children's security than a new environment with a stranger in charge?

Peter started school in Barnes. It would be better for him to stay on there for a year, let him settle down scholastically before the big move.

'I'm afraid I'm taking advantage of you,' he said to Laura.

'Rubbish. You are not taking advantage. I wish you'd stop fussing, Richard. Sit down and have a drink and tell me about your last African trip. Did you get to Salisbury? Are the Rhodesians still united behind Ian Smith? Do you really think he can persist with this UDI caper?'

Laura was much more interested in his travels than Rebecca had been. She had been wonderful over this last year. It couldn't have been an easy one for her, either. Her self-control was admirable. Her tears had been shed in private. Her attitude to the children and to himself had been compassionate and supportive.

By comparison his own mother had been a complete let-down, making it all too plain from the outset that she would not assume any form of responsibility for her grandchildren. She would have shown more mercy towards two rose-bushes threatened by blight.

'The Rhodesians think he will. Trade embargoes aren't working. They've just opened up a whole new market for sanction-busters. Petrol convoys are pouring in from South Africa. Portugal's with them – and France and West Germany have been pretty ambiguous in *their* attitudes.'

Chatting with Laura he was able to relax and open out, even if it was only about Rhodesia.

'You didn't see Caroline?' Laura asked when they had exhausted the topic of UDI.

'She was in Mauritius.'

They chatted on. Richard, who had intended to take Peter and Cassie home for the weekend, consulted his watch.

'It's nearly nine! What will Eileen think of me, forgetting about the children?'

'Exactly the same as she always thinks! Don't worry. If it's that late she'll have put them to bed already.'

'Here?'

'I can't imagine where else! Good heavens, you don't have to behave like a penitent. It wouldn't be the first or last Friday the children have spent here.'

'But I'm going to Lusaka again next week.'

'And they'll sleep here then.'

Getting away from the op and pop of London was a relief. In his present state of mind he was not up to coping with its cheerful vulgarity, its flip jargon, its scene-makers, its Raga beat. In Carnaby Street girls in wildly coloured vinyl and polyester outfits might have stepped out of a psychedelic hallucination induced by LSD. Edwardian jackets were in. Trousers had bell-bottom flares. He had no energy for any of it. He was – he knew it – a square.

But Lusaka now brought back poignant memories of Rebecca, even though she had never actually been there.

George Meredith met him at the airport. The sky was high and blue and the country smelt of wood fires and he wondered why White people could not take a leaf from an African book and dare to be themselves. Except that he couldn't relax here either.

'You're terribly something-or-other, Richard,' Chloe Meredith told him. 'Braced up. Unsprung. Got a woman in your life, have you?'

'No. Actually not.'

'You should have. You can't go on mourning Rebecca forever.

You should get married again. Better for you and better for the children.'

He took refuge in his drink, hoping that she would leave it at that.

'But what do you do about *sex*, Richard?'

'Chloe, don't intrude!' George said, cringing. 'Leave Richard alone.'

'Don't be boring, George. Richard is our friend. I'm concerned about him. You're not offended, are you, Richard?'

'No. Not at all . . .'

'You see? We'll have to *do* something. There are dozens of single women around. We'll give a party. Who shall we ask, George?'

'The Harrisons.'

'Of course, the Harrisons. I was thinking of single women. What about Daphne?'

'I'll leave it to you,' said George.

All week Richard was involved in a series of meetings. October in Zambia was known as suicide month. The rains had not yet broken. The sun blazed down. Inert black bodies lay under the shade of trees. Cicadas shrieked.

On Friday he drove back from town to the Merediths with sweat pouring down his back, thinking wistfully of an early night.

'Yoo-hoo, Richard, is that you?'

'You look nice,' he said to Chloe. 'Special occasion?'

'The party.'

But, of course. In Lusaka a party was an excuse for dressing up. Chloe was wearing a long gown and diamond earrings. The other women came similarly attired. Only one of them, a red-head, was mini-clad.

'Daphne Croft,' Chloe said.

Hadn't someone mentioned a Daphne? She was a slim woman in her early thirties with a good figure and excellent legs. The mini was six inches or so above her knees.

'Hello, Richard. Chloe told me about you. I gather you come out here quite often. You work with George.'

'That's right. I do.'

'So did my husband.'

'Did?'

'He lives down south now. We're getting a divorce.'

'Oh. I'm sorry.'

'Why are you sorry?' Daphne said. '*I'm* not. I can't wait to get rid of him.'

What did one say in reply to such a statement?

'Do you have children?'

'A couple, at school in the UK. *He* wanted to take them down south but it wasn't on.'

She had a glass in one hand. With the other – fingers splayed out – she was absently stroking her left thigh.

What did that signify? Availability? It looked that way.

At dinner they were seated next to each other. Daphne asked him well-informed questions about his work. She had been well-inducted, he thought. But then she was bound to have been. Her husband was one of us.

He realised that he had not caught her second name. 'Ah. You're *Grant's* wife.'

'Ex-wife. More or less.'

Grant, he recalled, had been a rather ineffectual sort. She had probably proved too much for him. No wonder they had broken up.

Across the table George Meredith was telling one of his jokes. As usual he repeated the punchline and the other guests, who had been waiting for him to do so, grinned and shook their heads.

No one was in a hurry to go home. At one A.M. Daphne made the first move in this direction and Chloe promptly suggested that Richard escort her.

'But I've got my own car.'

'Richard will drive behind you, won't you, Richard? It's so dangerous these days. Ever since UDI, Nkomo's men have been all over Lusaka waving guns.'

Richard complied. The roads were deserted. He had an idea

that gun-wielding guerrillas were a figment of Chloe's imagination, an adjunct to the seduction which she hoped was about to take place. In the morning she would want to know exactly what had transpired, whether the cure she had prescribed had proved effective.

Nevertheless he accepted Daphne's invitation to come in for a night-cap. The house had a semi-vacated look. Basic furniture. No photographs or ornamentation. Perhaps Grant had cleared out the memorabilia before leaving.

'Brandy?'

'All right.'

'I'll join you.'

She had a frighteningly heavy hand. He had already drunk too much. Tomorrow was bound to be hell.

She sat beside him on the sofa, close enough for her thigh to – just – touch his. When he had downed half his drink he took hers out of her hand, put it on the table, and kissed her.

'Mm – nice,' she said.

They kissed again. Chloe, he thought, would be pleased. They got up and went into the bedroom with Chloe silently cheering him on.

Daphne unzipped her dress and stepped out of it, leaving it in a puddle on the floor and revealing skimpy panties and a half-cup bra.

'Undo?'

She turned her back to him and he fumbled with the hook of her bra. Her body was as good as her legs. She had an all-over tan. He pulled off his own clothes, lay beside her on the bed and took her in his arms. She smelt of brandy and Chanel Number Five, all that poor dead Marilyn Monroe was said to have worn in bed. He guided her hand, kissed and caressed. Nothing happened. Not to him. Nothing was going to happen.

He rolled away from her, facing the other wall. 'I'm sorry.'

'You said that before.'

'I mean it. It's all my fault. You're terrific. It's just me.'

'It's like that sometimes,' she said, not unsympathetically.

'I must go.'

She didn't try to stop him. He got up, dressed, and – not looking at her – said, 'Goodnight. And thanks.'

'What for?'

He was left to wonder what Chloe would make of the débâcle; whether Daphne, over a game of Bridge, would spill the beans.

Should he send flowers? Waking in the morning with a splitting headache he decided that he would not.

Colleagues from the Johannesburg office had more appetite than Richard for swinging London.

'OK,' said Colin Newman, newly arrived and curious, 'where's it all happening?'

'Colin, I'm a bit out of it – '

'Come on, Richard. I've only got four days.'

They started off on the King's Road with Colin commenting on the names of boutiques: *'Granny Takes a Trip*! Kinky stuff, hey Richard! *Hung on You*! That's Jean Shrimpton, I'm sure of it. Can't you get your mother-in-law to introduce me?'

'I doubt it.'

They approached a pub. Colin, pleading thirst, dragged him in. They were still there at closing time when Colin caught wind of a party in a basement in World's End.

The door was opened by a huge coloured man. Colin – taken aback – recovered and surged forward. Inside couples were crammed hip-bone to hip-bone, gyrating to the sound of 'Sgt Pepper's Lonely Hearts Club'.

Colin and Richard struggled through to a second room where a dozen or so people were sitting cross-legged on the floor.

'They're smoking *dagga*!' Colin exclaimed. 'Back home this is for Coloureds. You do this, Richard?'

'Sorry to disappoint you.'

'Have you tried meditation? Some of those *oekies* – gurus – bury themselves alive. Have you been to India?'

'No,' said Richard. 'But the Beatles have.'

They moved on.

'They're clapping in there,' Colin said at the third door. 'What do you say it's a strip?'

Inside an applauding group had encircled a bed on which a couple were copulating.

'*Sies!*' said Colin, appalled.

They walked back to Richard's flat, lost in their disparate thoughts.

'The dolls in this town are *different!*' Colin said.

'They're kids, that's all.'

'You call that doll on the bed a kid?'

Richard said wearily, 'They come to Chelsea for the so-called Bohemian life. They buy new clothes and hang around and get dragged into seedy parties like that.'

'*Sies!*' said Colin again. 'I wouldn't let *my* kids grow up in this town!'

'Aren't you the one that's looking half slack enough this while back? I wouldn't take a lease of *your* life with the weight you're after losing!'

'*I'm* not thin, Eileen.'

'Not thin, is it? Scraggy I'd say. Will you look at the cut of your clothes?'

'I needed to lose a bit.'

'Indeed you did not!'

'You have lost a lot of weight, Richard,' Laura agreed. 'You'd better come to us for a weekend and let Eileen fatten you up.'

'All right, I will.'

'You come over here on Friday,' Eileen said, 'and I'll have fat back on your bones by dinner-time Saturday!'

It sounded like a serious invitation but he wasn't sure. On Friday he packed spare shirts and socks and underpants and, in case it was not, left the suitcase in the boot when he got to Barnes.

Laura opened the door. 'Disaster! Eileen's down with flu and I've been so damned busy, Richard, that I haven't managed to cook.'

'It doesn't matter.'

'It does. We asked you here for the weekend and you're going to be fed. I'll take you out.'

'You'll do no such thing. I'll take you. What about the children?'

'Eggs. That I did manage. And Eileen's not so sick that she can't babysit. We'll wait until they doze off and then sneak out. I fancy a dry sherry. What about you?'

'Good idea. Be generous,' he said. 'It's been that kind of week.'

'For me, too. Do you have many bad weeks, Richard?'

About to deflect this question with a facetious, 'Don't we all?', he found himself surveying Laura. As usual she was sombrely dressed in pale and dark greys. Fair hair tucked behind her ears. No make-up. She did not in the least resemble Rebecca.

He said honestly, 'I'm afraid so. Yes.'

'Because of Rebecca.'

He stopped, added truthfully, 'Not because I miss her so much,' and waited for Laura the bereaved mother to hit out at him.

'Poor Richard,' she said. 'Guilt is ghastly, isn't it?'

Seven words. Before he could stop himself many, many others poured out of him in a flood of explanation.

'It's more than that. It's more than having to live with the fact that I knew for ages that I shouldn't have married her. She was – just too young for me. My fault. And then – that last pregnancy. She didn't want another baby. You must know that. She didn't want a *second* baby, for Christ's sake. When the post-mortem diagnosed that she was pregnant I – '

'You're being too hard on yourself.'

'If she hadn't been pregnant she wouldn't have crashed. Sorry. I should shut up.'

'Why should you if you need to talk?'

'Not to you. I shouldn't do this to you.'

'You're not the only one who feels guilty, you know. She came here that day for a specific purpose. Probably to tell me that she was pregnant. Anyway, I put her off.'

'You think that's why she came? I don't think she knew she was pregnant. *I* didn't suspect it. I thought . . . I must have misunderstood her.'

'You see, I was busy,' Laura said. 'If she'd stayed here, rested – '

'It's not a crime to be busy.'

'And it's not a criminal offence to make love to your wife. It can't have been rape.'

He had run out of words but he was feeling much better. Thanks to Laura. The mother-confessor. Laura the absolver. She was ever a good confidante. Conversation with her flowed freely. He had always enjoyed her company, been disappointed whenever they had had to part. But tonight he wouldn't have to rush home. They had the whole weekend ahead of them.

'Richard,' Laura said firmly. 'You've got to stop blaming yourself and so, for that matter, have I. Let's not talk about Rebecca any more this evening. I'm going to check up on the children. Then we can walk over to the village and find ourselves something to eat.'

It was strange how dining *à deux* in a restaurant with someone you had known for years could be quite different from facing that person across a familiar table. Odd, too, the way an aura of intimacy could be artificially created by candles which neither of you had lit.

Facing Laura he was struck again by the dissimilarities between mother and daughter. This applied even when it came to ordering the meal. Rebecca would have shuddered at the fattening food which Laura selected and devoured.

He liked her healthy appetite. He approved of her altogether. It occurred to him that many men must have found her attractive over the years.

When they had nearly finished the wine he gave in to curiosity.

'Has there really been no man in your life since Klaus died?'

'The odd flutter. One-night stands mostly. I fled before involvement.'

'You loved him that much?'

That didn't draw such a quick response. Laura fiddled with her spoon, ate a mouthful of chocolate mousse, swallowed.

Finally she said, 'I did love him very much,' and leant back in her chair.

'How much?'

She laughed nervously. 'A lot. It was a long time ago, Richard. Before the war. I'm quite old, you know.'

'You're forty-nine. You're not old.'

In the candlelight she looked more ethereal than ever, fragile and pale. In appearance she was too delicate a creature to have survived the loss of her husband and only child. A woman in need of protection. But strong in mind. Tough as nails, Rebecca had once said. And the best company.

She gobbled up the rest of her mousse and refused coffee. 'I'll make it for us at home.'

'You sure you want me to stay for the whole weekend?'

'I'm sure. Your bed is made up.'

They walked along Church Road. When they were at the intersection Laura reached for his hand. It seemed entirely natural for the two of them to walk on with fingers entwined.

Crossing the Common he felt for his guilt, like a man searching for his wallet. It was not there. He could find no trace of it.

'It's beginning to rain.'

'Did you see *Singing in the Rain*?'

'With Gene Kelly?'

'Who else? I have this most ridiculous urge to dance!'

'What's ridiculous,' Laura said, 'about wanting to dance?'

'Good question. Rain's worsening. Better run.'

Hand-in-hand they scampered towards St Mary's Grove. He had left the car parked in the road outside the house. He let go of Laura's hand, lifted his suitcase out of the boot, hesitated, giving her the chance to say that she had changed her mind, that he should go back to Chelsea.

She didn't speak. She stood there waiting for him and he knew that he need not go home, not this night. Because once they had ascertained that Peter and Cassie were sound asleep, Laura and he would make love. As they would have done long before had he not chosen the wrong woman. The daughter not the mother . . .

He groped once more for his guilt. In vain. Laura had relieved him of it forever. His heart bursting with gratitude he followed her up the path.

H E woke in the guest room with his emotions as tangled as Laura's unfamiliar sheets. The events of the night before, so natural then, were mind-boggling now in their implications. Reviewed in cold blood his actions were those of a lunatic.

Laura. His mother-in-law. The children's custodian. Colin – any of his friends – would confirm that he had to be out of his mind. Crazed. But happy. As he still was this morning with two days – two *nights* – of the weekend ahead of him.

Was Laura awake yet? He could hear no sounds of stirring. Her bedroom was adjacent to his, a much larger room that stretched down the right-hand side of the first floor. The bedrooms where Eileen and the children slept were on the left, the single bathroom and separate loo off the landing.

It was not a house designed to facilitate illicit lovers. Creeping upstairs to Laura's bedroom the night before he had waited with trepidation for a child to appear, wide-eyed and chatty and in need of attention. This had not happened, and when he and Laura were safely inside the room she had locked the door.

'You think they'll hear us?' he had whispered, still nervous.

If one of them were to bang on the door and demand entry, Laura had said, he could hide in her walk-in cupboard, at which point they had been reduced to giggles.

But Peter and Cassie had not woken and nor had Eileen, and desire had eclipsed fear.

Happy. Back in the mainstream of life. What next, he wondered? Ideally, there would be a (discreet) knock on the door and Laura would come in. She would be wearing a white housecoat and carrying a breakfast tray. Sausages, bacon and eggs, he thought, and coffee, not tea.

The door did open but it was Cassie who entered and climbed into his bed. 'Daddy!' she said, rubbing her cheek against his. 'Oof – scratchy beard!'

'I'll shave, just now, specially for you.'

'Will you?'

'Of course. I can't let my beautiful daughter get all scratched.'

Her face was pudgy and rounded and her hands dimpled. 'You're very squashy,' he said.

She frowned. 'What's squashy?'

'Soft and cuddly. Nice.'

'I want a puppy,' she said.

Who else had said that?

Before he could formulate an answer to this, Peter paddled down the corridor and got into the other side of the bed.

'No one's up,' he said, aggrieved. 'Eileen's *still* sleeping and Laura's door is shut.'

'Does she normally leave it open at night?'

'So she can hear us,' said his son. 'Cassie is only small.'

This further evidence of the tenderness of Laura and her importance in the children's lives added to his confusion.

What if last night unbalanced that relationship? Where then would the children be?

The odd flutter, Laura had said – one-night stands. After which she had fled. What would it do to Peter and Cassie if she ran away?

He looked down at the tops of their heads. The rest of them was submerged under the bedclothes, their limbs wedged against his. Why had he not thought of them before Laura and he made love?

'Eileen's *dead*!' said Cassie suddenly.

'She is not!'

'She's dead! I saw!'

'All right,' he said. 'That's enough.'

No one else but Laura, and Eileen when she was conscious,

would put up with their tiresome fights.

'Good morning, Richard!'

Laura – and in a white housecoat at that! No tray – but it only mattered that *she* was here, that she hadn't run.

'Hello.'

'Did you sleep well?'

'Never woke. Terrific.' (But that was because of you. Other nights I toss and turn for hours.)

The sight of her soothed him. He longed to be able to reach out for her. To hold her in his arms would have been enough. But Peter and Cassie were resettling themselves on either side of him. Laura was a luxury out of his reach.

'And you – did you have a good rest?'

'Wonderful,' she said. 'I can't remember when I've last slept so well.'

In white she was gossamery and feather-light and if he couldn't take her in his arms he could at least make an open declaration of her worth.

'*You're* wonderful,' said Richard. 'You are the most marvellous woman I've ever met. Isn't she, children?'

The practical difficulties remained. Conducting a love affair with your mother-in-law could be nothing but problematic while your children slept under her roof. Eileen, in her way even more of an incipient danger than the children, was also up and about that same day.

'Are you better?' Richard asked when she and not Laura had produced bacon and eggs.

'Nicely, thanks. No use complaining. You'd get nothing for it,' she said, and sat down at the breakfast table with Laura and himself, eroding their privacy.

Eileen was as sharp as a new blade in his razor. Tolerant about everything else, she was not lenient in sexual matters. He remembered how, in Rebecca and his courting days, she had been critical of hand-holding and caresses and late home-comings. Certain models had incurred her wrath, their morals called as dirty as a pig's crubeen. The Sixties, by challenging established mores, had deeply offended her.

But Laura had never upset her. Laura might have 'fluttered' but not in Barnes. Or not until last night. But this relationship was no one-night stand, or he hoped it was not. How then to do it justice?

'What are we going to *do*?' he hissed when Eileen was out of earshot.

Thankfully, Laura did not pussyfoot around asking him what he meant.

'We'll have to go to your flat.'

'Tonight? Won't Eileen mind staying with the children? It's Saturday. Doesn't she want to go off.'

'She doesn't feel up to going out. She wants an early night. Otherwise we'll have to work out a strategy – if you want to go on, that is.'

'Why wouldn't I?'

'Because you've allowed yourself to get carried away and I daresay you've had second thoughts this morning. Because I was Rebecca's mother. Because of the children. Because I'm older than you.'

'If you love someone, second thoughts along those lines are irrelevant.'

'Is that a statement you're making?'

'Statement: I love you.'

'So we'll work out a strategy.'

Even at the beginning, Richard was irked by the need for masquerade. Even when he and Laura were at the stage of wanting to make love incessantly they were inhibited by timetables and the necessity to placate Eileen and the children. The pleasure he derived in bed was marred by having to get out of it on a cold night to drive Laura home.

Occasionally Laura stayed over in Cadogan Gardens, a treat which involved elaborate fabrications about out-of-town assignments.

'God, I hate lies!' Laura said.

The constant requirement to conceal their feelings and censor their words in the presence of the children added strain.

Close shaves were inevitable. One weekend Eileen took a break and they were able to stay in Barnes. Richard, creeping out of Laura's bedroom in the small hours, met Peter on the landing.

'Why are you coming out of Laura's room?' Peter mumbled.

He was half asleep. Richard guided him to the lavatory and, in the morning, waited uneasily for Peter to raise the subject again.

When he did not, Richard did obliquely: 'Certain amount of wandering in the middle of the night.'

Peter reached across and helped himself to a piece of toast.

'Who was wandering?' he said innocently. 'Cassie, I suppose.'

'I thought it was you.'

'Me? I *never* wake up, not at night anyway.'

And it was not just Eileen and the children they had to deceive but friends. Neither of them wanted to issue Press statements about their relationship, not yet. They were on a hitherto unexplored and unschematic pathway leading to heaven-only-knew where, and they did not want to become the focus of even affectionate speculation.

Although he did not say so to Laura, Richard dreaded his colleagues at work getting wind of the situation. There were, he knew, certain people who would have liked to see him make a thorough fool of himself. In his professional life he seldom made mistakes – he saw to that. No one suspected that he was actually terrified of failure, but some resented his efficiency and the speed with which he had been promoted.

His blood ran cold at the thought of the nudge-wink routine: '*Stacton's having it off with his mother-in-law! How about that!*'

But when he weighed these drawbacks against the sum of his love for Laura their total was insubstantial. Whereas the love was made up of exactly the right measures of stimulating companionship and satisfactory sex.

Why hadn't he recognized Laura's potential for him at the beginning of their acquaintance and married her, instead of being led astray by her daughter's beauty? Answer: because he had been a fool.

And now – even though they weren't married – he was positively uxorious about her. And why not, since she was warm, compassionate, generous and honest – and just terrific in bed.

With the dawn of love for Laura had come the humbling doubt – what did she see in him? How come he had managed to pin her down? She had run from all other men.

She parried inquiries by saying mockingly, 'It's because you're family, Richard. You're *safe*, don't you see?' but he thought that there was in this dismissal an element of truth.

At other moments Laura would insist that Richard had miraculously healed her, making it possible for her to love again, and he wondered if there might not come a time when the patient would dump the doctor for a more charismatic man.

No such man materialised but another rival did, one that had actually been present all along, had Richard but noticed. Laura took her camera with her wherever she went. Her devotion to it became an increasing irritant.

'What on earth are you lugging that thing around with you for?'

'For obvious reasons. All photographers do. Does it worry you?'

'Not in the least.'

But it did. He was – he admitted it to himself – jealous of Laura's camera. Small as it was it was a symbol of that enormous part of Laura's life from which he was denied access.

Laura – quite reasonably, he said to himself – kept her professional life to herself. She did not want him around when she was taking pictures. Nor would he appreciate Laura pfaffing around in his office from Monday to Friday. And yet – most unreasonably, he agreed – he disliked being excluded from her studio. He wanted the right to roam freely in all areas of her life, an aspiration which even he condemned as petty and possessive.

Meanwhile, there was her camera, leering at him, even in bed.

One night in the middle of love-making, his hand caressing her breast, Laura said suddenly, 'Don't move, Richard! Stay lying exactly like that,' and she reached out across his body and seized her camera.

'God, woman, what are you doing?'

'Beautiful,' she said. 'Your thigh – like that, against mine. Wonderful shot!'

'I absolutely refuse to pose for porn.'

'It's not porn. It's just a marvellous angle. You're so puritanical. Stay still!'

'I am not puritanical! You're not going to sell the photograph to *Nova*, are you?'

All the trendy photographers worked for *Nova*. The magazine explored aspects of modern living as no other British publication had ever before done. Its covers were bold and brave and gaudy, its photography and layout highly experimental. It was, Laura said, the most exciting thing that had ever happened to magazine publishing but he had no intention of letting his left thigh appear in its pages. He said so in more categoric terms and Laura laughed.

'My God, but you're vain!'

'And you talk too much! *Next* wife – ' in his mind she *was* his wife – 'next wife will be the daughter of a Trappist monk! What's more your hair is too short!'

'So is yours. Much good you'd be pulling the birds on the King's Road!'

'Not as good as you are at recording that scene.'

Her mind and imagination were wide open to change. She would be like that at eighty, he thought, at a hundred, which was why she would never grow old, never lose her allure for him.

'Do you really think my hair is too short?'

'No. It's fine. Really. I was just getting my own back.'

'Not that I want to grow it.'

'It's pretty the way it is,' he said. 'And you're very pretty. I can't believe my luck. I can't understand why the other men failed and I succeeded.'

Laura had put her camera on the bedside table and was lying in the cradle of his arm. She moved her head so he could not see her face.

'Don't you?'

'No, I don't. Why me?'

There was, he thought, nothing special about his personality. Quite the opposite. As a child he had been aware that his mother had regarded him as the runt of the litter. Although she had been a zealous gardener even in those days, Richard's image of her had been as a Master of Hounds, willing her husband and sons to hearken to her command and ensuring that they were whipped in when they strayed from the pack.

Her sons had grown up and diversified, at which point she hadn't cared much whether they came or went any more, but her judgement of Richard as merely passable still coloured his view of himself.

Why me, he wondered, and it did not cross his mind that Laura, too, might lack confidence in her personal worth.

She was not coming back with an answer to his question. Her eyes were closed but she couldn't have fallen asleep. Surely not?

Testing, he kissed the top of her head. 'I wouldn't really like you with flowing locks.'

She stirred. 'Why not? Because of my age?'

'Because hippy women don't turn me on.'

What he wanted was to get back to where they had been a few minutes earlier. He shifted position and saw Laura's camera on the bedside table.

So tiny, so innocuous-looking – and so deadly, in terms of what it could do to a good erection. He turned on to his side away from the camera and its implications. 'Darling . . .'

'I'm going to New York next month,' Laura said. 'It's for American *Harper's*.'

'New York?'

'I'm so pleased I can't tell you. This is going to be *the* year – I can feel it. *Vogue* and *American Glamour* are coming up trumps, as well. New York next month and Tokyo in September.'

'When did you learn all this?'

'It's been on the boil. I've only just got confirmation about New York.'

But what about us, Richard thought – what about the family? *We're* not going to New York. I, the *children* need you here. Peter and Cassie hated Laura going away. They said so frequently, Cassie in particular. Cassie worshipped Laura, followed her grandmother round the house when she was present and moped when she wasn't there. And here was Laura calmly announcing that she was going to New York. Wasn't it enough that she went all-too-often to Italy and France?

'You're not listening, Richard.'

'I *am* listening.'

'I'm not at the top yet. I'm not up there with Penn and Avedon and I want to be and I haven't got youth on my side. Not like Bailey or Donovan.'

I want you here, Richard thought. But that was unfair. He was going to be away a lot himself this year.

In Zambia the legality of the ownership of the country's mineral rights had been called into doubt. The mines were owned by companies and shareholders. The right to operate them was outside the government's control, a state of affairs which President Kaunda was determined to end – within the next two years, it was generally felt. When that happened Richard's company would concentrate their efforts in South Africa. In this connection he would be over and back to Lusaka and Johannesburg more than he would have liked. Leaving the children not under Laura's jurisdiction but, increasingly, under Eileen's.

Eileen was loyal, devoted and capable but she was fundamentally a simple woman, a nanny and an untrained one at that. More to the point, she was an employee. She was not related to the children as Laura was. The children might benefit from Eileen's common sense and disciplinary tactics but they should also have a maternal influence in their lives. Or the next best thing. Laura, in fact. On whom neither they nor he had the right to make demands.

Uxorious as he might be about Laura, she was not his wife. He had not even succeeded in making love to her tonight.

'. . . Twiggy for a cover,' Laura said.

Twiggy, big-eyed, bony and beautiful, was the year's top model – that much he knew. Of what Laura had been saying previously he had lost track.

So might he lose touch with Laura herself. For he hadn't succeeded where other men before him had failed. He had never pinned her down.

In September, when he returned from Zambia, she was in Japan. He told himself that he should have been grateful to have learnt of her plans in advance.

Laura was still not used to the concept of liaising with him about her intentions. He told her the details of his diary weeks in advance. Laura made arrangements to go abroad and sprung them on him at the last minute, completely disrupting their private life.

It drove him mad and yet he did not openly object. He went along with it, as he did with many situations about which he had inner reservations and no one, least of all Laura, knew what he felt.

He missed her horribly when they were apart. This was not new – all days and nights without Laura were bereft – but it was getting worse. He had the feeling that neither of them was entirely in control of their futures, that they were on two different fairground dippers, whirling around and unable to get off.

It was the travelling that did it. He always was thoroughly disorientated after a long trip, and so was Laura.

They were both rushing around too much. It was bad for the

children, and bad for their own relationship. It had to stop. Their lives needed restructuring. Face it, he said to himself, we need to marry. Whatever people may think.

And why not, since they loved each other; had a responsibility to protect that love? The age difference was of no consequence. It wasn't as if he wanted children by his second wife.

Peter and Cassie's reaction mattered. How, he wondered, would the children take it? Would it cause complications – ridicule at school? Daddy and Grandma? Even though Laura was not exactly a 'grandma' person – whatever that meant?

He was mulling over this at work when the phone rang.

'Richard?' Jane, personal assistant to Donald Forbes, the managing director.

'Who else?'

'You free for a few minutes? Donald would like to see you.'

Telling Donald – announcing it at the office. That was another horror to be overcome. Donald, meanwhile, was in an affable mood. Coffee was ordered.

'I've been thinking, Richard.' Donald toyed absently with a ginger biscuit. 'Are you absolutely set on staying in London?'

'What have you got up your sleeve?'

Donald laughed. 'You haven't answered my question.'

'I'm in the process of adjusting to it. Give me an alternative so I can complete the process.'

'Fair enough. How would you feel about a transfer to Johannesburg?'

Richard whistled. 'Johannesburg?'

'You've always been an Africa man at heart. Not a bad lifestyle down there for a fellow in your position. Good for kids. Education. Servants. Social life. Golf. And several steps up the career ladder.'

'How many precisely?'

'The top job, Richard. Blandford's retiring. You know that.'

'I do. I hadn't thought along those lines.'

'Then do. Go out there. Take a look around. You've still got six months in which to make up your mind.'

'Go when?'

'Six weeks from now?'

'Suits me,' Richard said.

Johannesburg, he thought. Fantastic climate, seductive lifestyle, friendly people. The top job. Appropriate for him to arrive with wife in tow.

How would Laura fit in? She wasn't exactly cut in the same mould as your average corporate wife. If they went to South Africa she would have to give up working for international magazines and fine down her career ambitions. That might not suit her.

So put it to her, he thought. All she can do is turn you down. The alternative was to marry her anyway, rule out South Africa – and go on living the same unsatisfactory lifestyle. The one advantage would be that subterfuge would end.

But – the top job. An environment which would make it easy to raise children. Which way is it to be? Laura, come home from Tokyo and put me out of my agony.

She did so with armfuls of presents for the children and himself. She looked different. What was it? Hairdo? Eyeshadow?

Cassie said, 'You're wearing a pink coat, Laura. You never wear pink!'

'Moment of madness,' said Laura, her cheeks getting pink as well. 'I thought – I . . . Do you like my coat, Richard?'

'Lovely. *You* look lovely. You must wear that coat this evening.'

'Where are you going?' Cassie said resentfully.

'Nowhere until you two are asleep.'

But then, he thought, we'll talk. I'll tell Laura about the South African offer, put my cards on the table, ask her to marry me.

'Where would you like to eat?' he said.

Laura thought. 'Why not the Savoy?'

G ETTING out of the taxi, in the foyer, it was still all right.

He helped Laura off with her new pink coat, took off his own and carried both of them through to the men's cloakroom where he ran into a rule that he promptly wanted to break.

'*Ladies* next door, sir.'

'Are you inferring that this isn't my coat – that *I* can't wear pink?'

The attendant became confused. 'No, no, sir. Not at all.'

'Well, then,' said Richard grandly and strode back into the foyer to rejoin Laura.

It was all right when they were having a pre-dinner drink.

The Savoy was altogether an all right place, he thought, leaving one with the surety that, whatever unsavoury incidents might occur out on the Strand the hotel would continue to operate on the same patrician level.

Pleading jet-lag Laura declined a second sherry and they went into the River Room.

Richard had been to the Savoy on many occasions since the evening he had proposed to Rebecca, but only for business lunches. He had not been there with a woman. Not with Laura. Not with Rebecca's mother . . .

Suddenly the past hit him hard. Instead of Laura he saw Rebecca facing him across the table. What had Rebecca been wearing that night? He couldn't remember. He could recall only her overall beauty. They had talked then about South Africa, about the massacre at Sharpeville. Rebecca had been deeply shocked by the atrocity. And after coffee he had produced the ring and asked her to marry him . . .

'In Japan I realised just how right Quant's clothes would be on Oriental women. I liked Japan, Richard. They're so meticulous, so polite.'

He had been about to repeat himself. To discuss South Africa. To propose. How could he have been so insensitive? To propose here to Laura would be to insult the memory of Rebecca. Laura would think that.

Laura was talking about her next Famous Faces assignment.

'. . . was splendid in *This Sporting Life* . . . certainly deserved the Best Actor Award . . .'

He gazed at his plate, listening to Laura in a vague kind of way but acutely aware of Rebecca whose presence was so powerful that he was half convinced that she and not her mother was sharing the table.

'Richard,' Laura said, 'you're doing terribly badly over there.'

He swallowed, shook his head and made an effort to eat. 'Shouldn't have had such a large lunch. What were you saying?'

'I was telling you about – '

It *was* Laura over there. She of all people would understand his current reactions. When he was able to talk about them. He couldn't do that here.

Waiters came and removed plates, replaced them with others. Richard regained partial control of himself. It would be all right again, he thought, when he and Laura were in bed and he could hold her close.

He glanced surreptitiously at his watch. Ten o'clock.

'I guess you're as tired as I am,' Laura said. 'Let's not wait for coffee. I'd like to go home and sleep.'

'Home? You mean Barnes?'

'Yes. Straight home. We're both exhausted.'

'You're not coming to Cadogan Gardens?'

'Not tonight. I've had it and you're whacked as well.'

No, I'm not, Richard wanted to shout. But Laura was drooping.

He fetched their coats, the attendant watching to see which he would put on, and they caught a taxi to Barnes. On the way Laura proved that she was tired by falling asleep.

He woke her gently.

'Sorry,' she said. 'Oh groan,' fumbling in her bag for keys to open the front door. 'So weary I can't tell you.'

With Eileen in residence Laura, he knew, would not invite him into her bedroom. He followed her into the hall and hugged her tight. The relief of being free to just embrace her! He closed his eyes. In his arms Laura felt limp, so inert that she might well have dozed off again. If only he could carry her upstairs to bed, stay overnight, wake beside her in the morning. *Talk* . . .

When they were married lying in bed and talking would be routine, instead of luxury. No more driving round between Chelsea and Barnes. No more sleeping in separate beds. No more . . .

The faintest noise – a creaking beam? a scuttling mouse? – distracted him. He opened his eyes. He was facing the stairwell. At the top of the stairs a small, all too human figure was sitting, silently watching them.

Cassie! Oh my God, he thought, that's done it. How long has she been there? What conclusions has she drawn?

Before he could feign nonchalance, detach himself from Laura and greet his daughter, the figure had upped and gone.

'Shit!' he muttered aloud.

'What?' Laura said sleepily. 'What did you say?'

'Nothing. Off to bed.'

What a life, he thought, letting himself out. When are we going to resolve it? The prospect of returning to an empty flat was not consoling.

In the morning he woke in a more optimistic frame of mind. The answer, surely, was to take Laura away for a few days. Somewhere quiet where they could be completely alone. Cornwall or Devon?

He left work unusually early and drove to Barnes to suggest this to Laura. She was still in her studio. Peter and Cassie and some of their friends were playing Swallows and Amazons in the garden. They ran in, greeted him affectionately, and rushed out in response to a shout. Cassie, as far as he could ascertain, was not harbouring dark thoughts about the previous night.

Presently the door to Laura's studio opened and a girl in a cheesecloth caftan came out. Seeing Richard in the sitting-room she called across the hall, 'Hello. You're Richard, aren't you? Heard about you. I'm Lorraine.'

Cockney accent. Beautiful face.

'Hello, Lorraine.'

She shook her head and her hair, which had been pinned up, fell down over her shoulders. It was stunning hair, golden-blonde and almost waist-length.

'Nice to meet you, Richard,' she said, and went upstairs.

Richard settled down with the evening paper. Lorraine came down and disappeared into the studio without talking to him again.

Eileen looked in. 'Fancy a cup of tea, do you?'

'Yes, please.'

'And scones? I've lashings in the kitchen.'

'You offer all the best options, Eileen.'

The joy of relaxing in Laura's house. It was truly his favourite place. He liked the way Laura had furnished it, the modern, unfussy décor and furniture. And the paintings. Just lately Laura had invested well in the work of several British artists. He approved her taste. Their attitudes to so many things were the same.

Salcombe? Brixham? Falmouth? Anywhere as long as they could have peace.

Eileen brought his tea and scones and Cassie returned briefly to share his feast.

'How are you, darling?'

'I'm fine, Daddy. Peter is a pain!'

'You can stand up for yourself, I think. And quite right, too.'

Shortly afterwards he heard her in the garden: 'Daddy says . . .'

All perfectly normal. No funny looks. In Cassie's eyes hugging

Laura was doubtless a natural thing to do. It was he, with his worries and inhibitions, who was out of line.

The children were still playing outside when Lorraine left the studio, waved a hand at him and departed. A car started up. Finally and not before time Laura herself came through.

'You look worn out,' he said.

'I am.'

'You're working too hard. Take a leaf from my book and relax!'

Laura didn't respond in the same light-hearted vein. 'Oh, Richard,' she said exasperatedly, 'I've had to reshoot. So annoying. Is there a cup left for me in the pot?'

'Yes. Sit down and I'll pour.'

'Thanks. I'm still thinking work. Lorraine – '

'Ah. The beautiful Lorraine. She of the caftan and the golden hair.'

There was a short silence. Then Laura said, 'You know Lorraine?'

'Not exactly. We've just met. It's beautiful hair. Is it a shampoo ad?'

Another pause. 'No,' said Laura at the end of it. 'No, it's not.'

The possibility that he might have said something wrong dawned on Richard. 'Um – '

'You have a fetish about hair, don't you?' Laura cut in.

'*Me?*'

Peter and Cassie, purple with fury, burst into the room.

'He *hit* me!'

'I did not!'

'You did! My face is bruise-ed!'

He wondered anew at his children's energy and blood-lust.

'Go and bath!'

'*Bath?*'

He might have suggested a dipping in boiling oil.

'Yes. This minute. And cut the fighting out.'

Laura had finished her tea. She got up with the air of one who is about to resume work.

'You're not going back into the studio?'

'I am.'

'You're crazy.'

'You may think so,' Laura said coldly, 'but others don't. Anyway, with this other job running down the track at me – '

'What other job?'

'I told you last evening,' she said. 'I'm going to Ireland.'

It was his turn to ice up. How typical of Laura to spring such a surprise just when he was about to suggest their going away.

'When?'

'Tomorrow. I told you . . .'

'You didn't tell me. And even if you did I think it's damned inconsiderate of you to rush around the world in support of your blasted career without considering how I or the children feel!'

'And what about *you*? You, I suppose, are static! Come off it, Richard.'

'That's different.'

'Why? Because you're a man? But you're the children's father, Richard. I'm just their grandmother.'

'For Christ's sake let's not fight. I want to talk to you. I've got to talk. Why don't you pack it in for tonight and – '

'Sorry. I can't. I have an early start in the morning and I still have work to do and I want to pack.'

'In that case I'll be off!' he said, as angry now as Peter and Cassie had been but minus their outlets for letting off steam.

Their feelings had to be taken into account and so had Eileen's. He couldn't let himself slam the door after he went out.

Having exited without saying goodnight to the children he dashed to Barnes before breakfast.

'Laura's gone already,' said Peter.

'To take a picture of Elizabeth Taylor,' Cassie announced.

'Has she?'

It was entirely possible. Elizabeth Taylor had been in London for a family wedding that same week. He had seen a photograph of her in the *Evening Standard*.

'Richard Button bought her a ring that cost one million dollars!'

'*Burton*,' Richard said distractedly. 'Well, I'm sure she deserves it.'

Gone already.

'It isn't Elizabeth Taylor, stupid,' said Peter. 'It's Richard Harris.'

'From Limerick,' said Eileen. 'Did you not see him in *This Sporting Life*?'

'No.'

This Sporting Life? Who, in the last twenty-four hours, had also mentioned the film?

'He won an award.'

Laura had said that. At the Savoy. Of course.

'Do you have Laura's number in Ireland?' he asked Eileen.

'I do.'

She presented it to him, said pointedly, 'I'd phone her now if I were you. She having left here this morning a long string of misery.'

'She was unhappy?'

'Woeful put out. "Take a hoult of yourself," I said to her, "for the two of yous will be back together yet"'

She looked meaningfully at him. You villain, Richard thought. You've known all along.

He went to the phone, picked up the receiver, dialled the operator.

'Dad?'

'Not *now*, Cassie.'

'But I want to tell you something.'

'Ssh.'

Go, he wanted to add – vamoose. Let me talk to Laura in peace.

Cassie plonked herself down on the floor by his feet.

The number he had requested rang incessantly. Ten, eleven, thirteen times. He was about to give up when a female voice, not Irish, answered breathlessly, 'Yes, who is it?'

'Could I speak to Laura Conway, please?'

'She isn't here yet.'

'When are you expecting her?'

'I couldn't say.'

'What hotel *is* that?'

'What did you say?'

'Da-ad?'

'Be quiet! What? I can't hear you. The line's very bad.'

The voice at the other end gabbled incomprehensibly. Frustrated he put the receiver down and very nearly tripped over Cassie.

'How often must I tell you not to interrupt when I'm on the phone?'

'But I was trying to tell you. It's not a hotel. It's *Harriet*'s number. Eileen didn't say.'

'Harriet or Harris – make up your mind!'

Cassie pursed her lips. 'It's Harriet *now*, Dad. Laura's gone to Tipperary for the weekend.'

'That was Harriet on the phone?'

'I s'pose so,' Cassie said.

Ditched, he thought. Dumped in favour of Charles and Harriet. Unless she's gone to Ireland with another man.

'You said she was taking pictures in Ireland.'

'Not till Monday. Can't *we* go somewhere, Dad?'

He took them to London Zoo. The heavens opened and drenched them. Cassie lost the buckle from her sandal and had to be carried on his back. At rock bottom, he trailed them off in search of lemonade. They sucked on their straws, making horrible noises that jarred on his nerves, and squabbled intermittently.

Then, as Peter took his place in a queue for chocolate, Cassie accused him, 'Laura went away because of you.'

'What *are* you on about?'

'You were horrible to her and she told Eileen and then she phoned Harriet and said could she come over for the weekend. I heard.'

'You shouldn't be listening in.'

But he wasn't cross. Perplexed, yes – and relieved.

I wasn't horrible, Richard thought, only hurt by Laura's attitude. Surely that was obvious? Apparently not. Our lines got crossed and Laura ended up as miserable as myself. What a mess. The kind of imbroglio that comes out of working too hard. It has to stop – has to, or we'll both go mad.

'Laura cried.'

'She did?'

'Because of you.'

'Not because of me. Because she's tired. Because she needs a rest.'

In Devon or Cornwall. But Ireland could be just as reparative. He could join Laura there. He could phone again when he got home and set it up.

Restored, he allowed himself to be steered to the aviary. They all went back to Cadogan Gardens and he saw that the children were bathed and fed before making his second call.

There was no reply from Tipperary, then or later on. Out to dinner, he thought, disappointed but not too upset. In the morning he tried again. Still no reply. Where *were* they?

He buoyed himself up by ringing Donald Forbes at home and arranging to take the following week off, allowed the children to gorge themselves on hamburgers and chips and tried on countless occasions to get through to Ireland without success.

On Sunday evening he handed Peter and Cassie over to Eileen.

'Are you off over?' Eileen asked.

He had given up on deception. They were conspirators now, he and Eileen. He told her about his failure to find Laura.

'Ah, sure, maybe they've gone to Kilkee for the weekend.' Kilkee was a holiday village on the coast of Clare.

'Why would they go there?'

'Isn't that where she's taking the pictures? I have the phone number of the hotel where she'd be staying.'

'What would I do without you?'

What indeed? Would Eileen come with them to Johannesburg – that is, if they went? He didn't care where they lived any more, as long as they were together.

He reached for the phone. And then he got the idea of surprising Laura. He would just turn up . . .

'You *sure* she'll be at this number tomorrow night?' he called out to Eileen.

'And Tuesday, and after that she'll be back.'

No, she won't, thought Richard. We're taking the week off.

He phoned the hotel. The voice that answered was unmistakably Irish.

'Do you have a room for tomorrow night?'

'Do you want it with bath or without?'

'With, please.'

'Oh, thank God,' said the voice at the other end. 'We haven't any without.'

He flew to Shannon, hired a car and drove the twenty or so miles to the coast, the line of which was a succession of caverns and chasms and extravagantly shaped rocks.

The village of Kilkee was built along a sandy, crescent-shaped beach with a massive rock outcrop acting as a reef.

He booked into the hotel and inquired about Laura.

'She's off out taking photographs,' the receptionist said.

She would be. But he had succeeded in tracking her down. He asked if Charles and Harriet were also staying at the hotel and was told that they had dropped off Miss Conway and afterwards left.

'Miss Conway didn't say when she'd be back?'

'No, but if you want her in a hurry she's at Newfoundout along with Richard Harris.'

'Is Newfoundout far?'

'You can walk there if you want. It's past the Pollock Holes and the Diamond Rocks. Where the golf course is.'

He took the car. He had only driven a short way when the road ran out. To his right was a vast stretch of black rocks broken by a series of natural swimming pools. Ahead was a cliff walk; on his left a golf course.

According to the receptionist Newfoundout was further along

and actually part of the breathtakingly high cliff from which the redoubtable Mr Harris had dived before swimming across the bay to George's Head. It was beginning to make sense. Laura would want to photograph the actor at the scene of so daring a feat.

There was no one around, just gulls screaming and swooping, and below the Atlantic pounding against the cliffs. It was almost beyond belief that anyone would have the nerve to dive down into its depths from such a height. The awesome sight of ocean and cliffs was inducing a sense of desolation in him. Lonely and longing for Laura, he began to have misgivings about turning up.

Laura was on location with a major star. Neither of them might take kindly to his butting in. He might be better advised to turn back and connect up with Laura at the hotel.

Then he spotted two figures ahead. Laura and the actor. Richard Harris was standing profiled against the skyline, red hair gleaming. Even from a distance he radiated an elemental, almost mystical aura. It was quite conceivable, after all, that such a man might plunge from this cliff down into the sea.

Laura's picture would convey this message. Camera in hand she was oblivious to everything else. Richard, as far as she was concerned, might not have been there. Photographer and actor were together in a world from which onlookers were excluded. From which *he* was forever shut out.

Laura's world, he thought sadly – inaccessible to people from his, whatever Laura might say. However Laura might respond to him physically, however she might purport to love him, her world was of more importance than their affair.

He would not be doing her any favours by proposing. Why hadn't he realised that until now? For even if she accepted – and she might even do that – she would live to regret it. She would be bored to tears as his wife. She might stick with it, might continue to care for him, might pour affection over the children, might never, ever desert her post, but deep down she would be resentful at having been deprived of her career.

231

So run, he said to himself. Run not so much for your life, but for Laura's. Move fast – for any minute now she will turn and see you and it will be too late.

But Laura remained where she was. It was Richard who wheeled about, retraced his steps and almost ran back to the car. In all of ten minutes he was at the hotel.

'You found her, did you?' the receptionist said in her friendly way.

'Look,' said Richard, 'I'm terribly sorry about this but, after all, I can't stay.'

'All right so.'

'I wonder – could you do me a favour?'

'It would be a pleasure.'

'Don't tell Miss Conway that I was here.'

He produced a ten-pound note. The receptionist took it and tucked it into the pocket of her blouse. 'I never saw sight nor sound of you. Safe journey home.'

She didn't seem to find his behaviour in the least bit odd. The Irish were ever tolerant of eccentrics, he thought, and thank God for it.

At Shannon he waited three hours for a flight to London. He couldn't ever remember feeling more unhappy, not even when Rebecca had died. Because, in a sense, Laura, too, was dead – or their affair was moribund. He was at the beginning of mourning.

Laura would grieve, too. He would not be able to provide consolation – anything but. To help both of them he would remove himself from the scene. In the morning he would tell Donald he was leaving at once for Johannesburg. Donald wouldn't mind.

And in a few weeks he would tell Laura what decision he had made. To a large extent his mind was already made up.

He went to the bar.

'What will you have to drink, sir?'

'A double Paddy,' he said.

THE hotel, part of a large shopping complex in the central city, was adjacent to a department store and a soaring office block. Richard's room on the nineteenth floor provided an excellent view of concrete buildings and man-made mountains of tailings and rocks from disused gold mines.

The city had been built on the grid system. In the early mining days, corner sites on what was to become Africa's most advanced town had commanded the highest prices. To this end the mining commissioners of the Boer Republic of the Transvaal had ensured that camps were laid out in small blocks. Ninety years later the result was tidy but monotonous.

It was a city with its roots embedded in gold and its people divided: affluent Whites luxuriantly housed in its chic northern suburbs; the unblest Afrikaaners, Portuguese and Spanish immigrants tucked away in the south. And further south still the Indian suburb of Lenasia and beyond that the south-west township of Soweto, official home for one million Blacks.

Within these divisions were others with which Richard was already familiar. In the northern suburbs – where, today, he was to lunch – Jewish businessmen and their families congregated in one area; wealthy Afrikaaners in another; and those of British descent in a third.

On previous visits Richard had been faintly irritated by these inter-White social partitions. Now, in flight from chaos, he craved order and regimentation. The concrete metropolis beneath him could not be termed attractive but its functionality had an appeal.

Why in any case criticise Johannesburg since it was soon to

become his adopted city? Shortly, he and the children would be taking up residence here.

Loose ends remained to be tied up. Before returning to London he would have to buy a house, employ staff and book the children into appropriate schools. The London flat would have to be let. Not sold. The volatility of Africa underlined the need for a bolt-hole.

Much to do. But easy work. Less simple would be the task of extricating the children from Laura and Eileen. As to detaching himself permanently from his love . . .

He had been in Johannesburg for a whole week without phoning Laura, an Herculean achievement, but not one of which he was particularly proud. The mere thought of Laura cast shadows over the otherwise brilliantly sunny day. The invisible chains of love stretched out from London to Johannesburg to bind him to her.

But maybe she wasn't in London. Maybe she was in Paris or New York or Tokyo. If she only remained static, he thought, there would have been no need for a break . . .

No thinking of Laura! In any case he had to be making tracks, not standing around in a hotel bedroom brooding about love.

The Newmans had asked him to lunch, a *braai* – or barbecue – in the garden of their Parktown home, a come-casual get-together.

He took the lift to the ground floor. Uniformed Africans wearing the masks of courtesy and deference rushed forward to open doors and bring around his car. Expressing thanks and donating tips he marvelled at their tolerance and patience. What would happen when their reserves of both ran dry? Was he doing the right thing by the children in bringing them here?

To get to Parktown he drove through Hillbrow, the most densely populated square mile in the whole world. High-rise apartments soared up further than he could see. Outside a shopping centre a group of Hell's Angels were assembling on Japanese motor-cycles modified to look like Harley Davidson choppers.

At the Fontana café he bought a box of chocolates for Helen Newman and was accosted on his way out by a small Coloured boy who asked him timidly for ten cents to buy a bun. Richard gave him fifty cents. The child was not much older than Peter, a scrap of humanity classified Black by the law, a waif lost in the Nowhereland that lay between Blacks and Whites. God alone knew where his parents were, or who they had been.

The car had heated up. Sweating, he rolled the windows down and drove into what had once been Johannesburg's most gracious suburb. In Parktown the new aristocracy who had grown up out of the gold rush had flamboyantly recreated a European lifestyle. In this suburb, where land had originally been purchased for prospecting, massive mansions of twenty rooms and more had sprung up in a multitude of styles – Gothic, Renaissance, Georgian, mock-Tudor and Scottish baronial.

Some were a compilation of several styles in one, revelling in turrets and spires, gables and cupolas, art-nouveau ironwork and complexities of vivid stained glass.

The men who had built these mansions had imported not only the timbers, doors, light fittings and plumbings but also the artists who had painted the walls and decorated the ceilings. To run them they had brought out English butlers and governesses, valets and coachmen, housekeepers and maids from France and cooks from Ireland.

No Afrikaaners had lived in this suburb and no true Afrikaaner ever would. To the Dutchmen and their descendants Parktown had long been a hated symbol of British rule, its origins reflected in the names of its streets.

The Newmans lived in Victoria Avenue. Whoever had designed their house had started off with a pleasing Georgian façade, a central doorway on each side of which were two rectangular windows based on pedestal-aprons and surmounted by plain friezes and cornices.

But then – instead perhaps of framing the doorway with Corinthian pilasters – the architect had gone wild. A grotesque and badly-proportioned porch had been added and embellished with hideous gargoyles. To the right ran an incongruous *stoep* from which a pedestal supported a smaller balcony. Along this a shoal of dolphins swam.

Richard shuddered and rang the doorbell. The oak door was promptly opened not by a French maid but by a sturdy African woman in a black dress and a crisp white apron.

'Good morning, Master,' she said.

Richard was temporarily blinded by the move from intense sunlight into the interior of the house. He could hear the chatter of voices and the clank of glasses. Adjusting his vision he saw an open white marble stairway and an extraordinary mural along the right-hand wall, a riot of Italian Gothic depicting haloed figures, a church, a castle, mountains . . .

The maid stood waiting.

'Sorry,' he muttered and followed her through the house on to a patio where a number of people in swimsuits and casual clothes had gathered around a kidney-shaped pool.

They were sun-tanned and healthy-looking and the women were elegantly slim. By comparison he felt physically and mentally washed out, a laughably pale Englishman perspiring in clothes designed for another climate.

'Richard!' Colin said. 'Come in. Have a drink. What will it be?'

South Africans were hospitable, friendly and curious to the point of intrusion. And positive in their approach to life.

'Vodka and tonic, please.'

He presented the box of chocolates to Helen and was kissed on each cheek.

As was normal on these occasions the party was broken up – further divisions! – into two groups: men in one, women in the other. The men, he thought, would be talking business or sport; the women, children or maids.

Colin conducted him towards his peer group where a cricket match at the Wanderers' Club was being dissected. From this a discussion evolved about the way the Springboks had been hassled and harried by Peter Hain's Anti-Apartheid Movement during its UK tour.

John Vorster and his government were scathingly criticised for barring the MCC from visiting South Africa two years before because of the inclusion on the team of the Coloured, Basil d'Oliveira.

'Bloody Rock Spiders!' somebody said. 'What can you expect?'

Richard finished his drink and accepted another. On his last visit the sports' impasse had also been discussed in similar terms but he did not object.

One of the women dived into the pool with a resounding splash. She emerged from the waist up, shaking the droplets from her hair. Another woman hovered on the edge of the pool. They were both wearing one-piece bathing suits. In public swimming pools in Johannesburg bikinis were banned. Last year, he recalled, the *Nederduits Gereformeede Kerk* had been waging war on mini-skirts. A drought had been seen as God's punishment for the fashion's evil cult.

The woman at the edge of the pool glanced round and he saw that she was older than she appeared to be from the back, nearer thirty than twenty. Her silvery-blonde, shoulder-length hair was shiny and thick and her eyes very blue. She was long-legged and slim and extremely pretty and no doubt she was married to one of the men discussing cricket.

'Don't swim now, Sophie,' Helen Newman called to her. 'We're going to eat.'

On an iron grill over a pit, steaks, chops, the spicy sausages known as *boerewors*, and *sosaties* – an assortment of curried meats slotted on to skewers – were being turned. Salads had been laid out on a table.

Helen gestured to her husband. 'Doll, it's ready.'

'Come on, Richard, help yourself.'

A plate was put into his hand. He piled it high with meats, wandered over to the table to investigate the salads and found himself next to the blonde.

Her swimsuit, although modest, was covered by a towelling wrap.

'Sensational salads!'

'Let me help you,' said the blonde.

Though South African women often looked as if they had stepped off a film set they were not, as a breed, confident with their menfolk, who regarded them as subservient. As a result the women were deferential and submissive.

The blonde was even prettier close up, a honey of a woman with a honey-coloured tan; and yet there was a naivety about her that came from living so far from the mainstream.

She was planets apart from the women he met in London – as different from Laura as she could be, the only common factor being the colour of their hair. He must stop thinking of Laura.

'Whose wife are you?' he said.

'No one's. I'm divorced. That's my son over there.'

Children of various ages and heights were queuing for food. Her son was about ten years old.

'Do you have other children?'

'No. Just that one.'

'He looks like you.'

'People tell me that. *I* think he resembles Helen.'

'Helen?'

'I'm Helen's sister. I'm Sophie Jurgens.'

'That's a German name.'

'Yes, my ex *is* German. And you're Richard Stacton. Colin said you'd be here today.'

'He's never told *me* about *you*.'

She let this go. She had filled her own plate and was standing as if waiting for him to make the next move.

'Let's get some shade, shall we?' he said.

Side by side they walked to a ring of chairs arranged in a semi-circle under a tree. He was lucky to be with friends, not to be on his own. With sport and films prohibited on the Lord's Day, a South African Sunday would otherwise have been deadly dull.

Where was Laura, he thought? How was she spending this

day? Sooner or later, he supposed, they would be forced to talk on the phone. He would have to contact the children. Laura might answer.

We *can't* have parted, he thought. I haven't really made this decision. Surely not . . . Sitting under the trees, thousands of miles away, he felt closer to Laura than ever.

'Helen says you have children, too,' said Sophie. 'How many?'

'One boy. One girl.'

'And they're coming out here to live with you.'

'Oh, yes. Their mother is dead.'

'How sad. And they're – how old?'

'Nine and seven.'

'Have you organised schools for them?'

'No. Before that I have to buy a house.'

'You'll be looking for servants,' said Sophie. 'I might be able to help you about that. You have to be so careful. But my maid's sister is out of a job.'

'That sounds promising.'

'About schools – Rob – my son – goes to Pridwin. I'm very pleased with it.'

'And for my daughter?'

'Saint Katharine's. It's in Parktown. Very near here.'

'What a fund of information you are. Perhaps I should consult you about my house.'

She started to list the best suburbs. The other chairs in the semi-circle had filled up. The man next to Sophie was telling a story about how two friends of his had come to divorce.

'. . . Pekinese. Snappy thing but she was crazy about it. Anyway, they were driving up from the Cape and Jenny kept nagging about giving the Peke a run. So he pulls up, grabs the Peke out of her arms and slings it into the bush. Then it was put-foot and on to Bloem without a stop!'

His audience giggled.

'That's a *horrible* story,' Sophie said. 'I can't believe anyone would do such a thing.'

She looked genuinely upset. To divert her Richard steered the subject back to the house market.

'Forest Town, you said.'

'Or Parkview,' she elaborated. 'I do envy your house-hunting. I just love going around and seeing what's for sale.'

'Then why don't you come with me? It would help a lot.'

He expected her to say that she couldn't, that she worked during the week or was otherwise busy.

'Would it?' she said. 'Then I'd like to be of help.'

The estate agent was a woman of about forty with a superb body, an artificial smile painted on to the face of experience and a bouffant hairdo.

She wore a tight polyester dress with splotches of purple and yellow on a black background, four gold chains studded with diamonds and precious stones, and gold ankle-strapped sandals. She was driving a red Mercedes.

'Hop in, doll,' she said to Richard, studiously ignoring Sophie who climbed into the back.

The dismissal annoyed him.

'You all right back there?' he said to Sophie.

In contrast to the woman beside him she was supremely elegant in a pale blue linen dress and shoes to match.

'I'm fine,' she said, smiling shyly.

'We're seeing this one first,' said the estate agent, and shoved a piece of paper on to his lap.

'Parktown North? But I thought we were going straight to Inanda. The property there is the one in which I'm interested.'

'*Afterwards*, doll.'

'This isn't what I had in mind.'

'Look. Just look is all I ask.'

Richard gave up. He leant back, grateful that the Mercedes had air-conditioning.

Unlike the city centre, suburban Johannesburg was very attractive indeed, or at least the northern area which he knew best.

Jan Smuts Avenue, along which they were currently speeding

was particularly appealing, with large houses set back in luxuriant, well-maintained gardens. Africans in overalls hosed, mowed and weeded, some of them Zulus with discs as big as the top of a tea-cup gouged into the extended lobes of their ears.

They reached a set of traffic lights and turned off the main road. To their right was a small artificial lake surrounded by pretty parkland.

'Zoo Lake is just to die for, isn't it?' observed Sophie. 'I take the dogs here every morning for their walk.'

'How many dogs?'

'Just two. A poodle and an Alsatian.'

'I'm really pushing the buyer on this property,' the estate agent said. 'I might get it down a bit for you.'

They pulled up at a gate with a 'For Sale' notice prominently displayed.

Richard took stock of the property. 'It isn't what I – '

'Take a look,' said the estate agent. 'What trouble is it to me to show it to you?'

She set off along the pathway waving a bunch of keys.

'Honestly!' Richard said. '*Shall* we take a look?'

'I suppose so,' said Sophie.

A dog was barking inside the house. As they neared the front door someone shouted, 'Shut *up*, Scrappy!' from the interior.

'She's in,' the estate agent said unnecessarily, and the door opened to reveal a bare-footed maid with a duster in her hand.

'Madam's got guests.'

'She wants to sell or she doesn't wanta sell?'

The maid looked lost. The question was obviously beyond her power to answer.

'She's got to make up her mind,' said the estate agent. 'She isn't sitting on oil.'

'Look – ' Richard began and caught Sophie's eye. Her blue ones were twinkling with merriment. The heaviness which had been weighing him down since leaving London lifted a fraction.

They went back to the car. The property which had interested him all along was in Inanda, pony and polo country. *His* house came complete with tennis court, pool and rolling lawns.

Its lych-gate was over-topped with thatch.

'This is a real classy house,' the estate agent said. 'If you want class you've got to have it – hey?'

'Exactly!'

A gardener opened the gate. The Mercedes oozed its way up an imposing tree-lined avenue to a paved parking space in the middle of which was an enormous oak tree.

'Classy – hey?'

He stared at the back of a double-storey thatched residence, flanked by a series of white-washed out-buildings.

'Guest cottages?'

'Servants' quarters. Luxurious, aren't they?'

'Not electrified.'

'You want that They burn it down?'

He was beginning to feel like the maid in the previous house, continually confronted by questions to which he could not reply.

The estate agent, he thought, was probably the most monstrous woman he had ever met. He and Sophie followed her round the side of the house to its front. Here a central *stoep* curved out into a half moon. Over it was a thatched porch supported by poles.

A second gardener stood aside to let them pass. A maid with downcast eyes showed them into a vast sitting-room, its roof open to the rafters. Doors led, presumably to bedrooms, from a minstrels' gallery.

'I like it already,' Richard said. 'Sophie what do *you* think?'

'I love it.'

Every bit as appealing as its appearance was the price of the house. In England, he knew, it would have bought a nondescript semi-detached.

They went upstairs. Within minutes he had clinched the deal. After that it seemed appropriate to invite Sophie to dinner.

'To celebrate,' he said.

Once again she accepted without demur, with the proviso that he stop first at her place for a pre-dinner drink.

'You can meet Rob. You know – my son. He'd like to hear about Peter and Cassie.'

He was touched by her recollection of the children's names. It crossed his mind that he should phone and tell them about the house. But that might mean getting Laura on the line. He shied away from the thought, replaced it with practical considerations.

By this evening Sophie was hoping to have tracked down her maid's sister. It was, she had said, much easier to recruit a gardener. And she had come up trumps, too, where schools were concerned, with a promise to introduce him to the staff at Pridwin and Saint Katharine's. The South African school year began not in September but in January, which suited his plans. November was almost upon them already. The children would have some six weeks to settle in before meeting their new classmates.

By New Year they would have made friends with Sophie's son. He envisaged the three of them leaping into the pool and playing tennis. All thanks to Sophie. What a nice woman she was. Would she also help him to furnish the house?

He listened to the radio news. There was no television in South Africa but he did not think he would miss it, not in this climate.

Bathing and dressing, he mused about the good life he and the children were going to have: sunshine, outdoor living, plenty of sport. The novelty would help Peter and Cassie get over the break with Barnes.

He would recover, too. And maybe one day he would find a replacement for Laura. That woman would not have a career. South African women did not suffer from constant jet-lag. They stayed put, looking after their husbands and children and homes and gardens. The Sixties, which had liberated British women, had not altered their lifestyle one whit, not as far as he could see. Women like Sophie – well-mannered, gentle, delightfully feminine – were creatures of the Fifties and no worse for it.

Sophie in particular was very sweet. He must stop on the way to her house and buy her flowers.

Unaware that he was humming, he combed his hair, checked his tie and set off down the corridor to the lift. Waiting for it to arrive he thought he heard the telephone ring in his room. But he did not go back.

Less than a week later his plane touched down at Heathrow.

He had left Johannesburg in what was for him lately a relatively light-hearted state. Unusually, he had slept on the flight, and instead of having a muzzy head and a sluggish body he felt alert and rested.

At Sophie's suggestion he had left most of his clothes behind at her place – 'Why take them all the way to London only to bring them back again in a few weeks' time?' she had said sensibly – and travelled with hand-luggage.

With his travel bag over his shoulder and his briefcase in his hand he sauntered through the customs hall without arousing interest.

It was still only six-twenty A.M. The flight had been fifteen minutes early. He could grab a taxi without fear of getting snarled up in the morning traffic, go home, shave and shower, and be at the office before nine A.M.

He emerged from customs into a sea of bodies, three international flights having come in within a few minutes of each other.

Back to the rat-race! But not for long.

The woman in front of him gave a cry of joy and was hugged in a most unBritish manner by a grey-haired man. A hippy with dirty feet bumped into him without saying sorry. God, he thought, who needs people en masse? South Africa was far from Hippyland and you couldn't call the Transvaal with its vast veld and rolling hills a built-up province. Even bustling Johannesburg was a mere village in comparison to London. Only a few weeks . . .

'Richard?'

Someone had put a hand on his arm. *Laura*! Her touch sent a charge through him. All the emotions he had switched off this last week were reconnected.

Only a week? So much had happened in those few days . . .

'Hello,' he said warily. 'What a surprise.'

'I thought I should come to meet you.'

'You came by car?'

'Yes. You came through incredibly quickly. I've only just got here.'

'I just brought hand-luggage. It was good of you to come.'

He could hear himself sounding formal and disengaged, which was how he wanted to be with Laura. He reminded himself that it was all over between them, that he must not – for *both* their sakes – become entangled again. Inside his head a conflict was raging between instinct and common sense, sapping his energy. The lively man who had disembarked from the plane was fast fading, like an old sepia print.

Laura flinched. The urge to embrace her was powerful. Instead he clutched at his travel bag as if it was a shield that could protect him from himself.

'Where are you parked?'

'One up.'

She was wearing her pink coat. Her hair was freshly washed and her cheeks were flushed. She might have been any wife welcoming back her husband from an overseas trip.

But she was not his wife and she never would be.

'How are the children?'

'Fine. A bit disappointed that you didn't phone, but they'll get over it.'

He let that pass.

'They didn't want to come out with you?'

'Whatever ambitions they had on that score weren't sustained through the night! They were fast asleep when I left.'

An Asian family with two trolleys loaded with luggage came between them. I'll have to tell her at once, Richard thought. I

245

can't drive all the way to Barnes making polite conversation, feeling like a hypocrite.

The car park was full. Laura peered around for the car. 'I think it was one up.'

'There it is. Do you want to drive?'

'Not particularly.'

She gave him the key. Inside the car was evidence of the children having been there: crumpled paper from an Aero bar, a pair of discarded socks.

Shit, he thought, hating the thought of what he had yet to say and do.

He reversed out of the parking bay and drove down the ramp and Laura in her pink coat sat beside him, her lips sealed. She had no true comprehension of what was wrong between them. In her eyes they had quarrelled and could now make up.

Shit!

'We've got to talk,' he said. 'I need to have half an hour with you on our own. Is that all right?'

'I know we've got to talk.'

Her conciliatory manner made it worse. Better if she had taken an aggressive stance, if a fight had developed, providing him with an excuse to make the break. It couldn't be made in the car – that was too cold-blooded.

'In that case can we go to the flat?'

It was even worse than he had expected. Laura launched straight into an explanation about a woman called Lorraine.

He could not recall Lorraine, could not imagine why, after mentioning her, Laura should burst into tears and carry on about her hair being too fine, and how old she was, and how she had never been a beauty, even when she was young.

'But you *are* beautiful,' Richard said, bewildered by this. 'And age never came into it.'

'But it must matter,' wailed Laura. 'I'm eight years older than you.'

'Why should that matter?'

246

He shouldn't have asked her that because she perked up and he had to remind himself again that there was no way – *none* – that the relationship could be saved.

If it could be – if it could be made to work – he would have taken her straight to bed which was what he wanted to do anyway. Instead, he went into the kitchen and put the kettle on with the declared intention of making her tea.

While he was doing so Laura went to the bathroom. She came into the sitting-room with her face newly made-up and faith shining out of her grey eyes.

'Sorry about that.'

Lovely as she was she would never fit into his new life in Johannesburg. Her ambition and personality would never be satisfied by the Transvaal.

But there was love for him written all over her face and his own feelings for her were so intense that he couldn't contain them.

He put the tea tray down and was about to step forward to embrace her, to tell her that, in spite of having accepted the transfer to South Africa, bought a house and furniture, employed servants and booked his children into new schools, he was going to change his plans.

She wouldn't like it there so, for her sake, he would remain in London. They would get married – if that was what she wanted. And as for the demands of her photographic career, surely, in the face of such affection, they could work things out?

They . . . He froze, stared. Laura's handbag, unfastened, was lying on the coffee table. Inside it was her camera. It had travelled with her to the airport at six A.M. It would always be with her.

His heart hardened. Laura and he could never marry. She was already wedded to her career. All the compromises in their relationship would be his, not hers. They could never work it out.

'Tea,' said Laura. 'Just what I need.'

Shit, he thought, and he poured the tea and told her that he was leaving her and she wept again.

*

247

After a while she seemed to regain control of herself. She said, no, she didn't want a lift to Barnes. It was extravagant but she would catch a taxi from the rank in Sloane Square. There was no point in his coming to Barnes, she said. The children would already have gone to school. He should come in the afternoon by which time she would be out of the way . . .

While she was saying all this Richard was standing by the window.

She got up and came towards him with her coat over her arm and he thought that she was about to kiss him goodbye and he clenched his hands.

She did no such thing. She wrenched open the window, admitting a blast of cold air, and threw her pink coat out of it.

'You can't – you'll catch your death of cold,' he said idiotically, but she was already running across the room.

The door shut behind her. Richard was rooted to the spot. The downstairs door slammed. Laura appeared on the pavement.

'Wait!' he shouted. 'I'll drive you – '

She didn't look up. She ran along Cadogan Gardens hailing a cab.

Her pink coat lay where it had fallen, in the middle of the road. Bright as it was passers-by did not notice it. As he watched, a car drove over one of its sleeves.

He closed the window and sat down with his head in his hands, thinking numbly that he should shower and go to work.

He did all these things in the end, after half an hour had gone by. But before doing so he went into his bedroom and picked up the phone and dialled a Johannesburg number and got through to an African maid.

'Is that Mrs Jurgens' house?' said Richard. 'Can I speak to the madam, please?'

SOPHIE

1970 – 1971

THE day before Richard made the break with Laura, Sophie was taking shelter indoors from a thunderstorm. The first white cumulus clouds had appeared at noon, ice-cream dollops which had turned black in the afternoon. Fingers of forked lightning flicked out of the clouds, illuminating a sky purple and red with rage.

In the middle of this Sophie's mother, Geraldine Ward, called with the air of one who has news to impart.

'Hannie has been to see me.'

'My ex?'

'Who else do I call Hannie? He's moved back to Jo'burg.'

'Hannie has?'

'Just this week past. I was glad he came to see me. We always hit it off.'

'What did he want?'

'I'm coming to that. It was so nice to see him again – '

'Mother, get to the point.'

Mrs Ward sighed. 'I've never really understood what happened with you and Hannie. You never talk about it. But I do think you should try to be friendly, for Rob's sake.'

'So that's what it's all about. He wants to see Rob.'

'Well, why shouldn't he? He's Rob's father, after all. He was granted custody rights, Sophie. You shouldn't come between them.'

'I don't want to discuss it,' said Sophie coldly. 'Yes, Seraphina, what do you want?'

'Sugar is finished, Madam.'

'Take some money and go to the shop.'

'They put *five* spoonfuls in their tea,' Mrs Ward said when the maid had gone. 'They drink the tea and then they spoon it up. There must be something missing in their make-up.'

'You're not thinking of driving back to Pretoria in this weather, are you? I think you should stay the night. Rob would be pleased about that.'

'You see everything through that child's eyes,' said Mrs Ward, but she did stay, and she was still there the next day when Richard phoned.

'*He's* not wasting any time, is he?' she said when Sophie returned to the lounge after taking the call. 'What's he like?'

'He's charming. You'd approve!'

'When is he coming back?'

It was not easy to keep secrets from Mrs Ward. Did I manage to keep her from finding out about Hannie, Sophie thought?

She did not have to hide anything about Richard Stacton. Still it might be preferable if her mother did not intrude upon the relationship. Richard was very English and therefore likely to be reticent about his affairs.

Not that they were having an affair . . .

'In a few weeks – hm. What does Rob think of him?'

'Rob liked him. But then Rob is such a friendly child. Richard has a son about his age. We think they'll become friends.'

'I thought you said he had two children.'

'He does. The girl is younger.'

'Three is a nice size for a family,' Mrs Ward said. 'It would be very good for Rob to have other children around the house. Not to mention a father.'

'Mother, please. Are you stopping for lunch?'

'I've got Bridge at two so I can't. Sophie, please will you think again about Hannie seeing Rob?'

It was much more pleasant to think of Richard. Sophie changed into her swimsuit and lay by the pool, upgrading her tan and indulging in recollection.

Richard was a gentleman without any of the brashness that

characterised South African men. Like them, he was a go-getter. But he had a subtlety that they lacked. Unlike them, he apparently enjoyed the company of women.

Growing up, Sophie had dreamt of a Richard, an Englishman of the calibre of those who appeared in British films. In South Africa there were lots of men with English blood in their veins, descendants of the 1820 Settlers or others who had emigrated from England in more recent years. But these men were happier being together in clubs. They preferred watching rugby or cricket to being with their wives. They did not cosset their womenfolk and they considered those who did so to be unmanly.

Richard wasn't like that. And Rob *had* taken to him. That was the second most important thing, the first being that any man who entered her life should be good for Rob.

It *was* excellent that Richard had children of his own. His concern for their welfare had given her added insight into his personality. Richard would never endanger Rob. Not like Hannie . . .

Her shoulders were getting pink. She reached out for the suntan lotion. Dabbing it on, smoothing it into her skin, she thought of Hannie's request.

What had got into him to have made it? Surely he knew that she would never, ever allow him to see Rob? As far as that relationship went, Hannie was dead. Rob understood that. He knew his father had acted so badly (but that, naturally, was all he knew about Hannie's behaviour) that he had been outlawed.

Since he was an exceptionally equable and loving child, Rob had accepted his mother's ruling. There was always the worry that later, in adolescence perhaps, he might ask questions which could not be answered. But he wasn't making inquiries now and he might never do so.

As for Hannie's pathetic request, it was of little or no concern. Irritating, yes, and puzzling, but not a threat. Hannie would never dare to see Rob without her permission. Hannie was no fool. He knew that she had the upper hand where Rob was concerned.

She checked her shoulders. Ten more minutes and that would be enough. She must not burn.

She rolled over on to her stomach and saw the maid Seraphina coming up the driveway after having been to the shops.

Sending a servant on an errand inevitably meant giving them an hour off work. Seraphina knew most of the other maids who worked in this road and would have stopped for a chat. They were always popping in and out of their employers' homes. You returned home to find another girl wolfing down great hunks of bread and drinking tea and talking to Seraphina. Either that or the two of them would have disappeared out to Seraphina's room, leaving kitchen and phone unattended.

There was nothing you could do to stop it, any more than you could check what men Seraphina had in her room after sundown. Under the law men were not permitted to stay in these rooms overnight, not even husbands, but the rules were always flouted. You just had to turn a blind eye and hope that whoever was there wasn't a *tsotsie* who would burgle the house or stick a knife in your back.

Seraphina had paused half-way up the drive. She was standing there as if she needed a rest although she had not walked far. There was something about her stance, the way her free hand spreadeagled out over her ample stomach that made Sophie catch her breath.

So Seraphina had stood during her last pregnancy. Her condition then had sickened and frightened Sophie so that she had barely been able to tolerate having the girl in the house.

But – the baby had been a boy. And afterwards Sophie had felt sorry for Seraphina and had allowed her – illegally – to keep the child with her in her room.

It hadn't worked out because Seraphina, not wanting to leave the child alone when she went to the shops, had wrapped him in a blanket and hoisted him on to her back and the neighbours in the next house but one had complained to the police.

For this offence Sophie had been fined and Seraphina forced to take her child – who would be nearly two by now – back to live with her mother in Natal along with her two older children.

And here she was, getting pregnant again. Didn't they ever learn? The baby had doubtless been conceived after a casual encounter. Africans didn't care much about patrimony. The baby, illegitimate or not, would be welcomed into Seraphina's family. Whatever its sex.

It might be a girl . . . Sophie felt physically sick at the thought. She had lain down in the garden with Richard on her mind, allowing herself to get enthusiastic about the prospect of their meeting again. But Seraphina, simply by standing in the avenue, had pushed Richard out of her mind and let Hannie get in again.

Twelve years before, when Sophie was only eighteen, she had been standing at a bus-stop in Hillbrow. She had just done her Matriculation but she had not yet passed her driving test so whenever she wanted to go to town she had to catch a bus.

Hillbrow wasn't town as such but her mother had asked her to drop some material off at a dressmaker's in Kotze Street. So there she had been, filling in the time by holding an imaginary conversation with her father who wanted her to go to secretarial school as Helen had done.

'All girls should be trained for something.'

'Why? I'm not going to work. I'm going to get married and have babies. What's wrong with that?'

'You mustn't get married too young.'

'I'm not young. I'm eighteen. I've left school already.'

It was a drowsy afternoon and the bench on which she had failed to get a seat was occupied by somnambulant people.

'Believe me, you're young!' her father said silently inside her head, which was when she glanced down the street and saw someone else waiting at another bus stop.

He was a young man with very blond hair. She noticed him for two reasons – one because he looked rather like herself (how odd); and two because he was naively standing at a bus-stop reserved for Blacks.

How funny. He must be a foreigner to South Africa. No one

who lived here would be so stupid.

Shame, Sophie thought. Her own bus was almost due but the two stops were only a few yards apart.

She went over to the young man. 'Excuse me, but you're at the wrong stop. You should be in our queue.'

'I should?'

She had been right. He had a foreign accent.

'This stop is for Blacks.'

'Ah. Ja. Blacks.'

He must be German. He followed her back to the correct stop and waited beside her.

'Thank you,' he said. 'I am only now coming here.'

The bus was late. In the interim Sophie learnt that her companion had only recently arrived from Stuttgart to stay with his uncle and aunt.

'They are here in Johannesburg since 1948.'

That was the year the Nationalist government had come to power. British immigration had thereafter been discouraged in favour of German.

'Why did you come? Are your parents dead?'

'My father yes, in the war. My mother and my sisters are alive. But now it is bad in Germany. My uncle and my aunt are rich. They say to me come here.'

His uncle and aunt lived in Sandhurst, a suburb of which her mother would approve.

'What does your uncle do?'

'He is buying hotels. He has three.'

That, too, was encouraging.

'And are you going to work for him?'

The young man shook his head.

'No. I do not like to work for family business. Today I have been for interview for Fraser's Stores. Do you know this company?'

Fraser's Stores traded, primarily to Blacks, in the rural areas of South Africa and the British Protectorate.

'My father is Sir Ian Fraser's attorney,' said Sophie proudly.

'Ja? Then we are friends.'

The bus came. They got on, sat next to each other and exchanged names and ages. He was Hans Jurgens and he would be twenty next month.

Close to, the resemblance between them was stronger. Sophie had heard that people who looked alike were often attracted to each other.

Hans *was* attractive, although his skin was pale as could be and he had a spot on his chin.

Those were the days before Geraldine Ward, widowed, had moved to Pretoria. The Wards were living on the Oxford road.

Just before Sophie's stop one of the power transmission poles that linked the trolley bus to the overhead wire became detached. The bus stopped and the traffic came to a halt. The conductor got out.

Hans looked out of the window, fascinated by what was going on. From under the bus the conductor pulled a very long bamboo pole with a hook on one end. With this he attempted – unsuccessfully – to coax the end of the pole back on to the wires.

While this operation was being undertaken the passengers were resigning themselves to baking in the sun.

'I'm getting out,' Sophie said. 'Would you like to come home with me and have a cool drink?'

'Ja. Thank you.'

'Are you being met in Rosebank?'

'Excuse, please?'

'Is your aunt going to drive you from Rosebank to Sandhurst?'

He shook his head.

'But the bus terminates in Rosebank. How are you going to get to Sandhurst from there?'

'I will walk.'

'Walk?'

White people didn't walk from suburb to suburb, only Blacks.

'I do not have a car so I walk.'

Things must be very bad indeed in Germany to make people accept such notions.

Her mother was home. Sophie introduced Hans. Mrs Ward

summoned up cool drinks and cakes, took a liking to the young man and offered to drive him home. By then he had taken Sophie's phone number.

The following day he phoned to say that he had got the job with Fraser's. Almost as an afterthought he asked Sophie out.

Within the month they were inseparable. Over the next year Sophie gave in and did a secretarial course. But she never worked. At the end of the year Hans was promoted. He bought Sophie an engagement ring.

Her father capitulated. He, too, liked Hans. Six months later they got married.

She was not the only one in her circle to marry young but she felt that she was doing better than the others who had.

Hans was going places. She drew vicarious pleasure from her husband's potential. Power excited her. Money was secondary. Sex further down the line of her priorities, in spite of her genuine feeling for Hans. She had expected bed to be more romantic, less carnal than it proved to be, but they got by.

Pregnant with Rob, Sophie was happier than she had ever been in her life.

Seraphina was trudging up the drive to the house. Sophie got moving, too. She decided that she would have a light lunch, salad and fruit – she must not put on weight – and get her hair set before picking Rob up from Pridwin. The majority of her friends had their hair blow-dried but it didn't last. And she could do with a manicure.

'Seraphina?'

'Coming, madam.'

She pronounced it 'medem' as they always did.

'Lettuce and tomatoes and cucumber. Are the avos ripe?'

'Yes, madam.'

She *was* pregnant.

'No meat?'

'On second thoughts I'm not hungry.'

What if Seraphina gave birth to a girl? Her other children were boys, all three of them.

I couldn't bear it, Sophie thought. If it's a girl she'll have to leave. And once again she thought about Hannie and the terrible thing he had done to herself and Rob.

There should have been other children. She had banked on two, spaced out with a couple of years between their births.

Meanwhile, there was glorious Rob, most enchanting of babies, to monopolise their attention. Hannie, like herself, was besotted with his son.

He was an excellent father then. He got up at night to tend the baby. He had no inhibitions about changing nappies or giving bottles. He couldn't do enough, for either of them. Sophie's happiness had spread out like the sun over the veld.

There was one little drawback. After the birth, sex between herself and Hannie was never quite right. She had never been that enthusiastic about lovemaking and – with Rob as proof – she began to think of it only as a means of procreation. And they weren't ready yet for another baby. So, in a way, sex was unnecessary, a relief to Hannie but a bit of a trial for her.

But it wasn't a serious problem. Most women, Sophie thought, had to contend with their husband's demands. It wasn't as if she didn't love Hannie, or as if she refused to give in to him in bed.

Hannie was promoted again. His work for Fraser's took him around South Africa, into Swaziland and Lesotho, where the company had a chain of rural trading stores. Hannie adored Swaziland which he said was racially advanced. Apartheid had never made inroads there, Swaziland being a British Protectorate, and not falling under the rule of the NATs. But, said Hannie, Whites in Swaziland are less obsessed with race than Rhodesians or Kenyans. In those countries people who purport to disapprove of apartheid still believe in their own superiority.

It was the kind of conversation that made Sophie uneasy. She was glad none of her friends were present to hear Hannie saying these things. They would conclude that he was dangerously Liberal or that he was developing Communist inclinations instead of fundamentally being a kind person who got on with Blacks. He did tend to treat them as equals, even when he was at home. He should know better than to do that.

She didn't voice these criticisms to Hannie himself, or to anyone else either. She never argued with men. By nature she was loyal.

'You must take me with you to Swaziland one of these days,' she said, not wanting to go but trying to appear enthusiastic about his interests.

'Yes, I must,' said Hannie. 'Why don't you come with me on the next trip?'

Sophie vacillated. Rob was nearly two, a bad age for long car journeys. A holiday in Mbabane did not appeal to her. She would have preferred to fly to Cape Town and spend a couple of weeks in the Mount Nelson Hotel. Down there she would be able to relax. She should be having another baby but, so far, she had failed to conceive.

'Maybe the trip after next . . .'

So Hannie drove on his own to Mbabane and it was fortunate Rob was not in the car with him because just outside the Swazi capital he collided with an African bus.

No one was killed and only Hannie – who had not been at fault – sustained injuries, breaking an arm and a leg.

The first Sophie heard of this was when Fraser's contacted her to say Hannie was in hospital. He remained there for three weeks but Sophie did not go to see him because Rob got mumps.

Hannie understood that she couldn't abandon Rob in his favour even if Helen *had* volunteered to stand in. And he was being well looked after in Mbabane hospital, albeit by African staff. It was odd to think of her husband being intimately tended by Blacks, but Sophie only gave this passing thought.

He was not quite himself when he came home. She put this down to delayed reaction after the accident and to Hannie being uncomfortable in plaster in the summer heat.

When the casts were removed he continued to travel but he didn't again suggest a joint visit to Swaziland. Nor did they get around to a holiday in the Cape. Hannie said he couldn't afford the time, having been off work for so long.

Sophie did not become pregnant again. Worried, she consulted a gynaecologist and was reassured that nothing was wrong, it would happen in due course.

But they didn't make love that often. On the one hand that was a relief, but on the other hand, how could she get pregnant without regular sex?

Hannie, she thought, was rundown after the accident. He would recover and revert back to being his old passionate self. But a year went by and then another year and Hannie remained passive. Rob was four and badly in need of a brother or sister.

Sophie began to run out of patience with Hannie. He should snap out of it, she thought. All he had done was break an arm and a leg, both of which had mended. Neither his brain nor his genitals had been damaged in the crash.

His integrity as a man, however, was unimpaired in her eyes. Hannie was just as generous, just as hardworking as ever, and just as devoted to Rob.

One day she decided to sort out his wardrobe, and sell off his shabbier clothes to Seraphina. There was one jacket which she disliked. She checked the pockets in case Hannie had left money in there, and found a dirty handkerchief, a few cents and – in the inside breast pocket – an envelope with a Swazi stamp.

There was a letter inside the envelope. She had never spied on Hannie, never before felt the need to do so, but she instinctively felt that she should read it.

It was short, to the point, but it administered a *coup de grâce* to her marriage.

'Greatifications!' it said.

My brother Dhlamini will get married on 14 June. Please come for this. You will not mind that you are the only White person there!

Our daughter is well and beautiful,
My love,
Christina.

Hannie didn't try to deny it. He came out with the whole story explaining that Christina was a nurse, that she had looked after him when he was in hospital and that he was the father of her child.

Sophie did not ask how old the child was or what name she had been given. She was motivated by only one thought – the need to get rid of Hannie.

It was not only the heinous offence he had committed against herself that tortured her, although forever afterwards she would feel dirty, knowing that Hannie had slept with a Black woman and then with her. Africans were riddled with VD. Everyone knew that. It was a miracle that he hadn't passed an infection on to her.

He had. But the sickness was in her soul, not her body.

It was not only what he had done to her. What he had done to Rob was infinitely worse. Hannie had created a Coloured half-sister for his son. To Sophie, this was as if he had sired a monster of iniquity. For that reason, she said, he must never, ever see Rob again.

In vain Hannie pleaded with her to have mercy. Sophie was adamant. If Hannie attempted to visit Rob she would have him gaoled. Sex between the races was forbidden by law.

Hannie could have pointed out that his offence had been committed in Swaziland where South African law did not apply. But Hannie was crippled by guilt. Faced by the force of Sophie's wrath he retreated.

He gave Sophie a divorce and a huge settlement which ensured that she never would have to work. He paid for Rob's education and he put money aside for his son in a trust fund. Even Sophie had to admit that he could not be faulted on these scores.

Before they parted she made him swear that he would never

divulge the reason for their divorce. Rob must never know of the existence of his Coloured sister. No one must. She did not even tell her parents, or her sister what had occurred.

She glared at Hannie and she wondered if he was mad enough to consider marrying this Christina when the divorce came through. Suppose he did and suppose the story came out through that?

But Hannie was not going to get married again, he said. Once was enough. He was going to get out of everyone's way and move to Cape Town. Where doubtless in due course he would take another Black mistress – or a Cape-Coloured.

And perhaps he had, thought Sophie, stepping out of her swimsuit, getting into the bath, and afterwards putting on fresh make-up and a newly-laundered dress – pale yellow, one of her best shades. Perhaps he had.

Hannie was German, after all. Germans – as everyone realised after the war – went in for depravities.

Richard, being an English gentleman, would never behave like Hannie.

A MONTH later Richard made another phone call to Sophie, from Johannesburg.

In between he had called on several occasions from London, asking her what she was doing and telling her how it was going at his end. According to him the children and work were eating up every minute of his time, which was what she wanted to hear.

Here he was back for good, looking forward – so he said – to seeing her and to introducing Rob and herself to Peter and Cassie.

'Bring them round. Rob's just dying to meet them.'

'Why don't you two come here? Are you free tomorrow? Being Saturday I know Rob won't be at school but – '

'We are free,' said Sophie.

Rob was playing cricket but for once he could get out of it. 'Can't you, darling?'

Rob pulled a face. Even with his nose and mouth contorted he was a beautiful boy, thought Sophie – blond and blue-eyed, with long, sun-tanned limbs.

'It's difficult, Mom.'

'*Try*. Richard's children are pining to meet you. They don't know anyone here. They must be lonely and you know their mother is dead.'

Rob had a soft heart, which could ultimately work to his disadvantage. She worried about that. He also had charm which worked. He was allowed to go to Inanda for lunch.

Sophie had asked if she could help to prepare the meal or at least bring along some salads but Richard had declined. Eileen, the children's nanny who had come out for six months to help them settle in, was going to cook.

How grand to have a European nanny. Sophie imagined a tall, upright, uniformed figure with total control over her charges.

It was a shock therefore when Richard's door was opened not by Seraphina's sister Veronica but by a dumpy woman in a crimplene dress whose gaze was as steely as her hair.

'There you are so,' she said to Sophie, not in the least deferential.

'Good afternoon,' said Sophie formally. 'I'm Mrs Jurgens. My son and I have been invited to lunch.'

'Don't I know that already? Will you come on in. We're in the sitting-room.'

We? Surely Richard didn't allow this unfashionable creature to sit in the lounge as if she was family?

Put out, she followed Eileen – for who else could it be – into the house.

Richard was sitting in one of the easy chairs which she had helped him buy.

'Sophie! How lovely to see you. Shall we sit outside?'

'I'd *love* to sit in your nice garden.'

She was looking forward to being alone with Richard. They had a whole month on which to catch up. Veronica brought coffee.

'I don't take sugar,' Sophie said – and Cassie came into the garden and sat at Richard's feet.

'Dad, can we phone Laura this evening?'

There was a moment's silence. Then Richard said, 'Maybe. We'll see.'

'She said she'd be back today.'

'Did she?'

'You know. Please, Dad. I haven't seen her for ages. She's been in France for a whole month.'

Richard grunted.

'Dad?'

'Who's Laura?' Sophie asked.

There was another silence, after which Richard said,

'My mother-in-law. The children's grandmother.'

So that explained Laura.

After that the two families got into the habit of meeting at weekends, sometimes at the Stactons' but more often at the Jurgens' so Eileen, said Sophie, could have a break.

These get-togethers yielded positive results. The friendship strengthened between Rob and Peter. Sophie's relationship with Richard developed, too.

Some Saturday evenings and once or twice during the week Richard and Sophie went out on their own. They got along well together. Sophie was a good listener although Richard told her more about his work than about his private life in London.

Before long he would try to take her to bed. Sophie was not averse to the idea. The days when a woman held out until after marriage were forever gone, even in South Africa – at least, at their stage.

She was confident that Richard would propose. He was in dire need of a wife. Two months had gone by and in another four Eileen would have gone. The children had to be mothered. Richard's beautiful house required a woman's touch.

Running such an establishment was a full-time job. Veronica and the garden boys should be chivvied up, flowers arranged, dinner parties given, all of which Richard must have realised.

She sensed that he was letting the situation develop naturally. When frumpy Eileen had been packed off and she and the children were completely at ease with each other, he would ask her to marry him.

One Sunday afternoon they were all gathered round the Jurgens' pool. The rains had abated earlier than usual and people were talking of drought. Sophie was basking in the sunshine, watching Rob and Peter compete in the pool. Richard was at the far end, treading water and encouraging the boys.

Cassie had been messing around on the verge, with her armbands on. She could barely swim, unlike her brother.

'Keep going!' Richard shouted to Rob and Peter.

Cassie came over and sat down in her father's chair. She

looked slyly at Sophie and said, 'Did you know that Laura is coming out here?'

'Laura?'

This was news to Sophie. Richard had mentioned nothing about a visit from Laura.

'Are you sure about that?'

'Oh, yes,' said Cassie airily, 'Laura told me. I spoke to her on the phone.'

She looked up expectantly, waiting for Sophie to ask her more questions. Noticing this, Sophie did not comply.

It was unfortunate but she just could not take to Cassie. The child was not sympathetic, not like Peter. She was cunning and, in her father's absence, hostile to Sophie.

'She's coming to live with us,' Cassie announced.

'Is she?'

Sophie sounded cool. She was not going to give Cassie the benefit of knowing she was upset. Coming to live here, she thought. This was worrying. Richard's mother-in-law would be a different kettle of fish from Eileen. Laura would hold smart dinner parties for Richard – fill the empty role of mother to his children.

But there, she thought, it would stop. Richard wouldn't go to bed with his mother-in-law! So she needn't worry.

'Yes, she *is* coming!' said Cassie fiercely. 'I know she is!'

'That's it, boys!' Richard stated. 'I'm getting out.'

He pulled himself out of the pool and as he did so Cassie jumped in.

Sophie waited until he was sitting down before saying, 'I hear Laura is coming out,' in a mildly interested voice.

'Sorry?'

'Cassie says that Laura is coming to live with you.'

'Absolutely not.'

'So it's just a holiday?'

'Not that either.'

'Why would Cassie say so?'

'Wishful thinking,' Richard said, looking sad. 'Laura and Cassie were very close. Cassie misses her. And you know how

267

children tend to fantasise.'

'Yes,' said Sophie although she did not know.

Rob was not a fantasist. Why should he be? He was perfectly happy in the secure world his mother had created.

'Anyway, Laura's too wrapped up in her work to take holidays,' Richard said drily.

'At her age?'

'She's not old! My first wife – Rebecca – was much younger than me and Laura herself was a very young mother. As for her work I don't think she'll ever give up.'

'What does she do?'

'She's a photographer. She's very well-known: Laura Conway. You may have heard of her.'

'Laura Conway! Is she your mother-in-law? But she's as famous as David Bailey!'

'I daresay she is,' said Richard. 'Anyhow she's not coming out here.'

At the end of the third month they left Eileen in charge of the three children and drove down to Cape Town. The journey took them through the Karoo desert.

The forecasters had been wrong about the drought. It had rained that week and the *vlektes* were flooded with flowers. The bare twigs of the grey-black bushes which, as if by mutual arrangement, grew at regular intervals from each other, had sprouted leaves. The car windows were right down and Sophie could smell the scent of the blue-green brackbosch, the Turkish figs, the kaporbos and the bitter karoo with its yellow blossoms.

As she gazed out the sun went down and under the pink and gold clouds the hills turned purple.

'Isn't that incredible!' exclaimed Richard and he drew into the side of the road and turned off the ignition. 'You can't say this isn't romantic!'

He put his arms around her and kissed her lips first and then – having unbuttoned the front of her dress – the swell of her breasts.

One thing led to another and, although Sophie was terrified that another car might come along the road or an African loom up out of the bush, they made love, right there on the front seat.

It was the most shameful thing Sophie had ever done. Afterwards her dress was crushed and shockingly damp and her face was pink.

Richard was elated and he only laughed at her rueful face. 'You're very sweet,' he said.

And then, while she was still in this rumpled condition, he proposed.

The circumstances were quite inappropriate, to put it mildly, but Sophie accepted.

'Excellent!' said Richard, almost as if he was clinching a business deal. 'Then let's go ahead and get married as soon as possible. I'd like to do it before Eileen goes home so you can move in and get the children organised.'

It was rather too clinical an approach for her liking. But she thought about Rob and how important a father figure would be to him and she understood Richard's feelings.

'In April?'

'Terrific. We'll set it in motion when we get back.'

The moon was out. Sophie was just about to suggest driving on when she heard a curious sound.

Thunder? No, not thunder. Hooves. In the moonlight, against a *koppie*, she saw a dust-cloud rise. Out of it sprang a herd of Springbok, moving like cumulus, some leaping high into the air, their delicate dancers' feet scarcely touching the dry, red earth. Perhaps in flight from a panther, they were heading for the decapitated Swartberg mountains.

'My God,' Richard whispered. 'But this is a wonderful country.'

But it's full of danger, she thought. Out there jackals are roaming in search of young sheep. *Roikats*, dreaded killers, are prowling, and snakes – Cape cobras, Boomslangs – and ant-bears and baboons. The night-prowlers.

All of a sudden she thought of Hannie and of the fearful

danger to Rob. And she saw not the desert bathed in moonlight but her own garden – the avenue in from the road. And coming up it a brown-skinned girl with curly hair and a look of Rob . . .

This girl would know what embarrassment her presence would cause in a northern suburb home. But that wouldn't stop her from making demands. She might have a chip on her shoulder but she would ask for recognition.

When she was snubbed by Sophie she would accost Rob. Rob would be devastated. He would ask whether or not the girl's claim was false. He might not even have to ask. The resemblance between him and the girl might be stamped on her face . . .

He would be mortified. Or – worse – he might be sorry for the girl. His heart was that soft. Without proper guidance he could develop liberal tendencies as he grew up.

If he went to Wits university he might get involved with the more extreme student elements, hold up posters saying FREE MANDELA.

Especially if the girl turned up.

And what would Richard think if she did? He would wonder why his wife had not told him about the girl.

But I don't want to talk about it, Sophie thought, not even to Richard.

'Are you cold?' asked Richard, hugging her tight. 'You're shivering, you know. We'd better move on.'

'Yes . . .'

The Springbok had gone but she continued to stare out of the window, trying her level best to banish thoughts of the girl.

As Sophie had longed to do with Hannie, they booked into the Mount Nelson Hotel.

The Mount Nelson was one of the last bastions of Colonial-style gracious living, a pink-washed stucco edifice set high above the Botanical Gardens on the lower slopes of Table Mountain. It was owned by the Union Castle Line. First-class passengers off the mail boat from Southampton stayed there before heading north on the luxurious Blue Train as Richard and Sophie were going to do at the end of their week in the Cape.

They retained the hired car so that they could drive around the Cape Peninsula. They went to Stellenbosch and Richard was charmed by the vineyards and the Cape Dutch houses. They lunched at Lanzerac, a three hundred-year-old homestead converted into an hotel. Richard marvelled at the great slave bell which still stood in the grounds. They had a day out at Milnerton for the races and Richard won. They made love again but not very often.

On their second last day in the Cape they drove to Muizenberg beach for a swim. The route took them through Lakeside, the Coloureds' suburb.

One saw Coloured people all over Cape Town but seeing them en masse was even more unnerving. Sophie reminded herself that the Cape Coloureds were a race apart, a mixture of the original Dutch and Huguenot settlers, Malay slaves and Africans.

'Fascinating people,' said Richard. 'I've read a lot about them.'

Sophie curled her lip. 'Dreadful degenerates! They're lazy and they drink.'

'The vineyard owners caused the drink problem by paying them partially in wine and partially in cash. What chance did they have? Anyway, I shouldn't think they *all* drink!'

It was going to be one of *those* conversations. People who came out from the UK thought this way at first but they soon learnt. As Richard would. She remained silent and let him carry on.

'Imagine what this country might have been like if people hadn't been discouraged from inter-breeding. The concept of colour wouldn't exist.'

'Oh, but I think it would,' said Sophie, goaded into speech. 'It's natural to stick to your own kind.'

'Is it?'

She must not argue with him. He wouldn't like it, and more to the point he wouldn't listen.

'Once, in Lusaka, I came down in a lift with a husband and wife and their two small boys,' Richard said. 'One of the boys had light skin and black curly hair and his brother had dark skin and blond hair. Something went wrong with the lift and instead of opening at the ground floor it shot up again. We adults started talking. We were in there, going up and down, for about twenty minutes and we got to know each other quite well. Finally the lift stopped and the door opened and we were able to get out and go our separate ways. Afterwards I couldn't remember which of the adults was Black and which was White. You see, it was completely irrelevant.'

'What a strange experience,' said Sophie.

She hoped Richard would never tell this story at a party.

Richard said, 'But it wasn't *strange*. Don't you understand – that was the point.'

She let Seraphina go back to her family two months before the baby was due. It was a nuisance being without her – the temporary girl wasn't as well-trained – but it was a relief not to be confronted with that enormous swelling and to wonder, in spite of herself, about the sex of the child.

She still worried about Hannie being back in the Transvaal. He had not been back to see her mother again or, if he had, her mother hadn't said so.

Then, out of the blue, he wrote to Sophie. She recognised his handwriting on the envelope and she trembled with anger at his nerve. She almost threw the letter away without opening it. But Hannie had never attempted to make direct contact with her after the divorce. If, now, he was going to make a nuisance of himself, she should know how his mind was working.

She took the letter into her room and shut the door as if its contents were a poison that might otherwise seep through the rest of the house. Inside the envelope was a sheet of paper. She read it.

Dear Sophie,
A very sad thing has happened to me. Six months ago my little girl died of lymphatic leukaemia. She became

very tired and then she began to haemorrhage and although she had radiation treatment it did no good.

I know you will find this hard to understand but I loved both my children and now there is only Rob. Please will you let me see him? It has been terrible all these years wondering about him –

Sophie didn't read on. All that mattered she had already absorbed from the second sentence.

The child was dead. Having learnt of the horror of her birth she had now learnt of her demise in the same manner.

Dead and no longer, therefore, a threat to Rob. The scandal of her existence could be buried along with her body and no one that mattered need ever know.

Sophie sat down on the edge of her bed marvelling at the timing of the letter. How fortunate that Hannie had written now, rather than when she was married, living in Inanda. She might have been forced to explain the letter to Richard. But not now.

A sad thing has happened to me, Hannie had written. But not to *me*, Sophie thought happily. This is the best wedding present I could have had.

She did not finish the letter. What was the point? Hannie's confidences and pleas were lamentable. What would become of him in the end? Not that she cared. But she might capitulate and let him see Rob occasionally. Once or twice a year.

Or maybe she wouldn't. She would have to think seriously about Hannie's request.

She felt reborn – as young and carefree as she had been after Rob's birth. The child was dead, had been buried six months ago and she had not known.

Still holding the letter she got up and went to the dressing-table. Her pretty, flushed face bore witness to her elation. She brushed her hair and applied spray and put more lipstick on. She picked up her list book. She must not sit here idling. There was, after all, a wedding to be organised.

T HEY didn't immediately tell the children of their plans.

'Wait for the appropriate moment,' said Richard, which meant as far as *his* children were concerned.

Rob would be pleased that she was marrying Richard. The two of them hit it off splendidly, as she and Peter did.

Cassie was something else. Sophie didn't see that much of her any more. Cassie, it was explained, had a lot on her plate. She was having extra coaching in Afrikaans which was why she couldn't come to the Jurgens' for lunch. She couldn't accompany the others to the drive-in as she was spending the night with a friend.

It took Sophie a while to realise that Richard was making excuses for his daughter – that Cassie was avoiding her.

Eventually, Richard gave up waiting for the appropriate moment and they broke the news. As Sophie had anticipated Rob was glad.

'Richard is a good *okie*, Mum.'

Okie was an Afrikaans word. English-speaking people used it as they did several other Afrikaans words: *lekker*, which meant 'lovely' and *voetsak*, a coarse 'get lost'.

These words sent shivers down Sophie's spine.

There were other expressions, too, which she found distasteful – 'my china', for 'my friend' and 'going for a jol' but these, at least, had English derivations. Afrikaners, despite the fact that they were running the country, were South Africa's lower class. They had started out as poor farmers and their language, bastardised from Dutch and Malay, had limited vocabulary, grammar and grace.

Whereas she and Rob came from 1820s Settlers' stock, the aristocracy of South Africa.

Gently but firmly she reminded Rob of that. 'So don't use those ugly Afrikaans words.'

'Richard says the 1820 Settlers were poor and dispossessed debris from economic depression,' Rob replied, parrot-fashion, 'after the Napoleonic wars.'

'Did he? Anyway, don't worry about it now. I'm thrilled you like Richard and I think we'll be very happy living in Inanda.'

'And Peter is pleased, too.'

'Did he say so? He's a darling boy.' In need of discipline, Sophie thought, but she could cope with him.

'Cassie isn't.'

'Isn't what?'

'Isn't pleased that you're marrying her dad.'

Sophie pursed her lips and lifted her chin. 'I daresay she'll change her mind in due course.'

'She hates you, Mum.'

'Why do you say that?'

'Because Peter says she does.'

Sophie swallowed. 'Does he? One doesn't want to take these statements too seriously. Go and ask the girl to polish your shoes and I'll take you to Hyde Park.'

An elegant shopping centre had been recently opened off Jan Smuts Avenue. It meant that all one's shopping – groceries, clothes, books, everything – could be purchased under one huge roof.

This development obviated the need to drive into central Johannesburg where more and more Blacks shopped these days. The city proper was not what it had been a few years back.

Hyde Park Corner, however, was more sophisticated in terms of its merchandise than town had ever been. The clothes shops were simply divine. Rob could have a milk shake and look at toys and books while she peeped into that new Italian shop. Cheered herself up. Instead of thinking of Peter's remark.

*

They would have a romantic honeymoon. Europe in the spring.

'I don't think we can go away,' Richard said.

'Why not?'

'Because of the children.'

'But, doll, that's not a problem. Mother will move in. And Helen's only in Parktown, after all. They'll take charge.'

'It's not as simple as that,' said Richard patiently. 'I'm sure your mother and Helen would be delighted to help but – '

'But what?'

'They might find Cassie difficult. She's still in the process of adjusting and – '

'No, they won't,' said Sophie, determined not to be done out of a honeymoon by a peevish child. 'Mother is very sensitive. She understands what these last years without Rebecca must have been like for the children. She'll make a big fuss of Cassie. She *adores* that child.'

This was stretching the truth. Cassie has the makings of a beauty, was what Mrs Ward had said – an opinion with which Sophie had disagreed.

'Even so.'

There was an obdurate streak in Richard, Sophie had learnt. He went along with a situation for ages and then all of a sudden – sometimes when you least expected it – he dug in his heels. And all because Cassie might prove difficult. Cassie who was – just – eight years old.

'But Richard – '

'I'll make it up to you,' Richard said. 'We'll have our honeymoon at the end of the year instead. Cassie will be all right by then. It's just a question of allowing the dust to settle.'

What dust, thought Sophie angrily. *I* haven't stirred it up. Why should this wretched child dictate the terms of our lives?

But Cassie had done so this time. She only had to look at Richard's face to get confirmation.

'You know best, doll,' she managed to say. 'After all, we have each other and that's what counts.'

'You're a wonderful woman. I couldn't have contemplated

marrying anyone who hadn't a child herself. It makes all the difference. You understand how complicated the whole thing is.'

I understand that I'm being done out of my honeymoon by an eight-year-old child, Sophie thought. No chance of Paris in the spring for us, because of Cassie. She must be taken in hand.

'I do understand,' she said to Richard. 'We'll sort it out.'

It could be that Eileen was colluding with Cassie against herself. Eileen was due to leave. Maybe the child would prove less edgy when she had gone.

On the evening of Eileen's departure, Richard was held up by a late meeting at work. Peter had pulled a hamstring at rugby that week and was still in pain with his leg up so it fell to Sophie to take Eileen to the airport, and to Cassie to see her off.

The journey to Jan Smuts was uneventful although Cassie sat on the back seat with Eileen so they could hold hands.

The tearful farewell anticipated by Sophie did not take place. Eileen, with surprising strength, remained in control of the situation and said, 'None of that now,' warding off hysteria.

Without speaking, Sophie and Cassie walked back to the car. Cassie got into the front, leant back in her seat and folded her small hands.

Still in silence they headed for town. An African – probably one of the many who had never passed his driving test – signalled left and turned right. Sophie blew the horn. The African turned down his car window and shook his fist. Some of them were becoming quite militant lately, thanks to Liberal Whites who voted Progressive and joined the Black Sash.

They flashed through the suburbs – Linksfield, Glenhazel, Waverley, Melrose – lights from houses gleaming out of the pitch darkness.

Then Cassie spoke. 'He doesn't love *you*,' she said. 'He loves Laura. And Laura loves him.'

Sophie was shocked rigid. Still, she retained her composure – not that Cassie could see her face in the dark.

'What *are* you talking about, dear?'

'Laura and my dad,' said Cassie clearly. 'They love each other. Didn't you know that?'

'I'm sure they do. Your father must be very, very fond of your grandmother after all she's done for the two of you.'

'They're lovers,' Cassie said. 'They sleep together in the same bed.'

It was Sophie's turn to drive badly, although no one hooted at her for cutting the corner. She was telling herself that Cassie was obsessed by the subject of sex – that the decadent Sixties had done that to English children so they imagined all grown-ups getting into bed.

The breakdown of discipline over there had resulted in men growing their hair and everyone taking drugs and the madness of free expression which had grown out of the music of the Beatles and that Mick Jagger man. She just had not realised the extent to which Richard's children had been influenced.

That was all there was to it. All there ever could be. Richard would not sleep with his mother-in-law.

'I don't think, dear, that you're telling the truth.'

'Yes, I am,' said Cassie. 'You ask Dad.'

Richard would be worried by Cassie's obsession but he would laugh her story off.

Sophie told him only because she was concerned for Cassie, not because she needed reassurance that the child was making it up.

Richard *was* worried. But he did not laugh.

'Good God,' he said. 'I hadn't a clue that the children – that Cassie knew about that.' At which point he confessed to having had a long affair with his mother-in-law.

Had she given way to her emotions Sophie would have screamed. But one did not lose control in the presence of a man.

When Sophie was under pressure she sought around in her mind for a compartment into which the source of her problem could be slotted. In that way now she considered the persona of Laura so it could be filed.

Laura Conway was an artist like David Bailey. Photographers these days were. Sophie's compartment for artist was sub-headed *sybaritic, unreliable* and *debauched*.

Having thus filed Laura it was far simpler to understand why Richard had bedded her. Being a man – all men were carnal by nature and easily tempted – he had fallen prey to a voluptuary. Eventually he had come to his senses and seen the light, broken off the affair.

He had not realised that the children – Cassie, anyway – had suspected, and was not upset about that, which was a point in his favour. But he had been careless. Gently and sympathetically Sophie said one could not afford that – not with children around. Not that she wanted to make him feel guilty . . .

Having spoken she wept. That was wise. Richard put his arms around her and held her tight. What there had been between Laura and himself was all over, he said. What counted now was *their* relationship – his and Sophie's. Didn't she know that?

'Then you don't love her any more?'

Richard hesitated. 'It's over,' he said at last. 'I'm marrying you, not Laura . . .'

The wedding was taking place at the end of June. The ceremony, presided over by a magistrate, was to be held at Richard's home

Sophie would have preferred a summer wedding. It was a pity to waste that beautiful garden setting, but it was already quite cold and she resigned herself to an indoor reception.

The day itself was chilly and crisp but the sun still shone. Sophie was wearing lilac, a crêpe wool dress with a hat to match. The outfit had come from Italy where women still dressed as women and not – as in England – like young girls.

She was defying tradition by dressing in the bridegroom's house on grounds of practicality. Sophie and her mother drove to Inanda three hours before the wedding was due to take place with Sophie's dress and hat on the back seat of the car.

'No looking!' Sophie said to Richard when he came out of the house to meet them. 'Turn your eyes away! And you shouldn't be seeing *me*, either.'

'I haven't looked – I swear!'

'Mother did a wonderful job with the flowers, didn't she?' Mrs Ward had worked hard the evening before, arranging lilac and blue flowers.

'*Wonderful!*' said Richard in that too-hearty tone men adopted when they had failed to notice something of major significance.

Sophie took the dress and hat up to the room in which she was going to change and left them there. Her hair had not yet been set. She had recently switched hairdressers. Melvin was queer, which she always found off-putting, but he could work miracles.

'I'll be back shortly!' she said gaily to Richard when she came downstairs again.

'So I should jolly well hope!'

'Are the children all right?'

Rob, at his own request, had slept at Inanda the night before.

'They're fine. Don't you worry about a thing except looking beautiful.'

Melvin performed wonders and applied extra hair spray to support her hat. Sophie gave him an extra rand as a tip. She was going to look every bit as gorgeous as Melvin predicted.

At Inanda Mrs Ward was bossing the staff and putting last-minute touches to the tables.

'You should be getting dressed, Mother.'

'So should you. The hair is *divine!*'

'Do you think so?'

Sophie floated upstairs as if she had already been drinking champagne. The pleasant sensation abruptly abated. Cassie was sitting on the floor of the minstrels' gallery. There was nothing odd about that. Children were always sitting in peculiar places. It was the expression on Cassie's face that got to Sophie: a smug, self-satisfied look.

'Cassie, dear, why aren't you getting ready?'

'Ready for what?'

Sophie's hand twitched. The child needed a good smack on the appropriate spot. But not today.

'For the wedding, dear.'

'Oh, *that!*' Cassie said in a what-does-it-matter voice.

It was as well for both of them that Sophie was – always had been – remarkably self-controlled.

She went into the bedroom in which she was to change. Her dress was lying where she had left it on the bed. But her hat was missing.

She looked around, thinking that her mother had moved it for some obscure reason. She couldn't see it. And it wasn't in any of the cupboards, either. What idiot had removed it?

She went out on to the gallery and called down to Mrs Ward, 'Mother, where's my hat?'

'What is it?'

'My hat – where's it gone?'

But Mrs Ward didn't know. Nobody knew – or if they did, nobody confessed.

Sophie was on the verge of swearing out loud. The minutes were rushing by and she didn't have a hat. It was much too late to go out and look for another one, not that she was likely to find one that would match her dress.

'We'll have to put flowers in your hair,' Mrs Ward said.

'Don't be silly!' Sophie snapped. 'I want my hat!'

It was a beautiful hat, wide-brimmed and swathed with lilac silk. How could it be lost?

'We can't find your hat.'

'I know that, for Christ's sake!'

'There's no need to speak to your mother like that!'

As a last resort Melvin was summoned to the house to re-do her hair and to introduce into it a lilac blossom.

He came reluctantly and only after being massively bribed to abandon another client and he kept on asking what had happened to Sophie's hat.

'I don't know,' Sophie said sulkily. 'If I did know you wouldn't be here.'

'Oh, so it's like that, is it? Our nerves are in shreds. Are we worried about what is going to happen tonight?'

He was revolting. She would tell her friends to shun his salon. But he saved the day with her hair. The wedding was slightly delayed but Sophie, so everyone said, was a lovely bride.

She had more or less forgotten about the hat when, coming out of the bathroom, she almost fell over Cassie sitting upstairs again.

'What are you doing up here, dear? You should be downstairs with our guests.'

'I was searching for your hat,' said Cassie.

She smiled insolently and Sophie, looking down at her, realised who the culprit had been. She would never know what had happened to it, whether it was at the bottom of the rubbish bin or buried in the garden, only that Cassie had removed it from the bed.

The sabre-rattling phase of their relationship was over and war had been declared. Sophie had survived the first assault but it had shown her all too clearly the extent of the enemy's hatred and the lengths to which her small assailant was prepared to go.

She was not going to engage in hostilities – not today – but she could hold her ground.

'How kind of you, dear,' she said, 'but you needn't have bothered. The flower looked so much prettier than the hat would have done. Losing it turned out to be a blessing in disguise.'

Cassie's face fell. Victory to me, after all, Sophie thought.

After dark, when the guests had gone, the battle recommenced.

Sophie was suffering from a sense of anti-climax. There was nothing left to do now but go to bed.

Richard, having different reactions, said, 'Thank God *that's* all over!' which did not help.

'I think I'll have a bath.'

'I'll lock up. I'll be with you shortly.'

Upstairs, Sophie poured a liberal helping of oil and foam into the bath. She needed to unwind. She could feel herself getting tense.

But she was reassured by the sight of her wrap and negligée. They were so pretty: rose pink trimmed with silver grey lace. She had done the bedroom over in these same shades.

She carried the wrap and negligée on their satin hanger through to the bathroom and immersed herself in bubbles.

'All right, darling?'

Richard had come up. He had his own bathroom on the other side of their room. She called out, 'Yes – marvellous,' and heard him turn on the shower.

Lovely, lovely peace. It was so soothing lying in the bath that she almost dozed off.

Quite soon – sooner than she would have wished – sounds from the bedroom indicated that Richard had finished his shower. Well, he would have to wait a little longer for his bride to emerge. She topped up the bath with more hot water. The nail varnish on her index finger had chipped already. What a nuisance. But she was too relaxed to care much about it.

Blissful tranquillity. And then the calm was shattered by the scream of a child.

Sophie jerked up into a sitting position, scattering water all over the floor.

'Dad – Dad – come!'

A break-in, Sophie thought. In spite of the security system a kaffir was in the house.

She almost fell out of the bath, reached for a towel, wrapped it round her and wrenched open the door, leaving her wrap and negligée dangling from their hanger on the back of it.

'Richard?'

But Richard had gone to the rescue. Muffled screams were still emanating from one of the bedrooms. Please, please, Sophie thought, don't let it be Rob.

She ran out on to the gallery as Richard came out of another bedroom carrying Cassie in his arms.

'My God, what happened?'

'She's had a nightmare.'

'A nightmare?'

'She's been having them a lot since Eileen left. Poor little darling. Never mind, sweetheart. Daddy's here.'

'So it's just that she's missing Eileen?'

'I'm afraid so. Don't worry. We'll take her into our bed and she'll settle down.'

'Into our bed?'

Sophie had never allowed Rob to share her bed, not even in the wake of Hannie's departure. That kind of cosseting was unhealthy from everyone's point of view.

'Why not? Poor little Cassie. We'll get rid of those horrible nightmares, won't we, darling?'

Sophie went back into the bathroom, dried herself and very slowly put on her wrap and negligée.

When she returned to the bedroom Richard and Cassie were in bed. Cassie was spreadeagled across the middle of the mattress and Richard was on his side on the edge. They were asleep already! How could they doze off like that? What was Richard thinking of, letting the child sleep in their bed? And on their wedding night, too!

Tomorrow, vowed Sophie, she would lay down the rules pertaining to this behaviour. After tonight Cassie would be banned from the marital bed. Tomorrow . . . Tonight she – like the other two – should get some sleep.

Except that she did not manage to do so, or hardly at all. Cassie wiggled and kicked and managed to occupy most of the bed. Sophie and Richard lay on opposite sides, along the ridges of the mattress.

Nevertheless, Sophie must have slept for a little while. She woke with a jerk and to her astonishment found that the mattress was damp. So was Cassie. The child had wet the bed! At eight years of age, Sophie thought. She must be extremely disturbed. What had she done, taking on such a responsibility?

The mattress would be ruined. They would have to have another one delivered today.

Her back ached from lying in the unnatural position she had been forced to adopt. In the bathroom she discovered that her negligée, too, was damp. It was all just too much.

Back in the bedroom Richard slept on. But Cassie was awake and glaring at Sophie with those large brown eyes.

'I wet your bed.'

'I know you did.'

Cassie let the conversation hang in the air. I *can* handle it, thought Sophie. I may not like doing so, but I can.

But Cassie on the warpath proved a formidable force. There were no more wet mattresses but the next attack also culminated in the bedroom. Having given much thought to the problem Sophie went in search of her step-daughter. She located Cassie in the garden, perched on the branch of a tree.

'I want to talk to you, dear.'

'Do you?'

'So please come down.'

Cassie did so. When she was on the ground she said, 'See what I've got. It's a chameleon.'

Sophie shuddered. She detested lizard-like creatures.

'Horrible,' she said instinctively, and Cassie smiled in the way Sophie was beginning to dread.

'In Afrikaans a chameleon is called *trapsoetijies*. It means slow-coach. It's because chameleons take so long changing colour to hide themselves.'

Coming from Cassie, this pertained to a chat. Sophie was encouraged.

'Cassie, I want us to be friends,' she said. 'We're all a family now and we must try to get on with each other.'

At that Cassie clammed up again. Sophie persisted.

'I know I'm not your real mother but she would be happy seeing that you were well looked-after.'

Cassie was staring at her hand on which the chameleon was resting.

'*We* can be happy, too . . .'

At that Cassie took flight and scampered off across the garden leaving Sophie as frustrated as she had been before.

She did not manage to get the child on her own again before

Richard came home. And then all three children had baths and an early supper and went to their rooms.

When it was the adults' turn to go to bed Sophie thought again of Cassie and told herself that it was early days yet, that the child would come right. This optimism faded the minute she turned back the bedclothes. She could hardly believe her eyes.

'Richard! Look!'

The chameleon – grey like the sheets but clearly visible – was on Sophie's side of the bed.

'How did that get there?'

'Cassie did it!' Sophie said bitterly. 'She just doesn't like me.'

'Now, darling, don't say that.'

She shouldn't say so but Cassie could. Cassie could castigate Sophie in a letter left on the dining-room table for all to read. A letter to Laura – of course. *You wouldn't take to Sophie, either. She's stupid and ugly and mean.*

And surely it was Cassie who hid the household accounts so payments were missed out and rude letters were sent and Richard became annoyed.

Who else – before a dinner party – stirred sugar into the pumpkin soup? Not the boys. It wasn't Rob who cut the strings of his new tennis racket. Or drove a nail into one of the tyres of Sophie's car so she missed a book-club lunch. And it wasn't Peter, either.

All winter the campaign went on. Sophie tried being firm.

'This must stop, Cassie. You have to accept the situation. I am married to your father. We love each other and that is that.'

'He doesn't love *you*,' said Cassie scornfully. 'He loves Laura.'

In the end Sophie couldn't take it any more. And neither could Richard.

'It's not going to improve, is it?'

'I don't think it is.' She didn't like admitting failure in Richard's eyes but she had to say so.

Richard sighed. 'It might be better all round if we send her back to England.'

ANUMBER of unwelcome truths now emerged. For months, it transpired, Cassie had been begging Richard to let her go home. Home, that was, to Laura.

Worse, Richard had discussed this possibility with Laura on the office phone, not once but several times.

'Laura's very keen to have Cassie back,' he reported. 'But I kept telling her to wait and see in case things got better.'

Sophie felt betrayed. Richard and Laura had been liaising on the phone behind her back. Why didn't you tell me, her heart screamed at Richard. But – as a wife should be – she remained outwardly calm.

Her image of Laura, until then lightly sketched, became more defined. She visualised Laura as a large, gypsy-like woman, in bright flowing clothes. Her favourite colour was red and she wore gold bangles on her arms. Her thick dark hair – Cassie's hair – streamed down her back.

Laura was amoral, irresponsible – and a threat. Richard must not be allowed anywhere near her lest he get back into her clutches. Therefore, *he* could not take Cassie back to England. Which meant that Sophie would have to do so.

She did not present the idea to Richard in quite those terms. It would have been foolish to reveal her hand to a man.

'We're not sending Cassie away for *good*, doll,' she said to Richard. 'I want her to leave with the feeling that I care about her. If *I* hand her over to Laura that message will sink home. When she sees her grandmother and her stepmother making arrangements together for her welfare she'll understand that we adults are a united force. That's very important when one's dealing with children. It makes them feel secure.'

'You're very good about these things,' agreed Richard. 'I'm sure you're right. When would you think of going to London?'

'There doesn't seem much point in waiting, Cassie must be settled.'

'No, I don't suppose there is. I'd better have another word with Laura and book the tickets.'

Another call to Laura. Soon there would be no further necessity for Richard to contact his former mistress. Once Sophie could claim acquaintance with Laura, *she* would make the calls and monitor Cassie's progress.

In the light of the journey she had to make she reviewed her wardrobe. On previous trips to Europe she had found that clothes suitable for life in South Africa, no matter how sophisticated they were, looked wrong over there.

It was something to do with the light. Happy colours, even the deep pinks and the lilacs of which she was so fond, had a curious way of looking vulgar when transplanted to the UK. So that meant buying new clothes in London.

'Laura wants to meet you at Heathrow,' said Richard after the call had been made.

'How kind. But there's no need for her to get up at that ghastly hour. We get in at five-thirty A.M. It just wouldn't be fair. No, I'll take Cassie with me to the hotel and Laura can come over at lunch-time and pick her up.'

In the interim, Harrods could be visited and suitable clothes acquired for the confrontation. Then the hand-over, two more days for London shopping, and back to Johannesburg.

Now that Cassie had succeeded in getting her own way Sophie imagined she would be easier to handle. But in fact the converse was true. Cassie's hostility now extended to Richard, as if he was rejecting her instead of merely acceding to her wishes. In the mornings her eyes were red as if she had been weeping. At table she glowered at the boys who were getting along famously. So disagreeable, thought Sophie, counting the days to departure.

At Jan Smuts there was a painful parting – painful for Richard because Cassie flatly refused to kiss her father goodbye. Bristling with anger she flounced into the departure lounge and from there on to the Boeing 707 which was to take them to Heathrow.

Having ensured that Cassie's seatbelt was fastened, Sophie switched off. She had armed herself with a sleeping pill. During this last night with her troublesome step-daughter she would at least be able to sleep.

It was raining in London. How on earth did people tolerate living in such an awful climate? It was soft rain, too, just the kind guaranteed to play havoc with her hair which – after the long flight – was already going flat. Harrods, she recalled with relief, had a hairdressing salon.

'What do we want to go to Harrods for?' said Cassie when the plan was outlined.

'I have some shopping to do there.'

'You mean clothes.'

'Yes, and I must get my hair done. You can have yours cut at the same time.'

'No, thanks. Eileen will do that for me.'

'Just as you like.'

After this morning, Cassie would not be her responsibility any more. Eileen could hack away at the child's hair to her heart's content.

'I'll stay in the hotel while you're out.'

Richard had booked them into the Churchill in Portman Square.

'I'm afraid that won't be possible. You'll have to come with me.'

She expected a protest but Cassie, for once, complied. It was a fag having to drag her to Harrods, knowing she would sulk all the while they were there. But – perhaps counting the hours to her reunion with Laura – the child was resigned rather than sullen.

A taxi was summoned to take them to Knightsbridge. They stared out of opposite windows at the crowds in the streets. Since both the men and the women had long hair Sophie could not always establish their sex. But, in the main, the men wore flowered shirts and ties and velvet jackets and the women flamboyant floating garments and masses of beads.

It was as if hordes of Romanian gypsies had taken London over. Sophie thought again of Laura, another gypsy, destined to disturb the lunch-hour equilibrium of the Churchill Hotel. She was both uneasy and intrigued by the prospect of meeting Richard's former mistress. Not that she *need* feel concerned . . . Laura never would have fitted into Richard's world. In this one, she would melt into the landscape.

'Look!' said Cassie. 'Hot pants!'

A long-legged girl in abbreviated shorts was crossing Oxford Street. Sophie gazed at her pert bottom on which a label – easy to read even at this distance – had been affixed.

'Everything Inside Is Pink!' it proclaimed. Honestly – what next?

Harrods – refreshingly – was the same as she remembered it, free of the hippy influence.

Trailed by Cassie, Sophie tracked down, tried on and purchased a pretty pale grey dress with a jacket to match. In the hairdressing salon her stylist was wearing off-white foundation and nearly-black lipstick but she did exactly what Sophie asked.

Cassie had slumped in a nearby chair and was almost asleep.

'T'n't she good!' said the stylist.

'She's just marvellous.'

'She doesn't look a bit like you. Must take after her dad.'

'Perhaps a touch more hairspray.'

The final result was pleasing. So far so good. But Sophie had reckoned without the vagaries of British weather. Before they had left the hotel the rain had stopped, for the day, Sophie had thought. Now, it was belting down again. There was a long queue for taxis outside Harrods.

Sophie hauled Cassie back into the shop and bought an umbrella, pale grey with white spots.

'What about me?' asked Cassie. 'I'm going to get wet, too.'

'No one will notice if *your* hair gets damp.'

Back in the queue Cassie stamped in a puddle drenching Sophie's feet. At the hotel she realised that, despite the umbrella, the rain had flattened her hair.

She fluffed it up, refreshed her make-up and put on the new dress and jacket. Laura, she thought, would be late. That sort of person would be.

But, on the dot of one, the phone rang and reception announced that someone was waiting downstairs. The Bangle Lady . . .

'We'll be down at once,' said Sophie, her stomach twitching.

She was seized by last-minute nerves. She was perfectly dressed for the part but could she play it? A Valium would have helped but it was too late now to take one.

Cassie was leaping from one foot to another.

'Don't do that, dear. Think of the people in the room below.'

'I don't care about *them*,' Cassie said. 'And I don't care about you, either. I want to see Laura.'

They went downstairs in the lift. The foyer was quite crowded. No sign of a gypsy. All the women looked more or less like herself . . .

'*Laura!*' screamed Cassie suddenly.

Heads turned. A human cannon, Cassie shot across the foyer into the arms of a slight, fair-haired woman.

That was Laura Conway? That mousy creature wearing – how annoying! – a silver-grey mid-calf skirt and a long-sleeved blouse?

The skirt and blouse were beautifully cut and undeniably stylish. It was Laura, not they, who was dull. And yet Sophie felt as if the soles of her shoes had grown tiny wheels. An unseen director appeared to be propelling her downstage left, towards her predecessor.

She rolled to a halt in front of Laura and Cassie and delivered her well-rehearsed lines.

'Laura! How are you? I'm Richard's wife.'

Close-to, Laura did not look her age. And somehow she conveyed the impression of being Someone . . .

'Hello, Sophie,' she said. 'You must be very tired after your long trip.'

She did not shake hands. She was holding Cassie close, stroking and soothing the child who had been overcome with tearful emotion.

'I'm surviving,' Sophie said, trying to smile.

Her lips, as if they had already been stretched to the maximum, lacked flexibility. Laura Conway, so unpretentious in appearance, so polite, was more unnerving in the flesh than in theory. And they still had lunch to get through. At the thought of food an army of butterflies declared war inside Sophie's stomach. But . . .

'I'm *starving!*' said Cassie, still sniffing and clinging leechlike to Laura's frail frame.

'You will have lunch with me, won't you?' Sophie was forced to say. 'I did book a table.'

'Thank you. We will.'

Why wasn't Laura nervous of *her*? Maybe she was. Maybe she was putting on a brave face for Sophie's benefit.

If so, it did not prevent her from enjoying her meal. Sophie, leaving most of her food untouched, watched Laura consume broccoli soup, roast lamb and chocolate mousse. Why wasn't she fat if she ate like that?'

The other odd thing was that Laura seemed genuinely concerned about Sophie's welfare.

'You're staying until Thursday? What are you going to do? Do you have friends in London – no? But you'll be lonely all by yourself.'

This approach, while overpowering, had the effect of playing into Sophie's hands where Cassie was concerned, uniting the grown-ups.

'What a foul day!' observed Laura prior to departure. 'Have you got comfortable shoes for walking in London? It's hell on the feet.'

'I did bring boots.'

'You *must* see the new Biba boots. Every girl in London pines for a pair! They've been queuing outside the shop. Nothing puts them off, not even the IRA! There was a bomb-scare the other day and Stephen FitzSimon – that's Barbara Hulanicki's husband – they own Biba, as you must know – Simon told everyone to leave the shop. But the girls wouldn't go without their boots!'

Whether or not Laura intended it to be, this was one-upmanship. Sophie did not know about Biba, which was probably part of that London Bohemia to which Laura – however she looked – belonged at heart.

Confronted with alternative values Sophie had a habit of poking fun to reduce the threat. She laughed lightly. 'Well, I doubt very much if *I'll* be queuing up!'

But Laura's mind was elsewhere.

'You must come and see us in Barnes before you go. There are a few things we need to chat about.' *On our own*, signalled her eyes.

What could one say but yes? Dreading it on one level. But, on the other, appreciating the advantage of being able to tell Richard – *Laura and I are friends.*

Therefore, in the future, you keep out of it. Leave Cassie to us.

Going to Barnes meant being able to inspect Laura's house. Having learnt her lesson about Laura at their first meeting, Sophie had no preconceptions about what it would be like.

From the outside it was a traditional English detached residence just inside a cul-de-sac. The entrance hall was painted a warm orange, which made a pleasant contrast to the grey world outside.

The sitting-room walls were Wedgwood blue. Huge, comfortable sofas covered in off-white were dotted with cushions in orange, pink and yellow. Further colour was added by the shelves on either side of the fireplace which were stacked with books. A real fire was blazing in the grate. Flowers – orange and pink and yellow – had been informally placed in a pottery jug on a small table.

More noticeable than anything else were the paintings – quite a collection: people and interiors; a remarkable drawing of a horse lying down; an oil on canvas, all greens and yellows, showing two tiny figures in a vast landscape.

'Are you interested in paintings?' Laura asked. 'I have a friend, David Wolfers, who owns an art gallery. He looks for artists who have a poetic streak as well as the ability to draw. Charles Duranty, for instance.' She pointed at the oil on canvas.

'And the horse?'

'That's by Elisabeth Frink. She's wonderfully talented – and a great one for championing freedom and human rights.'

A liberal, Sophie thought. She was beginning to feel uneasy again, left alone with Laura. Neither Cassie nor Eileen were around.

'Cassie's not here?' she said, trying to sound as if she was disappointed.

'She and Eileen have gone to the cinema. I wanted to have the opportunity to tell you what I think. About the Cassie situation, I mean. Richard told me how hard it has been for you.'

'Yes,' said Sophie with feeling. 'It *has* been hard.'

'Cassie seems to be angry with Richard. He said so and I have to tell you that she's confirmed it herself. She maintains that she doesn't ever want to see him again but that will pass. What *I* want to say is that I'm happy to have her here for as long as necessary. Forever if needs be . . .'

Forever. What a relief.

'You're very good.'

'I'm not good at all. I just love Cassie.'

There was a distinct catch in Laura's voice. Surely she wasn't about to cry?

But Laura did not cry. She pulled herself together and went on to talk of more practical things – Cassie's schooling; pocket money; Eileen's role.

'I'm glad I've been able to talk to you, Sophie,' she said at the end. 'Richard told me how worried you were about Cassie's security. I'm sure it *will* help if we three give her the impression of being united.'

Richard told me: I do wish, thought Sophie, that you'd stop saying that.

She managed a smile. After all, Laura was forcing herself to be nice for Cassie's sake. They had landed in this together and they might as well see it through.

'. . . off on Thursday?' Laura was saying. 'Cassie and I will see you off.'

'You don't have to bother.'

'On the unity front it might be wise. I'll pick you up at the Churchill and drive you to Heathrow.'

The weather remained foul. Sophie put on a thermal vest and her winter boots, which were zipless and tight-fitting, and considered her recent acquisitions in relation to luggage space.

She was bound to be overweight. Free of Cassie she had returned to Harrods and gone slightly mad. Richard wouldn't mind – he was a darling about clothes bills – but the customs at Jan Smuts might take a different view.

She had to sit on her suitcases in order to close them and then found that she had not packed her new silver-grey dress and jacket which she was forced to squash into her overnight bag.

Once again Laura turned up at the scheduled time. A grim-faced Cassie was sitting in the back of the car. Sophie got into the front thinking that – in spite of Harrods – she could not wait to get home. It was almost impossible to see through the rain. Laura's windscreen-wipers, at full speed, were still ineffective, so she had to concentrate fiercely on driving which obviated the need for polite chit-chat.

'There's a trolley,' said Laura when they got to Heathrow. 'If you go in we'll park and join you inside.'

Her suitcases registered horrors on the scale.

'You're well over,' said the ground stewardess in that school-teacher manner affected by certain Britons. 'You'll have to pay, I'm afraid.'

'Heavens, Sophie,' said Laura, veering up beside her, 'are you travelling in *boots*?'

'My feet are cold.'

'They'll swell on the plane. Are you wearing stockings? Absolute madness. I know. I travel so much. Do you have any other shoes in your hand luggage?'

'Well, of course. For when I arrive.'

'I think you should put them on now.'

Another instance of the school-teacher lark. It was irritating having Laura speak to her as if she was a child, and more so with Cassie present. Laura's comment about being a seasoned traveller was also annoying, inferring that Sophie was not. Still, it wouldn't do to get home with swollen ankles. She sat down on a vacant seat and rummaged in her overnight bag for her high-heeled shoes.

'Such heels!' observed Laura. 'You really are a glutton for punishment!'

She said this quite affectionately but Cassie smirked. And then the boots would not come off. She tugged and pushed to no avail.

'Here, let me help,' Laura intervened, but she didn't do any better.

'Can you wiggle your foot?'

'I don't think so.'

'They're *stuck*!' said Cassie with satisfaction. 'They'll have to cut your feet off when you get to Johannesburg!'

'Cassie, that's enough,' Laura said. 'Let's try again.'

This effort merely succeeded in dislodging Sophie's stockings so they hung like elephant skin around her slender ankles. Her face was red from exertion.

'Can I be of any assistance?' said a man's voice.

They all looked up. The man was forty-ish, sun-tanned, with black hair greying at the temples. *Clark Gable*, Sophie thought. He was certainly an American.

'Thank you,' she said. 'You can be.'

She stretched out one shapely leg. The American, who grew

more delectable by the minute, manipulated the boot.

'That's it!' he said triumphantly.

'You *are* clever!' Sophie said.

Men, even gorgeous men like this one, needed flattery.

'Let's have the other one!'

'Thank you,' said Sophie when the boot was off.

'My pleasure, ma'am!'

Laura and Cassie had been relegated to the background while this was happening. Laura was quite bemused. Perhaps men weren't in the habit of rushing forward to remove her boots. So much for her being the experienced traveller.

Her shoes on, Sophie became aware of Cassie's scrutiny. The child's face, tight-lipped and pinched, had hatred written all over it. Sophie shivered. Why did Cassie hate her so much? It was most unfair. She had tried so hard, been so kind to the brat.

'Please tell Richard that he mustn't worry,' Laura said, tidying up the loose ends. 'I hope you manage to sleep on the flight. I never do, I'm afraid.'

'I'm sure I shall. Richard booked me first class. It makes such a difference. Bye-bye, Cassie dear. Don't forget to write to Dad. Thank you so much, Laura, for all you've done.' She kissed Laura's cheek, but not Cassie's lest the child act up.

She was finally rid of them both. She went through passport control into the departure lounge and sat down to wait. Perhaps the handsome American was booked on her flight. That would be pleasant. Better still if they were sitting together. She had not the least desire to be unfaithful to Richard, only the need to be reassured that she was charming.

But she did not spot the American and after a while she could not remember his face. Whereas Cassie's was imprinted indelibly on her mind – her hatred and hostility. Quite frightening . . .

But it was nonsense to think that way. There was no necessity to fear Cassie. She was only a little girl, only eight years old. The child who *had* been a terrible threat was – mercifully – dead.

CASSIE

1981 – 1986

CASSIE had been awake since four A.M. and up since five. This early morning activity would not expedite the postman, due to deliver her A-level results this very day, but it was no morning for sloth.

Upstairs in their bedrooms Laura and Eileen were not sharing this viewpoint. Cassie made herself a second cup of coffee and re-read the letter she had composed to the BBC Appointments Board.

The letter was concise – one page only – well-written and designed to show Cassie Stacton as a positive person with a sharp understanding of current affairs.

Her eyes ran over her list of school achievements. Winner of the Debating Society Award. Prize for Drama – Best Director. Laurels for History and English Literature. These awards had been gained prior to sixth-form college. It now remained to be seen whether the move to Collingham Tutors had paid off, as she had convinced Laura it would.

She was confident enough about History, in particular the European paper on the Rise of Nazism which had played into her hands.

English Literature, a subject which she loved, was more problematic. Why were Shakespeare's *tragedies* always on the A-level syllabus instead of his comedies? 'Hamlet' had thoroughly depressed her. And it was common knowledge that the examiners, too, were a pessimistic, cynical lot who might take exception to the manner in which she had answered their questions.

Might but shouldn't. Because she had thoroughly and

methodically versed herself in the woes of the doleful Dane and, after all, one either knew one's subject or one did not.

All over the country other school leavers would be in this state, biting their fingernails and drinking black coffee and waiting for the crucial envelope to be dropped through the letterbox.

Hundreds of them – thousands probably – would also seek jobs at the BBC. But how many of them would hand-drop their applications to Portland Place, as she intended to do, instead of posting them?

Hers would get there first! But nothing more could be done until her results arrived.

Oh, come *on*, she willed the postman. Do get moving!

But it was Laura who did that.

'Hello, darling,' she said, kissing Cassie's cheek. 'I might have known you'd be up early. Stop worrying! You're a bona fide winner, my girl!'

'And you're my life-support! Where would I be without you?'

'In Johannesburg, I imagine!'

Cassie laughed. That she of all people could be in Johannesburg was ludicrous. Since leaving the city ten years before she had never been back.

Richard, Laura and Eileen had all begged her to go there during the school holidays but Cassie had resisted. Finally Eileen had pronounced her a bold thing not to visit her daddy and her brother and forecast that she would get her come-uppance in the future. That should have been the end of it. Should have been but wasn't . . .

'I had another letter from Dad yesterday suggesting I take a year off and spend it out there. Did I tell you?'

Laura shook her head. 'Poor Richard. He never stops trying. Coming here specially to see you – '

'Mostly on business trips. And he always has that ghastly woman hanging on his arm.'

'Not literally! And she *is* his wife.'

'Well, I wish she wasn't,' said Cassie fiercely, and then the postman turned in at the gateway. From where she sat she could see him coming up the drive.

'The shit's about to hit the fan! Laura, *you* open that envelope. I can't bear it if I fail!'

'You won't fail, you idiot!' Laura said, but she went into the hall and retrieved the envelope and tore it open.

'Tell me! I can't wait either!'

'Two A's and a B.'

'You're not serious! A's for *what?*'

'History and English Lit.'

'Brilliant! I didn't care so much about Psychology. You're not making it up, are you? I *have* actually passed?'

'When do I tell lies?' Laura said, hugging her. 'You clever girl! Let's phone Richard and let him know.'

'You do that,' said Cassie, 'I'm going to photostat my results and let the BBC know how well I've done!'

Her strategy worked. The BBC called her in for an interview at which she was able to demonstrate how charming she was, how ambitious, and how politically aware. In due course a letter arrived offering her a three-month contract as a researcher on a new television programme called Global Report.

For a school-leaver the programme was manna from heaven, giving Cassie the opportunity to travel as well as gain experience in television.

She went to Japan, as part of a team investigating the effects of the unprecedented birth-rate on society. In what was then the Soviet Union, Global Report filmed a day in the life of *Izvestia* and recorded an analysis of the role of journalists and the Press behind the Iron Curtain.

The producer filed his own report on the progress of Cassie Stacton. Her contract was renewed. Soon – much sooner than even she had dreamt – people were saying that she had a brilliant future in television.

Somewhere along the line she had slimmed and grown her hair long and cultivated an image far more glamorous than those of her colleagues.

At Television Centre blue denim bordered on the obligatory. Cassie refused to wear jeans. She did not want to look like everyone else. She made sure she was noticed by coming to work in fashionable clothes, samples that Laura had acquired in the course of her work.

She was even more of an infidel where men were concerned. Inevitably, they asked her out. Cassie automatically rejected the invitations from married men and made use of those that were single.

Men, too, could be used as sexual objects, she thought. As people, they didn't matter too much. They could be taken up and used as escorts and duly dropped when their interest grew too strong.

So Simon came into her life only to be ejected after a couple of months. Adam was a pleasant companion for a short while but nothing more. He was followed by Sebastian who also failed to stay the course.

What *is* it with Cassie Stacton, people asked – particularly women. Cassie was not popular with her own sex. Women were jealous of her. As her range reached out to cover other programmes as well as Global Report, there were one or two female producers who said point-blank that they would not work with her.

Cassie didn't care. There were more than enough good programme-makers within the corporation who respected her talents and wanted her on their shows.

Some of them secretly wondered just when Cassie Stacton would pinch their jobs. But Cassie was not a behind-the-scenes operator. She was ambitious, but not fanatically. She had never resolved to get ahead by stabbing others in the back. It was possible, she thought, even in the Eighties, to climb with grace if you were sure of your steps.

So she manipulated only her lovers and no one guessed that, deep-down, Cassie Stacton was frightened of the power of men. As a result of which she had made just one vow since growing up – that she would never allow herself to fall in love.

Four years after joining the BBC, Cassie was still living in Barnes with Laura and Eileen. Other girls of her age had moved into flats which they shared with friends. Cassie was not interested in community living, exchanging confidences about her sex life and queuing for a bath.

You're living with your *grandmother*? people said in amazement from time to time. Whereupon Cassie shrugged. Laura was a much more interesting companion than a girl of her own age. So what if she was well into her sixties? Where her work was concerned Laura was at a zenith, and showing no signs of slowing up.

Only Eileen was showing her age. Her eyesight was bad. Another of her relations had been summoned from Clare to act as a back-up. But Laura . . . Well, there was *one* change. Laura's hair was white now, instead of fair. Otherwise she might have been fifteen years younger.

Laura in her sixties? Ridiculous! But, anyway, thought Cassie, she's still my best friend. How many women could say that of somebody three times their age? It was a tribute to Laura's intelligence, Laura's sensitivity and Laura's courage in always telling the truth.

So naturally they were happy living together. And then Laura, to her surprise, turned the tables.

That year – 1985 – Cassie had been abroad on several occasions with Global Report. It was the end of the women's decade. A special one hundred-minute film entitled 'Forty Years On' reviewed the basic needs of the last forty years through the eyes of five women in five different parts of the world: Latin America, Spain, Africa, India and Indonesia.

The programme included coverage of the Ethiopian famine. Addis airport was chock-a-block with aircraft bringing in food supplies. There was difficulty obtaining permission to film, difficulty moving around the country. The team hitched a lift in a Libyan plane. There were no seats – they perched on sacks of grain.

Korem Camp was a nightmare, the hotels in the area no better than pig-pens. At night Cassie lay on a bug-ridden mattress listening to mortar shells overhead.

It was heaven to come home. From the doorstep she could hear Laura talking on the phone. 'I *insist* that you give me a new machine. I don't care two pins what the engineer said. He doesn't know what he's talking about.'

Episode four of the washing-machine saga. The appliance in question was only four months old but it had sprung a leak. The company which serviced it had found a bra wire wedged in the outlet pipe and informed the manufacturer. But the leak was in the drum and Laura had hotly denied that the wire – which had come from one of her bras – could have been at fault.

'Rubbish! Absolute rubbish! Tell me, Mr Johnson, do *you* wear a bra?'

The phone was put down with a bang and Laura, pink-cheeked but stimulated by the skirmish, came through to the hall.

'Bloody man! Darling, you're back! How was it?'

'Horrendous. We just freaked out. Peter got malaria from bed-bugs and we all had bad tummies. How have *you* been?'

'Fine.'

There was a barely perceptible pause and then Laura added, 'Your father's been here.'

'He has? So I suppose you were subjected to a visit from the dreaded stepmother?'

Another little pause. 'Actually not. He came on his own.'

'Huh! Business, I suppose?'

'Not entirely. Anyway, darling, get yourself organised and I'll tell you all about it.'

She did so in rather a roundabout manner.

Cassie said, 'I cannot tell you the relief of being home! I could kiss the ground this minute!' and Laura came out with:

'You know, darling, you should move into a flat of your own.'

Just like that.

'But *why?*' Cassie demanded. 'Are you trying to get rid of me?'

'What a thing to suggest! No, it's just that – you should be building a life of your own.'

'That's exactly what I'm doing at the Beeb.'

'I don't mean that. Your *career* is flourishing.'

'Well then!'

'*Not* "well". Wrong. You should be having an emotional life.'

'For heaven's sake, I'm not a virgin!'

'Even if you were I wouldn't suggest you moved out to rectify that. It's that you don't form *steady* relationships with men. You string them along for a few months and that's the end of it. It's not right, darling. And if you had your own place – your own *space* – it might be different.'

'And then again it might not,' said Cassie. 'What started your mind moving along those lines?'

'Richard, primarily.'

'The interfering old sod!'

'Hang on. Don't get mad. He wants to buy you a flat.'

'I don't need his bloody charity.'

'Don't be hasty. You don't get an offer like that every day of the week. Most people I know would grovel for it.'

'Grovel indeed!'

'Use your head! A flat would be an insurance for your future. And it isn't as if Richard can't afford it.'

'Can he? With all those trips Sophie makes to Harrods?'

'You're being bitchy. Look, let Richard do this for you. You don't have to move in if you don't want to – or not immediately. You can always rent the apartment out – put the money in the bank.'

'So he's not making conditions?' Cassie was cooling down.

'No. But we both feel that you should think about living on your own.'

'Huh!' said Cassie again.

The subject was put on ice. Richard, however, stayed put in his daughter's thoughts. Every time he came to London he contrived to see her alone, hoping, in a pathetic way, to patch up their differences. The offer of a flat was the latest in a series of bribes he had made in this connection. All the others – the offers of holidays, of a car for her twenty-first – Cassie had turned down and Richard, as she had intended, had been hurt.

But – a flat? At London prices even a one-bedroomed apartment was out of her present range. Richard would buy for cash. The investment would eat into his overseas savings, infuriating Sophie. It might even cause a row between husband and wife. What fun, thought Cassie.

Thinking like that was vile. Laura would most certainly condemn it, as she had proscribed similar thoughts, expressed out loud, in the past. But I can't help it, Cassie said to herself. Sophie has a negative effect on me – she always did have. And all these years on she still arouses in me the same antipathy I felt towards her when I was a child. The need to harm her – not just hurt, but *harm* – wells up inside me so I'm almost possessed. And yet – hypocrite that I am! – I'm outwardly polite nowadays when our paths do cross.

Don't think of Sophie, said common sense, intervening. Turn your thoughts to positive matters. For instance, the flat.

It seemed that she was going to accept Richard's offer; that it only remained to thank him for it and to look for a suitable property which he could buy. And furnish on her behalf. That, Laura insisted, was part of the deal.

She found herself considering colour schemes – wandering in to Habitat and the Conran Shop. Not that there was any hurry to move out of Barnes, even when the flat *was* located. She could, as Laura had suggested, rent it out, stay where she was. And yet . . . Living alone was not really such a bad idea.

The acquisition of the flat brought Richard and Cassie into more frequent contact.

Cassie's question, 'How much are you prepared to pay?' was answered by, 'In the region of £50,000. The lease should be upwards of ninety years. Make sure the managing agents are efficient and that the service charges are not too high.'

Cassie posted out half a dozen sets of details from estate agents and began her preliminary investigations.

She was attracted by Bayswater with its lively, late-night buzz and cosmopolitan feel. Queensway, with its kebab houses and East European restaurants, was aeons away from the King's Road, home of Punk.

The right apartment was located in Moscow Road, diagonally across from the Greek Orthodox Church with the green dome on the corner of Ilchester Gardens.

Richard was phoned and agreed to fly over to complete the deal. He came alone and stayed in Barnes, instead of in a hotel.

It was October by then and there was in the air an autumn nip. And yet Cassie had a sense of renaissance, a new beginning that did not only apply to herself but – oddly – to Richard and Laura.

She could not precisely pinpoint the evidence of that resurgence. Richard and Laura were not sleeping together again or being overtly affectionate. It was much more subtle than that. But there it was, this new life, in their smiles and eyes.

It was there the day all three of them went to see the flat. A navy blue Rolls with OYL on the number-plate was parked in the street outside.

'Signs of affluence?' Richard said and they all laughed.

But afterwards Cassie was angry with herself for softening towards Richard, all the more since Laura was looking so happy being with him again.

'We've done well,' Richard said, meaning Cassie and himself. 'You won't be able to move in for a couple of months so why don't you come out to South Africa for Christmas? I've been trying to persuade you for years.'

But Cassie was already battening the hatches down. 'Sorry,' she said, 'really. It's not my scene.'

Once again, Richard was cut to the quick. But Cassie, in dismissing South Africa in three words, tempted Fate.

The following year – 1986 – was the tenth anniversary of the

Soweto riots. The BBC was planning an unusual documentary to mark the event. At Television Centre Cassie was approached about the project.

The producer explained, 'This book, *Twelve Shades of Black*, was published in the year of the riots. It's a series of interviews with Black people living in the townships in and around Johannesburg. We want to find out what has happened to those twelve people since 1976. At least one has been murdered – possibly more.'

Johannesburg, thought Cassie.

'You'd want me there?'

'Of course. We're going to recruit one of the Black journalists from the *Rand Daily Mail*. It's not easy tracking down people in the townships. You know – you've been there – '

'Not since I was eight.'

'Pity about that. I thought you had family in Johannesburg.'

'Yes, I do,' said Cassie more positively, not wanting the job to slip out of her hands. Which it did not.

She told Laura. 'Guess what – I'm going to Johannesburg of all places!'

'That's amazing! What brought about such a change of heart?'

'You've got me wrong. I'm not going there on a holiday. This is work.'

'How fascinating,' said Laura when the project had been outlined. 'I wish I could go with you. I always fancied doing an Africa book.'

'Did you?' This was news.

'I've always secretly envied Eve Arnold's work. Those wonderful pictures of China.'

Eve Arnold's *In China* had won the National Book Award. The recipient of many other prizes, Miss Arnold was also a member of Magnum, the collective which gave photo-journalists artistic freedom and control over their rights. Magnum photographers risked their lives to bring back superb pictures from the world's trouble spots. Laura was not a member of the collective even though it had been co-founded by her old friend, Robert Capa, and Henri Cartier Bresson.

'You should be part of it,' Cassie said.

'Why? I don't take risks. Magnum would maintain that I opted for a fantasy world instead of reality and that's perfectly true. Anyway,' said Laura, briskly, 'I made my choice and I became rather rich as a result. Enough of that. You'll obviously be seeing something of your father in Johannesburg. Will you stay at the house?'

'Are you mad? Stay with the vile stepmother? Not me. We're all being put up at the Rosebank Hotel.'

'But you will *see* Richard?' Laura sounded concerned.

'Yes, yes,' Cassie said, 'I'll look him up. And I suppose I'll have to dine at Inanda at least one night. Think of the strain of sitting across the table from *her* on a mid-summer evening!'

She sighed hugely, raising her eyes to heaven, inviting Laura to laugh at the horror of this. But Laura didn't laugh.

'Because, darling, I don't think he's happy these days.'

'Isn't he? Well, he brought it upon himself.'

'I pick up nuances,' Laura said. 'I think he may be bored.'

'She *is* boring. Smug and self-satisfied and narrow-minded. He was a fool to marry her. You don't seriously think that they're breaking up. You don't think that, do you?'

'I shouldn't imagine so,' Laura said, disappointingly. 'Only that, so to speak, he's rumbling a bit.'

Cassie eyed her. 'Just how often do you two speak on the phone?'

'Now and again,' Laura said, and her eyes were sparkling with life.

Honestly, Cassie thought. She could be my age, or younger. And what does Dad think he's doing, phoning her up?

'If he phones again before I go don't say anything. I just want to arrive.'

'I won't. I promise. And don't *you* repeat what I just said.'

'Would I do that?'

The doorbell went. Laura chortled, 'That will be my new washing machine!' and exited, gloating.

Cassie switched on television. Mastermind was due to start in five minutes. She stared blankly at the screen, thinking of Richard. *He's rumbling a bit.*

He deserved to suffer, she thought. Yet Laura's assertion that he did tugged at her heart. From deeper down other thoughts pushed their way upward. Complex thoughts of Richard and Sophie and the past. Ugly thoughts, powerful, frightening thoughts which gnawed away at her soul. Thoughts that were infused with anger and the need for revenge.

She did not seem to have any control over these thoughts.

'You're awfully late getting here,' said Laura in the hall. 'You'd better have a cup of coffee before you go.'

No control . . . Terror seized. For a moment she was tempted to run to Laura for help. But Laura was in the kitchen supervising the installation of the washing machine. And she, Cassie, was a grown woman, not a little girl. She must stop running to Laura when things went wrong. Somehow or other she would have to gain control over her thoughts.

Magnus Magnusson's face appeared on the screen. She turned up the volume and huddled into her chair.

I T was a city with little respect for its history, a fact borne out by its obsession with demolition and the substitution of new structures for old. Much of what had been built in the 1950s had been razed to the ground by financially driven developers.

The lack of continuity had its effect on Cassie, driving in from Jan Smuts airport in the hired car. Johannesburg was restless, disquieting and hyperactive.

In Parktown the demolishers had been driven by ideology rather than money. Part of the suburb had been appropriated by the Nationalist-controlled Transvaal Provincial Administration, determined to destroy this symbol of English-speaking wealth and power. In place of the fantasy mansions of the Gold Rush millionaires were public sector buildings, including an enormous eyesore hospital perched on the crest of a magnificent skyline.

Private enterprise had done its bit, too. In the gardens where English flowers had once blossomed were dun-coloured brick office blocks.

There were other changes – yet to be experienced – of which Richard had spoken. Central Johannesburg had 'gone Black'; Whites went shopping in the huge suburban centres which had sprung up over the last decade.

One change was only too obvious, as she found when she pulled up at a Greek café to buy a bar of chocolate. A group of Blacks were gathered on the pavement. They looked at her with open hostility, their eyes burning with hate and resentment.

They always felt that way about us, Cassie thought. The

313

difference is that – today – they're showing their feelings. The masks have dropped.

At the Rosebank Hotel she experienced, on an even more personal level, another break with the past.

'It's Stacton, not Sampson,' she said to the head porter.

The long journey from London, the pressures of the environment into which she had stepped, were getting to her by then. She sounded more abrasive than she felt.

The head porter was Black.

'Don't speak to *him* like that!' said one of the White receptionists. '*He* knows his job.'

'There's a message for you, Miss Stacton,' the porter said, unruffled by the small contretemps.

He passed across a folded slip of paper. Her eyes skimmed over the message. The Black journalist from the *Rand Daily Mail* had confirmed their arrangement to meet this morning.

'Thank you.'

The porter returned her smile. 'Thank you, madam.' A page was summoned. 'Take Miss Stacton's case to her room.'

She thought fleetingly of Richard. Tomorrow, not today, she would make contact. There wouldn't be time until the afternoon – not if Gibson Mosala from the *Rand Daily Mail* took her out to Soweto.

And in the afternoon she would have a rest, then make notes about whoever she met in the township.

Gibson Mosala was in the lobby when she came down.

'Cassie Stacton?'

No lack of confidence here – and no hatred either.

'Fancy a coffee?'

'Thanks.'

There was no reason – not any more – why a Black could not drink or dine in an hotel once reserved for Whites. All the same, eyes watched their progress out on to the terrace. A White girl in the company of a Black man was obviously suspect. Things were changing, but not that fast.

She had brought with her a copy of the book from which the

314

idea for the programme had come. Gibson had one, too.

'I've tracked down many but not all of these people,' he said. 'The artist, Durant Sihlali, is still in Soweto. He lives in Jubulani, in Muja Street. I've arranged for us to see him today if that's OK with you?'

'That's fine.'

'The poet, Wally Serote, got a bursary to study in the United States and he's there now. I'm almost certain that "Hlubi" was murdered. But I will check.'

'Hlubi' was Detective Sergeant Ophen Chapi of the Murder and Robbery Unit, the man who had boasted to the author of the book that his reputation for strength was enough to ward off would-be attackers.

And here was Gibson speaking casually of his death, as if murder was an everyday occurrence in his world. But then Soweto *was* a violent place.

'Sarah Mashele, the Inyanga, can be found. We will go to her consulting rooms. But not tomorrow. On Fridays she is closed.'

An Inyanga, Cassie already knew, was a healer. Mrs Mashele was a healer *par excellence*. The people of Soweto paid on hire-purchase for her herbs and medicines and charms, as a result of which Mrs Mashele lived in a double-storey house in Dube, the township's most élite suburb, and owned three cars. If you were clever you could make money wherever you lived. There were millionaires – Black entrepreneurs – in Soweto.

'So today we see Sihlali. Shall we go?'

'Suits me,' Cassie said.

Her first impression of Soweto was of a dull and apathetic township slumped in inertia. The houses, squat brick bungalows, were almost all exactly alike, hundreds and hundreds of them facing each other across unnamed, untarred streets.

There were no flowers growing in the gardens and only, very occasionally, a despondent, stunted tree. Under one, a white goat sat, soaking up the sun. The car moved towards Jubulani in a cloud of dust. Through the open window Cassie smelt the pungent aroma of wood-smoke and *dagga*, South African cannabis.

Twice, the sight of Caspirs, the huge tanks used by the South African army, reminded her forcibly that a state of emergency had been declared in the republic. These tanks were manned by sun-tanned recruits doing their national service. Black youths of the same age shook their fists or gave the Black Power sign as the Caspirs cruised by.

Durant Sihlali was small and shy and neat; his water-colours lyrical, gentle and reminiscent, some depicting the period when he had lived in a tin shack.

Some were of Old Pimville, a Black suburb, also demolished now; of flooded homes after heavy rains; of women washing clothes; of a home about to be wrecked.

'It's beautiful work,' Cassie said as the artist put his portfolio aside to talk about change.

They lingered in Muja Street for a couple of hours before Gibson said with a start that he had to get to work. 'I'm on the afternoon shift. We'll come back to Soweto tomorrow but right now we'd better be going.'

Getting out of Soweto, thought Cassie, was easier said than done. There were no obvious landmarks, not unless one counted the burnt-out cars.

'Pinched,' said Gibson, matter-of-factly. 'This place is crazy. Frustration. Boredom. Booze. Illegitimate kids running wild. Killings every night. Crazy.'

They turned left. The car windows were up now but the dust was getting through. Cassie sneezed and felt in her bag for a tissue.

'Sorry!'

She sneezed again. Dabbing her nose she saw ahead a group of figures, waving sticks.

'Looks like trouble,' Gibson said in a toneless voice.

The crowd was shouting. Smoke was billowing up from an invisible fire.

'What do you think is going on?'

'Listen, in Soweto something's *always* going on. I think maybe we should stop and you get out and lie down in the back.'

'Are you serious?'

'There's a blanket on the back seat. Pull it over you and don't look up – OK?'

Getting out of the car she could smell burning rubber. She wrinkled her nose with distaste and got, as Gibson had suggested, into the back of the car, lying down and reaching for the blanket.

'Over your head – right?'

'I'm going to boil down here.'

But Gibson was already revving up. Cassie braced herself for an abrupt turn but he drove straight on.

The noise from the crowd had reached a crescendo. Wild shrieks of encouragement – screams of anguish or pain. Cassie cowered under the blanket. The car rumbled on, alternately hitting holes in the road and small obstacles, probably stones. The jerky movements, the heat induced by the blanket, concentrated Cassie's full attention on her stomach. The last straw would be to vomit in Gibson's presence.

The shrieks had died down. They must be over the worst.

'Can I come up?'

'No, not yet. I'll tell you.'

She eased from her stomach to her side, hand over her mouth.

The car turned on to more even ground. She guessed that they were on the road that led past Baragwanath Hospital. Out of Soweto. Safe. Hopefully.

'OK,' Gibson said. 'You can sit up now.'

'What was *that* all about?'

'The usual things. This township has a murder rate five times higher than New York – you knew that?'

'What happened back there?'

'A man was necklaced. Don't ask me why. I don't know why. But that was what happened.'

*

317

The afternoon passed slowly. Cassie wandered around the Firs Shopping Centre, not wanting to buy anything and not wanting to be on her own either. The screams of Soweto still seemed to rebound in her ears.

She *had* been warned – should have expected something like that to occur. The township was in uproar. All the time buses were being petrol-bombed; homes, churches and clinics burnt; rivals, dissidents and informers murdered.

'Render South Africa Ungovernable': the slogan used by the African National Congress and the United Democratic Front.

It was all happening – but not at the Firs. Here, life was proceeding as normal. Well-dressed women were looking in the boutiques, drinking coffee and coming in with children newly picked up from school. How many of those women knew what was going on less than twenty miles south of here, Cassie wondered, watching them wend their way up and down the escalators. Most would prefer to keep their heads in the sand and enjoy the good life. *eGoli*, the Africans called Johannesburg – the city of gold. It was still that for some.

She stayed at the Firs until the centre closed, then walked back the short distance to the hotel. Until now she had never really minded being on her own. The rest of the team were not due to join her until Tuesday. Suddenly the prospect of spending four evenings in her own company was unbearable. Ergo – phone Dad. As usual, he would be thrilled to hear from her, would drop whatever other plans he might have had for the weekend in her favour.

He wouldn't drop Sophie, though – he'd count her in. Shit, thought Cassie. But it was dark already and the blackness outside was underlining her desolation. Richard would long since have left his office. She reached out for the phone and dialled his number in Inanda.

Almost at once the call was answered by a maid. 'Hello, who is this, please?'

'Is Mr Stacton there?'

'Who is speaking?'

'It's his daughter, Cassie. Is my father there?'

'Plizz hold on.'

A male voice on the line. 'Hello?'

It wasn't Richard.

'Peter, is that you?' said Cassie.

'No,' said the voice at the other end. 'This is Rob.'

Over the years Cassie had behaved as if Rob did not exist. This had been easy enough. Rob never came to England. Nor did Peter. Although she classified her brother as a traitor he was family nevertheless. Peter was worthy of birthday and Christmas cards – Rob was not. Rob was Sophie's son – an automatic outcast and best ignored.

All efforts on Richard's part to break down the barriers had failed as hopelessly as his attempts to lure Cassie to Johannesburg. Photographs of Rob had been sent, along with others of Peter. Cassie had refused to look at them.

All the same, news of Rob had infiltrated over the years. There was his sporting prowess: Rob had won the Victor Ludorum in his matriculation year. His scholastic achievements: third in the top grade.

After school Rob, like Peter, had done his national service. He had taken a B. Comm. at the University of the Witwatersrand and now had a job, although what, precisely, he was doing, Cassie was unsure.

As an adult it was more difficult to ignore Rob. Like now, for instance . . .

'Oh, hello, Rob,' said Cassie in her most nonchalant voice. 'It's Cassie here.'

That was as far as she got.

'Cassie! You sound very close. Are you here.' He actually sounded pleased.

'Yes, I am. At the Rosebank Hotel.'

'That's incredible. What are you doing here?'

In spite of herself, Cassie unbent. 'A programme for BBC Television. I'll be in town for about three weeks.'

'Hey! Aren't you guys sick of our problems yet? I tell you, *we* are!'

'I think we've got a nice angle,' said Cassie.

She could hear herself sounding smug and defensive but Rob didn't notice – or mind.

'Anyway, it's great to hear from you. When can we see you?'

'We' she thought?

'I'm trying to work that out? Is my father there?'

'No, he isn't. The folks are down in the Cape for a week. They left this evening.'

'And Peter?'

'Out *jolling*.'

Having a good time. Unlike herself.

'I see.'

'Listen, what are you doing? Are you with people? Because if you're on your own, so am I. Why don't I come round and take you out to dinner?'

She should have declined. She should have told him that she had a report to write. Which she had. But she could do it tomorrow – or on Saturday or . . .

'I *am* on my own,' she said. 'Dinner sounds like a good idea.'

Cool and controlled and not wildly enthusiastic about meeting her step-brother. Who – it had to be remembered – was Sophie's son.

'What's your room number?' Rob said. 'I'll be with you in half an hour.'

He was bound to be dull. His mind would be closed. He would be insular and complacent. Miserable or not, she would have been better off alone this evening. Too late to phone and get out of it. He would already have set out. Short of feigning sudden illness she was stuck with him.

The phone rang. 'Miss Stacton. Mr Jurgens is waiting for you in the lobby.'

'I'll be right down.'

She walked past the lift and down the stairs. The lobby was

a-buzz with activity – diners making their way to the various restaurants, guests arriving late, men and women on their own, waiting expectantly.

She looked around, saw a desirable man sitting in a chair reading *Time* magazine, hoped he was staying in the hotel, saw a fair-haired horror running to fat, pot belly protruding over his belt, waiting at reception.

That would be him all right, she thought. Sophie's son, complete with beer-gut. She could still run for it – simply fail to materialise. Only that would mean answering to Richard. She was, after all, an adult, not an eight-year-old girl. She might feel much the same as when she was young but she had to act differently.

'Excuse me,' she said to the head porter. 'You said Mr Jurgens was here.'

'Yes, Miss Stacton. He's sitting over there.'

In the chair. Reading a copy of *Time* magazine. *That* was Rob? She went over to him. 'Rob?'

He leapt up, smiling so charmingly that she was taken aback. The smile said a lot about him, told her that here was a man who had been greatly loved and was confident, in the nicest possible way, as a result. There was nothing cynical in this man. Life had not yet hurt him. He might believe that it never could.

He was blond and blue-eyed and gorgeous and, now that she saw him close-up, much like his mother in looks.

'*Hi!*' he said. 'Great to have you here! You're just like your pictures. Dad has photos of you all over the house.'

Dad?

'Does he?'

'You live up to your photographs! My friends are always asking when my sister's coming out.'

My sister?

That fraternal smile. But Rob wasn't her true brother. He was Sophie's son and if he didn't remember who he was he'd have to be taught.

Being in his presence was extremely strange. He was

physically very attractive. She could already feel herself being drawn to him on that level. But he was *Sophie's* son and the demons, alerted to this, were getting to work.

'Do you like Chinese food? The Lien Wah is pretty good. I booked a table.'

His eagerness to please put her in mind of a puppy – a Golden Labrador, Cassie thought. But there was nothing canine in the way he moved. He was athletically graceful. She remembered that he was an excellent sportsman. Would he talk of rugby or cricket all through dinner?

Instead, he asked her questions. He was interested in everything about her – her life in England, her work, even her relationship with Laura.

He was much brighter than she had thought but he was somehow innocent in the way people are when they have not travelled far from their home environment.

'I mean to do the Europe bit. Everyone else did,' he said at one stage. 'But I guess everything I want out of life is here, in South Africa.'

He smiled again in that sweet way, inciting Cassie's demons. *My sister* indeed, she thought. Rob might be both personable and artless but his smile was a challenge.

'**H**E'S a nice chap but he's not in her league,' Richard said on the phone five weeks later. 'She'll chew him up and spit out the pips.'

It was seven A.M. – nine A.M. in South Africa. Richard would already have been at work for an hour.

Laura, sitting up in bed, pressed the remote control and silenced Breakfast Television. The avuncular, reassuring face of Frank Bough gazed back at her from the screen.

'Then the sooner that happens the better. She'll come home and that will be the end of it.'

'Not here it won't be,' said Richard grimly. 'Chaos pends.'

'You really think he's in love with her?'

From where she sat Laura could reach the table on which the essentials for making morning tea had been placed. She switched on the kettle.

'Completely enthralled. Poor chap.'

'They're sleeping together, of course?'

'Living together, more or less. It's a tiny flat. They're looking for a cottage.'

'I see.'

'Sophie's on tranquillisers. I must say, we were all caught on the hop. I mean, who'd have expected it – Rob and Cassie of all people. Peter says he was stunned.'

'He's against it?'

'*Look,*' Richard said inappropriately, 'it's so patently wrong. They're mismatched. He's a fine chap – bright, hardworking, sincere, but not that strong. Not for *her.* And then there's all this ghastly tension between herself and Sophie. Sometimes I think – '

The line went dead. The kettle came to the boil. Laura put the receiver down and made tea, opened the biscuit box and selected a chocolate gold grain. At once the phone rang again.

'Richard?'

'Ah, there you are. You know the minute I heard Cassie saying that she was going to stay on I knew something was up. I don't know how she's fixed things with the BBC.'

'Isn't she missing work?'

'I daresay. She mentions doing something for the SABC. They'd have her like a shot, drat them. Not that I wouldn't want her here under other circumstances. Except that I do worry about the future. The townships are in a bloody mess. Fifty per cent of our Black people are under twenty. The chances of most of them getting jobs are pretty remote. What have they got to lose by rioting? Anyway, to get back to Cassie . . .'

Laura chewed her biscuit, letting him run on. The action had hotted up – Cassie had seen to that – but the conversation she was having with Richard was in a sense the same one they had been conducting for years. The predominating theme: the welfare of Cassie. But there was more to it than that. The calls – necessary, but also once acutely painful from her own viewpoint – had long since lost their capacity to hurt.

The phone was Richard's life-line to her – she had come to understand that. If he had not used it to talk about Cassie he would have found another excuse. In the light of which her own pride had taken early retirement.

'She has a sadistic streak.'

'Only where men are concerned.'

'Only! A psychiatrist would say she is punishing me through her boyfriends for marrying Sophie.'

'I daresay she is.'

'She could have kept it out of the family,' said Richard. 'I dread going home.'

The peace of the day shattered, tea cold, Laura got up. Still in her dressing-gown, she wandered through to the studio, thinking about Cassie.

Over the last few weeks, ever since getting involved with Rob, Cassie had been evasive. They had only once spoken on the phone in that time, at Laura's instigation, although afterwards Cassie had written a short but cheerful letter. The kind of letter you wrote to someone when you were keeping your relationship with her on ice . . .

And now they couldn't talk – for the simple reason that there was no phone in Cassie's flat. According to Richard phone installation was an on-going problem in Johannesburg. You could wait months before being given a line. A fat lot of good that was going to be.

She went through her daily ritual of checking up, making sure that records had been kept of each roll of film, whether they had been numbered and labelled with the lens and the right F-stop. Notes should also have been made of garments worn by models, and of lighting changes.

She frowned and fussed. But Dodgy, newly recruited and so far impossible to fault, hadn't slipped up. She hoped that he had already organised the film for this day's shoot, checked that camera equipment was in perfect order. The knowledge that he was as much of a perfectionist as herself did not stop her looking for mistakes.

'Checking up on me, are you?' Dodgy asked, coming in silently.

'Don't creep up on me. It's nerve-racking!'

'Your nerves are made of steel wire!'

'And don't make me laugh, either. I've got a lot on my mind.'

'Paris,' said Dodgy happily.

Laura was taking him with her to shoot the Yves Saint Laurent Couture Collection. The storyline had already been decided in conjunction with American *Vogue*. The Saint Laurent Press office had been contacted and given precise details of what would be required – not only the clothes but all accessories.

As usual, when shooting haute couture, Laura and the

magazine had agreed to stick as closely as possible to M. Saint Laurent's original presentation, down to the same pink bow which he had chosen for a particular model's hair.

The photographs would be a final testimony to an extraordinary study in perfection, one that would have commenced six weeks earlier with the arrival of the designer's sketches in his salon in Avenue Marceau.

Laura had told Dodgy what happened thereafter. At the top of the salon was the *Premier d'Atelier*, thirteen workrooms divided into two sections: *Le Fleu*, where the softly flowing lines were made, and *Le Tailleur*, which produced the tailoreds.

The minute the sketches arrived they were whisked upstairs and translated into *toile* for the first fittings meeting with M. Saint Laurent. Once the *toile* translation had been pronounced perfect, designer and *atelier* decided which fabric should be used. Then, working by hand, the design would be cut, sewn and tried first on a dummy and then on a living model. Once again, M. Saint Laurent had to approve the result. Sometimes it took several weeks to produce one dress.

'He always shows his haute couture on a Wednesday, doesn't he?' Dodgy asked.

'That's right. And sometimes the *atelier* and the embroiderers work all the previous night.'

And meanwhile the perfect dress would have to be matched to the appropriate model. Fittings would have been held in the downstairs salon at which M. Saint Laurent would have decided whether this or that design looked best on a Black girl, or a blonde, or a brunette.

'*That*'s overloading your mind?'

'Not just that,' admitted Laura. 'Actually, to tell you the truth, I'm worried about Cassie. I think she's up to no good.'

Richard was thinking much the same. After talking to Laura he scratched his head reflectively and gazed into space. Laura had been wrong in thinking he had been at work since eight: he had got to the office at six, a good two hours before anyone else.

This had been a pattern for him of late. He slept badly, got up before daybreak and swam several lengths of the pool before dressing and driving off, leaving Sophie fast asleep in their double bed. Anyway, he couldn't talk to Sophie, not about Cassie. And not much about anything else.

'Blast and damn!' he said out loud and the intercom buzzed.

'Mr Stacton, you haven't forgotten your appointment with the dentist?'

'No, Jenny, I haven't.'

But, of course, he had. He looked at his diary. Nine-fifteen. Bugger that.

'Jenny, on second thoughts, cancel it. But I'll still be out for an hour or two.'

'Do you want me to make another appointment?'

'Yes, please do.'

The small flat Rob and Cassie shared was ten minutes' drive away. Cassie, just possibly, might be at home.

As luck had it she was. The flat had a communal pool. He found his daughter stretched out beside it with her nose in a book.

'Hello, darling.'

'Hello,' said Cassie in the off-hand, unenthusiastic voice she apparently reserved especially for him. 'What brings *you* here?'

'We need to talk.'

'Oh? What about?'

'About Rob.'

Cassie had oiled herself before lying down. She repeated the process now, fiercely concentrating as if that was all that concerned her.

'What about Rob?'

'Do you love him at all?' Richard felt silly asking the question.

Cassie looked at him slyly. '*You* love him as if he was your own son, don't you?'

'Well. Yes. I do.'

'As much as you love Peter – or me.'

'Does that upset you?'

'Not particularly.'

'Anyway,' said Richard, doing his best, 'we seem to have got away from my question. Darling, I'm anxious about this. Are you in love with him?'

'I think he's beautiful,' said Cassie, looking at her legs. 'He looks very like his mother, doesn't he? So I suppose I feel about him as you do about her.'

Richard did something daring. He reached out, took the bottle of sun-tan oil away from Cassie and squeezed her greasy hand.

'I want *you* to be happier than I am,' he said pointedly. 'I want you to choose wisely.'

Cassie softened. 'You're fed up with her, aren't you?'

But this was treacherous territory.

'Let's say – with *here*, with the society as a whole.'

In the brashness of Johannesburg he had once seen White vitality and panache. Like most Whites he had allowed himself to be effectively anaesthetised by separatism. He had been blind to the iniquities of apartheid. His disillusionment had been gradual. Today it was a stifling malaise.

It was the age of designer labels. The wave of materialism which was sweeping the West had hit Johannesburg hard. Only this morning he had noticed that Born-Again Christians were flaunting designer fish symbols on the rear of their Mercedes.

He tried to explain to Cassie: 'I've become repelled by the greed and vulgarity I see around me.'

Yes, he knew there were changes going on, but in his own affable circle was a conformity of attitude, a suspicion of harmless eccentricity that he found it increasingly difficult to tolerate. And he could only castigate himself. For years, Blacks had been mere shadows moving through his home and across his garden attending to menial tasks.

'It's dawned on me finally that I knew none of them as *people* – that I'd completely failed to communicate across the racial divide except at arm's length.'

To all of this Cassie listened with unusual sympathy. Then Richard made a gaffe.

'So, you see,' he said, 'that when an outsider like myself can fall into the trap it becomes easier to understand what it's like for someone who was born ensnared. It wouldn't be fair to blame Sophie for my discontentment.'

He was trying to convince himself as much as Cassie. But the mere mention of Sophie's name in a compassionate context was enough to sabotage the momentary closeness that had grown up between father and daughter.

That bitch, thought Cassie savagely.

The softness was gone. Looking at her, Richard saw Cassie the stranger again. Cassie the uncaring, the invidious. Back on course.

'You were asking me just now about love,' she said. 'But did *you* love Sophie when you married her?'

She picked up the bottle of oil, screwed its top back on, tossed it into the grass and dived into the pool.

'Don't forget – you're coming for supper this evening,' Richard called out.

There were times when Cassie was genuinely fond of Rob, when she acknowledged that he was one of the nicest people she had ever known.

Bed was nice, too. More than nice – delicious and, up to a point, satisfying, which was to say that while his emotions were engaged hers were not. Which had always been par for the course, according to her standards.

There were other times when the demons took over, when she knew that she was intent on wreckage and couldn't be stopped. Times when she wondered if perhaps she was not going mad. Times when she desperately wanted to talk to Laura. But phone calls were unsatisfactory – not that she had daily access to a phone, anyway.

When Richard had left she got out of the pool, tied a towel round her hair and went into the flat to get dressed. The cottage which she and Rob had seen had to be secured. She had an afternoon assignment at the SABC. And then – dinner with The

Folks, as Rob euphemistically called them.

She dried her hair, scowling at herself in the mirror. Peter's nickname for her was Flame Lily Sis. Rob had told her that. This flower, Peter had pointed out, was flamboyant – yellow or orange in colour – highly ornamental – and poisonous.

Rob had laughed this off. And Peter . . . But she had seen little of Peter. He was currently down in the Cape on an extended holiday. He wouldn't be present at supper tonight. She wondered if he knew that Rob had proposed – was always proposing. Just as she was always fending him off – in that respect, anyway.

'*I couldn't conceive of life without you, Cassie.*' How often in the last couple of weeks had Rob said that?

Flame Lily Sis – what a nickname!

Her hair was dry. She shook her head, ran her hands through it, checked herself once again in the mirror – and the demons clocked in.

'We've got the cottage,' Cassie announced when Rob came in. 'I've organised everything.'

'You're amazing!'

He went to the fridge and took out a beer. 'Want a drink?'

'No thanks.'

'What else did you do today?'

'I swam – tanned – worked. And Our Father Who Is in the Republic paid a call!'

'Dad came around?'

'He did.'

'What brought that about?' said Rob, sinking into an armchair, stretching out his long legs and drinking from the can.

'He wanted to know if I love you or if I am trifling with your emotions. How hypocritical can you get?'

'Come on, Cass. Dad's a good *oke.*'

'Like hell!'

'He's been fantastic to me – '

'Lucky old you.'

' – and to you. What about that flat? He's mad about you. He used to talk to us about you a lot when we were kids.'

This only served to exacerbate Cassie's irritation.

'You always think the best of everyone, don't you?' she said.

'Is that so terrible?'

'It can be. Have you ever read *Candide*? You should. It would teach you about yourself.'

'You're being smart. Don't make him pay such a high price for marrying my mom.'

The can was empty. Rob fetched a second one, set it down on the floor next to his chair, and undid his tie.

'He had another woman in England before he came out here,' Cassie stated.

'And that's wrong?'

'I haven't finished. They were crazy about each other.'

'And?'

'She thought they were going to get married. I know she did.'

Cassie the organiser was far preferable to Cassie the intense.

'Go on.'

'Don't mention this to Peter whatever you do. It's just between us. But Dad ditched her, left her – wham! – and came out here to marry your mum. But do you think he severs the other contact? No, he does not.'

This hurt. Rob's face showed it. 'How come you know all this? You've met the woman?'

'Of course I've met her.'

'What's she like?'

Cassie the intense became soft and wistful and oddly appealing.

'She's wonderful. Brilliant. Too clever for him. Masses of integrity. *Fun*. We all – everyone loves her.'

'You must have got really close to her.'

'I did. She's the greatest. That's why I can't forgive what he did. Why I want to make him *pay* for it . . .'

The intensity was back and with it his realisation of her pain.

'Cass,' he said, gently, 'you've got to forgive him. I mean, we've

331

all been through it. My parents also got divorced.'

'You don't see your father, do you?'

'I didn't – not for years after they broke up. But then Mom relented and we did see each other now and again.'

'What made them split?'

'Mom never talks about it. But a couple of years ago he got a bit drunk and he told me he had an affair with another woman and Mom threw him out.'

This was interesting. 'Who was she?'

'I don't know. He didn't say. One of Mom's friends, maybe. He's gone back to live in Germany. He told me before he left that he still loves Mom. Listen, we're going to be late – '

'Oh, God!' Cassie said. 'Supper at Inanda. What a bore!'

Sophie had not aged one whit in ten years. Her skin was smooth and silken, her hands well looked-after, her nails long and red. Her lips were also red, coerced into a smile of welcome that was patently insincere.

'Richard, darling, get the children a drink. So, Cassie, you haven't got tired of South Africa yet?'

'I'm afraid not.'

'It's always a revelation for anyone from overseas to see what we have to put up with from the Blacks – especially someone from the BBC. The violence is too terrible. They're worse to their own than they are to us. Although you wouldn't believe the number of break-ins since the troubles started.'

While Sophie was speaking a maid – her face carefully devoid of expression – offered snacks.

'You can go out to a movie and come home to find that the house has been stripped. Doll, tell Cassie what happened to you on the way to Zambia.'

Richard coughed.

Rob said, 'Oh yes – this is an interesting story. Go on, Dad.'

'This was a few months back,' said Richard. 'Just before you came out, actually. John Henderson and I were going to a meeting in Lusaka in his Cessna. John didn't get his act together.

We were late leaving and then he said we'd have to refuel at Messina. Only thing – the aviation fuel service had closed down for the night and there we were, stuck on the border with Zimbabwe. Pitch dark. Mossies everywhere. No food. No booze. No rugs. Nobody. And then this African pitches up – '

'Nothing to do with the airport. He just *crept* up, didn't he, doll?'

'Not quite. He was very well-dressed and extremely courteous and he asked us if we'd like to eat at his house. *Pap*, we thought, but we were so hungry we didn't care.'

'Can you imagine eating *pap!*' Sophie said.

Richard's eyes narrowed. He went on: 'It was just an ordinary African house from the outside but when we went in – beautiful furniture, rugs. Oil paintings on the walls! And then his wife came in. "I'm not sure if your religion will let you eat pork," she said, "so I've cooked a chicken as well." We had the most fantastic meal. Turned out she'd been a cook in Johannesburg for twenty years. And now here she was, playing hostess to the kind of people who used to employ her. And she did it beautifully. Isn't that great?'

'I think it's disgusting!' said Sophie promptly. 'I mean all those things – the furniture and the rugs and the paintings – they must have been *stolen*! Probably from her employers – or maybe even friends of ours. You should have looked more closely at the paintings, Richard. You might have recognised them.'

Cassie was seized by an overwhelming urge to shock Sophie. The demons had been hard at work all day trying to take her over. Now, it seemed that they had. She felt as if she was being carried along by a stream of events. She had not yet finished her first drink but she might have had three, so light did her head feel.

'What a fun story!' she said to Richard.

Her father beamed. 'It is, isn't it?'

'It almost made me forget our news.'

Our news, said Rob's eyes – what is that?

Wait for it, Cassie thought.

'What news is that, darling?' Richard asked.

'Rob and I are getting married,' Cassie said.

Sophie spluttered and choked so that for a couple of minutes the spotlight was on her. But the reaction of all three of Cassie's listeners was still obvious: Sophie's rage, Richard's distress and Rob's radiance.

When it was plain that Sophie was not, after all, going to choke to death, Cassie embellished her tale.

'We'd like to do it quite soon. I mean, why muck about once the decision is made? So we thought – let's get married at the end of the month.'

By now, even Rob was looking amazed.

'The end of the month,' Sophie said faintly, groping at her pearls.

'You two are the first to know,' Cassie went on. 'In the morning I must phone Laura and tell her, too. Can I do that from here? Of course, she'll have to come out.'

Sophie flinched. Still, she rallied, prepared to put on a show.

'Well,' she said, 'you've certainly surprised us but we're just thrilled for both of you, aren't we, doll?'

'I'm not – '

'And naturally we'll have to hold the reception here in this house. Richard knows so many important people. They'll all have to come. And Rob – all your sporting connections. But you can leave everything to me, Cassie. I just adore weddings. Remember how beautiful ours was?'

She was on the verge of hysteria but she coped. Richard, too, tried to pretend that he was pleased.

'This calls for champagne.'

'You're right,' said Rob.

CASSIE married, Laura thought. And no doubt blaming me because I didn't go out for the wedding. But, really and truly, how could I have gone? And, anyway, I had already arranged this shoot with Michael down in Haselmere.

Muttering to herself, she double-checked the contents of the car boot. Her three Leicas, including the new Leica R.6. Six lenses. Polaroid back-up. Tripod *and* monopod reflectors. Three 2K Tungsten lights. Light meter. Everything that should have been there was present and correct.

'You don't trust me or something?' Dodgy said, sliding in on the driver's side.

'After the bear . . .'

This was a touchy subject. After Paris they had shot an important campaign in Madras involving as a prop not only an elephant but a teddy-bear.

The bear, as they discovered in India, had not been packed. At vast expense Dodgy went back to London to fetch it, returning, so Laura insisted, with the *wrong* bear, for there had been two, a beige one and a pink.

'How could *I* have figured that out?'

'Would *I* use a pink teddy-bear in a shot?'

'Then what was it doing in your house?'

I can't believe she's married him, Laura thought. What made her do it?

'You're getting yourself psyched up,' Dodgy observed. 'Cassie getting to you, is she? And her being married – when was it?'

'Yesterday. You know very well. Haven't I been telling you all along? And you're driving too fast!'

Michael Roberts was Fashion Editor of *Tatler* at that time and for the shoot he had requisitioned a splendid mansion in Haselmere, part Tudor, part Georgian. Inside this mansion six teenage boys recruited by Michael were having their hair cut. One of the victims was protesting vociferously about this treatment as Laura and Dodgy walked in.

'I look *terrible!*'

Michael grinned. 'Nineteen forties,' he said to the others. 'And he had a terrible haircut *before!*'

Michael worked in his own unique way. Other fashion editors obtained the clothes for a shoot and thereafter devised a story. Michael started with an idea, sent sketches of clothes and accessories around to designers and made everyone, including the photographer, fit in with his overall plan.

This approach could and sometimes did lead to tantrums. Michael remained unmoved, insisting that 'the only ultimate relationship is *me*, in charge of the idea,' and refusing point-blank to play a subordinate role even to famous photographers.

'Who's here?' Laura asked.

'Everyone, darling,' which, as well as those present, also included the hair-stylist, Michael's assistant, the make-up artist, and one top model flown in from New York.

'Where's the model?'

'Liane? In her room. Not Fitting In!'

Laura groaned. A moody model was bad news. If one member of the team refused to fit in the whole concept of spending these few days together in the country could be jeopardised.

'Oh, my glory!'

At dinner-time, when the others went out to eat, Liane was still ensconced in her bedroom.

'Keep her thin,' Michael said. 'We're going to do a funny take on English sexuality, on the oddities of being English. Nanny and boarding-school syndromes and mother love and deprivation. I want a 1940s' football sequence – hence the hair. Liane – if we ever see her again – is the girl who's moved into a stately home next door to a boys' school. The boys will turn up in various guises to look at her – the postman and so forth. And I want a Flash Harry in the bushes, with watches in the linings of a check coat. Dodgy, that will be you.'

On shoots, assistants often doubled as models. Laura perked up. This sounded fun. Michael's ideas were conceived as a series of vignettes that flowed like a film, but were shot as stills. Close-ups interspersed and balanced with action pictures. Michael acted as director of narrative while the inter-reaction between models was played upon and recorded.

Laura tried to think more about all this than about Cassie. She ate a very good saltimbocca washed down with Orvieto secco and followed by lemon sorbet.

'You're beginning to relax,' Dodgy said.

But that served to remind her of why she had been tense.

Cassie married. At what point would she chew up Rob and spit out the pips?

With the exception of Liane they were all up at six A.M. and ready to shoot by eight.

Laura was beginning to wonder if Liane actually existed or if she was not a figment of Michael's vivid imagination. Michael was mischievous and liked to play tricks. Especially on herself. Perhaps he hadn't flown in a model at all?

'Where's this girl then?' said the cheekiest of the six boys, the same one who had protested so loudly about his haircut. *'We're* ready.'

The boys were wearing knee-length shorts and shirts with numbers emblazoned on the back. Their shorn hair had sent them back forty years and their ears stuck out. They had the dazed expressions of teenagers dragged too early from their beds.

At least the weather had held up, Laura thought. There was every possibility that – a little later – the sun might come out.

Where *was* Liane? Before she could make inquiries herself a very beautiful, very slender, very young blonde in a Janet Reger *negligée* came out on to the steps of the house.

'Hello, Liane. I'm Laura Conway.'

'Why are all those guys running round in those weird Bermudas?'

Liane's accent was undiluted Kansas, not New York.

'Never mind.'

'Her hair is wrong,' said Michael.

Laura, ready to take a polaroid shot, considered Liane.

'I don't think it is.'

'It's wrong. And there's more make-up on her left eye than on her right.'

'Michael,' said Laura through her teeth, 'I'm not blind. And would you prefer to take the pictures instead of me?'

'Of course I would!'

Someone – the most vociferous of the boys – guffawed at this. The sun, which had been thinking of coming out, sulked behind a cloud.

'Let's get this straight,' Laura said. 'It's either you or me in charge.'

'You know I never play a subordinate role to a photographer.'

'And *you* know that *I* can't bear being crowded.'

They had been down this path together before. Michael seethed. Laura growled. Eventually, the hair was adjusted to Michael's requirements and the eye make-up repaired.

'She's just got out of bed. She's yawning. She doesn't know anyone's around – '

'Thank you, Michael. I know the scenario. You've made it perfectly clear to me.'

'There's lipstick on her cheek.'

Finally they were ready to go. Laura examined every detail of the polaroid shot. No more lipstick smudges. Michael, a living camera, was standing behind her.

'OK. Liane. I want the transition from being half asleep to shock when you find you're being watched.'

338

The would-be voyeur was hitching up his shorts.

'Watched by *him*?' Liane said. 'I don't get it.'

Some photographers reduced models to tears. Laura had never bullied but toyed now with the concept of boxing Liane's ears.

'*Yawn!*'

Liane complied. It probably was the real thing. The polaroid was a dream. Liane, coaxed, repeated the yawn for the Ektachrome shots.

'Good girl, good girl! That's great – that's great!' Michael encouraged.

Now for the shock. Which didn't come. Liane's lovely face showed only ennui.

Michael said laconically, 'Just do as I say and she'll give us what I want.'

I will not, simply will not have a blazing row with him, Laura said to herself. Even though both of them are quite insufferable and the picture won't work. However, I'll take it and Michael can eat his words. Liane's boredom is there for all to see in the polaroid and that's what the Leica will get. And then – miracle of miracles – Liane went into severe shock. Her mouth opened and her eyes widened and Laura shot two rolls of fresh, spontaneous pictures while the image held.

The voice behind her said again, 'Great, great. Wicked!'

Everyone else was giggling – they were all convulsed. Not surprisingly. Two of the teenage boys were standing on her left where she hadn't spotted them. They were clad, not in football gear, but in striped pyjama bottoms and black, padded bras.

'What on earth . . . ?'

'Something had to be done,' said Michael sweetly. 'I thought of turning the hose on her but this was better.'

'You total monster!' But now Laura had the giggles.

'Wicked shot?'

'Wicked shot.'

She was still laughing when a car came up the drive, stopped – and Cassie got out.

*

'I knew I couldn't go through with it,' Cassie said, 'I knew it all along. It was just a question of when I'd call it off.'

'You are quite, quite vile.'

'I know. I didn't expect it to be so bad. I mean – the hospital. And Sophie – oh, God, you've no idea what she was like!'

'One thing at a time,' said Laura. 'Go back to the beginning. But I'm going to need a stiff drink before you start.'

Weeks before the wedding date – ever since announcing her engagement – Cassie had suffered sleepless nights. Sleeping tablets were prescribed, after which she had hideous nightmares. She didn't want to make love any more. Rob put it down to pre-wedding nerves and continued to be sweet, considerate and selfless, which didn't help.

In the daytime, two Cassies operated side by side: one listlessly caught up in the pre-wedding maelstrom, the other driven by the demons whose hold on her only tightened as the weeks went by. The pressures built up on every level.

On the morning before the wedding Rob brought her coffee in bed. He was not going to work. A number of small pre-wedding chores remained to be done. The cupboard door was half-open. Cassie could see her wedding dress on its hanger, an asymmetrical column of cream silk.

She was never going to wear that dress. She had always known that, deep down, even when she had gone out to buy the garment.

She was not going to marry Rob.

'I'm going to make sure the trestle tables have arrived,' he said.

They were without a phone, only due to move into the cottage after the honeymoon.

Only they were not going to have a honeymoon.

'I'm not going through with it,' said Cassie number two while Cassie one squirmed.

'With what?'

So she had to say: 'I'm not going to marry you, Rob,' and watch the happiness slowly drain from his sun-tanned face.

But the real nasties were yet to come. Rob, once he had registered the truth of what she had said, began to weep like a desolate child. His capacity for tears was apparently infinite. Since the one way she could stop the flow was out of the question – there was no going back now – Cassie took refuge in action.

'Rob,' she said when she was dressed, 'I'm going to find a phone and let Dad know. We can't forget the practicalities. The magistrate must be told. *And* the guests – '

'You can't do this to me,' said Rob through his tears. 'I can't live without you, Cass.'

Cassie the first nearly capitulated but the demons were stronger than pity. There were further pleas, a fresh flood of tears, but she went in search of a phone.

Richard was out of his office. Like Rob, he too would have had a list of pre-wedding chores.

'Please tell him I'll call back in half an hour,' she told his secretary. But Richard was still out at the end of thirty minutes.

Cassie wanted to run – to flee from all the drama that was bound to ensue. She was yet to find out the extent of that drama and if she had known she would indeed have fled.

But, concentrate on the practicalities, she said to herself. She couldn't spend the rest of the day in the hotel from where she had made her call. She couldn't dodge Rob all day, either. She would have to return to the flat to fetch her clothes and her passport. Because, of course, she could not stay on in Johannesburg, not after this *débâcle*. She would have to fly back to London as soon as possible and pick up the threads of her career.

Facing Rob was a miserable prospect but it had to be done. Feeling every bit the reprobate she let herself into the flat. It was deadly quiet – no radio, but no sounds of sobbing, either. Thank God for that. Maybe Rob had gone to Inanda to weep on Sophie's shoulder. That would figure.

'Rob?' she called tentatively, all the same, and got no answer. He *had* gone out. It might not even be necessary for them to meet again. She could pack, go back to the hotel and book her flight. Relieved, she went through to the bedroom.

So much for optimism. Her worst nightmare had become reality. Rob was sprawled across the bed. His eyes were shut. He appeared to be in a deep coma. On the floor was the empty bottle which had contained the pills to make her sleep.

The next phone call was to the ambulance service. Rob was rushed to hospital to have his stomach pumped out.

Richard was located, Sophie summoned, the full story elicited from Cassie in the hospital grounds. That was after they knew that Rob would live. Sophie was out for Cassie's blood. A row between the two of them was inevitable – even Richard expected that.

'I hope you're sorry for what you've done,' Sophie began. 'He could have died because of you. You could have killed him!'

'Steady now,' murmured Richard. 'It's all over.'

'It's not *all* over! He nearly died! All because of her!'

'The point is that he didn't die. He's going to be all right, he's asleep, they'll tranquillise him, he'll get over it.'

'Of course, he'll get over it! He'll be glad yet that she broke it off. Heaven knows, he's well out of it. *I* always knew she was a sly, cold girl. If he'd listened to me – '

Sophie ranted on.

' – and look what you've done to your father and myself. The expense. The embarrassment. All the phone calls I'm going to have to make. The cream of Johannesburg was coming to this wedding. Oh, I could just die!'

The demons got to work.

'That's all you care about – the embarrassment,' Cassie said. 'Keeping face!'

'How dare you speak to me like that!'

'*You're* the cold one, not me. You never did have a heart, Sophie. No wonder your first husband had an affair!'

There was a split second before the volcano erupted. The voidance was preceded by Sophie's scream.

'How did you know that?'

'Rob told me, of course.'

And then – while Richard and Cassie stood stunned – it all poured out: the details of Hannie's affair with a Black woman; the birth of a child. An eruption of hate and fear vomited out in the hospital grounds.

Once begun it was impossible to stop the flow. Sophie had kept silent for too long. She shrieked at Cassie: 'Well, what would *you* have done under the circumstances? I was *tainted*, don't you understand?' unaware that Cassie had not got the whole story from Rob; that Rob himself did not know it all.

When she had sicked everything up Sophie, still looking green around the gills, fell silent. Cassie, too, was struck dumb.

'Yes, well,' said Richard reeling under the series of shocks and groping for a lifeline, 'I think we should all try to calm down and take stock of the situation. Cassie, it might be best if you moved into the Rosebank Hotel for the night. I don't think you should stay in Rob's flat . . .'

Inanda was not mentioned as an alternative; Richard knew better than that.

He was seeking a peace settlement. But that was not the end of the drama. The next episode was to be staged later that night. Cassie did not witness it. It fell to Richard, on the way to the airport, to tell her what had occurred, leaving out the more intimate details.

All the phone calls cancelling the wedding had been made. Cassie's flight home had been booked. Richard and Sophie had been back to the hospital to visit Rob.

Richard told himself that all he wanted to do was get into bed and make love to his wife. This wasn't quite true. He did indeed want to make love, but not to Sophie. Still, he went on deceiving himself until they were in bed and he had snuggled up to her back. He put his hand on her thigh.

'Leave me alone,' she said.

She was not by nature a passionate woman, as he well knew,

but she was not in the habit of rejecting his advances. She had never before told Richard to leave her alone.

'I suppose,' he said, 'that you're angry with me because I'm Cassie's father.'

'That's not the case.'

'Then why are you being so cold?'

'*Cold?*' said Sophie angrily. 'That's what she called me – '

'She being Cassie.'

'Who else? She humiliated me. She knew all about – *that*. She's known all the time. *Rob's* known all the time. Hannie told him! I knew I shouldn't have let him see Rob again.'

'Pull yourself together,' said Richard, cold himself now. 'So what if Rob's known all along? It doesn't seem to have harmed him.'

Sophie sat up. 'Don't you understand anything? Of course it's harmed him. Can you think of anything worse for a child than that? Or for me. Hannie slept with an *African*, Richard. While he was married to me. It makes me feel tainted.'

'Christ Almighty!' Richard said.

'I hate swearing. You don't normally swear.'

'And I don't normally have to listen to this kind of crap.'

Sophie edged to the other side of the bed. 'I won't put up with being spoken to like that.'

'It's about time somebody spoke to you like that. I should have done so years ago. I was wandering around with blinkers – that was the trouble. I didn't see half of the things I should have done. I didn't see through you.'

Sophie switched on the bedside light. She was wearing a peach satin negligée. Her skin glowed in the light. Her hair shone. She was, he thought, a very lovely woman – to look at. But what he could now see of her personality he did not like at all.

He did not even desire her, he thought. After the trauma of this day he had wanted sex as a relaxant – that was as far as it had gone. And now – now it did not even go that far.

'I think you're horrible!' Sophie said, and it struck Richard that she sounded like a prim schoolgirl instead of a woman in her forties.

Prim schoolgirls were a turn-off where he was concerned. Sophie might be lovely but he did not share common values with her, he did not respect her, he did not like her any more . . .

Good heavens, he thought. 'You're pretty horrible, too,' he said. 'Only you don't realise that. You think that you are a much nicer, much more sensitive woman than you are, but that's just the part you play, Sophie. You used to be quite convincing in that role. You took *me* in. But it's narrowing down to an audience of two – Rob and yourself.'

'Peter likes me.'

'We don't see much of Peter, do we? Maybe *he's* seen the light as well!'

'That's what you think, is it?'

'Let me tell you what I do and do not think,' said Richard. 'I think that you are a narrow-minded, prejudiced puritan. I think Cassie was probably right – that you did drive Hannie into another woman's arms. I don't give a shit what colour that woman was. Unlike you, I don't believe that every African has syphilis, gonorrhoea, or any other sexually transmitted disease. I don't think I can go on being married to you . . .'

'I think that I can do with another drink,' Laura said.

Cassie poured it out.

'Are you going to give me a rocket?'

'In a moment. I'm still gathering my wits. Are they going to get divorced?'

'I'm sure they are. He's moved into the Rosebank.'

'And Rob?'

'I should imagine he'll go and stay with Sophie in Inanda. They can comfort each other.'

'You are foul,' said Laura in a heartfelt voice. 'Ruining everyone's life.'

'I know I'm ghastly. I know I'm a split personality.'

'Ruining your *own* life.'

'I know. I know. I can't help it.'

'I am very, *very* worried about you. Rob is a completely innocent person. To behave so vindictively to him is appalling.'

Cassie eased her left foot out of its shoe and wiggled her toes.

'He *is* better off without me.'

'You can say that again!'

Still, he's young – he'll get over it, Laura thought. It's Cassie's obsessive nastiness towards Richard that worries me most. But perhaps this is the end of it. Perhaps, at long last, she's got the poison out of her system.

'Are you writing me off altogether?'

'I should!' Laura said. 'You've been absolutely vile.'

'I know that.'

Truly the end of it? Think positive . . .

'But you're still my girl . . .'

DOMINIC

1991 – 1992

DOMINIC Lethbridge was normally a punctual person and on this particular occasion he had set out in plenty of time for his appointment. But even if he had been running late he would not have worried too much. He was considerate of women and they, in turn, thought that it was worth waiting for him; considered him, at twenty-nine, to be an exceptional man: bright, ethical, doughty, amusing and upwardly mobile.

Judged on looks, however, he did not measure up to Rob, and Laura, even if stuck, would not have used him as a model. On the surface he appeared a middle-of-the-road man: average height, average build, with light brown hair, hazel eyes and unremarkable clothes.

He was successful, not only with women, but also at the Bar, although he was not making as much money as his friends in Commercial Law. The cream of these friends were earning six figure incomes. They regularly wrote off their weekends and thought nothing of working all night.

When Dominic had opted for Criminal Law, completed his pupillage, and got his feet in good Chambers, he had expected to be reasonably busy but not as over-worked. This assessment turned out to be mistaken. Since most of their time was spent in court, criminal lawyers as a breed tended to put in reasonable hours. The exception was fraud – the area in which he had chosen to specialise. Nevertheless he had no regrets. What he was doing, he thought, was infinitely more exciting than other aspects of law.

He had been to Oxford and before that to Downside College

but right now he was in Chelsea, cutting across Cadogan Gardens on his way from Draycott Avenue to Sloane Street where, in Justin de Blank's basement he was to meet a girl called Sally for a pre-theatre meal.

On this evening in mid-September he had no presentiment that his perfectly pleasant life – no commitments, therefore no hassles – might be about to change.

He crossed the road, passing in the process the actor Dirk Bogarde whom he had seen a few weeks earlier in a magic film called *These Foolish Things*. The actor was clutching a delicatessen bag and Dominic was just wondering how often such people were accosted by effusive fans while doing their shopping when, in a ground floor window, he saw a pair of feet.

Initially he thought they belonged to a man. They were large and ensconced in black socks and the most curious thing about them was that they were upside-down. For a moment, while they remained immobile, Dominic thought that the feet must be part of a window display, that a shop – one which had as yet no identification – was about to open up.

Perhaps a pedicurist's or chiropodist's salon?

Then the feet moved, levitated, and he realised that they were attached to a pair of very beautiful legs, also clothed in black. Female legs, unmistakably.

Women's legs, upside down in a Chelsea window? It didn't make sense. He gaped uninhibitedly, fascinated by the sight and hoping to see more.

More, most delightfully, followed: a back view of knees, a pair of mind-boggling thighs, an exquisitely rounded bottom in tiny black pants. He was quite obviously asleep, lost in an erotic fantasy. He did not want to wake up.

What happened next was equally unreal. The bottom and the legs and the feet submerged. They sank slowly out of his line of vision and completely disappeared.

Dominic stood, shaking his head in disbelief. *Extraordinary*, he thought. Any minute now he would wake up with a jump. Instead, his old friends the feet reappeared and before his

350

bemused eyes the whole scenario was re-enacted. But only that one more time. Eventually, when he was quite sure that the feet were not coming back, he reluctantly got going again and rounded the corner.

It was only when he saw the health club sign that he realised he had been staring at a woman – or part of a woman – exercising in a gym, pulling herself up on bars to tone her muscles and keep in shape. That she had certainly done.

He gave in to an impulse that was, for him, unusual. He walked up the steps and went into the club. It was a most up-market place. A svelte Black girl asked if she could help and he said could he have membership details and a look around.

'Go ahead,' she said.

There was the sound of water lapping – a pool, a jacuzzi – the sight of a coffee shop; gratifying smells.

And then a girl in a black leotard appeared and walked towards him. She was quite stunning. Her hair was chestnut brown with red glints, wavy and almost waist-length. Her eyes were a very dark brown. She had a small nose with slightly flaring nostrils and a full, red mouth. She had a body . . . But he knew about that body. He had already seen it, upside down in a window. It was her.

He checked the membership fee, filled in the necessary form and wrote out a cheque. Which was why, that evening, he was late for dinner.

'I've joined a health club,' he announced to his companion for the evening. 'Did you know there's one just round the corner?'

'You've joined a health club?' Sally said. 'Where will *you* of all people find the time to work out?'

But he did. He went to the club the next evening and knuckled down to a series of exercises. She was not present. He went in to the coffee shop and ordered fruit juice and a piece of carrot cake as an excuse for staying on but she did not reappear.

For several days there was no sign of her. He was beginning to give up hope of ever seeing her again, let alone getting to know her. She might have been an overseas visitor using the club's facilities while she was in London. She might have gone back to her native land.

To add to his depression the necessity had arisen to buy some clothes. Dominic loathed this task. He was not interested in the design aspect and he did not need fashionable clothes as a confidence boost. Had society approved of the concept and the climate been more benign he would cheerfully have dispensed with them altogether.

When forced into it he bought in bulk – a dozen shirts, two dozen pairs of socks and a fistful of boxer shorts – so that he would not have to repeat the exercise in the foreseeable future. Having paid for his purchases with a faintly deranged air he then fled from the store with the alacrity of a shop-lifter. It was a wonder he had not yet been apprehended by a suspicious detective.

He went through this ordeal, carried his plastic bags into the health club, deposited them on a chair and wiped his brow with the air of a man who has escaped from enemy territory.

'You look as if you could do with a massage – talk about tension!' said one of the instructors.

'I can't tell you!' he said, groaning – and *she* strolled in.

'Hello,' she said to the instructor and cast her eye over Dominic.

She was no shy violet, but her lack of timidity only added to her attraction for him.

'Hi, Cassie,' the instructor said. 'We haven't seen you all week.'

She came over. 'I've been in Bristol,' she said. 'I'm doing the Roadshow and that goes out from the Bristol studios.'

Dominic filed this information away for future reference and looked expectantly at the instructor, a nice American woman who had once lived in Berlin, hoping for an introduction.

The nice American obliged. 'This is Cassie Stacton. Dominic here has just become a member.'

'Good,' said Cassie Stacton. 'Do you live in this area?'

'In Chelsea Green.'

'I *like* Chelsea Green. It's very villagey, isn't it? I was down there a bit earlier today, ordering a cake from the Jane Asher Shop.'

'A wedding cake?'

He cast a surreptitious glance at her left hand. No rings – excellent.

'A birthday cake. For my grandmother's birthday. One with a trumpeter on it and musical notes. She's keen on jazz.'

A pretty special grandmother, he thought. How special he had yet to find out.

'Do *you* live around here?'

'My father does. It was his idea that I join the club. He paid my membership as a surprise, to lure me over, as it were.'

'I must be off,' said the instructor, and went, leaving them on their own.

Terrific, he thought. Cassie Stacton, on the contrary, was not in a hurry, which was better still. They spoke for some time, long enough for Dominic to suggest coffee at the end of the class. Cassie accepted. At the end of the evening he knew that – just for once – he had been right to give in to impulse.

After their second date he told Sally that he couldn't see her again – that he had fallen in love with somebody else.

Sally and he had not been an item for long and her reaction to this news was more extreme than he had expected. He left her, feeling mean and wondering what he could have said to have aroused her expectations. He carried the burden of guilt with him as far as Bayswater but, once there, it more or less evaporated.

Cassie was cooking dinner for him. On the doorstep he considered his chances of getting her into bed after the meal.

She *seemed* interested. He pressed the buzzer and her voice answered, 'Dominic, is that you?'

Were there any other guests? Woe betide them, he thought. May they be suddenly stricken by a flu virus. May their cars break down. He was, at any rate, the first to arrive.

'I brought you some marguerites.'

'My favourites. Go through and I'll put them in a vase.'

He went in to the combination living/dining-room and noticed at once that the table setting was for two. His luck was holding!

The colours in the room had been taken from a large print of Bonnard's *The Green Blouse* which dominated one wall. There were other pictures, too, amongst them some originals. He had a small collection of English paintings in his Chelsea flat. He was inspecting one of Cassie's – a small oil depicting a house, a harbour and a dish of lemons left behind on a table – when his hostess came in with the marguerites in a vase.

'Do you like Mary Fedden?'

'Enormously.'

'I'm mad about her painting. Laura – my grandmother – bought that one for me from a gallery in Barnes. The New Grafton. Do you know it?'

'I sometimes go to their exhibitions.'

'Is that so? Then you might have run into Laura. She goes whenever she can.'

'Did Laura also buy this Anthea Craigmyle?'

'No. That was my treat to myself. Don't you love her sheep?'

'Mm. I bought a Charles Duranty from the New Grafton a few months ago.'

'Did you? Laura has several of his.'

The subject of Laura came up frequently with Cassie, he thought. He was close to his own grandmother, a landscape gardener, now widowed. He began to tell Cassie about her.

'She's taken up painting. Next weekend we're both going on a watercolour course.'

'*You* paint?'

'I'm going along to keep her company. She's potentially very good. Sixty-nine is a great old age to begin painting but that wouldn't deter her. My mother started studying medicine at forty-two. They're a formidable pair.'

'What did your father think about that?'

'He was right behind her. They don't have problems. They're

marvellous. They've always given each other space and they're still in love.'

'Great!' said Cassie, ever so slightly sarcastic.

'Well, actually it is. We're a lucky trio, my brother and sister and I, to have those kind of parents.'

'Aren't you?'

'I'm sorry. I know your mother is dead . . .'

'It's not that. I was only a baby when my mother died. I don't even remember her.'

'In that case,' said Dominic, 'why are you being so cynical? Some couples remain happy. I refuse to believe my situation is that unusual.'

'One-third of marriages end in divorce.'

'And two-thirds don't. Good news doesn't make headlines. All right, I know your father got divorced from his second wife but what about Laura? She seems a happy enough woman from what you say.'

Cassie frowned. Her mouth went down at the corners. 'Laura wasn't so wise, either. I can tell you that!'

'Then why don't you?'

'She fell in love with my father. They had a long-standing affair – then he ditched her. That, I would say, is a fairly unusual situation!'

He had to agree that it was. 'It didn't stop her from making a success of her life, though.'

'No, but she was terribly hurt when it happened.'

And so were you, Dominic thought. And Laura's probably got over it long since while you, my love, have not.

Talking about it also distressed her if he was to judge from the fidgety gestures she was making with her hands. How screwed up was she by this affair? It must have taken place quite a while back since her father had subsequently remarried and divorced.

Had he ascertained exactly when, he might have been wary of Cassie, deducing that here was a woman with a very long-standing problem. He thought that afterwards, when Cassie was

355

trying him to the limit of his patience and he knew some more but not all of the facts.

But he had gone in at the deep end. He was confident. His relationships with the female side of his family – his grandmother, mother and sister – had led him to truly like women. He had always been lucky in love.

But he had never before been deeply in love. He had never thought: this is the woman with whom I want to spend the rest of my life. Not until now. And here she was looking hurt. Instead of taking flight he stepped forward and fell into the love trap.

'She didn't find herself another man?'

'No, she did not,' said Cassie. 'She's the kind of person who loves rarely and deeply. There've only ever been two men in her life: her husband, my grandfather, who was murdered by the Nazis; and, more than twenty years afterwards, Dad. That's what she's like.'

I bet there were a few lovers on the side, Dominic thought. Only nuns are that pure.

Cassie was coming over as somewhat ingenuous, a paradoxical characteristic in such a worldly young woman. This artlessness only related to one person, as far as he could tell. And perhaps Laura Conway *was* a bit of a Grandmother Superior, hopping over the convent wall every twenty years?

Enough of grandmothers, he thought. He could smell apples. He was getting hungry. He was heartened when Cassie, instead of pursuing the subject of Laura's love life, asked if he'd like to eat at once.

When he said, 'Absolutely!' she produced an orange baking dish. Inside was turbot with apple and cider sauce.

'In Normandy this is traditional at first communion celebrations,' said Cassie.

'Are you a Catholic?'

'No, are you?'

'More in theory than in practice. You're a very good cook.'

For pudding there was a pear-and-almond cream tart – another speciality of Normandy. This entailed making and prebaking pie pastry which had to be chilled for a specific length of time before being placed in the oven. His hostess, he thought, had gone to a great deal of trouble preparing this meal.

The cheese was Neufchâtel, made in a heart shape.

'I was in France the other week,' said Cassie. 'I bought it then.'

'Working?'

'What else? The Roadshow is going Continental, starting with Paris – then Rome and Berlin.'

'Berlin is a city in which to find antiques?'

'Definitely.'

'Should be interesting,' Dominic said.

Just *how* interesting he had yet to find out.

All through dinner he thought how much he wanted her. But what were her feelings? She was not giving him a come-on. Her attitude now was so straightforward that it did occur to him she might only want friendship.

He was good friends with a couple of women with whom he had grown up. Platonic relationships with the opposite sex had worked for him. But that was not the relationship he wanted with this woman.

His confidence ebbed slightly. Sally had said that it was always easy for men. But Sally had been wrong. Now, for instance, he was uncertain what his next move should be.

Cassie's feelings for him were still unclear when she stood up from the table and said, 'OK. Let's have our coffee in comfort,' and transferred him to a sofa.

Coffee was percolated, pot and cups brought in on a bright red tray.

She sat next to him, but not too close. She poured his coffee and handed it to him in a sisterly way. Had he then misread the signals she had sent out in the gym? Or was she back-tracking? Had he bored her at dinner? He had talked rather a lot about Criminal Law, mentioning in particular one case of a woman wrongly accused of bringing about her husband's death.

'That client you told me about,' Cassie said suddenly, 'the

woman who was acquitted of murder – you really seemed to care about her!'

'Why shouldn't I care? It's not *always* about money and climbing the ladder.'

'Isn't it?'

'No,' he said, 'it isn't. Although money and climbing the ladder obviously enter into it.'

Cassie smiled. The edges of her mouth turned charmingly upwards, her nose wrinkled and two deep dimples appeared, one in either cheek.

He put his coffee cup back on the tray, reached out and pulled her towards him. She didn't draw back.

Kiss her, you fool, he thought, and did so tentatively. Now she, too, wanted more than friendship – her mouth told him that.

He kissed her more purposefully. Her eyes could not have become darker but the pupils dilated. She put her hands on his shoulders.

Yes, yes, yes, he thought. It's going to be all right.

He stayed all night and woke sated with pleasure, tender in more than one sense after his exertions.

Saturday morning. Beside him Cassie was still asleep, one marvellous bare shoulder visible above the duvet, most of which she had appropriated.

This is it, he thought – *the* relationship. This is not for Tuesdays and Thursdays. This is an every day, all-year *affaire de coeur*.

How then to build it? Are we going to live together? In which case will she move in with me or I with her? Will it be easier to let my flat or hers? Getting to work in Holborn is much the same either way. I don't know what the parking in Bayswater is like.

Fantastic skin-tone, he thought. God – the fucking was just terrific.

If I move in with her, what about Mrs Griffith? She's the best cleaning lady I've ever had. I can't let her down. Would she come over here? It may be too far for her. Does Cassie have someone else already? And what about my shirts? I can't expect her to take care of them. So do I still take them to the Chelsea laundry or is there a service in this neck of the woods?

He was longing for Cassie to wake up to discuss the future. But she was flat out – in need of sleep while his batteries were over-charging.

After half an hour the inactivity was too much for him. He eased himself out of bed and crept through to the kitchen to make himself coffee. Once there he found he was hungry again so he rummaged around for bread and butter.

Cassie wouldn't mind – would be like himself when she finally woke, all smiles and *bonhomie*.

What was she normally like in the mornings? It was odd to be so sure that you loved someone of whose personal habits you knew so little.

He meandered through to the sitting-room and contemplated the view from the window. It was not exciting – rather dull modern buildings. A pity the flat did not front on to the Greek church.

He was still standing there when Cassie padded in bare-footed.

'Hi!' he said, all warm and wanting to hug her.

'Hello.' There was frost in that voice. And the Cassie of the night before simply wasn't there. This girl was cold and withdrawn.

He was shocked rigid.

'I see you made yourself some coffee.'

'You don't mind?'

'Why should I? Excuse me, but I'll do the same.'

'Wait a minute. Before you do anything else, tell me what's up.'

Her face was a sheet of ice. She hesitated – then, 'Sit down.'

'Which is the electric chair?'

'Wha – ?'

But a thaw had set in. His Cassie was on her way back. Suddenly she laughed. It was a delicious laugh, spirited and impudent, and it made him believe – quite erroneously – that the ice had melted for good.

HE was the only under-sixty on the watercolour course but that was not why the weekend irked him. He spent most of it wondering what Cassie was doing, wishing he could be with her.

It was all the more frustrating because the following week she was leaving for Rome, to reconnoitre for The Antiques Roadshow.

He still had not established the reason for the big freeze-up. Presumably Cassie, too, was mesmerised by the degree of passion there had been between them on the night he had stayed at her flat. Maybe she had been in need of space so she could analyse the value of that passion. Which was fair enough. But something indefinable had happened since that night: he found that out when they next went to bed.

Physically Cassie was very much there, but intrinsically she was not. She had put on an emotional chastity belt which was every bit as tantalising to a man in love as a tactual appliance. Worse, because he couldn't verbalise his dissatisfaction, couldn't say, 'What the hell is this?' in case he scared her off.

But it was early days yet. Her childhood, he thought, had been far less stable than his, therefore her faith in on-going relationships couldn't be as strong as his own. It would have to grow.

He proceeded to cultivate the ground in which it could bloom, using as his tools love and patience. Nothing much seemed to be germinating in this rich soil when Cassie went off on her first trip to Berlin but he was not down-hearted.

On her return she said nothing of her nostalgic visit to Laura's

360

old apartment. Liking the players, they went to see Dustin Hoffman and Bruce Willis in the film version of *Billy Bathgate*.

It was much more violent than either of them had anticipated. The blood and the shootings proved too much for Cassie to take. Dominic had been holding her hand. Half-way through the film she started to tremble.

He leant closer. 'Hey! You know what? I've just realised that this is a *comedy*!'

No response. She sure wasn't easy.

'Come on,' Dominic said, 'let's go. I don't think I can stand another sighting of Bruce Willis in concrete boots!'

Outside, Cassie looked stricken. 'Horrible!' she said angrily, *as if he was at fault*. 'People being *shot* all over the place. So much blood!'

'They *were* generous with the tomato sauce. Hoffman was excellent.'

'*I* didn't think so. I'm sick of violence, aren't you?'

Then, with no connection that he could see, she began to talk of her visit to Berlin.

'It wasn't all levelled to the ground. Some of the old houses and apartment blocks are still there – if you can find them.'

'Might be fun to go there together sometime.'

'Might be,' Cassie said.

So much for that notion, he thought. The possibility of living together had never been raised. Crestfallen but not beaten he soldiered on.

The months between Cassie's first and second trips to Berlin passed without any perceptive change in her attitude.

During her absence Dominic wondered if she did not have another man at the BBC, someone with whom she had more in common. It was perfectly feasible. And yet somehow it wasn't.

In all other ways Cassie demonstrated that she was a person of integrity. If there had been another man in her life she would have announced it, he thought. In all other ways she appeared loyal and constant – abnormally loyal where her grandmother was concerned.

But, equally, there was much that he did not know about Cassie's motivations, much that she did not permit him to know. Well, he was not prepared to intrude. If information was not forthcoming he was not going to attempt to prise it out.

Cassie had said she would phone the day she got back from Berlin. When she did not, Dominic was despondent. Was their relationship stretching out to snapping point? Were they growing away instead of towards each other? *Was* there another man?

But the next day Cassie did phone.

'Sorry. Something happened. I had to stay on.'

'That's all right.'

'I thought I might come over.'

'That's even better.'

Dominic's flat in Chelsea Green had once served as his grandparents' town pad. His grandmother had left it to him in her will. Meanwhile she rented it to him for a pittance on the understanding that her bedroom and only her room be left intact lest she felt like an evening in London.

The arrangement worked magnificently to Dominic's advantage. His grandmother put in an appearance once or twice a year, they went to the theatre and to art exhibitions, she asked him how he could stand the over-crowding and coaxed him to the country before leaving on the afternoon train.

From a window he watched surreptitiously for Cassie to arrive. When she did he quelled the impulse to rush to the door, fling it open, and cheer her return.

She was wearing a flame-red suit. He thought wildly of rushing downstairs, taking her across the road to the florist's and buying up the entire stock of brilliant blossoms to lay at her feet.

Lie low, he counselled himself.

'Good to see you.'

How about that for restraint, he thought, and Cassie produced a duty-free bag containing a bottle and said, 'And you. So much has been happening. I can't believe I've only been away for a few days.'

'You must tell me all about it.' More moderate words.

'I *will* tell you,' Cassie said. 'In fact, I have got to tell you or I'll go crazy. You can't imagine what went on in Berlin.'

She told him in bed. She described in detail what had happened in the SSB hall and in the apartment in Metzer Strasse. She said that she was handling a potential landmine in terms of Laura and explained what she intended to do.

Then she began to speak of Laura again – of Laura's days in Berlin.

'I kept thinking of her all the time I was there. It was so hard to find traces of those days but when I went to her apartment I could see her – *and* Klaus – both of them walking along Joachim Friedrich Strasse.'

'You never told me that you went to her apartment.'

'Yes, well I did. The first time I went to Berlin. I'm so glad I did. It made all the difference. It made my grandfather come alive. Does that make sense?'

'Yes. Go on.'

'He must have been a wonderful man – somebody special. You had to have real guts in those days to oppose the Nazis. No wonder Laura never wanted to marry anyone else. Or not until – '

She stopped, floundered. She's going to cry, Dominic thought. All her defences were down.

He kissed her, a peck of a kiss intended to comfort rather than to arouse. She snuggled in closer, put her hand round the back of his neck, encouraging him to kiss her again. Tenderness became passion – became a passion as intense as that of their first night. She had unlocked the emotional chastity belt. She was ready for him in every sense.

'I love you,' she said, eyes dark, tears falling, but not for Laura.

He was sure that he had her for ever, that she would never again erect barriers between them. He fell asleep holding her in his arms – and woke in the morning to find her gone.

He phoned her flat.

'Oh, hi,' she said nonchalantly, as if the lovemaking of the night before had been his illusion. '*You*'re up early.'

'Why did you go?'

'Well, you know, it was terribly late – nearly four. And I prefer to wake up in my own bed.'

Every one of the barriers was back in position. From that day onwards they were fiercely reinforced, supported in due course by the admiration she engendered in other men, on which she played.

Dominic did his level best to break down the defences but he had also to contend with his own dignity. By the evening of Laura's exhibition he had been provoked almost beyond endurance.

The morning after the retrospective, Cassie was going to Belfast to work on a one-off programme for BBC Northern Ireland.

She phoned before she left. 'Could I ask a favour of you?'

'Sure. What is it?'

'I can't find the gadget for my answering machine – the remote interrogator.'

'So you want me to pop round to your place and check messages while you're away.'

'Would you mind?'

'I'll do it,' he said.

'And then I'll phone you. What are you up to this week?'

'This and that,' said Dominic, putting up some defences of his own making. 'Anyway, not to worry. I'll sort everything out. Be careful over there.'

'I won't be wandering far. The Europa Hotel is just round the corner from the BBC.'

The next call was internal. 'Dominic. Mr MacCarthy's here.'

Gerard MacCarthy was a charming Irishman, charged by the company for which he had worked with fraud and misrepresentation. He was a fine-looking man in the Richard Gere mould with black hair, smutty blue eyes, an up-beat attitude to life and enormous charisma – a sun-god, despite his colouring.

On their previous meeting MacCarthy had outlined his problem to Dominic. The company in question had been pursuing business interests in Eastern Europe. According to the charge, MacCarthy had side-lined several of these propositions and then raised funds to initiate them independently.

Misrepresentation was said to have been carried out in a variety of ways. Bribery and corruption were fairly common in the Eastern European countries with which he had been dealing. The company had been told that certain officials would have to be paid off through a Belgian bank in order to secure business.

The company now maintained that the money it had paid out in good faith had not been put into the pockets of the officials but into MacCarthy's and, to a much lesser extent, into those of an employee of the Belgian bank.

'You and I both know they shouldn't have been bribing the officials,' MacCarthy said. 'But it's common practice. I can threaten to expose that, Mr Lethbridge, but I'd rather not. There are good men in there I don't want to see brought down. One of them is a friend of mine. I worked with him in Johannesburg ten years ago.'

'You lived in Johannesburg?'

'For twelve years. You can't let down friends that go back that far, even to save your own neck, now can you?'

He was not to be trusted, Dominic thought.

'Which company were you with in Johannesburg?'

MacCarthy supplied the information and Dominic made a mental note of it. Johannesburg ten years back, he thought, when MacCarthy had left. Richard was out there then – he might have met him.

He dialled Richard's flat. 'It's Dominic here.'

'Hello, how are you?' said Richard warmly. 'The exhibition was a great success, didn't you think? What an achievement . . .' He praised Laura at length.

'I wanted to ask you something,' Dominic said at the end of it, and went on to explain.

'Gerard MacCarthy? Doesn't ring a bell, I'm afraid, but I can check him out. Why don't you come around tonight and have a drink? Cassie's away. Laura's taken herself off somewhere. We've been deserted.'

'Tonight?'

'Tonight. This evening. Whenever you finish work.'

This was at seven. He parked the car in its residents' bay outside his flat and walked to Richard's apartment.

The red-brick Victorian building in which Richard lived was stolid and reassuring, like his own impression of Richard. For security reasons the names of those who lived in the block had been omitted from their buzzers. Dominic pressed one of them and almost immediately Richard's voice said, 'That you, Dominic?' over the intercom, and the huge metal and glass door creaked open.

Richard greeted him. 'Did you notice that the table is missing from the hall downstairs?'

'I can't say I did.'

'The lock on that bloody door jammed and they were in like a flash. The same night a tramp came in and slept on the stairs. Not that I mind that. Have a beer.'

Richard's flat was pure Conran: brave autumnal oranges, reds and yellows. Those elements of Africa that were present – two paintings and a couple of carvings – were of a high standard. One of the carvings, a large seated woman with begging hands, was positioned on the table on which Richard was putting their drinks.

'Takes you back to the tramp,' he said. 'I like Kumalo's work. He combines traditional African sculpture with Expressionist thinking. About MacCarthy, it turns out that he worked for one of our subsidiaries. Not surprising – the business community in Johannesburg isn't that large. His function was to operate the Counter-Trade Desk. Counter-Trade, as you no doubt know, is essentially barter.'

'Go on.'

'MacCarthy's role was to offer mining equipment in exchange for commodities in those Black Africa countries which fell under his brief. He used all of his considerable personal charm to get his foot in the door, build up trust. He met people who saw him as someone who could assist them in their offshore wheeling and dealing, people who wished to place contracts in Western Europe. They were in a position to organise government contracts in return for which they could expect a commission shared out on an agreed basis.'

'You found all this out today?'

'It wasn't difficult once I'd actually traced the fellow. The company is still smarting. They discovered, you see, that MacCarthy had been cutting himself in for commissions which should have gone to his employers. Our friend is not popular in Johannesburg.'

It was getting dark. Richard's face was almost obscured.

'Thanks for checking that out. It confirms my suspicions.'

'That's *all* you wanted to talk about, is it?'

'What makes you think there could be more?'

That produced a belly laugh. 'You're involved with my daughter. The way I read it she's fallen in love with you and she's mighty annoyed about that!'

'That's one way of putting it. By the way, *I* love *her*, too.'

'You have my sympathy. She's trouble – like all idealists.'

'That's how you see her – as an idealist?'

'Totally. And once committed, painfully loyal. As she is to Laura. Not that Laura is undeserving of her loyalty, mark you. Laura is the most remarkable woman. Quite simply The Best. But she's also a human being. Like the rest of us, she has faults. But to Cassie she's a saint. Sometimes I wish that she had a less perfect image of Laura. She's all wound up about her. She has a neurosis like the inside of a golf ball. If one could unravel that . . . Anyway, that's *your* problem. I totally failed. Have another beer.'

'I think I could do with it.'

'I hope,' said Richard carefully, 'that *you* do succeed. In my opinion you're the right man for my daughter, pain in the neck that she is.' There was too much love in his voice for Dominic to take exception to this remark.

They sat on drinking and talking until after ten, by which time it was too late, Dominic thought, to go across to Bayswater to check Cassie's answering machine. He walked home to Chelsea Green in a subdued state, stopping at the Europa Food Store in Draycott Avenue to buy a carton of milk. Should he or should he not phone Cassie at the hotel of the same name in Belfast?

He decided in favour of doing so, only to be told by an Ulster voice that Miss Stacton was not in her room. The now familiar feelings of uncertainty and jealousy moved in for a takeover. Richard was hoping that he would succeed with Cassie. But he couldn't continue to operate in this unsatisfactory way – not any more.

It's got to be make or break, he thought. When Cassie came back from Northern Ireland he would tell her so. He started to imagine what his life would be like if they were to part. It was a diabolical prospect.

Driving to Bayswater in the morning he was still in a bad mood. A cab-driver who cut across his path bore the brunt of his fulminations.

Cassie's flat, barren in its owner's absence, did little to cheer him up. The answering machine was sending out red flashing signals. He eyed it warily. What if one of those messages was from a rival for Cassie's affections, like that pretentious egghead producer from Radio Two over whose head he had so badly wanted to pour his drink? For all he knew the twit could be with her now, over in Belfast.

He blipped the 'play' button and was relieved when the first message proved to be from a girlfriend suggesting lunch, and the second from the dry cleaners confirming alterations done to an emerald-green suit.

He was just about to re-set the machine and head for work when the phone rang again.

Still twitchy, he picked up the receiver.

'Cassie Stacton's flat.'

'May I please speak with Miss Stacton?' A foreign voice – a German intonation.

'She's not here, I'm afraid. My name is Dominic Lethbridge. Can I help you?'

'I wish please to have the telephone number of Laura Conway. I am an old friend calling from Berlin.'

'Hold on,' Dominic said, 'I'll find the number for you,' and, as an after-thought, added, 'Who's speaking please?'

'Dr Paul Eisermann,' the old friend said.

All along Dominic had been intrigued by the personality of the man who had so willingly handed over the photographs and the bureau.

Who *was* this altruistic character and what was the motivation behind his action? No one parted that easily with valuable possessions, not unless he or she felt they had to do so.

Cassie believed that guilt was at the back of it – that the old man must have stolen the objects in question from Laura's apartment and then – believing himself to be in the firing line – concocted a story about having known Laura when they were young. But if that was the case why now was he on the line from Berlin trying to make contact with Laura?

This was running through his head while he looked for the phone book. It wasn't there, or, if so, he couldn't spot it. Cassie's filofax, also containing Laura's number, would be with her in Belfast.

'I'll have to call you back, I'm afraid. What's your number?'

The caller hesitated. 'Miss Stacton is not there?'

'No,' said Dominic, irritated at having to repeat himself, 'Miss Stacton is in Belfast.'

'Belfast. Do you please have her telephone number there?'

'I do. But I doubt if you'll get her. She's doing a programme for the BBC and she'll be at the studios already.'

'Ah! You are sure that you will find the number for Laura?'

'I did say I would.'

'Because, you understand, I have seen her on German television at the exhibition of her work.'

Dominic looked at his watch. What had possessed him to drive to Cassie's. He was now going to hit the rush-hour head on. And here was this old man waffling away on the phone.

'I'll call you back,' he said firmly and was about to put down the phone when Dr Eisermann said, 'Are you the husband of my granddaughter?'

Dominic could see the phone book now out of reach on a table. The search for Laura's number would have to wait. He stayed on the line.

Sometime later, having volunteered to do so, he rang Laura's home and got through to Cecily.

'How are you?'

'Fine. I thought you might be Jonathan,' she said. 'You know – your friend from the Arts Programme.'

'No friend of mine.'

'No? Anyway, he promised to phone. Are you looking for Laura, because she isn't here. She's pushed off – left me one of those "Don't worry. I'll be back" sort of notes, very unlike her.'

'Is she in Paris, do you think?'

'Could be. I don't know. I'll give you that number. If you talk, tell her *Options* has done a brilliant profile on her work.'

'Will do.'

Laura, however, did not answer her Paris number. Disastrously late for work, Dominic plunged into the rush-hour traffic. It was vital that he make contact with Laura.

In the Strand he recalled Richard mentioning her going away the night before. But Richard did not know her whereabouts either. Throughout the day Dominic tried Paris several times without success.

At six he was still at work. Then Cecily phoned in.

'I've had a thought. There's an exhibition this week at the New Grafton. Laura said she wanted to buy one of the paintings that will be on show.'

'Would she come back specially for that?'

'I think she might. Unless she gets someone else to queue for her.'

'Queue – you have to queue up?'

'The gallery operates on a first-come first-served basis. You can view the paintings the day before an exhibition. Then, if you fancy something, you come in early the next morning for a ticket. The gallery opens at nine but people start queuing long before that, from six-thirty sometimes.'

'I see,' Dominic said thoughtfully. 'I'll bear that in mind, Cecily. Thanks a lot.'

LAURA had never been a devotee of hotels, although circumstances had often forced her to stay in them when she was overseas on shoots.

In Paris she had always preferred the privacy of her own apartment to the luxury of the Crillon or the Georges Cinq. Now she had done what she hoped was the unexpected, booking into the Lancaster Hotel in rue de Berri.

This meant that she was staying absurdly close to her empty apartment in rue Jean Mermoz. She was of a generation whom war had made wary of waste: surely no one would imagine her doing such an extravagant thing.

Extravagant but essential. It was imperative that she go underground for the time-being. In London after the exhibition she had felt hideously exposed, as if someone had walked up to her in the street and ripped off her clothes. In Paris, at least, she would not have to face the hurt and the curiosity she had seen on Cassie's face. In Paris she would not be obliged to lie to Richard, telling him that everything was fine when he could see for himself that it was not. In Paris she could make an attempt to cope with her emotions.

So she had thought on arriving at Charles de Gaulle. But in Paris she found herself in just as much turmoil as she had been in London. In the faces and bodies of young Parisians she saw aching echoes of Klaus and Gebhard and Paul.

In Paris she learnt that she had not exorcised the old pain, merely buried it alive. All these years it had been waiting to stab her with surprising strength. But Paris was alleviating in the sense that Cassie and Richard were not present to witness her distress, plague her with questions and offer comfort which she could not deserve.

Despite the turmoil there were people to see in Paris: on the second day she called in to the offices of Spanish *Vogue* in rue Saint Dominique.

Here, Lisa Lovat Smith, the magazine's pretty blonde fashion editor, had been making some changes in décor.

A magnificent hand-carved screen depicted aspects of the male form. On each door were massive posters of a boy in an hotel bedroom, the lower half of his body covered by a sheet.

'The place looks like a shrine to Michael Roberts!' Laura said, noting Lisa's Chanel suit and her silver Karl Lagerfeld rings. 'Have you seen him lately?'

Before Lisa could answer a door opened and a tall figure in a cream linen suit, melon tie and black-and-white check cap came in. It wore a red and grey tie adorned with beige and grey horses and there was a vivid hankie in its breast pocket.

'*Michael!*' Laura exclaimed. 'It's *good* to see you!'

Since they had so recently met in London and Laura was not normally so effusive, Michael Roberts looked surprised as well as pleased.

'What did you think of my article on the Italian menswear collection?'

'Brilliant! Outrageous without being malicious. Mind you, I thought that Giorgio . . .'

They were soon at affable loggerheads, arguing the merits of Armani and Versace and Valentino.

'You did get the flowers?' Lisa said to Laura. 'We loved your last shoot. By the way, there's a rumour going round that you're going to retire. It's not true, is it?'

'Me – *retire?*' She was back in familiar territory. The pain had temporarily subsided.

Finally Lisa announced that she had to go out. 'I'm doing a story on Chanel. I have to see Giles,' and Laura accepted Michael's invitation to continue their chat in his apartment.

'I want to show you some of my fashion paintings for the *Sunday Independent* mag.'

Michael's apartment was in Saint-Germain, in rue Saint André des Arts. Walking in the old fashioned streets was in itself a palliative.

'I can't think why I never bought a flat in this quarter,' Laura said. 'But I'd go for the rue de Fürstenberg. That marvellous square with the paulownia and the white-globed lamp posts and the ghost of Delacroix lurking in the background.'

Michael lived on two levels. Downstairs was an extensive library of books, magazines and newspapers – back copies of the *Sunday Times*, the *Sunday Independent*, *Tatler*, *Vogue* and other publications in which his work had appeared.

In a single room upstairs was his bed, his canvases and his paints.

'How's the book?'

'*In Sicily*? After the way recession hit publishing last year I thought it would never come out.'

'And your paintings?'

'I've done some new gouaches.'

'You're really going it,' Laura said – and a bell in her head rang.

Paintings – the exhibition at the New Grafton, she thought – that's tomorrow. A mixed exhibition, and in it will be two or three paintings by Mary Fedden, one of which I would like to buy for Cassie. Which means going back . . .

'Blast and dammit!'

'What have you remembered?'

She explained.

'You can't send Cecily?'

'I could if I had already made my choice but I haven't seen the paintings.'

'So go back.'

'There's a bit of a problem – '

This she very nearly explained to Michael. A twinge of pain made her decide against talk of the past.

Concentrate on the present. I suppose, thought Laura, that I could *sneak* back, catch a late flight to London this evening, get up early, secure the painting I want, and hot-foot it back here until the dust settles.

If it ever does.

I might drive back. No, I told Dodgy to have the car serviced. Which means I won't have a car at my disposal when I do get home.

In the morning the whole of the south-east was immersed in fog. Laura got out of bed at five-thirty, unaware of this fact and planning to walk to the New Grafton Gallery once she'd had her bath.

She felt like an intruder in her own home, taking care not to leave evidence that she had been there overnight. Dodgy and Cecily had the run of the house. They would be hurt as well as mystified by her in-and-out flit.

They had both doubtless been phoning her apartment in Paris and getting no reply. She had been in there only once, to switch the answering machine off and thus keep them all at arm's length.

She shouldn't have gone that far. How could the studio function in such circumstances? Cecily might be super-efficient, Dodgy might – quite rightly – conclude he was heir to the throne, but they were both very much subject to her rule.

When she was back in Paris she would blithely phone in, explain that she had been madly busy, and apologise profusely for having been out of touch. That, she owed them.

The heating had not yet come on in the house. It was quite chilly. The temperature outside must have dropped during the night.

Ghastly setting off without having had tea, but the sacrifice had to be made. If she was going to camp out on the doorstep of the New Grafton she did not want to need to go to the loo in the first half-hour. She put on a coat, wrapped a scarf around her ears, opened the front door – and stepped into opacity.

Barnes was lost in the mist. Good heavens, she thought, this is a drag. She was tempted to stay at home until the fog had lifted, put the kettle on, make tea, get back into bed. Other people would be reacting in the same way, telling each other that this was no morning for standing about in queues, abandoning the project. But some wouldn't be put off. There would be other rivals for Mary Fedden's work. They couldn't be allowed to have first choice. And perhaps it wasn't as bad as it looked out there. Fog fell in patchy swirls. Nearer the village the visibility was probably very much better.

She shut the door behind her, set off down the pathway to the gate, stepped into the road. Not that she could see the road. Like her feet, it had disappeared into the fog. Right now those feet were required not only to cross the invisible road but to continue her journey across part of Barnes Common, a lonely spot in the mist.

Laura had not slept well the night before and it was only because she was over-tired, she told herself, that her imagination began to get out of control.

She had spent most of her life in this area, knew every house, every tree. But now, by each gate-post and behind every tree, an assailant was waiting for her – or so she feared.

Be logical, she said to herself. What pervert in his right mind would be up so early? What insomniac pervert is going to attack a woman of seventy-five? But perverts were not in their right minds and little old ladies were just as susceptible to rape and murder when mad men roamed.

Still, she made herself walk on, across Queen's Ride, over the Common until she reached Rock's Lane. After that there was another stretch of open ground after which – if she was lucky enough to survive so far! – she would ultimately find herself on Station Road.

When she did so unscathed she said, 'Thanks for that,' lest there be a benevolent God, and strode on, more confidently, to the Methodist Church and the Green.

The white pond was partly visible, though not the white

railings on the opposite side. She could just make out the outline of the solid Sun Inn. Nearly there. A lone jogger ran past and was swallowed up in the mist.

She reached the gallery, realised with satisfaction that she would be first in the queue since no one else had turned up, noted that there was a Mary Fedden in the window. Melon and rose and moon (or was it sun?) behind two diagonal pale green lines. Yes! That was the one. Cassie would think so, too.

Now to wait. In the past, when she had embarked upon a similar caper, she had brought with her two cushions on which she had happily sat for an hour and a half. She had left the cushions at home, not wanting to be bothered with them as she was going straight to Heathrow from the gallery. But I could have left them with David, she thought. *He* wouldn't have minded. Her feet were aching from the walk. Her legs were cold. Why hadn't she had the foresight to put on boots?

A milk car clattered past in the fog. From an indiscernible tree a starling squawked. It was seven-fifteen A.M. Where were all the other people who should have been in the queue? It was infuriating to think that they were still in bed, sipping tea and planning to roll up, all warm and fresh-faced, in an hour from now. How could they be content with second place?

At half-past seven a car pulled up and a bearded man in a striped blazer got out, opened the back door, reached in and took out a parcel.

'Hello,' he said to Laura. 'I'm Tom Coates. I'm having an exhibition here and this is a painting I want to drop off. Can I leave it with you?'

'That's very trusting.'

'It's not trusting,' said Mr Coates. 'I know who you are.'

I am a woman dying from hypothermia, Laura thought.

Ever so slightly the fog had lifted. Near the gallery was a pink house with a false window on one side. On this window an artist wit had painted a nun with a made-up face.

Church Road was waking up. Commuters drove past, gazed at Laura from their car windows. Inside those vehicles the heaters would be on. I am a misanthropist, Laura thought.

A man and a woman joined the queue, then two women. Another man approached holding a paper cup in his hand. Coffee, thought Laura. He doesn't know I could kill for that!

The man reached the gallery and stopped. Laura squinted, looking from the cup up to the man's face.

'Good heavens,' she said, sounding to her own ears like the starling. 'Good Heavens, what on earth are *you* doing here!'

'Providing you with coffee to warm you up,' said Dominic the saviour. 'You're turning blue, did you know? Cassie's sitting in the French patisserie along the road. She wants you to join her. I can take your place in the queue. Hold on though – I'd better explain.'

Even before he began to do so Laura knew instinctively that the game was up.

Laura's disappearance had troubled Cassie all the way to Belfast. Where could she have gone, and was her flit directly linked with her distress at having been given the bureau?

The aftermath of the retrospective hung over Cassie like the effect of a particularly vicious bilious attack. And she had, too, the unsettling conviction that her own life was about to move out of her control.

The trip to Northern Ireland only exacerbated this condition. Her least favourite cameraman, Mr Moronic himself, was on the team and at his most pessimistic. On the way her suitcase got lost, leaving her without a change of underwear and little time to shop.

Belfast was a city in perpetual mourning: in Ormeau Street she remembered the savage killings carried out by Loyalist paramilitaries in a bookmaker's shop earlier in the year.

The programme she was making concerned the effects of the continual violence upon the children of Ulster. Meeting six- and seven-year-olds whose parents or siblings had been murdered was an acutely unnerving experience.

Her least favourite cameraman emphasised the hopelessness

of the situation and it was his pessimism that caused Cassie to alter her travel plans when filming had been completed, rerouting via Dublin on her own. This meant a train trip – there were no flights between Belfast and the southern capital. The two cities were poles apart: one, most tragically, in the grip of the past; the other laughing in the present.

In Grafton Street there was a plethora of well-dressed women. Street musicians sang and played. For a fee a man would recite your favourite Yeats' poem. The shopping centres and the Dawson Street bookshops were packed with people who had no fear of bombs. In Bewley's one hundred-year-old coffee house she allowed herself one cherry bun. But wherever she went she thought of Laura – and she longed for Dominic.

Alarmed by the extent of this need, she kept away from the phone. For as long as she could remember she had been terrified of falling in love and losing ascendancy over a man. All year round she had been wary of caring too much for Dominic. This had happened in spite of herself and it was every bit as annoying as Richard had said. So that now – even buying a suit and sweater in Brown Thomas's – she found herself thinking how much better things would be if Dominic was present.

She thought this on the plane to London and as a result she came through the customs' hall scowling and ready to snap the head off any official who might accost her. None did. She strode into the concourse not looking round, since she did not expect to be met, with her hostility to crowds and noise mounting by the minute. All the while thinking of Dominic and then of Laura and then again of Dominic.

Shit, she said to herself, and she was still cross when Dominic himself emerged from the crowd.

Her heart, in the way of those in love, missed a beat. She very nearly said, 'Dominic, it's wonderful to see you! I've missed you so much!' which was what she thought, but she was – just – able to restrain herself and substitute, 'What a *surprise*!' holding on to her cool with the last of her strength.

'I must warn you, there's going to be another one!' Dominic said, having kissed her.

'Not Laura – nothing's happened to Laura?'

'Relax on that. I've taken the rest of the day off. We have to talk. We'll go to my flat.'

'It isn't true,' said Cassie wildly. 'It can't be true. Laura wouldn't lie.'

'I think it is true. Dr Eisermann and I spoke for ages on the phone.'

'He's making it up.'

'In that case what's eating Laura? It's something to do with the bureau. You tell me what Dr Eisermann has to gain from lying. He has this affair when he's young and that's all there is to it, as far as he knows. A mutual acquaintance tells him Laura's gone back to England and asks him to look after her bureau and her photographs. And then war breaks out and all through the war he's working at the Jewish Hospital and he has enough horrors to contend with. He marries a nurse and they have a daughter and somehow they survive only to spend years on the other side of the Wall. You expect him to be thinking of Laura all that time? Come on!'

Cassie fought back. 'So he thinks I'm his granddaughter. Why did it take him nine months to work that out?'

'It didn't. He realised it at once. But he couldn't spring that one on his daughter – not then. His wife had just died. It was a sensitive time.'

'And why now?'

'He saw Laura on television. It gave him a jolt. He told his daughter. She said he should phone. She sounds to me like a nice woman.'

'She is.'

The fury was dying down. Cassie pulled her hair around her face and hid behind it. Dominic watched and waited.

'If only I could speak to Laura,' a muffled voice said. 'I would if I knew where she was.'

'I might be able to help you there,' said Dominic. 'But don't you think you should talk to Dr Eisermann first? I have a confession to make – I told him you'd phone.'

'You've got a nerve,' said the muffled voice.

After this Dominic sat tight. Cassie remained in retreat behind her hair. Several minutes went by.

Then, 'All right then! I *will* phone!' said Cassie, still sounding cross.

Laura, coming in to the patisserie, saw her sitting at a window-table. Cassie was wearing a cerise pink Paul Costelloe suit and she was studiedly turning the pages of *Image*, the Irish magazine.

'More coffee?' Laura mouthed.

Cassie shook her head. She did not smile.

Laura placed her order, 'Coffee, please, and two ham and cheese croissants,' and took these across to the window-table.

'Hello, darling,' she said.

'Hello.'

Cassie closed the magazine and put it into her bag.

'I know what you're thinking,' said Laura, 'I just don't quite know where to begin.'

'Well, *I* just want to say one thing,' said Cassie, which in Laura's experience was what most people said as a prelude to a far lengthier speech. 'I can't *believe* that you lied to me and I don't understand you of all people acting the way you did. You always made such a fuss about the need for honesty and having integrity in relationships and if screwing around when you're married isn't lying I don't know what is.'

'Screwing is an ugly and inaccurate word.'

'Fucking then. Whatever you like!'

'Don't you want one of these croissants? They're very good.'

'No, I don't!' Cassie hissed, conscious that they were attracting attention from other tables. 'And I think it was just terrible the way you took everyone in. Mother. Father. Your parents. *Me!* You didn't let my grandfather in Berlin know I existed!'

'He didn't attempt to contact *me* all those years.'

381

Cassie's eyes flashed. 'You can imagine what he went through during the war. It's a wonder he survived the holocaust.'

'I believed he hadn't.'

That registered.

'Well, he did,' said Cassie, slightly mollified. 'I didn't realise any Jews got through the war in Berlin but I was wrong. He told me about it on the phone. They weren't allowed to use public transport or cinemas or taverns but there was a *centrale* near the zoo underground where they could meet on Sundays. He said it was too depressing to go. He and his wife just went on working at the hospital, expecting to be taken off to a concentration camp at any moment.'

'So your grandfather married a nurse?'

'I can't even be certain that he *is* my grandfather,' Cassie said bitterly. '*He* seems to think so. But for all we know my mother could have been Klaus's child, after all. You're the only one who can tell us that – but maybe you don't know whose child she was, not if you were sleeping with both of them.'

She stared at Laura, challenging her to speak the truth. Sitting up very straight and making a huge effort to keep the wobble out of her voice. Not quite succeeding, but putting on a brave show. Panic, though, in the big brown eyes.

Tell me the truth, implored her eyes. Eyes like Paul's.

You must try to understand, Paul the idealist had said over fifty years ago.

How very alike the two of them are, Laura thought, slowly taking in the implications of what Cassie had said.

Whose child?

'Darling Cassie. There couldn't be any doubt. You are Paul's grandchild. Your mother was his daughter. And I was not sleeping with both of them, only with Paul.'

Cassie glowered. 'What was wrong with Klaus?'

'Nothing,' said Laura. 'And I want you to know that I loved him. But I also loved Paul. I loved them both in different ways, but Klaus was gay.'

She stopped, waiting for the pain to return, as it had done in

382

Paris. It did not. And outside a pale sun was breaking through the fog.

'I should have told you,' Laura said. 'I was wrong. Try to understand.'

GOING BACK

'IT'S a rotten month for Berlin,' Richard said, 'November. Bound to be cold and wet. Why didn't you persuade the fellow to come over here?'

'Cassie was dead set on our going there.'

'Not much of a city either! Parochial – '

'Now it's the capital again all that's changed.'

' – and ugly. Soulless. Gloomy Soviet war memorial. And the Institut für Wasserbau und Schiffbau painted blue and pink and green! That's my recollection, anyway.'

'Cassie's is totally different. The nightlife is the best in Europe, I'm told.'

'Raucous and shady.'

'It was shady before. That was a part of its charm.'

'I haven't told you about the scaffolder,' Richard said, dropping the subject of Berlin. 'I've been watching him all week out of the sitting-room window. I thought he was part of a renovation scheme on the right-hand side of the gardens. Turns out he was planning a break-in. He's been caught in the act.'

'Good God! How high up?'

'Three floors. None of us is safe. I'm seriously thinking of moving from Chelsea. Round your way, I thought. I've always liked Barnes.'

'It *is* pleasant.'

'It's a pity you're going away. I've found a new restaurant, the Depot. Good spot – but not much fun on your own.'

'You're not without friends.'

'I enjoy *your* company, as you very well know.'

'I must go,' Laura said reluctantly. 'I still have to pack. You're a darling to phone.'

'Why wouldn't I?' Richard said, getting the message and ringing off.

Underwear, belts, bags, shoes. The shoes – two pairs, both black – were encased in bags. She put all these things into her suitcase, added a black-and-white Prince-of-Wales check jacket, a black skirt, a black-and-white spotted blouse, a white sweater with a black trim. Not trousers. The forecast had been for reasonable temperatures at this end. Her black coat could be carried until she reached Berlin.

From her wardrobe Laura took her latest acquisition, a bright red dress by Geoffrey Beene. She looked in the full-length mirror, holding the dress against her body. It could be worn not only with the black coat but also with the check jacket, accessorised with silver jewellery and a red hankie in the breast pocket.

She rummaged in her jewellery box, found the hankie mixed up with her gloves. What would Cassie have to say about the dress? She might not even notice it, being so much in love.

The change in Cassie. The miraculous change. She paused in her packing to consider that. The transformation had followed swiftly upon her own revelations. Cassie had listened and pondered and – yes – Cassie had understood. Had gone further – had said that in Laura's shoes she would have done the same. That ghost had been laid.

And afterwards Cassie had somehow unravelled her knots and everything had come right between Dominic and herself. She had moved into his flat in Chelsea Green and plans were being made for a spring wedding. A church wedding, too, with a long dress and Richard giving the bride away and Peter being encouraged to fly over to act as usher.

But not, of course, Rob – he being married to somebody else. Not Rob and not his mother. For which, thank heaven.

Meanwhile Cassie's enthusiasm was directed towards Berlin. This reunion had been entirely her idea and she was still carrying everyone else along in her excitement. Everyone else being Dominic and Laura. Not Richard.

Richard thought the expedition was a big mistake. But Cassie had no doubts that she and Laura and Dominic were going to have a wonderful week with her German relations.

The lines between the two cities had hummed as she and Paul's daughter made all sorts of plans.

'I've told her that we don't want to be met at Tegel,' Cassie had said. 'It's better to start afresh in the morning when you and Paul are rested,' as if, thought Laura, Paul and I are two old dodderers with a foot in the grave.

But it was impossible to resist Cassie. It had always been hard to do that but the new Cassie was even more lovable – more compassionate, more mature – than the Cassie of yesteryear.

Passport and credit cards. Tights.

Such a pity darling Richard couldn't come. Or hadn't wanted to do so, under the circumstances.

He felt left out – no doubt about that. Those little digs he had made about Berlin.

Vanity case. Make-up remover. Cotton wool. Maquisatin crème. Bright red lipstick to match the dress.

'Want a hand with anything?' Cecily said, looking round the door.

'No thanks, darling. Dodgy here?'

'He's gone to Shepherd Market to find a fake leopard-skin backdrop. Peter Jones didn't have anything like that in the fabric department.'

'I knew they wouldn't.'

Dressing-gown and nightdresses. Anything else?

But in terms of packing her mind had switched off. One clear image did persist: of Richard sitting alone at a restaurant table.

Not much fun on your own.

Dining with Richard would have been so pleasant, Laura thought. She snapped her suitcase shut.

Any private misgivings Laura had about the excursion she was able to quell on the plane.

All went according to plan, although the stewardess, a tall girl with her hair in a plait, had problems with a drunk who dropped a bottle of duty free Moulin à Vent as she approached with her trolley. Glass splintered all over the cabin floor and an ugly red stain appeared on the carpet. The drunk, swaying, got up to help, breathing fumes over Laura's head. No pain in that – except for the stewardess.

It was not really like going back since, in the past, she had not travelled by plane to Berlin. She retrieved a substantial splinter, wrapped it in a tissue and put it into her hand luggage for later disposal.

At Tegel she was diverted by the sight of a small blond child biting his father's hand, an occurrence that was swiftly followed by a whack on the boy's rump. The child bellowed with rage and was walloped again. Laura grimaced but she did not feel even a twinge of pain.

And then Cassie's enthusiasm began to take over.

'I wish it wasn't dark. The Tegeler See is supposed to be such a lovely place. If it was light we could have seen the lake.'

'We can always come out here later in the week,' Dominic said reasonably.

'Yes, let's. There's supposed to be a Russian cemetery somewhere around here and a church with onion spires. Some of the Czar's family are said to be buried there, and the graves are marked with the Cross of Saint Andrew.'

That brought it back. Laura had never been inside the cemetery but she could dimly recall the entrance to the churchyard – a covered gateway with bells and Russian-style carving.

It was more the reference to the Russian influence than to Tegel itself that got her memory going so she could hear again the sound of the balalaika, remember the taste of borscht and blinis and shashlik; see Kitty, dead these twelve years past, sitting at a table in the Coq d'Or restaurant.

The pang of pain was quite sharp.

Pull yourself together, she commanded silently. Fool! For it isn't as if you haven't heard the sound of the balalaika since those days, or eaten blinis, either. You have been to Russia, for God's sake! Cut this out!

They caught a taxi into town. Cassie had booked them into the Berlin-Hotel Kempinski on the Kurfürstendamm, recommending it as quiet and central with an outdoor dining-room and an indoor pool.

It was most odd to see the Kurfürstendamm in its rehabilitated state, looking so different from long ago that Laura thought pain would leave her alone.

'You must see the Kaiser-Wilhelm Gedächtniskirche before we book in,' Cassie said, so they took a look at the church.

It wasn't as if Laura had never seen photographs of this landmark. They had been on thousands of postcards, in books, magazines and newspapers: she had known very well what to expect.

And yet she hadn't. It was the basic manner in which the partly destroyed church with its bomb-scarred towers was propped up that brought the past into the present.

She had been quite categoric with Cassie about not visiting Joachim Friedrich Strasse, aware that Klaus would be there. But now he seemed to step out of these ruins and beckon to her.

It wasn't as if we ever worshipped here together, she reprimanded herself. I don't think we ever even went inside. What is *wrong* with me?

Klaus did not linger long on the Breitscheidplatz, no doubt being put off by the modernity of its shops and cafés and nightclubs, and perhaps Cassie sensed that he had been present for she urged the taxi on.

'The clock in the tower is still working,' she said to Dominic. 'I've been reading up on it – they call the original church the Broken Tooth, and the new extensions, the Lipstick and the Powder Compact!'

'Berliners always did have a knack for irreverent names,' said

Laura, determined to cope with her ache. 'What are you two thinking of doing this evening?'

'That depends on *you*. Dominic and I have open minds on the subject, don't we, darling?'

'Completely open minds,' said Dominic, which meant that what they truly wanted to do was explore Berlin on their own.

We are still great friends, Cassie and I, Laura thought. But Dominic has become her *best* friend, which is right.

Youth to youth. And tomorrow they intend to hand me over to Paul.

'I hope you won't mind,' she said with a straight face, 'but I would like an early night. The minute we get to the hotel I'm going to my room where I will order a glass of wine and a sandwich and get into bed.'

'If that's what you want,' said Cassie, trying to look disappointed and completely failing, 'then Dominic and I might go to Kreuzberg. Everyone says that it's *the* place to hang out.'

'Just be careful. I've heard that it can be rough.'

'Be careful indeed!' said Cassie. 'You're one to talk.'

The taxi pulled up outside the hotel. To Laura's relief Klaus was not waiting. That brief sighting of him had already been too much to bear.

How understanding Cassie had been about Klaus, she thought. Thank God her generation does not judge people on the grounds of sexuality.

Forms were filled in – keys supplied.

'All right, darlings, I'm off.'

'You're sure there's nothing we can do for you?' Dominic asked.

'Quite sure, thank you.'

She had changed her mind about the sandwich and the wine. She had taken the precaution of having sleeping pills prescribed. She took one, went to bed, and put down the shutters on the past.

Going early to bed meant that she was awake and dressed long before the other two. Their appointment with the Eisermanns was for midday. Four hours to go.

Outside it looked like being a mild enough day. On the wide boulevard the bare branches of the trees did not sway. There was not a hint of rain. Laura decided to go for a walk.

She swallowed the last of her coffee in a single gulp, put on her black coat and went out on to the Kurfürstendamm.

No ghosts were strolling along the street, only people in modern attire going to work. The ghosts had turned away, horrified perhaps by too much contemporary glass and marble and steel, not in the least impressed with the efforts of the women who had rebuilt Berlin after the war. *Their menfolk being dead.*

No morbidity, please, said Laura to herself. Nevertheless she did come upon a ghost or two, first in the Café Möhring across the road from Wertheim's department store, and then again in the Art Deco elegance of Number 52.

Well, isn't it marvellous that these buildings have survived, she told herself – and stop looking for Klaus wherever you go.

Too far west along the Kurfürstendamm would bring her into dangerous territory, tempting her, after all, to walk along Joachim Friedrich Strasse and thus meet Klaus.

To do so would be an exercise in masochism! If she was to continue her walk she must head east.

This meant once again passing the Wilhelm Gedächtniskirche, but she was stronger after her night's rest, she thought, and she would simply stride past the church with her head straight up.

She did so without realising that it was nine o'clock precisely. On the hour the bells chimed out the melody written by Prince Louis Ferdinand and she started with shock. Heart pounding, she went across Breitscheidplatz and turned right into Budapester Strasse. This, because of the Zoologischer Garten, was a cheerful street. One day Dominic and Cassie might take their children here. Berlin would be a draw for them from now on.

Her feet appeared to be taking her to the Tiergarten but that was absolutely fine.

No need to grieve there, she thought. The trees and the flowers and the shrubs have been replanted so successfully that even very old Berliners are reported satisfied by the results.

And the Siegessäule survived the bombing, which is also heartening. *That* lady will bring me no pain. I associate her with Paul and he and I are going to be reunited in a few hours' time.

Her pace had slowed down but she could see the soaring golden figure above the naked branches of the trees. No women riding side-saddle passed her as she went, only two joggers and a cyclist followed by a panting dog with his tongue hanging out.

Such a pity that the trees were not at their best, but it was marvellous to know that they would put on new leaves in the spring – and every spring thereafter.

At the base of the Column of Victory was a hall. Once, that hall had housed bronze reliefs commemorating German victories. But hadn't the French insisted that these reliefs be removed after the war?

I must look in there during the week, thought Laura – and then she noticed the bench.

That is the very bench on which Paul sat when I first saw him, she thought – but, of course, it couldn't be. This bench is quite new. But positioned in more or less the same convenient spot.

If she stared at it for long enough a ghost would materialise. He would be tall and wide-shouldered and his hair would be dark brown, curly and thick. His eyes would also be brown, his nose narrow and his mouth wide and sensual. He would be a handsome ghost – quite outstandingly handsome – and he would sit on this bench and reach in his pocket for a medical text-book.

She kept on looking and the ghost did appear. His clothes were dreadfully old-fashioned and not well cut but Models One would go overboard to sign him up. She chuckled aloud at this thought.

The ghost on the bench was not sharing her amusement – well, he wouldn't, Laura thought. Paul always was a solemn personality. He was not born with the gift of laughter.

I do appreciate that those were grave days before the war. For all the Jews in Berlin. And yet many *were* able to laugh. Remember the wry wit of the cabarets?

I wasn't much fun myself! I, too, took myself rather seriously. I was ever too intense. Just like the ghost who's sitting over there. What a pair we would have made, had we ended up together!

What a dull couple we'll be when we meet at midday! What are we going to talk about? The passion we shared?

I can't remember any of it, Laura thought. That's the whole trouble with sex. It consumes you while you're indulging in it – and then it's gone.

Until the next time which, for Paul and I, is decades too late.

The joggers were returning, a young man and his girlfriend, both dressed in red. They ran towards her, drew up and – not knowing that a ghost was there – collapsed on to the bench.

'*Ich bin am Ende meiner Krafte!*' said the girl.

I'm worn out. I do remember my German, Laura thought.

In spite of this declaration the couple were soon back on their feet. They vanished along the path.

Laura looked at the bench. The ghost of the young Paul had not returned. She realised then that she would never again see him so clearly – that she would only find traces of him in the face and the body of an old man who lived in Metzer Strasse.

Since the bench was now unoccupied she sat on it herself. The golden symbol of victory soared above her head and she thought of Paul as he had been, and how he would be now.

How beautiful he had been. None of the models with whom she had worked could rival his looks. But that beauty would be gone. Like Berlin, Paul would have changed beyond recognition.

I have seen the Wilhelm Gedächtniskirche, Laura thought, and that is enough. I do not want to be forced to look at Paul. Not even for Cassie's sake. Cassie has her own relationship to establish with him. Mine is dead.

I will go back to the hotel, collect my case, pay my bill and go to the airport. I will take the first flight back to London and I will dine this evening with Richard. With whom my relationship is not dead.

Cassie will be furious at first but Dominic will reason with her. And when I've been able to explain my reasoning, she will forgive me.

She opened her handbag and took out a notebook and pen. She ripped out one of the pages and began:

Darling Cassie,
I've made a decision. I am going back . . .